D0644264

THE *DASH* OF DR. TODD

Other novels by Howard E. Adkins:

The Predators
The Scar
The Peccavi File
Strata
Hannity's Curse

THE *DASH* OF DR. TODD

Howard E. Adkins

SPRUCE PINE PUBLIC LIBRARY
142 Walnut Avenue
Spruce Pine, NC 28777

Copyright © 2009 by Howard E. Adkins.

| Library of Congress Control Number: | | 2009906150 |
| ISBN: | Softcover | 978-1-4415-3352-4 |

All rights reserved. No part of this book may be reproduced or transmitted in any form or by any means, electronic or mechanical, including photocopying, recording, or by any information storage and retrieval system, without permission in writing from the copyright owner.

This is a work of fiction. Names, characters, places and incidents either are the product of the author's imagination or are used fictitiously, and any resemblance to any actual persons, living or dead, events, or locales is entirely coincidental.

This book was printed in the United States of America.

To order additional copies of this book, contact:
Xlibris Corporation
1-888-795-4274
www.Xlibris.com
Orders@Xlibris.com
59979

ACKNOWLEDGEMENT

My great-grandfather was a physician who graduated from medical school in the eastern United States in the mid-nineteenth century. He traveled around Cape Horn by ship and practiced Medicine in Oregon Territory before moving to Idaho City, Idaho Territory, when gold was discovered there. He practiced in that mining boom-town until his untimely death. My information about his life is pitifully limited; even his medical bag was jettisoned long ago by an uncaring relative. My purpose in writing *The Dash of Dr. Todd* has been to explore some of the maladies and problems that undoubtedly challenged him, and the therapeutic constraints imposed upon him by the limited medical knowledge that existed in the 1850's and 1860's. In order to convey any real impression of these experiences, many sources of information are required. I am sure that I uncovered but a few of those that are potentially available, lying hidden and dust-covered out there somewhere, but my goal in writing The Dash of Dr. Todd was not to provide an exhaustive review of the Medicine of that era, but just to explore and convey an impression of the physical and mental stresses, the triumphs, frustrations and defeats that probably assaulted my great-grandfather.

For details in the whaling portion of *The Dash of Dr. Todd*, I am indebted to Robert Cushman Murphy and his *The Logbook for Grace*, an excellent window into nineteenth century whaling practices observed first-hand during that author's months spent on board the *Daisy*. What I found to be the virtual bible of the Medicine practiced in the 1850's and 1860's is a multi-volume tome entitled *The Cyclopedia of Medical Practice*, edited by John Forbes, MD, MRS, in England in 1845. Other sources were *Lectures in Materia Medica* by Carrol Dunbar, M.D., *The Complete Herbalist* by Dr. O. Phelps Brown, and *Genito-Urinary and Venereal Diseases and Syphilis* by Robert W. Taylor, M.D., all of that time period. The Chinese doctors contributed greatly to medical care in the Frontier West, often being more successful in their treatments than their Caucasian counterparts. An excellent source about their activities and formularies is found in *China Doctor of John Day*, by Jeffrey Barlow and Christine Richardson. An invaluable source about Idaho is *History of Idaho*, by John Hailey, whose life in the middle of the nineteenth century was that of a packer, Indian fighter, and a molding force in the development of Idaho's territorial government, as well as being a very competent historian and writer. I am grateful to John Ocker, M.D. and David Rice, M.D. of Boise, both of whom generously made their libraries of very old medical books available to me.

Howard E. Adkins, M.D.
Boise, Idaho 2009

DANIEL LOCKE TODD, M.D.

1825-1868

Eighteen twenty-five *dash* eighteen sixty-eight: a man's life summed up on a gravestone, as though his birth and death are the only cardinal facts of his existence. Certainly, a Mozart concerto is much more than the first and the last notes or even the total number of notes contained in the work. It is the manner in which Mozart arranged those notes, the themes they demonstrate, and the sentiments they elicit that give the composition its beauty and importance. In the same sense, the *dash* on the gravestone really represents the whole fabric of the life of the deceased and consists of a complex weft and warp of events, emotions, and actions—all the threads that produced, day by day, the cloth of that man's life. At least some of those threads are undoubtedly worthy of note in the existence of any man. The story that follows is the *dash* of Daniel Locke Todd, M.D.

PROLOGUE

It had been an even hotter September than usual throughout the southern hemisphere but particularly from Colombia all the way north to the Yucatan. Sweltering land temperatures heated the shallow offshore waters of the Gulf of Mexico to almost 30 degrees Centigrade in some places. These tropical waters then transferred untold tons of moisture into the air and created a muggy, suffocating, vapor-laden atmosphere of almost palpable density. Being so near the equator, the earth's rotational torsion, the so-called Coriolis Effect, was appreciable. In the virtual absence of any vertical wind shear, a huge area of low pressure near the water surface was slowly set into a huge convection movement by this phenomenon with mounting winds at the outer margin. As this current of moving air gained strength and ascended, the centripetal wind flow also increased.

Gradually, the angular velocity due to the Coriolis Effect grew to produce a true cyclonic curvature to the air flow and a huge whirlwind, of sorts, was the result. The irresistible force of these upthrusting air currents even carried boobies, frigate birds and noddies higher and higher until they eventually plummeted back to earth at the periphery of the system, frozen to death. Great clouds of mosquitoes also were carried upward until each insect became the nucleus of an ice particle. Gradually, more and more heavily water-laden air continued to be added to the system. As condensation of moisture occurred during the ascent, the cooling of the air released an enormous amount of previously latent energy. That energy produced increasingly stronger winds and violent lightning storms that could be seen to illuminate the sky at the margins of the storm. These winds caused progressively greater intake and uplifting of ever larger amounts of very humid air with further release of energy. The mercury in an aged barometer on an idling ship in the Gulf below dropped an inch and this change was actually associated with the surface of the water in that area rising up by *one foot*—water was literally being thrust upward by the decreased pressure of the atmosphere above it. The evolving process thus increasingly continued to feed upon itself.

The evolution from a tranquil tropical depression into a violent tropical hurricane took place over a period of only four-and-a-half days. Now, while winds near the center of the storm remained either non-existent or only a few knots at most, the velocity farther out in the maelstrom reached 147 knots as it passed northwest of Cuba. Inching forward at a speed of only 9 knots, the storm center traveled in a north-south pressure trough and tracked first northwest through the Gulf but then began to swing northeast, across the tip of Florida, to progress along the coast of the Carolinas. The storm had lost some energy in crossing the land mass of Florida, but the hurricane quickly regained strength as it once more traveled over water. It was now releasing a torrential downpour of water, churned by the horrendously violent whirlpool of air. Its winds are gusting to 153 knots.

PART ONE

THE WHALES

1849

CHAPTER ONE

At first, the *Southern Cross* encountered only rapidly building swells that soon became huge. They were oily-smooth and far out of proportion to the mild winds, but everyone commented on the strange, almost dusty-red appearance of the shifting air stirring above them. Then, the winds mounted and gradually edged into a truly squally southeaster with rain, weather that was an unwelcome change from the sunny skies, strong following breezes, and swift sailing that had sped the clipper ship south from Boston during the past week.

The ship was a fast, Baltimore-built, gaff-rigged topsail schooner and Daniel Locke Todd, extremely proud of his recently awarded M.D. degree, was delighted to be sailing in her to San Francisco. Once there, he eagerly anticipated moving on to the gold fields of California, not to seek the yellow metal but to pursue an adventurous, yet hopefully useful, life there in the practice of medicine. If graduation had been earlier in 1849, he could have traveled overland more economically, but there was no way he could set off from Boston in mid-June, reach St. Joe, Missouri, arrange transportation in a wagon train, and hope to beat the winter snows over the Rockies. He had even made the great sacrifice of selling the watch given him by Dr. McClure in order to purchase passage on this ship that was sailing around Cape Horn. By mid-fall, at the latest, he hoped to be starting his practice. It was a truly exciting prospect.

Daniel Todd, a stocky, auburn-haired man who looked more mature than his twenty-four years, was thriftily dressed. His very frugal life had been a struggle up to this point but, now, he exuded a confident optimism in his future. Indeed, he had politely voiced his impatience at the delay when Captain Trover had explained that, even though they would hug the coast as far south as the Carolinas, they would then sail east-southeast toward the Cape Verde Islands and almost to the coast of Africa to pick up the trade winds that would then propel them around Cape Horn. Daniel had felt there surely was a quicker, more direct route and he was painfully eager to get to California.

The staysails and driver luffed as the wind of a new squall suddenly shifted again and moved in off the larboard beam. The whipping canvas added its chattering bit to the mounting noise of the storm. O'Donnell, the Bos'n, moved closer to Todd and shouted, "Best get below, Doctor. The glass is fallin' somethin' fierce."

"I've sailed little catboats back home in some stiff breezes but have never weathered a storm at sea on a real ship. I wish to remain on deck to watch, if I may," Todd replied.

"Come to my quarters then. I'll borrow ye a slicker." O'Donnell turned and headed below, totally untroubled by the wildly plunging deck. Todd unsteadily followed with some difficulty, donned the proffered oilskin coat and hat, and returned to the deck.

The squall spawned a torrential downpour, the wind raged ever more violently, and the seas rapidly built to mountainous proportions. Watches had been secured and struggling seamen had long since been sent aloft to shorten sail until only skysails remained to maintain the *Southern Cross'* way as she now ran before the wind. Supper had been biscuit and cold ham since cooking was impossible. Darkness settled in and quickly became absolute except for the feeble island of light surrounding a ship's lantern that hung near the binnacle. Earlier, it had twice been strongly suggested to Todd that he go below, but now his strength and presence were welcomed by Captain Trover, O'Donnell and the helmsman in their struggle to keep the helm from being twisted out of their grasp as the storm warped the vessel and challenged them for its control.

Suddenly, Trover screamed, "My God! My God! We're lost!" Squinting against the lashing rain, Todd saw what had terrified the captain. Barely visible in the wind-lashed darkness, a gigantic storm surge, swelling as high as the mainmast, overtook them out of the black storm from astern. It was so huge that it dwarfed the ship and, to the feeble beings on the poop deck, it seemed as though a new world was violently engulfing them. Had they been able to observe the entire scene as detached witnesses, they would have beheld their ship being lifted higher and higher on the face of the wave but plunging forward as it slid down the massive scarp until, finally, the keel of the *Southern Cross* almost reached the vertical as the bow of the ship dived toward the depths below. The four men dangled from the now horizontal helm. Then, as her bow plunged deep into the trough and the crest of the wave broke, the ship somersaulted forward as many tons of water crashed down upon her, smashing her in the gurge. Todd would never know the mechanics of how, when he was thrown aside, he had not been crushed amid the splintering masts and crashing spars as all four of those on deck were churned into the suffocating black maelstrom of the sea. The poor unfortunates trapped down below deck had no chance at all. All the barrels and crates of cargo shifted in the hold and crashed against the now-dependent under-surface of the weather deck, wrenching it away from the beams of the vessel. *The Southern Cross* literally exploded into match sticks under all the altered stresses on the hull and the weight of hundreds of tons of water that had crushed it from above. A flailing Todd was only aware of hitting the water and then being pummeled, sucked, tumbled and plunged farther and deeper into an inky abyss.

The blackness that enveloped him was so absolute that he would have screamed his terror had he been able. Instead, he clamped his mouth tightly against the almost overwhelming desire to breathe. In his panic to orient himself and find the surface somewhere above him, he was surprised that he noted the tepid temperature of the water even as he struggled, second by second, against the overwhelming urge to breathe. He knew that to do so would be fatal. Would it ease that explosive hunger in his lungs if he let out just a little of the air he had gulped so hastily before his plunge? If I do, he thought, I won't be able to stop and I'll suck my lungs full of water and die! Where is the surface? Am I being pulled down by the ship? *Which way is up?* Just then, he thought he could feel bubbles stream past him so he kicked and made frantic clawing movements with his arms to follow them. Am I diving deeper? Oh, Mother—I'm going to die! I can't hold out! Mother—I can't . . .

As he burst above the surface, the wind struck his face with such a physical force that it was like an actual blow to his head. Todd gulped air so hungrily, along with the salty mixture of spray and rain, that he gagged and coughed. As he flailed to keep afloat, he saw that it was no less black on the surface of the water than it had been in its depths. He could see absolutely nothing. It was only the brief slackening of the wind that indicated to him when he was momentarily in a trough and protected by the mountainous swells; when he was atop one of them, the wind shredded the night and drove its lacerating rain horizontally into his face with such force that he could neither breathe nor open his eyes. He turned his back toward it and tried to relax and just float on the surface. He could not; he had to swim to stay afloat. His hand struck a piece of flotsam so large that it felt solid and unyielding. He could not identify the object his hand encountered, but he finally located a handhold and clutched it with all of his strength.

Todd screamed to locate any other survivor, but the wind screamed louder and flung his shouts off into the night to be lost in the nearly liquid blackness. Why is the wind so noisy, he wondered, when there is no obstruction for it to blow around? Accepting its meager hint of salvation, he closed his eyes and clung fiercely to the wooden sanctuary, giving thanks for his survival to the God he had abjured in the past.

- - -

Dawn emerged hesitantly through great sheets of rain and horizontal spray ripped from mountainous seas, bringing only feeble relief from the horrors of the night. The shape of his "life raft" gradually emerged out of the fading darkness and Todd could identify it as a fractured section of mast that was still attached to a sizeable piece of decking. It resembled a snaggle tooth that had been torn from a jaw and had taken a fragment of gum tissue with it in the extraction. The ship must have been crushed asunder and its debris scattered by the weight of that incredible wall of water. He realized his survival thus far was miraculous but he feared the end was inevitable and surely could not be too far in the future. How long could he last in his present state?

He was unsure how much those early winds or the later hurricane had affected the course of the *Southern Cross*. Certainly, the closer they had still been to Cape Hatteras when the full fury of the storm arrived, the better were his chances now of being rescued. The farther the ship had traveled southeastward, the less likely it seemed that any surviving vessel might chance to pass close enough to find him. He grimaced at the probability of that unpleasant prospect. But as long as there is life there is hope, Todd told himself as he clung to his uncertain haven. Realizing suddenly how exhausted he was, he gathered a length of rope that trailed from the mast like a strand of seaweed and looped it under his arms, tying it so as to harness himself to the wreckage and give the aching muscles of his arms and shoulders a rest.

Other than an indescribable gratitude for still being alive, the only emotions crowding Daniel Todd's mind now were those of fear and crushing loneliness. How he yearned for the sight of another human being. Even if that person were dead, it would validate the reality of what had just happened to him. Otherwise, his survival of the sudden nightmare in which the stately schooner had simply ceased to exist was so incredible that his brain found it hard to fathom. Perhaps I am actually dead now; perhaps this heaving water is actually that fabled River Styx, just more turbulent than anyone ever imagined, and I have to swim my passage—Charon's boat doesn't exist. Perhaps I'm really on my way to Hell—or this *is* Hell and I'm already there. Am I condemned to an eternity of this? He slumped into the supporting strands of rope, allowing the mast to cradle his body. In his utter exhaustion, he slept.

- - -

When he awakened, the leaden sky was still disgorging torrents of water but now the downpour angled more vertically; the wind had diminished to less than gale force and no longer was ocean spray being stripped from the swells to add its salty seasoning and produce the suffocating horizontal confusion of water that the darkness had held. Todd roused and turned his face upward to catch as much water in his mouth as he could; the downpour was still so dense that he found it difficult to breathe in this position, but he realized his survival depended on fresh water. If only he could catch it and store it. When his belly could hold no more, he again called out repeatedly to attract the attention of any other possible survivors. The wind no longer was a deafening competitor, but he heard no response to his cries.

He looked at his hands. The skin was wrinkled and puckered in spite of the wetness of its surface. It would be better, he thought, if I could be on top of the mast boom instead of staying suspended here in the water. He untied himself from the fractured mast and struggled up to straddle it. Once on top, he slowly inched forward until he reached the section of deck still attached to the snag. This fragment was perhaps four by seven feet in its dimensions, its shorter measure being held nearly vertical and, although it offered no surface that he could utilize as a raft platform, the portion of deck did serve to stabilize the mast and keep it from rolling in the water. Finding no perch more secure than the one he already had, a wet, despondent, and frightened young man reversed his position on the mast and leaned back against the section of deck to await whatever Fate held in store.

- - -

Nobody will know or even care that I'm dead, Todd thought ruefully. Father didn't even attend my graduation from medical school, let alone know that I had left for California. Passing thoughts of other acquaintances came to mind. Medical school classmates, all very involved in plans for their new careers, had reacted with politeness but with a casual disinterest when he mentioned his plans to go west. And Elizabeth, who had made it very clear that she considered any further contact with him an inconvenient complication in her life, did not know that he had departed Boston on the *Southern Cross*. How depressing it is, he agonized, that nobody on this entire planet other than myself gives a tinker's dam whether I live or die. He almost wept when he thought of his father's unreasonable anger, the painful memory of which had festered all these years.

"Through adversity, perhaps you will find God." Those had been the very last words the Reverend Thomas Blakely Todd had flung at his son after ordering him from the parsonage and from the life of the sanctimonious minister. Reared from birth in the bosom of the Hadley Congregational Church's devout Connecticut Valley assemblage by his strict and demanding parents, young Daniel had been the dutiful son, even when his newly widowed father dictated his future by enrolling him at nearby Amherst College to study for the ministry. But the more he read the writings of great minds and the wider flight his own thoughts were free to take, the more Daniel began to question the devout but narrow teachings of his childhood. His late mother had always urged him to have an inquisitive mind and to explore any path that interested him, but his father's rigidity of thought and very literal biblical beliefs had been too dictatorial and overpowering for him to overcome while he was still living in that household.

Daniel's new patterns of thought gradually spawned that defiant certainty so characteristic of inexperienced youth and lent an undiplomatic recklessness to his expression of his newly formed opinions. He now realized that his disdain for the narrow but traditional judgments of his father had probably been well seasoned with a revolutionary desire to defy the man. In any case, he had decided that he was not meant to be a minister and that Medicine, with its mysteries, truly offered the career path he wished to pursue. Instead of discussing his new choice with the Reverend Todd tactfully, he had thought he must challenge his father and he prefaced the argument he was certain would follow by boldly announcing he had become an agnostic and, therefore, a life in the ministry was no longer possible. The explosiveness of his father's angry response and the bitter recriminations that did indeed ensue were so intense that Medicine was not even discussed. Much of Daniel's long-suppressed bitterness finally was exposed and only added fuel to the contentious exchange. The final result was not just his father's denouncement of him as a son but, also, disinheritance and loss of any financial support for his final year of study at Amherst.

The fin of a shark sliced the surface nearby, interrupting Daniel's reverie. Panic caused him to draw himself as far as possible up the slight incline of the broken mast. He watched the circling predator warily and wondered if it could see how precariously he now perched. Would it lunge upward and drag him once again into the sea? Finally, to his relief, the fin disappeared but the terrifying awareness of the lurking danger remained.

Only now did he realize that he still wore O'Donnell's slicker. Stripping it off and draping it over the section of decking, he decided it was time to take stock of his assets. It didn't take long. Other than the clothes he wore, the slicker and a length of rope attached to the mast segment seemed to be all he possessed. Feeling in his pockets, he discovered that he did have his Barlow pocket knife and a pauper's purse containing fifty-three cents. The former would be useful. As he surveyed his surroundings, he became aware of other scattered flotsam and wondered if any of it might contain food or water. Searching in vain for any other survivor or even a dead body, he tried to paddle with his hands and propel his "raft" toward the nearest pieces of wreckage. For the first time, he noticed the thick mass of seaweed just below the surface of the water and surrounding his mast segment, all of it seemingly buoyed by small brownish, berrylike bladders. He guessed that this must be the famous Sargasso Sea he had heard about. Either the *Southern Cross* had been driven into it by the storm or the violence of the maelstrom had shifted the floating mass to where he now was.

Panic gripped him again. He feared becoming entrapped and thought, what if I can't get free of its grasp? Surely, ships try to avoid it and that thought bred even greater doubt that a vessel might ever see him and save him. He faintly remembered hearing that even most sea life avoid the Sargasso Sea and that meant he had less chance of somehow taking a fish for its life-saving food or moisture. The shark fin he had seen would seem to refute that bit of information, although Daniel was not anxious to have that sort of a companion, even in the Sargasso Sea.

When the sun was high above him, one piece of flotsam had drifted close enough for him to make out the letters stenciled on its side—SALT COD. No help there; just reading the words made his thirst worse. How he wished that rain was still drenching him. Was the storm just last night or was it the night before? He shook his head and tried to clear his thoughts. Maybe the fogginess of his mind was the effect of the hot sun; he propped the skirt of the slicker above his head and tried to retreat as far as possible into its shade.

"I have to think of something else," he said aloud, just for the sake of hearing a voice.

Into his thoughts, an image of the grandfatherly Dr. Patrick J. McClure gradually drifted.

Even Daniel's seeking out Dr. McClure had been indirectly the result of one of his father's attitudes. When he had realized that his newly disinherited state left only an apprenticeship in Medicine as the pathway into that profession, he had set out to petition one of Hadley's two doctors for such a position. The only occasion on which the Todd family had sought any medical care whatsoever was when Mrs. Todd had developed pneumonia. The fact that her course had been steadily downhill and that the Reverend Todd had blamed Dr. Joseph Stewart's incompetence for her death led Daniel to approach the alternative choice first. Hadley was not a large town so he knew who Dr. McClure was but had no more than a speaking acquaintance with him. He relived the moment in 1843 of their first encounter in front of the doctor's house.

"I am flattered, Mr. Todd, that you wish to apprentice yourself to me. However, I am an old man and near the end of my career; it would not render justice either to you, to me or to your future patients were I to agree," the old doctor had said.

"You have an admirable reputation, sir, and I could ask for no better teacher, I am sure." Todd had continued to plead his case by disclosing some of his personal story and how his studies at Amherst had thus been cut short. It may have weakened his cause when he said, "I had hoped, upon graduation from Amherst, to study Medicine in Boston or in Philadelphia but, alas, I am now without the financial support of my family. I must find other avenues into Medicine.

"Please help me, sir," Daniel continued. "I could help compound your medicines—I have read chemistry and botany in addition to my regular studies at Amherst—I could relieve some of your burdens by acting as a nurse for your patients and perhaps even, under your supervision, make sick calls for you. I could tend your horse and perform household duties to compensate you for my food and lodging. Please, Dr. McClure, don't turn me away."

"So, you are willing to settle for second best, are you? Can't go to medical school and so you will accept a simple country doctor as your tutor?" The old man thoughtfully filled his pipe and then sucked flame from a sulfur match into its bowl, puffing out clouds of aromatic smoke in the process.

"Of course," he finally continued, "four out of every five of our present doctors gained what medical skills they possess by serving an apprenticeship. They are 'doctors' in name only. They don't hold any actual degree conferred by a university for completing the studies at a true medical school."

The doctor puffed again on his pipe and said, "You seem a well-spoken young man and, if you have completed all but one year at Amherst, you obviously have academic skills. You should persevere and finish there. Find a way to go to medical school as you had hoped, young man. That will make you the best doctor that you can be."

He turned to leave, saying, "Now, I must visit the Sandhursts. I told their man that I would be there some time ago. I am happy to have gotten to know you better, Mr. Todd."

The old doctor shuffled toward his buggy and, with a lameness of age compounded by fatigue, slowly hoisted himself into the buggy. The light trap rocked in protest.

Daniel watched the old doctor's carriage move away down the tree-lined street and he felt a genuine disappointment. His reason for choosing Dr. McClure over Dr. Stewart had not been all that compelling in the first place, but he had liked this old gentleman immediately and now found this dismissal very saddening. Perhaps he's right, though, Daniel thought. Perhaps I should get a job until I can save enough to finish Amherst and then go on to medical school. I'm eighteen. With a good job, I could work a year, study a year, work another year. I could earn my medical degree eventually.

Daniel had been pondering these possibilities when he heard a mounting clatter on Elm Street, just around the corner. It reached a crescendo and ended with an echoing crash. There was silence then except for the frenzied squeal of a horse in pain. Daniel trotted swiftly in that direction. A jumble of wreckage confronted him. Dr. McClure's horse was motionless in its traces and appeared dead. The team hooked to the heavy grain wagon both were struggling to stand but neither seemed able to get to its feet. Their shrill brays of agony were pitiful.

Todd had been the third person to reach the wreck and he helped the other two untangle the wreckage. Amidst the splintered shambles that had been his buggy, Dr. McClure lay in a grotesque heap and there was a grimace of pain on his face. They found no sign of the other driver.

Dr. McClure groaned at each movement of his limbs as the rescuers extracted him, and then he pulled Todd close to him and muttered, "Get Dr. Stewart, my boy—my right hip is broken, and I'm not sure what else. Don't bother looking for the other driver. That runaway wagon was empty when it hit me." Dr. McClure fainted.

How many times Daniel had looked back on that accident and mused over how pivotal it had been in his life.

CHAPTER TWO

The sun sank into a bank of clouds that stretched all across the western horizon. It was a dark and colorless sunset, as grim and bereft of beauty or hope as Daniel felt his own prospects to be. The griping hunger in his belly would have overwhelmed him had not his thirst been so much more distressing. He could actually hear the rasping sound that his tongue made when he moved it across the flaking surface of his lips. At least, he thought sluggishly, nightfall will bring some relief from the baking heat of that sun. As he shifted his weight on the mast, he wondered how many hours of the afternoon he had stuporously lain in that one position. His stiffened limbs resisted, but he moved them anyway—stretching, bending, stretching, bending.

For the thousandth time of the day, he scanned the horizon, now darkening swiftly in the east. Then he saw it! Was it real? Were his eyes playing tricks on him? No—it was actually a sail! A SHIP!

The sun, no longer visible from his position at sea level, still cast a faint glow on the distant skysail. Croaking garbled shouts in a maniacal burst of energy, Daniel climbed as high on his island of debris as he could get and waved the slicker. He continued to wave it frantically until darkness finally enshrouded him. He imagined that he could see the faintest hint of light, perhaps a glow from the distant ship's lantern. He tried to convince himself that the vessel was slowing or changing course but, sobbing with disappointment, he was forced to admit defeat when even that indistinct glimmer blinked out. It had left him! The lonely, terrifying blackness of night settled in on him once again. At least, tonight he could see a moon and the stars, but their very remoteness only intensified his lonely plight.

Finally, Daniel let his head sink onto his arms, and he concentrated on counting in time with his pulse. He had no real purpose in this exercise, although the beat of his heart convinced him that he was still alive, and it was a way to pass the seconds and minutes and hours of thirst and hunger before daylight once again returned. Perhaps the ship will still be out there in the morning after all, and they will see me. He gradually became aware that he was having difficulty in focusing his thoughts enough to keep the proper count. Eighty-one, eighty-two, eighty-seven . . .

- - -

He awoke once more in the strangling embrace of deadly black water, and he clawed frantically, seeking a way to safety. His head struck something solid, and he realized he was not having a horror-filled nightmare; he had fallen from his perch on the mast. Holding onto the slippery wood, he gulped air to quiet his panicky heart and rubbed at the sea water on his parched lips. What a temptation it was to drink his fill, but he fought the compulsive ache of his thirst. Instead, he stretched his cramped and aching limbs in the warmth of the surrounding water and wondered why he had not relieved the tedium of the past hours by easing down into the sea before. Then, sluggishly, he remembered the sight of that shark fin slicing the surface above it and he quickly clambered out of the water.

I've got to stay awake—Medicine—you're a doctor—think of that . . .

- - -

Todd dredged his memory and saw Dr. Warren gaze at the new students who clustered around him and announced, "Gentlemen, this poor wretch will provide the opportunity to introduce you to Medicine. His remains, the Massachusetts Medical College of Harvard University, and I will launch you into an exciting, challenging, and most rewarding life."

With that, the Hersey Professor of Anatomy and Surgery plunged a dissecting knife into the cadaver's belly and opened it with a flourish. Bloated intestines billowed out of the incision; some students crowded closer, others shrank farther back into the group.

Undoubtedly, this bit of showmanship was performed by Dr. Warren to impress the new medical students properly because, in time, Daniel became aware just how scarce were the fresh bodies that came from the Almshouse. Any cadaver, when it became available, was carefully prepared before the lecture by prosectors, honor students who were given the privilege of personally dissecting bodies for study in order to best demonstrate particular anatomical details. How those structural minutiae had been drilled into his brain! Origins and insertions of muscles, architectural form of bones until he could identify most just by their feel, course and relations of nerves and arteries and veins—details, details, details.

To test himself now, Todd thought of the Median Nerve—it leaves the cubital fossa by passing downward between the two heads of the pronator terres, then behind the humeral head of the pronator terres, until it reaches the deep surface of the flexor digitorum sublimis, which separates it from the flexor carpi radialis and the palmaris longus . . .

Daniel sadly shook his head and thought, if there is a God in the Heavens, surely he would not allow such vast tracts of knowledge to be crammed into my brain and then waste it all by letting that mind die and rot unused. What a waste! But then, he thought of Nature's profligacy in its extravagant overproduction of sperm or pollen or fish eggs or whatever—always, always present in far greater numbers than are necessary to their purpose. The thought that he might be one of those profligacies added to his despondency.

- - -

Exhaustion forced Daniel into little snatches of sleep, but whenever he was startled back into consciousness, he compulsively searched the faint line where the black-black of the sea met the blue-black of the sky for any hint of that sail. Each time, he was disappointed. In his boredom, he searched the sky for constellations that he could identify. The July heavens were crowded with stars, but he was ashamed of how few he knew. Eventually, he identified Ursa Major in the northwest and Ursa Minor in the north. The brilliant Vega was visible slightly to the east. He studied the clusters and searched for others he recognized. There's Libra and Sagittarius in the south, with Scorpius in between, marked by its brilliant Antares. Having exhausted his celestial knowledge, Daniel was forced to think of other things that might take his mind off his unrelenting thirst. With death seemingly so near at hand, his thoughts dwelt on the morbid.

He pictured Dr. Channing, Boston's leading *accoucheur*, that night at the Boston Lying-in Hospital. The patient was thin, malnourished and weakened by her chronic poverty, which was why she had come to this charity obstetrical hospital for the delivery of her child. When Daniel first saw her in his capacity of attending medical student, he was alarmed and immediately called the nurse. This startled lady panicked also when she saw the presenting hand and immediately sent for Dr. Channing. Fortunately, it was the good doctor's habit to spend at least some hours of his day at this institution, which had been founded primarily through his efforts, and he was still in the building. He soon strode into the room with reassuring authority.

"What is the problem here, young man?" he had asked, directing his question to Daniel rather than to the nurse.

"I found her with the baby's arm protruding, sir," was the medical student's response.

The patient was groaning with her almost constant contractions. Between two of these spasms, Dr. Channing carefully felt the woman's abdomen. "When did her water break?" he asked the nurse.

"Shortly after she came to the hospital four or five hours ago, sir. She has been in labor since, but there was no sign of that arm until just a few minutes ago," the nurse replied.

"What is your name?" he asked of Daniel.

"Todd, sir."

Motioning him aside, out of the hearing of the patient, Channing said to Daniel, "Well, young man, we have a bad problem here. As you know, this baby is what we call a 'transverse lie', so its head was not down into the pelvis when her labor started. Without that as an obstruction, all of her water, as well as eventually that arm, came out when the membranes ruptured and now the wall of the uterus adheres tightly to the baby. We probably won't be able to rotate its position in the womb; that's why it is so important to do that maneuver early in labor. Remember that. If we can't remedy this situation, probably both the baby and the mother will die."

Turning to the nurse, Dr. Channing ordered, "Get some help in here to hold her legs."

While he was removing his coat and rolling up his shirt-sleeves, Channing said to Todd, "When there is prolonged labor without the head acting as an opening wedge against the cervix, the upper uterine segment gradually becomes thicker and the lower uterine wall becomes paper thin. If it ruptures and tears across the broad ligament and through the uterine artery, the woman bleeds to death."

Channing inserted his left hand between the labia and into the uterus, alongside the protruding arm. Between contractions, he gently pushed upward on the shoulder of the infant while massaging the mother's belly wall with his other hand in order to rotate the baby. His efforts were unsuccessful.

"That dry uterine wall is virtually gripping the baby. I can't rotate it, so I'll try to bring a foot down. I should be letting you do this, Todd, but we are in a very delicate situation here."

Daniel was perfectly happy merely to be observing.

Dr. Channing seemed to be exploring higher into the uterus with his left hand. "I must avoid compressing the cord." He stroked downward several times with his right hand on the woman's belly wall, as though trying to move part of the baby downward toward his internal hand. "Ah, I've got a foot," he exclaimed, biting his lower lip in his concentration.

Carefully, Dr. Channing began to withdraw the foot and the baby's arm was slowly retracted back into the womb. Suddenly, the mother gave an agonizing scream as blood gushed from the birth canal and she fainted. Channing realized that the uterus had ruptured and he quickly began pulling on the baby's leg while continuing to press firmly on the belly from above. He knew he could not save the mother, but he was trying to deliver the baby alive. As one leg emerged, the other uncoiled from its flexed position and came out, followed by the hips and finally the abdomen. Channing snaked first one arm and then the other down from their position alongside the baby's head. But now, the little head was hung up with the chin caught under the mother's pubic bone. Channing gently pushed the head farther back inside while rotating the body 180 degrees. Continued traction delivered the limp body.

"I'm afraid he is dead," the doctor said as he handed the baby off to the nurse, who slapped and rubbed the little body in an unsuccessful attempt to revive it. The unconscious mother had become deathly pale and soon she, too, was dead, lying in a great pool of her own blood.

Channing slumped in defeat and said to Todd, "There is a razor's edge between a very normal birth and a disaster such as this. We, as doctors, are supposed to make a difference, make more of them normal, but we are not always successful. Your goal as a doctor, Todd, must be to do a better job than I have just done here."

After washing the blood from his hands and arm in a nearby basin, the doctor donned his coat and, with a nod to those present, walked despondently from the room.

Every minute detail of that experience had seared its impression deeply into Daniel's brain. It had destroyed his vision of himself as a potential "Warrior Against Death" when he understood that even such a great doctor as Dr. Channing occasionally might be the actual agent of someone's demise. Fear, his own inadequacy and impotence, even the fallibility of great doctors—all had overwhelmed Daniel that night, even as he now felt so totally out of control of his own destiny. Utterly depressed, he slumped into sleep.

- - -

The long night finally was coming to an end. Daniel's thirst was maddening and had gradually crowded out almost everything else from his mind. Still there, though, was the compulsive prayer that he would see the ship. His agonizing anticipation mounted to an almost unbearable pitch as he strove to penetrate the veil of pre-dawn darkness. It was followed by crushing disappointment when he finally became certain that last night's vessel had truly gone. He sobbed his disappointment but could not shape his parched lips around the words to express it. He slumped down and lay prone on the section of mast. As he actually contemplated surrender and just slipping off into the gentle swells of the ocean, he was totally unconcerned that his limbs draped into the water. Perhaps it might be better, he thought, if a shark did suddenly end my life for me right now.

He was uncertain how long he had remained in the same position; he knew that he must be drifting in and out of consciousness. An alien sound edged into his awareness—a harsh, grating squawk. It sounded again and this time was accompanied by a stabbing pain in his neck. He bounded upright and a seagull launched into terrified flight. It circled in a varying radius above his head and seemed to be gradually coming closer to him again. He settled back onto the mast, his neck still smarting where the gull had pecked him. He kept his hands cradled on the mast with his head on them, turned so he could see the bird for part of its circling flight. Could it be possible that the bird might once more alight and he could *catch* it? He remained absolutely motionless.

The gull landed on the water and watched the immobile figure. It dipped its beak into the sea and then watched again. The whitish-gray head turned from side to side as it inspected him with first one eye and then the other. With a loud squawk, the gull slowly lifted into the air again. Its circling flight caused Daniel's spirits to plummet, but he remained still as death. Only his eyes moved as they followed the bird. Finally, when it settled to land again, it came to rest on the planking attached to the mast. After a seeming eternity, it jumped down onto the spar, not three feet from where Daniel lay. The bird was out of his sight, and the temptation to move so he could see it was almost overwhelming, but he resisted.

Then, there was a painful peck on his hand and another and another. He was certain the bird's beak was drawing blood, but he forced himself not to move. Then he felt the feet striding across his hand, followed by a piercing stab on his upturned temple. In an explosion of movement that surprised even him, Daniel swept his hands together and gathered the bird in his grasp. It struggled and thrashed its wings as it tried to lift into the air, but he clung to it as though it were his very life.

Any twinge of remorse that he might have had at killing another living being was overcome by the raw pain he still felt in his left temple and by his thirst and by the certain knowledge that he himself was close to death. Daniel grasped the seagull by the neck and spun the life out of it. Only then did some verses of the *Rime of the Ancient Mariner* come to mind and recollection of the vengeful price that was levied for that seaman's killing of the albatross. It was only a fleeting thought, however, and did not forestall him from his purpose.

He tore the skin and wet feathers from the gull's breast even before it made its last quivering movement. Daniel ripped a mouthful of flesh with his teeth and chewed it as a wild animal and not a man. The moisture his gnashing teeth extracted did wet the tissues of his mouth but not enough to allow him to swallow. He chewed and chewed until only a wad of nearly dry flesh remained. Unwilling to sacrifice this bit of food, he carefully deposited it above the water line on the mast. The liquid he wrested from the next mouthful of gull moistened his mouth enough that he was just able to swallow the solid remains. But hunger no longer really registered in his mind, so great was his thirst.

Daniel now carefully skinned the rest of the bird and flung this tissue and feathers into the sea. Logic began to assume control over his attack on his prey, and he extracted the Barlow knife from his pocket. Realizing that he could scrape the flesh from the bones more efficiently with a knife than he could with his teeth, he proceeded to dissect and eat the bird, mouthful after mouthful, until he had consumed the entire seagull—muscle, liver, heart, blood, and everything but the intestines. Even his extreme plight could not drive him to consume those. Finally, he sucked at the bones until they were stripped of every fiber and drier than his mouth.

His thirst was not satisfied, but he felt remarkably better. He studied the gull's bones and wondered if it would be worthwhile to crush them for their marrow but then remembered that in birds, bones were hollow in order to afford them lighter weight. Suddenly, the idea struck him; perhaps I can whittle fishhooks from them. What can I use for a line? Todd looked at the Bos'n's slicker and thought he might be able to cut narrow strips from it, but then his eye fell on the length of rope trailing in the water from his mast. He snaked it from the sea and set about untwisting a section to separate out its individual hemp fibers. Painstakingly, he twisted these into a tiny cord that was a fathom and a half long.

Next, he studied the pile of bones. He decided they offered two possibilities for hooks. He took the wishbone and shortened one branch of its fork. He sharpened the end of this part with his knife and then attached his cord to the longer branch. It was not a sturdy connection and involved untwisting the last inches of his cord, tying them in a series of knots around the long branch of the bone, and then finally tying the ends together through a hole he drilled with the point of his knife in the flared junction of the wishbone. He baited the "hook" with a section of the gull's intestine and threw it in the water after tying the free end of the cord to his wrist. To his disappointment, it floated on the surface above the layer of Sargasso weed. Well, perhaps *something* will find it and get caught, he thought.

Next, he fashioned two more "hooks" by tying the small bone of the middle segment of each wing to the larger bone of each; he surmised that they corresponded to the radius and the ulna of the human arm. The small bone angled upward from the end of the large bone and was secured there by multiple strands and knots of hemp fibers. These "hooks" were flimsy and probably would not support a fish large enough to take one in its mouth, but he could think of no other design.

The sun had climbed high in the sky and its heat drove Daniel to shade himself again under the skirt of the slicker. As he reclined there, snatches of Coleridge's poem once more swept into his thoughts:

> "All in a hot and copper sky the bloody sun, at noon, right
> up above the mast did stand, no bigger than the moon.
> Day after day, day after day, we stuck, nor breath nor motion;
> as idle as a painted ship upon a painted ocean.
> Water, water everywhere, and all the boards did shrink; water,
> water everywhere, nor any drop to drink."

Daniel closed his eyes and his poor excuse for a raft wafted rhythmically up and down on the gentle swells. "I'm better off than I was a few hours ago," he told himself without any real conviction in the haltingly spoken words that sounded so strange to his ear.

- - -

A tug on the cord at his wrist aroused him. It took a second or two for him to orient himself, but then he realized that a fish had struck his hook. He knew he must pull it in very carefully so that nothing broke in the process, but his sluggish muscles didn't seem to work. His vision was blurred, and he had trouble maintaining his balance on the mast; it was as though he occupied somebody else's body. It simply would not respond to the commands of his brain. Then he realized that there was no longer anything pulling on the cord. When he did manage to pull it from the water, the wishbone hook was just a shaft of bone tied to the string. The rest had broken away. His disappointment was beyond description, but his physical condition had become such that he was not even able to register his anguish. He groaned through the chalky, sandy tissue of his lips and tongue and collapsed in exhausted depression back on to the mast. It was as though even the air he wheezed in and out rasped all the way down into his lungs. Each breath was almost more of a struggle than it was worth. Daniel could no longer sort out in his mind how many tedious days had passed since the storm, but he wondered if he could last through another night.

He drifted out of consciousness.

CHAPTER THREE

Captain Ozias Corbet strode the poop deck of the *Ellie Mae*. The ship was an hermaphrodite whaling brig of 386 tons, two weeks out of New Bedford. She was 126-foot in overall length, two-decked, framed with oak and chestnut, planked with yellow pine, and copper-fastened. Captain Corbet, a well set-up Yankee of 54 years, had a basso voice twice too great in volume for his five-foot six-inch frame. His short, wiry and grizzled beard wrapped tightly around his chin and matched in color the profusion of tousled hair that peeked from under his captain's cap. His spirits were perhaps better than usual because he had just had his fill of griddle cakes for breakfast and the crew was working out better than he had thought they might during those first days at sea.

It was a beautiful sunny day and a decent following breeze created just a pleasant chop on the cobalt sea. Captain Corbet now owned a greater share of this sturdy ship than he had on its last cruise, and he looked about him with a swell of pride. Just two weeks before sailing, he had been able to buy William Church's 3 and 7/32 share in the *Ellie Mae* when that seedsman had encountered his financial difficulties. Captain Corbet and his wife now owned over half of the *Ellie Mae's* thirty-two shares—19 and 7/32.

The Captain paused in his promenade and bounced with impatient energy up and down on his toes. "Crowd a driver on the main, Mr. Maxfield," he bellowed at his First Mate. "Let's make the most of this wind, mister." With a nod of his head, he strutted onward past the helmsman.

Maxfield had just sent four men to rig the driver to the mainmast. Two dozen or so of the crew were also enjoying the sunshine while going about their assorted tasks on deck. Brewer, the Second Mate, was directing another half-dozen men in restowing some timbers that the *Ellie Mae* carried on the larboard main deck for mast and spar repairs; he was angrily complaining that their original lashings had loosened and he fumed loudly about "miserable lubbers with two left hands when it comes to bendin' a line."

Swan, the Cooper, had accumulated a great pile of planed shavings around himself as he went about his endless task of making barrels that the entire crew hoped would be full of oil before the voyage ended, overcrowding all of the ship's storage space.

Halbert, the Third Mate, was inspecting the Larboard Whaleboat. He silently admired the efficient beauty of the craft: thirty feet long, it was an amazingly seaworthy, double-ended boat built of white cedar. A six-man crew could row it swiftly, yet it could withstand the punishment of being towed miles by a harpooned monster of a whale and could sail back to the mother ship even if seas had become dangerously angry. Along with sail and spars, the whaleboat held a mast ready to be stepped. Stowed forward, along the starboard side, were the harpoons; opposite them were the razor-sharp lances in their wooden sheaths. The "waifs" or signal flags were stowed in the stern along with lantern, matches, flint and steel, all packed in a cask of hard bread. There was a cask of fresh water, the boat's compass, a blubber spade, knife and hatchet, grappling iron, line-drogue, piggins and bailers. Up forward, the heavy loggerhead was positioned far enough from the stroke oar thwart to allow space for the 200-fathom tub of heavy line to be stowed just before the whaleboat was lowered into the water. The loggerhead was so stoutly built into the keel that it could withstand the strain when the harpoon line was bent around it as the boat was pulled by a wounded whale.

Isaac Lawrence, a boatsteerer, slowly walked to the scuttlebutt immediately forward of the *Ellie Mae's* mainmast. Into the water keg, he inserted the "thief", a slender, cylindrical copper dipper that always hung from a peg on the mast and fitted easily down through the bung hole of the water cask. Drinking his fill, he finally grimaced and released his breath that he had stubbornly held against the water's bilgy taste. He knew that this resulted from tight bungs and the stink was due to the decomposition of any impurities that might have been in the water when it was put in the barrel. Isaac looked forward to the time in a month or so when the water would eventually work its way clear and finally improve in taste. He returned to his labor restowing the timbers.

- - -

Daniel had lost track of night and day. So parched had his body become that even his eyeballs had softened in their desiccation. Even simply squeezing his lids together distorted their shape so much that it further blurred his vision. There was nothing for him to look at anyway. He had long since despaired of seeing a ship so he simply lay on the mast with his eyes closed and made no effort to keep his limbs out of the water. His body was essentially in hibernation. His mind vaulted fitfully from memory to thought to dread and back again to memory whenever his brain crossed that fuzzy barrier between the conscious and the unconscious state. He no longer knew when he was actually thinking or when he was dreaming because he was never certain whether he was awake or asleep. He realized, though, that he was nearing the end.

- - -

Dr. McClure said, "Young man, you need a place to stay and I need some strong fellow who can take care of me, all laid up with this broken hip as I am. My housekeeper can't do it—she's as old as I am—and I have no family. I could even tell you a bit about compounding medicines, perhaps".

Daniel thought back to the meals he had prepared, the bed pans he had positioned and then emptied, the bed baths he had given, the groceries he had purchased. He thought also about the many hours Dr. McClure had spent just talking to him about cases he had treated, deaths he had witnessed, the joys and sorrows, the triumphs and failures he had had in his medical career. Daniel considered all the philosophy of life that the old doctor had bestowed on him—not the endless "thou shalt"s or "thou shalt not"s or the "fire and brimstone" threats such as the Reverend Todd would have preached, but the joy that could be found just in living, in dealing with people, in accomplishment, in leaving the world a little better place than you had found it.

Daniel remembered his own clumsiness as Dr. McClure talked him through the preparation of some medications for the doctor's bag, working zinc oxide and ferric oxide into lard to treat skin irritations; dissolving Turkish opium into alcohol to make laudanum; mixing the jalap and calomel to compound the Dr. Rush's Thunderclapper pills that McClure favored so as a laxative; and countless others. But perhaps the two sentinel events that remained in the forefront of Daniel's memories of the few months he had spent with Dr. McClure were first, an action of his own but still reflecting McClure's influence, and second, the final deed of the good doctor's life.

The first had come when a frantic messenger arrived at McClure's house and pleaded with him to come because Elias Turner was threatening suicide.

He apparently had gone out in his yard to shoot himself, and a neighbor had been trying to talk him out of it. The messenger said Turner would not talk to anybody but the good doctor.

McClure pointed out his helpless state and said, "Obviously, I cannot go to Elias, but I am going to send my young associate, Dr. Todd, and I am certain that he will be able to handle the matter."

Daniel, uncomfortable at the time because of falsely being represented as a doctor, could still savor the conflicting thrill of satisfaction and terror McClure's words had struck in his heart. He started to follow the messenger when the doctor called him back and said, "Wear a hat, for God's sake, and take my medical bag. Give him a gill of laudanum if you can get it down him. That will sedate an elephant."

When Todd arrived, Turner was out in front of his house holding an old flintlock pistol to his temple. "Where is Dr. McClure?" he demanded of the messenger.

"He's bedfast with a broken hip, but he sent his associate, Dr. Todd here, to talk to you."

"Don't you understand? I have to talk to Dr. McClure!" Turner screamed.

Daniel struggled to speak calmly and said, "He sent me to give you some medicine to make you feel better. Then you will be able to go to Dr. McClure's house yourself and talk to him without interruption."

Turner screamed, "You're just trying to trick me. Everybody tries to trick me."

Then Daniel took another tack and asked the inane question, "What seems to be the difficulty, Elias? May I call you Elias?"

Turner hung his head and shook it in wearied frustration, as though it was just too great an effort to try to catalog his problems.

"Please talk to me, Elias," Daniel continued, gradually forming some idea of what he might say.

"I just can't handle—can't solve all of these problems. And what will people—what will God think if I do this? I can't even commit suicide without facing another problem."

"Maybe you should be talking to your minister," Daniel countered, without really meaning it.

"You know what he'll say. Damn it, man, you *know* what he'll say."

"Well, no, Elias, I don't know what other people, or God, or your minister might say, except *don't*. All I know is what I think. I think you should try to look at all of this from some other points of view. That's what your brain is for. What if somebody stole your horse? You would be beside yourself because somebody stole something that was yours. Even worse, what if they had shot the poor animal? You would be incensed that they had so wantonly destroyed your magnificent horse. Now, isn't that so, Elias?"

"I suppose."

"All right. Now, look at your left hand; no, not the hand with the gun in it. You need to keep that up to your head so nobody can take it away from you, because we want you to have free choice in all of this. Look at the other one. Move your fingers. Move them as if you are letting them dance over the strings of a violin. Do that. Isn't that amazing? Your brain is listening to what I say, then it is telling those fingers to move, and they are doing exactly what you are telling them to do. That means you have to hear, to understand, to tell your body to act and it has to be able to obey. Does anybody you know have the knowledge and skill to build any sort of machine that complicated? What do you think, Elias?"

"No. No, I suppose not." Turner's body language showed him to be relaxing a bit. He seemed curious to know where Todd was going with this.

"And do you know what will happen if you pull that trigger? That piece of lead will tear through skin and bone; more importantly, it will simply make mush out of your brain. Not only will that brain no longer be able to hear, it won't be able to command your hand or your legs or anything else."

Daniel paused for a moment and then said, "The important thing is that you can't think when your brain is mush, so you can't find answers to these problems that are overwhelming you. True, your problems will no longer vex you because you will be dead and gone, but you will leave all of those unsolved troubles and even more besides to those who stay behind."

Turner seemed to be listening so Daniel continued, "If I were in your shoes, I wouldn't allow anyone to steal something so perfect, something as complicated and wonderful as my brain from me; and most certainly, I would not make mush out of it *myself* and on purpose. But, maybe that's just me. Maybe you think a busted head full of squishy jelly is the way to go. But, just remember how you would feel if somebody destroyed your horse—and this is infinitely more important.

"But, there is a very easy solution to all this," Daniel offered. "You don't have to shatter your skull and scatter your brains all over the yard. I can give you a drink of an elixir that will be the first step in letting Dr. McClure help you to find your answers. How about it, Elias? Have a drink and come talk to Dr. McClure. You know he can help. You know you need to talk it all over with him."

Seconds ticked by and Daniel feared he might have pushed Turner too far. Then, in a faltering motion, the man lowered the pistol from his head and Daniel slowly moved toward him, fumbling in the bag with shaking fingers for a bottle of Dr. McClure's laudanum. If there had ever been a doubt in Daniel's mind about going into Medicine, the elation he had felt after the Turner incident erased it completely.

The other cardinal event resulting from his association with Dr. McClure came at the very end of the old man's life. In spite of Dr. Stewart's good care, McClure followed the course of most elderly patients bedridden with a hip fracture and he developed pneumonia. Dr. Stewart's treatments of frequent dosing with Glauber's salts, quantities of Peruvian bark, frequent cupping, and constantly flooding the sick room with vapors from burning tincture of benzoin were all to no avail and McClure went downhill.

In his final lucid moments, he motioned Todd to come close and he weakly wheezed, "Listen to me, my boy. Stewart has had the necessary papers prepared and I have signed them. Mrs. Sylvester, my housekeeper, gets a small bequest for her service. I have grown very fond of you, Todd, and . . ." The old man had to stop briefly and pant in order to recover enough to continue. Clutching at Daniel's hand, he said in little more than a whisper, "I have great expectations for you as a man and as a doctor. Everything—house—all—all goes to you. Use it to go to medical school, my boy."

Exhausted, McClure's grasp relaxed and his hand slipped away and lay still on the coverlet. Very soon, he totally lost consciousness and within a little over an hour, his labored breathing ceased and the old man quietly died.

Even without the inheritance, Daniel Todd would have felt greatly enriched by his time with the wise and grandfatherly doctor. He had received far more filial direction from Dr. Patrick McClure in the short time he had known him than he had from his biological father in a lifetime. And the inheritance. How could he begin to put a true value on that? Its dollar value had been only meager after the estate had been settled but it was enough that, by careful marshaling and great frugality, he had been able to finish his studies at Amherst and attend the Massachusetts Medical College of Harvard University.

Daniel had often wondered if, immediately after the doctor's accident, the old gentleman had accurately forseen the final results his hip fracture would have and had asked Todd to move in with him in order to set in motion the relationship that eventually followed. Certainly, though, whatever the motivation for Dr. McClure's actions and his bequest and even beyond the money involved, the sentimental value of his generosity and thoughtfulness was beyond measure.

As though this brief lucid interval of his own and the reliving of such emotional memories had drained him in the same manner that McClure's final conversation had exhausted *his* final energy, Daniel faded out of true consciousness. Delirious, he saw flitting images of fellow students, was vaguely aware of Elizabeth's haughty disinterest in him, heard snatches of Materia Medica lectures, saw barbaric surgical demonstrations and even could suppose that he was the patient. All was confusion in his mind and the images were totally fragmented and surreal. Finally, even those thoughts winked out. If, at that moment, Dr. Todd could have had any objective thoughts, he would have realized that his death was very imminent.

- - -

The masthead lookout on the *Ellie Mae* sang out, "Floating debris a quarter league off the starboard bow."

Captain Corbet swung his heavy brass glass around and inspected the object. "My soul and body, so 'tis. 'Twill do for tryworks fuel and we may salvage some nails. Mr. Halbert, lower the Larboard Boat and recover those timbers. Smartly, now. We don't want to waste time an' wind."

The Third Mate and the Larboard Boat crew scurried for their boat, lowered it away and set smartly to the oars. The distance was not great enough to step the mast and hoist sail, even though the breeze was inviting. Wishing to impress the captain, all the oarsmen strained to pull ahead of the *Ellie Mae*. Captain Corbet was just as competitive and did not waver, so the ship and boat raced neck and neck. When the ship finally drew as near the wreckage as its course would take it, Maxfield, the First Mate, was ordered to come about and the *Ellie Mae* wallowed and slowed.

Halbert's boat also coasted. As it drew near the floating debris, Lawrence, the boatsteerer was the only one facing forward because the Third Mate was gazing back at the slowing *Ellie Mae*. He said, "Mr. Halbert! Look at that!"

The whole boat crew turned to look back at the flotsam and saw that a man's body was draped over the mast. "Is it dead?" was the question murmured by several of the oarsmen.

As the whaleboat drifted in and bumped the mast, Halbert reached over and felt for a pulse in the neck. "He's alive, but just barely. My God, look at his mouth."

"Let's give him some water," Lawrence exclaimed.

"No, as close to the *Ellie Mae* as we are, don't breach that water cask. Bring him aboard, and we'll get him back to the ship straight away," Halbert ordered. Many hands competed to bring the survivor aboard; the whaleboat rocked in response. "Pull together smartly, now, and make for the *Ellie Mae*."

Captain Corbet, impatiently watching Halbert's boat from his Quarterdeck, wondered why it was returning without the timber. "My soul and body, what's got into Mr. Halbert? Fetch me my trumpet," he ordered, reaching for his glass.

"Hmmph! He has something in the boat instead," he exclaimed, after his telescopic inspection. "Ahoy, the whaleboat. Why are you not carrying out my orders, sir?" he bellowed through the megaphone.

"We have a survivor on board, Captain," was the faint shouted response from the still distant whaleboat.

"Hoist him aboard," Captain Corbet shouted through his voice trumpet when the whaleboat finally drew alongside. "Hoist him aboard and then fetch that fuel, as I ordered." There was no note of humanitarian concern or curiosity in the Captain's voice.

When the unconscious body was lifted aboard, Captain Corbet inspected him in a cursory fashion and then ordered, "Douse him with a bucket of sea water and give him a thief's measure from the scuttlebutt. No more, at first."

Maxfield got the fresh water while Smithers tried to revive Todd with a bucket of sea water in his face. It had no effect. The captain returned to the Quarterdeck. Maxfield knelt beside the survivor and cradled his head while he dribbled a small amount of water into his mouth. At first, even that produced no change, but after a minute or two, Daniel's tongue moved against his lips. Maxfield dropped a few more drops onto Daniel's lips and he coughed feebly, his eyelids drifting apart.

"It's all right, friend, you're safe," Maxfield said.

Daniel tried to move more upright but was restrained. "Here, drink this," the First Mate said. In his eagerness, the prostrate figure spilled more of the water from his mouth than he was able to drink but, at least, it served to moisten his terribly parched lips and mouth. Daniel struggled to a more upright position and looked around at his blurry surroundings.

"You're safe, friend. You have been rescued by the whaler *Ellie Mae*. In a few minutes, we'll give you all the water and food you need. Just relax for now. You're safe." Maxfield's tenderness was a contrast to his usual rough manner and a surprise to the sailors looking on.

Daniel breathed a deep sigh of obvious relief and slumped back onto the deck.

Maxfield nodded to Smithers and said, "Take him to crew's quarters. Bed him on a mattress on the deck—not in a hammock—and you stay with him. Give him one of these dippers of water half a dozen times each hour. I'll look in on him later."

Several other crew members helped Smithers, as though the rescued man was a new mascot. They were all surprised when Captain Corbet appeared in the fo'castle with a tumbler of rum in hand. He knelt beside Todd and assisted the man in taking a sip.

The patient gave a feeble cough and gasped as the fiery and alien vapors mounted from his parched gullet into the back of his throat. He coughed again and rasped out, "Thank you for saving me. I can assist your cruise. I am a doctor."

Captain Corbet drew himself to his full authoritarian height and growled, "By my soul and body, sir, I am the doctor aboard the *Ellie Mae*. What I need is another oarsman." With that, he strode from crew's quarters, his diminutive height not even requiring him to duck his head to avoid the beams overhead.

CHAPTER FOUR

At first, the intervals between drinks of water were torture because it seemed to Daniel that the few mouthfuls each dipper held were completely absorbed by the dry tissues of his mouth and throat and never reached his stomach, so unsatisfied was his thirst. Still, he realized the wisdom of the captain's order and tried to endure the eternities between Smithers' visits by inspecting his surroundings. Crew's quarters, the fo'castle, was dark except for the subdued and scattered light entering through the grating above his head. In the gloom, he could see many hammocks that swung in unison like troops moving in lockstep as the ship plunged through gentle swells. Nearest to him in the room, there were several tables with backless benches attached. He tried to raise himself off the pallet laid out on the deck but he was too weak to summon the necessary energy. He had to be satisfied simply to allow his body to flow into the fabric underneath him. He couldn't suppress the tears of relief and gratitude that welled up in his eyes. He wondered how dry a man's body had to become before he could no longer form tears.

Smithers returned with another dipper of water and asked, "How ya feelin', mate?"

"Much better, thank you."

"What're ye called?"

"I'm Dr. Todd. Dr. Daniel Todd."

"Well, Dan'l, I'm Smithers. I heard the cap'n say yer a oarsman now. I guess ye scuttled that there doctor part somewhere back in the sea." Smithers chuckled at his own humor as he supported Todd's head and watched as he gulped down the water.

Todd wiped at his moist lips and was surprised at the bristly beard on his usually close-shaven chin. I wonder how many days I was out there, he puzzled.

"Hungry?"

"I'm sure I will be when I get another gallon or two of that water in me," Daniel replied as he slumped back on to the comfortable pallet. "As a doctor, though, I can assure you that now it is perfectly all right to step up the frequency of those water rations."

"Orders is orders, Dan'l. It's time ye learned that," was Smithers' reply as he straightened and mounted the ladder to the weather deck.

Todd drowsed fitfully between the frequent interruptions for his water and was feeling much stronger by the time he heard the echoing clang drifting forward from the quarterdeck; two bells rung close together followed by another two an instant later. The crew members, one by one, began drifting into the fo'castle from the galley, each with a mounded tin plate in one hand and a large tin cup of liquid in the other. Most cast curious stares and, occasionally, one or another would nod a greeting in Daniel's direction.

The pungent aroma of supper lent him the strength to rise to a sitting position and announce, "That food smells marvelous. I haven't eaten anything but a raw seagull in I don't know how many days."

Isaac Lawrence entered crew's quarters just in time to hear this rather plaintive comment and said, "Here, take this plate and sit up to the table, if ye can." He deposited his plate and cup and assisted Daniel on to the bench. Others inched sideways to give him room, but it seemed to him their withdrawal hinted more at distancing themselves from a pariah, a strange, weakened invalid.

Lawrence said, "I'm Isaac. I'm a boatsteerer and the one who saw ye on that wreckage. I helped bring ye back to the *Ellie Mae*."

"I'm Daniel," Todd said, having gathered already from Smithers that his medical degree meant nothing in this new world where Fate had deposited him. "I thank you for the rescue—and thank you for the plate of food." He looked down at the heaping portions of beans and sauerkraut and the massive chunk of bread. He would have consumed it in an instant, so great was his hunger, but there were no utensils.

"I'll fetch ye a spoon," Isaac said. "We all have our own." With that he headed back to the galley and Daniel sopped the bread in kraut juice and bit off a massive chunk of the most delicious food he had ever tasted.

Just as Isaac re-entered the fo'castle, a distant "Bl-o-o-o-o-o-w-s-s-s. Bl-o-o-o-o-o-w-s-s-s, off larboard beam . . ." could be heard from above and everybody at both tables scampered from their seats, tumbling over each other in getting up the ladder to the main deck. Bewildered, Daniel remained where he was and devoured huge mouthfuls of food, washing each down with gulps of tea. He was curious about the activities on deck but was too weak and too hungry to move from where he sat. Life was good, life was marvelous. As he chewed, he closed his eyes and gave thanks for his salvation; he was not clear in his mind to whom he was extending his gratitude but he was thankful to be alive.

- - -

Isaac knelt beside Daniel's pallet and roused him from his sleep of exhaustion. "Feeling better?"

"Oh, yes," Daniel replied, as he blinked the confusion from his eyes. "Where did you go?"

"Masthead lookout saw a pod of sperms and the Cap'n called away all boats. But, they sounded before we got to 'em and then it got dark All the boats returned to the *Ellie Mae* then. Can I get ye anything?"

"No," Daniel replied. "I'm feeling almost well. I even found the water cask myself and have made several trips to it. I admit that I'm not too steady on my feet, though."

"Get a good night's sleep. If yer goin' to be on a boat crew, the old man will surely issue ye 'slops' tomorrow and ye'll have a proper hammock." Isaac stood up.

"Slops?"

"Gear. Ye'll be sold everythin' a proper oarsman needs—clothes, knife, needle and thread, tobacca, everthin'," Isaac replied.

"I won't get much for fifty-three cents. That's the extent of my worldly wealth," Daniel remarked with a feeble smile and a shake of the head that reflected his despondency at the unexpected reversal his life had taken.

"Oh, it'll all be charged to yer lay of the eventual profit of the cruise. Never fear; the owners'll get their due. Now, I've got to go on watch at the helm. I'll see ye in the morning."

With that, Isaac Lawrence moved with tired steps up the ladder to the deck above and Daniel was left in the gathering darkness of the fo'castle and the night sounds of most of the crew, now already asleep in their hammocks. He was grateful for Isaac's friendliness. He just hoped that the man was a good teacher because the mysterious clanging of the ship's bell, now just finishing eight peals, reinforced the fact that he had a lot to learn about life at sea.

He turned over and luxuriated in the comfort and safety of a dry bed and the feeling of security it afforded, even though the deck beneath it gently plunged and tipped in the motion of a ship underway.

- - -

Daniel awakened and rose before the rest of the crew, making his unsteady way to the weather deck just as dawn was breaking. Full sunrise was still many minutes away and the undersurface of the cloudbank to the east was still black and seemed fused to the darkness of the sea beneath it. Only the billowing mounds of its upper reaches were faintly highlighted. The wind was fresh, but the temperature was pleasant. He inhaled deeply, enjoying his solitude in this alien world where he already was discovering how rare a prize was that condition. But, it was good to be alive and feel life about him. He no longer had to grasp at anything within reach to support himself; he felt immeasurably stronger but still not back to normal.

As dawn's light gradually diffused around him, a strange man hurried past and descended into the fo'castle. He apparently came with orders from the poop deck because, in just a moment, he came back up on the weather deck and, after a curt nod in Daniel's direction, returned aft. In just a few moments, three crew members stumbled out into the light, yawning and sleepily rubbing their eyes. Daniel assumed that two of the men were lookouts because they scrambled up lines to the two masts and stationed themselves in metal hoops far above the deck. The third man had to be the cook; he disappeared into a cabin off the main deck and, in a few moments, the clatter of pans could be heard from there.

When the sound of four peals on the ship's bell sounded, more crew members began to issue from the fo'castle, making their way in twos and threes to piss into a topless cask that rested on deck, lashed to the foremast. Soon, the deck was seething with activity, reminding Todd of an anthill recently stirred with a stick. An officer gave the order to "Swab down," and buckets on lines quickly hoisted water up from the sea, mops appeared and, in just a matter of minutes, the deck was freshly scrubbed. Throughout all of this activity, Daniel's presence was essentially ignored, as though he were a familiar, but inanimate, object. It wasn't until Isaac appeared on deck and came up beside him that any word was cast in his direction.

"Good morning, Dan'l. It looks good to see ye up and about," was the friendly boatsteerer's greeting.

"Good morning, Isaac. I was beginning to think I was invisible. The crew looks right through me."

"We're only a few weeks out of New Bedford and, except for a few of the ol' hands who shipped with me on the *Ellie Mae's* last trip out, many of 'em are still almost strangers to me, too. 'Most everyone is pretty much on his

3 4444 00247111 8   2010

guard. I s'pect we'll all be true shipmates, by an' by—an' ye'll be included. Ready for some breakfast?"

"I think I can eat every hour, on the hour. Lead the way," Daniel replied.

Isaac stepped into the noisy cabin that indeed did turn out to be the galley, handed a tin plate, cup, and spoon to Daniel, and said, "This is Fishcake, the cook. He's burned slum on board the *Ellie Mae* since way before Cap'n Corbet took command. Fishcake, say 'hello' to Dan'l, here. He's the one we delivered from Jonah yesterday."

The cook gave a single, silent nod of his head and, instead of offering a handshake, dumped a huge ladle of porridge on Todd's plate. It was followed by a massive chunk of last night's bread deposited in the middle of the thick lake of oatmeal, and then the cook nodded in the direction of the huge metal tea pot.

Daniel said, "Pleased to make your acquaintance, Fishcake," and proceeded to fill his tin cup with tea. He edged his way toward the fo'castle, followed by Isaac. "Does he ever talk?" he asked, over his shoulder.

"When he does, can either be chapter and verse or profanity that'll strip tar right off the deck. Best not to have him converse with ye more than necessary," Isaac replied.

They sat, side by side, at one of the fo'castle tables. Isaac nodded at the line of hands across from them and said, "That's Pinchot, that's Flaherty, Dugan, Lowell, and Calthrop. Mates, this is Dan'l Todd. Ye all know 'bout Larboard Boat fetchin' him from death's jaws yesterday. And that's Smithers next to ye, but I guess ye two have met."

Daniel nodded to each in turn and gave a general greeting, "Good morning. I understand from the Captain that I'm going to be an oarsman. I'll appreciate all the help any and all of you can give me because I'm definitely not a sailor. I do know starboard from larboard but that's about it." His self-deprecation resulted in a relaxation of the tension that had surrounded him even last night and an immediate warming of the atmosphere.

After a moment, Dugan said, "I hears ye says ye was a healer when ye came aboard. I could use yer talents. Ol' Lillie, in Bedford town, done went an' gave me the gleet 'fore we shipped."

"Well, Dugan, I'm sorry to say that I lost everything when the *Southern Cross* went down, so I have no medicines, but if it gets so bad that you can't pass your water, I'll use a quill from a pen or something to relieve you. That's a promise. Of course, if the pain and drip *is* intolerable, I could amputate right now, but you will have to loan me a knife."

Daniel's comment drew coarse laughter and further cheerfulness. Conversation drifted to the high prices asked for the gear they had been issued, hopes for an unusually successful cruise and quick return to port, and whether or not the ship would round the Horn to search for grey whales in the Pacific. Daniel was content to let the conversation flow around him and was pleased that it did not seem to be stilted by his presence.

He had wiped up the last of his porridge with the bread when a voice called down from the deck above, "Todd. Ye down there? The Cap'n wants ye."

Daniel rose and gave a questioning glance toward Isaac about what he should do with his plate and cup. "I'll care fer it," several voices chimed in competition.

When Daniel reached the deck, he found Mr. Halbert, the officer who had been in the rescue boat, waiting for him. Without a word, the Third Mate turned and went aft toward the poop deck. Daniel followed and near the helm stood Captain Corbet, feet planted wide apart and hands clasped behind his back.

"So! I see ye are recoverin', Todd. Let's do yer shipping papers." With that, he turned to a separate journal that was laid out over the ship's log in the charthouse and ordered Daniel, "Read an' sign this."

"On this day, _____ signed aboard the *Ellie Mae* in the berth of _____ and for his services he is to have _____ lay of the net proceeds for whatever oil and bone may be taken from this date forward.

Date _____   _____
                                  Master and Agent of Brig "Ellie Mae"

                                  _____
                                  His Signature

                                  _____
                                  Witness

"Oarsmen get a 1/185th o' the lay on this voyage, Todd. Sign it an' we'll issue ye yer slops," the Captain said.

Daniel bristled, "Look, Captain, as I told you, I'm a doctor, and I know nothing about being an oarsman. Just drop me off on the next ship you meet or port you enter, and I will reimburse you for this passage as soon as

I can get to some funds. I appreciate your saving me, but I'm not prepared to risk life and limb going up against your whales. Not even for 1/185th of the lay."

The Captain looked up into Todd's face and fixed him with a sour stare. Finally, he said, "It may be a year 'fore we meet another ship an' near that 'fore we make a port of call. Ye, sir, are partakin' o' my hospitality, my Christian spirit, an' my food an' lodgin'. If ye are not prepared to work for yer keep, we can always cast ye adrift again on yer sorry piece o' flotsam. By my soul and body, sir, ye are an ingrate. An ingrate, do ye hear me? Now, sign that article or prepare yerself for another swim."

Overwhelmed by the loud and militant reply, Daniel dipped the quill into the inkwell and was ready to sign. But, as a feeble challenge, he paused and said, "You must fill in your terms, Captain, before I will sign anything."

An angry Captain Corbet added the terms to the journal and then Todd printed his full name and signed it, carefully making M.D. stand out more boldly than the rest of the letters. With hesitancy and distaste, he printed "oarsman" after berth. "You did not fill in the date, Captain. I don't know what that is."

The captain added "July 2, 1849" and signed his full name. He then handed it to Mr. Halbert for his signature as witness and said, "Mr. Halbert, ye found 'im an' saw fit to bring 'im aboard. He'll be in the crew of yer Larboard Boat. Issue 'im slops and put 'im to work."

- - -

Todd strung his hammock in an empty space and grimaced at the tight crowding of the crew's berths; the hooks to which each hammock was tied had to be less than two feet apart. He inspected the "slops" for which he had just been charged. Everything was contained in a heavy canvas sea bag. Included also was a small bag Mr. Halbert had called a "ditty bag" and said it was to hold personal items and was to be hung from the hook at the head of his hammock. Also, there were blankets, a heavy coat, oilskins, boots, brogues, underwear, a bulky sweater and watch cap, sheath knife with the sharp point broken off—the Mate said it was for work and not for fighting—pipe, tobacco, and even needles and thread. Daniel thought, I'll look like a sailor even if I'm not.

When Mr. Halbert had taken him below to issue these slops to him, Daniel had been overwhelmed by the countless, tightly packed casks of all sizes that filled the hold of the ship. It was from one of these that his sea bag had been extracted. The Mate told him that everything goes to sea in casks—spare sails and rigging, flour, salt beef, hard bread, beans, tobacco, tons of fresh water, everything. He said that as the casks are emptied, they will eventually be used to store the whale oil as it is rendered; water might even have to be dumped if there is a sudden surplus of harvested oil.

Mr. Halbert had pointed out some casks with a capacity of fourteen barrels and other casks that ranged all the way down to tiny, slender ones that he called "wryers." Daniel was impressed by the apparent self-sufficiency of the *Ellie Mae* and realized that this might be a very long cruise.

His reverie was interrupted by a masthead lookout's call from far above deck, "Shoal of blackfins half a league off the larboard bow. Blackfins!"

Nearly exhausted by the day's efforts so far, Todd slowly made his way up the ladder to watch the activity indicated by pounding feet on the deck above. He heard the First Mate shout "Starboard and Bow Boats, prepare to launch."

Crews streamed into these two whaleboats, and they were quickly lowered from their davits, stopping short of the water and delaying casting off as the *Ellie Mae* took them closer to the gam of whales. When they did cast off, the oarsmen bent their backs and the sleek whaleboats skimmed the surface in the direction of their prey. Both boats successfully harpooned their blunt-headed quarry and were pulled swiftly along by their victims. One broke free before it could be killed by the harpooneer's lance, but that boat was successful in securing another. In less than an hour, both boats were alongside the *Ellie Mae,* and the dead whales were hoisted aboard and deposited on deck by heavy tackle.

"Best stand back, Dan'l, while these are bein' cut in," said Isaac, as he and other crewmen quickly set about slicing off large chunks of skin and blubber with cutting spades and casting them into the huge try-pots under which fires already were burning.

Todd was amazed how quickly the cutting-in was completed. Isaac returned to his side and said, "Now we'll be a bit more ginger in harvesting the melon blubber—that's from the junk an' jaw, ye know—'cause that's kept separate. It goes to watch oil an' is worth maybe $15 a gallon. It's prime stuff."

With that, Isaac and his mates began a careful dissection of the blunt heads of the two fifteen-foot-long carcasses. While that was being done, Fishcake sliced off slabs of the dark meat. Then, the remains were hoisted again and cast adrift in the sea. Sharks quickly collected and began devouring the carrion. The resourceful Fishcake now began fishing for the pilot fish that swarmed around the sharks.

Mr. Halbert approached and said, "Todd, ye seem well enough to watch. Bear a hand here with the Larboard Boat crew an' give her a swab down."

Isaac briefly cast his eyes heavenward in discontent and said, "C'mon, I'll show ye the drill."

Along with the rest of the whaleboat crew, Isaac took a bucket and handed one to Daniel. They went to the cask where he had seen crewmen urinating and partially filled their buckets with the yellow liquid. Then they stirred in ashes from the try-works and began swabbing the greasy deck where the whales had been flensed.

"It ain't pleasant," Isaac said as he wielded his swab, "but, sure as sin, it cuts the grease." After a vigorous scrubbing, buckets of sea water were used to flush it all down the scuppers.

In spite of it all, Todd chuckled to himself and reflected; well, at breakfast, I thought it best to mix with the crew and be accepted as one of them. There's no leveler or equalizer of personal worth quite like swabbing decks with your shipmate's urine to make those around you absolutely certain that you are one of them.

CHAPTER FIVE

During much of the week that followed, it was as though Todd had awakened in a totally alien world. It was a life that Daniel could hardly have imagined a month or so ago when he sailed out of Boston harbor on the *Southern Cross*—but he found himself enjoying what each new day presented. A freak accident involving some broken rigging disabled the Larboard Boat to which he had been assigned, preventing its involvement in a number of blackfin harvests until its repairs were completed, and allowing Daniel time for a gradual, although steady, recovery and an opportunity for him to acquaint himself with the ship.

He found that a whaler's crew was much larger than that needed to actually sail the ship. The additional numbers were needed to man all four whaleboats during the hunts. Each boat crew consisted of six men including a mate. A helmsman, some lookouts, and six or eight ship handlers, along with the Captain, had to remain on board the *Ellie Mae* to handle her while the boats were out. When no whales were being encountered, there was a surplus of crewmen and a great deal of busy work, such as scrubbing, flaking line, painting, and minor repairs, was assigned to the men to keep them occupied. Two boat crews make up the "starboard watch", and the other two crews are the "larboard watch." The watches alternate day by day in manning the mastheads and bow as lookouts and in working the helm and sails. There are no masthead lookouts during the hours of darkness. Throughout the day and night, the watches, or duty periods, are each four hours long except for the two "dog" watches, from eight bells to four bells and from four bells to eight bells in the evening (4:00-6:00 p.m. and 6:00-8:00 p.m.). The men composing the "starboard watch" or "larboard watch" rotate through these duty periods so, the purpose of the dog watches is to stagger the schedule so one person would not always end up with the same work period on his duty day, as he would if there were an even number of watches during the 24-hour period.

Daniel learned that there are two peals of the quarterdeck bell for each hour of the day, starting at 1:00 a.m. After eight bells, the count is started all over again, with eight bells being sounded at 4:00 a.m., 8:00 a.m., noon, 4:00 p.m., 8:00 p.m. and at midnight. Two bells are sounded at 1:00 a.m., four at 2:00 a.m., six at 3:00 a.m. etc. Daniel realized that it was a very good system since he no longer had a timepiece, nor apparently did any of the other men before the mast. Much of the ship handling, the shifting and changing of the sails appeared to be done by a small group of Cape Verde whalemen who seemed to keep mostly to themselves and were referred to by other crewmen collectively as the "Bravas".

Daniel had now stood several watches as a masthead lookout and had come to enjoy his time of solitude up there, although his first experience had filled him with panic. The ship had been pitching and rolling more than usual, he thought, as he looked up at the crow's nest high above him on the maintop and at the slightly lower one farther forward on the foretop. He had watched other lookouts as they scampered up the ratlines, and he had shuddered with apprehension when they reached their nest because each would then fearlessly lean out from the shrouds, hang from the edge of the crosstrees and then reach up to grasp the futtock shrouds, the lines from the upper mast that supported that platform. They would then dangle in space, their legs dancing an airy hornpipe, before they nimbly swung outward and scurried up onto their post.

Daniel was determined not to show the apprehension that gripped him but, as he reluctantly started to climb, each ascending step on the insubstantial crossropes found him less in command of his body and more reluctant to release one handhold so that he could reach on up to the next ratline. When he did arrive at the undersurface of the crosstrees, he was so frozen to the shrouds that there was absolutely no way he could force himself to imitate the other crewmen in their daredevil use of the futtock shrouds. He finally surrendered to the indignity of wiggling through the narrow hole in the crosstrees next to the mast, the so-called "lubber's hole", and wormed his way into the relative security of the encircling hoops, where he panted from panic and from his exertions but was flooded with relief at having survived the climb. Being a hundred feet above the *Ellie Mae's* deck, meant huge excursions of his perch in relation to the base of the mast and the rolling hull as the "crow's nest" swayed through great arcs of sky. Looking down and seeing the blue-green sea beneath him more of the time than the ship's deck caused panic to flood his being anew. It seemed to Daniel that the vessel must be tipping completely over on to its side, and that he would dip into the ocean long before the motion reversed, and he sped through the sky in the opposite direction. Gradually, by fixing his gaze on the horizon and the distant sea, as he was supposed to be doing as a lookout anyway, Daniel found he could relax and enjoy the remarkable view. He had spotted one pod of whales on his second masthead watch, but his inexperience drew jeers and ridicule from the crew because his quarry were finbacks and of no value. His vantage point from so high above the sea did afford a marvelous view of porpoises as they gamboled alongside the ship. He enjoyed watching them play and plunge along as though they were racing the *Ellie Mae*.

Swabbing, caulking, picking oakum, tarring seams, performing the many minor chores about the deck also allowed opportunity for Daniel to become even further acquainted with the ship. He was told that she was an hermaphrodite brig because she had two masts and that the mainmast could either be rigged with a square mainsail as a snow or with a fore-and-aft boom mainsail as a brig, as she was at the present time. She had four effective whaleboats, three suspended from davits along the larboard side—the Bow, the Waist, and the Larboard Boats. A fourth boat, the Starboard Boat, was in davits on the starboard side aft and was the province of the First Mate, Mr. Maxfield, during a hunt.

Forward of that, on the starboard side, was the cutting stage, a scaffold suspended over the side on which Mates stood to cut skin and blubber from whales too large to hoist on board. Daniel had not seen it used as yet. Forward of the cutting stage was an empty pair of davits that could house another whaleboat. A spare boat was slung from the "tail feathers", the davits at the fantail of the ship.

Between the foremast and the mainmast was the main hatch with its tarred canvas tarp that covered the actual hatch boards that made that access water tight. This opening was the major access to the hold of the ship. In front of the hatch was the try-works, a monstrous front-loading furnace of metal and fire-bricks, and two huge iron kettles perched securely on a rack above. These pots could be tipped so they drained their oil into a holding and cooling tank between decks. The poop deck was aft of the mainmast and housed the helm, binnacle and a small chart house. There was a second deck below the poop deck that housed the Captain's Quarters aft and the small adjoining Mates' cabins.

Forward of the hatch and foremast was steerage—the galley on the weather deck and the fo'castle below, which was the quarters for the crew. Beneath the galley was the huge holding tank where oil was sent from the try-works as it was boiled from the blubber and before it was finally placed in casks upon cooling.

Daniel could not complain about the food. Many times as a student, his fare had not been as varied and was never as plentiful. Occasionally, there was fresh fish when the cook was successful in his angling for triggerfish or pilot fish, or fresh liver was the fare whenever it was available because a porpoise had been harpooned from deck or on a hunt. Otherwise, meals were of salt meat, the so-called "salt horse", hash made from salt meat, fresh bread several times a week or hardtack the rest of the time, dried potatoes, baked beans, soup from dried peas, corn or beans, coffee or tea. Occasionally, the cook served a dessert of dried apple crisp, bread pudding, or duff. Of course, each meal consisted of only a couple of these items, but the quantity was always ample. Without fail, breakfast was the ubiquitous porridge, bread and tea.

Daniel had mastered getting into and out of his hammock and had even become accustomed to sleeping in the comma-posture that it produced. As a matter of fact, he found himself looking forward to the uninterrupted nights when his Larboard Watch did not have the duty, and he was assured the security of enjoying his personal area of the ship throughout the entire night. His new life was indeed tolerable.

CHAPTER SIX

"B-L-O-O-O-O-W-S-S-S! Sperm whales off the starboard beam! B-l-o-o-o-o-w-s!" The masthead lookouts almost danced their excitement because sperm whales were the prime goal of the cruise and also, a pledge of 5 pounds of tobacco had been made to the first lookout to spot a sperm that was eventually taken. Most importantly, the more productive the hunt, the quicker a full cargo of oil and bone could be obtained and the sooner the ship could return home, all hands the richer.

"Man all boats," Captain Corbet bellowed from the poop deck and all hands scurried to their stations. Line tubs were uncovered, lifted into each whaleboat and then stowed forward of the midship thwart. Gripes were cast off and harpoons and lances unsheathed. Isaac, the boatsteerer, sat in the stern of Larboard Boat.

"Lower the boats!" Again, Captain Corbet vented a voice seemingly twice too large for his dumpy body. The falls were cast off, and all the boats settled into the water. Daniel, Mr. Halbert, and three other men hung on to tackle and skidded down the slide boards to take their places in the Larboard Boat. Isaac Lawrence and Tolliver, the harpooneer, positioned themselves in bow and stern. Mr. Halbert directed Daniel to a place beside him on the stroke oar thwart. Dugan and Pinchot had the oars at the midship thwart. They pushed off from the ship and took a few shortened sweeps with their oars. The boat rose and fell on the gentle swells and drifted behind the *Ellie Mae*. She was already slowing, her square sails shortened and aback as she swung into the wind. The whaleboat's mast was stepped, the lugsail hoisted and, with Lawrence at the tiller, the Larboard Boat slid around the counter of the *Ellie Mae*.

Dugan stared ahead at the pod of sperms and observed, "Not much chance of a big bull in this gam. Usually, they's all by theirselves."

All four whaleboats abreast slowly approached the whales, and Mr. Halbert spoke softly, "Quiet men. Don't even shift yer quid."

Isaac excitedly whispered, "They're still soundin', so they're grazin' and ain't afeared of us."

"Quiet, Lawrence!" Mr. Halbert hissed. He directed Lawrence to steer toward the largest whale, and Tolliver stood up in the bow, his harpoon poised. "Bring me in dartin' range—wood to black skin, sez I," he muttered softly.

The whaleboat sailed up onto the monstrous back, and Tolliver thrust the harpoon downward, just in front of the hump. The startled beast shot ahead in an explosion of motion. In the boat, the sail and mast were quickly taken down. Isaac and Mr. Talbert moved forward so Lawrence could handle the line as it chafed around the loggerhead and the Mate was in position where he could lance the whale when the boat was close enough. The rudder had been quickly shipped.

After the initial run, the big sperm paused in its attempted escape, and a drogue tub was quickly attached to the line. When the whale resumed its plunging flight through the waves, the drogue slowed it noticeably. Still, spray swept outward like giant wings from the bouncing bow, and the entire crew was thoroughly soaked during their "sleigh ride."

"Forty-barrel bull," Mr. Halbert shouted.

The struggling whale alternately plunged ahead on long runs, sounded, spun, slapped the water with his giant flukes, and launched off again, dragging drogue and whaleboat behind as though they weren't there. Daniel couldn't believe the harpoon did not dislodge at the tremendous strain placed on it. In some of his soundings, the bull actually pulled the bow of the whaleboat completely underwater because Isaac, who was managing the line at the loggerhead, was either unwilling or unable to slacken it quickly enough. All hands had to bail and Todd marveled that men would subject themselves to these hazards on purpose. Just before another sounding, the big flukes broke water and then crashed down on the surface, narrowly missing the bow of the boat.

Mr. Halbert never got within range to thrust his razor sharp lance into a vital spot in the beast. Since they were almost out of sight of the *Ellie Mae* and the battle showed no sign of slackening, he broke out a bomb lance from its watertight cask. The next time an adequate portion of the whale's back showed above the surface, Mr. Halbert ordered all hands to row to a position parallel to the sperm. All backs strained to the maximum. The whale appeared to be resting when the Mate hurled the bomb lance. There was a muffled blast as it exploded in the bull's lungs. His death leap sent a great wave that nearly swamped the boat. The behemoth shuddered and then spouted a bloody froth.

"His chimney's afire!" Mr. Halbert shouted and all hands slumped onto their oars in exhaustion.

Using the harpoon line, the crew gradually pulled the whaleboat close enough again for the Mate to plunge his lance repeatedly between the whale's ribs until the bull finally died and turned fin out. Tolliver chopped a hole through the fluke and attached a line. A "waif" was hoisted—a flag to signal the *Ellie Mae* that they had a kill—and all hands relaxed with fresh water and hard bread.

Daniel could only guess how long the struggle had lasted. He was certain, though, that more than two hours must have elapsed since Tolliver had "darted" the huge whale, as the whalemen described any harpooning. He had had moments of fear, but this had been an experience he would always remember. He found he was actually enjoying his new life, and the sight of the *Ellie Mae* underway in their direction sparked a warm sensation of homecoming in him.

- - -

Two other whaleboats, in addition to the Larboard Boat, had had success in their hunt. Three sperm whales were secured alongside the *Ellie Mae* as she lay hove-to in preparation for the cutting-in. Two whales were tied up on the larboard side and the one taken by Daniel's team was "flukes forward" under the cutting stage on the starboard side. The leviathans were to remain there all night because it had been almost dark before the ship recovered all three kills. The four whaleboats had been triced up and secured to their davits, plug holes opened in the bottoms so all sea water could drain and "supper the watch" called. Captain Corbet had even issued a tot of rum to all hands in celebration of the successful hunt.

The next day, the crew was greeted with an early breakfast at eight bells and then all hands streamed on deck in the pre-dawn to stand by for the cutting-in. Daniel's job was to mince blubber in the "blubber parlor"; until some was available on which he could work, he was free to watch the flensing process on deck.

The whale under the cutting stage was secured by a heavy chain that was made fast to a massive bitt on the forward deck and passed out through the starboard hawsepipe to encircle the tail just in front of the flukes. This had been accomplished last night in the process Isaac had called "sweeping and fluking." The great blunt head of the whale was held close to the stern of the ship by a line secured to the beast by a harpoon.

The Mates, armed with razor-sharp cutting-in spades on handles about twenty feet long, leaned against the railing on the cutting stage over the dead beast and made a hole in his hide just behind the eye. A huge hook, suspended on a series of hawsers and blocks from the mainmast head, was inserted in this hole. All available hands, Daniel included since he was not yet occupied, were set to hauling at the windlass. As more and more tension was applied, the *Ellie Mae* began to cant over toward the whale which now acted as a huge anchor. Daniel strained along with the other grunting crewmen to the accompaniment of the groaning ship's timbers. He feared the mast might snap, but there was a sudden sucking sound as the blubber started tearing away from the whale. A bulky strip of skin and blubber, fashioned and shaped by the Mate's slashing cutting spades as they dissected the scarf, stripped away from the whale, causing the beast slowly to roll over and over in the sea. Daniel was reminded of his peeling an apple and striving to keep the ribbon of skin intact.

When the heavy strip of skin and blubber could go no higher because the tackle was "two-blocked", Tolliver, a harpooneer, thrust a long boarding knife through it in two places at deck level. A chain was then pushed through these holes and attached to a second hawser, the "port falls" of the cutting blocks. When that line fully supported the lower part of the blubber blanket, the upper part was severed by chopping through it with the boarding knife just above the new support, and the original blanket swung over the deck, still attached to it's hook. It was then lowered through the main hatch into the blubber parlor. Mr. Brewer, the Second Mate, ordered Todd and others below to start their work there.

It was hot and the air hung heavy with the fleshy odor of the blubber. Daniel imitated the other men as they wielded their knifelike mincing spades and cut one-by-two-foot blocks of skin and blubber from the huge blanket and then made many crosscuts that left the inch-thick flaps of fat connected to one another only by the thick gray skin, making a "bible" as they called it.

Everyone went about his work in silence except for Trumbull. It seemed to Daniel that this man always thrust himself forward in any group, whether it was at table in the fo'castle, at work on deck, or lying in his hammock shouting insulting commentary to anyone within earshot. This occasion was no exception.

The blusterer paused in his work now and roared, "Mark me, lads! Corkscrew Trumbull can play hell an' come up jack. He can stove the skull of any mother's son who claims Bedford town as his port." He sliced wantonly at the blanket of blubber, glowered at Daniel and added, "Or any fancy sawbones, either!"

Surprised by the man's sudden and unwarranted aggression, Todd bristled. He had only been in one fight in his entire life and was certainly not eager to answer this challenge, especially against a bully of Trumbull's size and one with such a lethal weapon in his hands. But, he could not ignore the gauntlet that had been thrown down and still earn the respect of the men around him. He took a step toward Trumbull with the appearance of much more aggression than he actually felt and ran his thumb along the knife edge of his own mincing spade.

"Well, Corkscrew Trumbull, your liver probably looks just like any other man's, and I've seen a lot of them in my time. You anxious to put yours on display, are you?" Daniel hoped his growling, thespian words sounded threatening and with no hint of a quaver to betray the fear he felt.

Just then, Mr. Brewer shouted down through the open hatch, "Turn to an' finish that last lot, ye slackers. Here comes another'n."

Todd and Trumbull glowered menacingly at each other but returned to their work. Daniel thought, I wonder if he's as relieved as I am.

Blanket after blanket was lowered into the hold, and the mincing continued. There was no more open conflict, but the atmosphere remained charged. Finally, Todd was sent to the weather deck with an armload of spades to be sharpened because they had been dulled in the work. He sought out Mr. Swan, the Cooper, whose sole duty during the cutting-in and mincing was sharpening spades at the grinding wheel that was set up on deck. Dull ones were deposited in one cask, blades down, and as the Cooper finished working on them, he placed them in another open cask with their knifelike edges upward, gleaming in the sunlight. The longer-handled cutting-in spades were carefully laid out on deck as soon as they were sharpened.

Daniel paused to look over the gunwale and saw the last blanket of blubber coming off the first whale. The carcass had great craters in its flesh where chunks of meat had been torn from it by sharks as it had rolled over and over during the flensing. Daniel watched the Mates on the stage punch many holes in the intestine with their long spades and then they smelled them after each thrust in the hope of detecting the presence of ambergris. Isaac had told him that ambergris was a rich but rare treasure that could be sold as an agent in the making of perfume. The Mates were disappointed in their quest this time. Now the body was cut through just in front of the flukes and those were hoisted on deck.

After the head had been severed just behind the condyles of the skull, the rest of the great body was cast off and allowed to drift away on the sea where the trailing sharks swarmed around it and set about stripping off the last of its flesh. Daniel had been told that the head accounted for about one third of the whale's body weight, so it weighed many tons and could not be hoisted on deck because of the possibility that it might break the hawsers or drive the foot of the mast through the keel, sinking the ship. The head was allowed to float in the sea, although it was secured close to the ship. Isaac had told Daniel that the fore and upper part of the whale's head was made up of the spermaceti "case" that could hold hundreds of gallons of that fine oil; near it was a massive amount of fat called "junk" which was quickly cut away and hoisted on deck to be treated as common blubber. The Mates carefully separated the case by cutting through the "whitehorse", a fibrous floor of the case itself.

Adams, boatsteerer on the Starboard Boat, was then lowered over the side in a bo'sun's chair on a line held by his boatmates. His job was to make the "fastenings", a spider web of cordage across the rear end of the case to form an attachment for a heavy line from the cutting blocks. Adams busied himself making this lacing with a two-foot-long "head needle". Daniel was impressed by the man's courage; three times before he completed his work, only the very skillful handling of his life line by the men on deck above had saved him from being crushed between the head and the rolling ship. Many sharks were killed by the slashing cutting spades of the Mates before the beasts could get to Adams' partially submerged body. Finally, tackle was secured to the fastenings, and Adams was hoisted safely aboard.

Now, the rear end of the case was hoisted to deck level, the bulk of the head still buoyed by the sea. A meticulous cut was then made in the case and a "case bucket", a long, slender, round-bottomed piece of equipment suspended by tackle from the foresail yard, was lowered into the slit. It was pushed in by a slender pole and repeatedly extracted so its contents could be dumped into butts and tubs on deck. The valuable spermaceti would be boiled separately later and stored in special casks.

"Todd! Quit yer gawkin' and fetch them spades to the blubber parlor," Mr. Brewer shouted in a voice so loud that it could be heard over the entire ship. "Damn it, move lively now, man!"

The cutting-in of the other two whales continued until dark and then fires were started in the furnaces of the try-works. The boiling would continue throughout the night, manned in six-hour watches. It was mind-numbing work; the seemingly endless task of casting bibles of slithery, minced blubber into the try-pots, draining the golden oil into cooling tanks and then into casks below deck, skimming the fibrous tried remnants of the blubber from the surface, draining them, and then casting them into the raging furnaces to fuel the continuing process.

Before Daniel's watch at the try-works, he had enjoyed a huge supper of baked beans and fried sperm whale meat. The old hands said it didn't compare in taste to the meat of a humpback, but it was certainly superior to either fish or "salt horse." After his watch, Daniel collapsed into his hammock, so exhausted that not even the uncomfortable heat that had invaded the fo'castle from the nearby try-works furnace kept him awake. His last thought before sleep overtook him was a quick mental calculation. Isaac had said that the hundred or so barrels of oil from the three whales should bring between $1600 and $1700. His 1/185th of the lay would be worth about $9.00—probably equal to the fees he would have earned from four or five office calls if he were in practice now instead of engaged in the endless hours of backbreaking toil he had just completed.

Well, maybe someday . . .

CHAPTER SEVEN

Sperm hunting was good. Days were filled alternately with successful hunts and the firing up of the try-works. Daniel gradually became confident in his duties and even found excitement in the pitting of his crew's whaleboat against the behemoths. One day, the Larboard Boat took a sperm whale that yielded forty-seven barrels of oil. In its death throes, it vomited dozens of small squid. Three of the larger ones were completely undigested and had tentacles over four feet long so they were turned over to Fishcake, the cook, for a calamary menu. Daniel had never eaten calamary before and found it to be delicious.

In late September, the *Ellie Mae* had anchored briefly in the roadstead at the Portuguese island of Santo Antao to take on fresh stores. All hands labored willingly as boatload after boatload of water casks, fresh vegetables, fruit, live pigs and chickens, and some fresh meat drew alongside to be hoisted aboard the whaling ship. The prospects of a change in diet brought smiles to every face and, surprisingly, even to that of the usually dour Fishcake. At first, Daniel eagerly scanned the harbor for any American ship he might transfer to, but then remembered that he was totally without funds and could not buy passage anyway. He realized how very far from home he was when someone commented that the dusty winds they had experienced on this Cape Verde Island were laden with sand from the African Sahara. It was over three months since he had embarked so optimistically from Boston and Daniel realized that he was destined to finish his tour on the *Ellie Mae*. Captain Corbet ordered her back to sea with the first tide after the last piece of stores was hoisted on board. He didn't want to risk having *any* of his crew jump ship. The anchor was catted up, full sail spread, and the ship continued on her quest.

Mr. Halbert, the Third Mate, continued to be steady and imperturbable. Daniel admired his efficiency and lack of bluster. He never demanded a show of respect, but there was an aura of command about him that made the "Mr." or the "Sir" automatic when any of the crew addressed him. He was actually respected much more than Captain Corbet, but the men were careful not to make a display of this.

Isaac Lawrence continued to be Daniel's friend and chief mentor. The bond between them grew stronger every day. Although very robust, with massive shoulders and arms, Isaac had a placid demeanor, much like Mr. Halbert. Daniel learned that, as a boatsteerer, Isaac would receive 1/100th of the lay and was probably in line to be made a Mate whenever a vacancy became available. He had a sweetheart in New Bedford and planned to marry her whenever he became an officer.

The rest of the fo'castle crew seemed to cluster into three main groups. There were the older hands, ones who had shipped on the *Ellie Mae's* last voyage. Three of these were in the Larboard Boat's crew and because of that fact and Isaac Lawrence's stout friendship toward Todd, he was readily accepted as a member of this group. There were the "Bravas", the Cape Verde whalemen who did most of the ship handling. And finally, there was the rest of the crew in steerage. They were a younger lot, in general, and many had not been to sea before. Trumbull had been on other ships in the past so because of that, his size, age and his naturally domineering character, he was able to play the part of the old sea dog and thus become the unsavory leader of that group. Perhaps if the old hands had put Trumbull in his place early in the cruise instead of merely ignoring him, he would not have become so obnoxious and powerful, Daniel mused.

When the weather was good and there was no hunting or cutting-in, the crew members who were not on watch spent their evenings after supper on deck to escape the heat in the fo'castle. Some just smoked or talked or listened to Flaherty play his concertina and sometimes even sang along. Not Trumbull; he was always pushing, wrestling, skylarking and being aggressive in some manner of word or deed. He was even worse when foul weather forced the crew to spend off-duty hours in the confines of the fo'castle below.

Ever since they had picked up the Southeast Trades on leaving Santo Antao, the ship had logged many miles each day, but there had been more frequent rain squalls. Late the previous afternoon, a hard gale had overtaken them. The captain had ordered all sails reefed save the fore topgallant, and the *Ellie Mae* began rolling scuppers under as waves overtook the ship in long combers. All hands were exhausted after nearly two weeks of dawn-to-dark labor from the hunts and harvests so the respite afforded by the storm was welcome.

Today, the sea was somewhat quieter, but the wind-whipped rain continued to drench those with the watch at the helm or at the mastheads. Those who were not on watch enjoyed their leisure in the fo'castle; there was a general light-heartedness and Daniel and Isaac were attempting to keep checkers from sliding off the mess table where they were playing under a ship's lantern that swayed and bobbed with each plunge of the vessel. Others of the crew were in their hammocks, all swinging rhythmically with the roll of the weltering ship.

As usual, Trumbull was commenting loudly on somebody's feeble attempt to grow a beard, someone else's clumsiness in the shrouds, one of the *Brava's* torture of the English language—on an on, endlessly. His commentaries were always cruel, but it was obvious that he thought them quite humorous. Usually, his own laughter was the only response to be heard. His ongoing prattle was just another of the several methods he used to maintain influence over those he felt he could dominate.

"So, ye're goin' to marry a Quakeress when ye make port again, are ye, Grover lad?" Trumbull queried as he lazed in his pendulous hammock with arms cradling his head as he waxed magisterially over those around him. "She'll trim yer sails, man. Are ye certain sure 'tis what ye want? I mean, a'givin' up yer freedom an' all the creature joys of rum an' loose women. Ol' Corkscrew sez 'tis a crime ye'll be committin'—a crime agin yerself an' all jus' fer a warm back in yer bed. That'll grow scripture-poundin' cold all too quick, I'm tellin' ye. Mark me words, Grover, or ye'll curse the day ye didn't."

Grover ducked his head, obviously insulted by Trumbull's comments about his betrothed but too intimidated to challenge the man. His reluctance just spurred Trumbull to continue. "Aye, I'm tellin' ye, what ye need, Grover, is to shed some o' yer ballast. When yer ol' snake is gettin' hard as a narwhale's tusk, ye need to scratch yer itch right here at sea an' not be a'lustin' fer what's waitin' back there in port. Mebbe ol' Lawrence there'll share the sea pussy he's found in that li'l doctor friend of his'n. Yessir, nothin's as good as sea pussy when ye've been months at sea. Ain't that right, Lawrence?"

All conversation ceased, and the only sound in the fo'castle was the groaning ship's timbers as they strained against the working of the pitching hull. Daniel was speechless at the idea that he could be considered a depraved "sailor's maiden", and his fury exploded. He stumbled to his feet to confront Trumbull, but Isaac rose faster and moved around the table, placing a restraining hand on Todd's arm. Lawrence advanced to the foot of Trumbull's hammock and glowered at him in silence for half a minute.

Then, in a voice absolutely malignant in its softness, he said, "Ye best learn yer place in this here crew, Trumbull."

With the swiftness of a striking cobra, Isaac whipped his knife from its sheath and slashed the rope that attached Corkscrew's hammock to its supporting hook. Trumbull crashed to the deck with a painful grunt that was followed by a curse. He struggled to rise, and Lawrence drew back his knife, cocking it ready to slash horizontally at the bully's throat.

"Try to rise or puke out one more such word about me or Todd an', as God is my witness, I'll mince yer throat like a piece o' blubber," Isaac warned.

Thoroughly daunted, Trumbull slumped back onto the deck as Lawrence calmly returned to his checker game. Someone chuckled up forward and, in a second or two, another bit of laughter was added to it. Soon, the entire fo'castle resounded with the gales of merriment, and nothing could have been more painful to Trumbull than this derision. In that brief exchange, his dominance over the crew had been shattered. Daniel watched as the bully, wilted in his shame, hung his head while he re-slung his hammock. It was satisfying to see him humbled in this manner, but Todd was certain he and his shipmates had not seen the end of this encounter.

Suddenly, almost as a capstone to the drama just ended, but one that eclipsed Trumbull's shame, Lowell suddenly pitched forward from his seat on the bench near Daniel and went into a seizure. His back arched, his fists clenched as they drew up tightly to his chest, his eyes turned back into his head and his whole body went into violent convulsive movements. Todd sprang to his side and, whipping the leather scabbard of his sheath knife from his belt, worked it in between Lowell's tightly clenched jaws and then compressed the carotid arteries in his neck. Shipmates grasped Lowell's limbs to restrain them until finally, the man relaxed and lay in slack unconsciousness on the deck.

"What's wrong with him?" Isaac asked.

"Epilepsy. A fit," Todd barked.

"Can you do anythin' for him?"

"Just leave him there on the deck for now," Todd replied. "If he doesn't have another one in the next little while, we'll put him in his hammock."

"What caused it? I've never seen him have one before. 'Course, he's a new man," Isaac said.

"Well, it's due to some sort of irritation of the brain. We don't know all that much about its cause," Daniel admitted.

"Can you treat him?"

Having been virtually ignored as a true doctor, Todd could not resist a professorial touch to his answer. "Not very well, even ashore, and probably not at all here at sea. There's no cure and the treatment is directed, in the main, toward simply reducing the frequency of the seizures. Some doctors recommend changing the diet; whatever the patient ate before, change it to something else, but favor meats, cream, and milk. Avoid fermented liquors. Some say that the scalp should be shaved once a week, taking all but a few ringlets of hair around the temples. Of course, Lowell here doesn't have all that much hair anyway. They do say that the scalp should be rubbed daily with a stiff brush. Some bleed the patient from the temporal artery during a seizure," he said, pointing to his temple, "to relieve pressure on the brain, but I think that pressing on the arteries in the neck is every bit as effective and certainly safer."

Daniel continued, "There are medicines—antimonials, mercurial purgatives, various antiphlogistics—but I've been taught that medicines that relieve disorders of the nerves—serpentaria, cardamomum, belladonna, opium and others of that sort—are the most efficient. They are probably the best, but we don't have any of those, anyway. The only thing we can do is to wrestle him like we just did whenever he has a fit and try to keep him from hurting himself. We must make sure that Lowell is never a masthead lookout again where he could fall to his death with a seizure."

Daniel shook his head in frustration and then said, "I think we can put him in his hammock now. He'll probably sleep for several hours."

- - -

Most days since they had picked up the Southeast Trades, the wind continued to speed them on their way south. As they drew ever closer to the equator, the air became stifling in its hot, suffocating mugginess and on this day, it barely stirred their canvas. Every inch of sail was hoisted, but the *Ellie Mae* was almost dead in the water. A spate of successful sperm hunts had produced so rich a harvest that hopes rose for an early return to port with full casks by the end of the year but then, a dearth of prey was encountered. There had been no sightings in over a week.

Suddenly, the main masthead watch sang out, "Huge sperm aft the starboard beam."

All hands excitedly thronged to that side of the ship. Indeed, a huge bull was spouting, and his spume blew in that forward arc so characteristic of a sperm whale.

"Away all boats!" the captain shouted excitedly.

In just minutes, the operation that had become such a routine quickly resulted in all four whaleboats careening rapidly toward their quarry, bows rising and falling as all backs bent at the oars to reach the whale first. Three times the bull sounded and then broke the surface, first on one side of the boats or then behind them, as though he was playing tag or hide-and-seek.

"He may make more'n a hundred barrel," marveled Mr. Halbert in a voice more excited than Daniel had ever heard from him.

Then on the fourth sounding, the bull was gone so long that everyone thought he had tired of his sport and had fled to another part of the seemingly boundless ocean. Suddenly, as if his anger had been whetted by the hounding persistence of his tormenters, he exploded from the sea in an ecstasy of rage and arched over on his side to crash down on the bow of the Larboard Boat. It splintered into a thousand tiny fragments. Three of the crew simply disappeared under the tons of flesh—Tolliver, the harpooneer who had been standing expectantly in the bow with harpoon ready; Pinchot, who was filling-in as one of the midship oarsmen; and Mr. Halbert, who ordinarily waited until the harpoon was set before he moved to the bow to use his lance but today, in his excitement, had made the move prematurely. Isaac was just in the process of moving to his station by the loggerhead. Todd, at the stroke oar, Dugan on the midship thwart, and Isaac were all catapulted into the air, and fell onto the bull's back, then slid off in different directions from the rough and barnacle-covered surface. All three dived frantically to escape the slap of the giant flukes.

When Daniel finally sputtered to the surface, gasping for air, he was confronted by a huge, unblinking Cyclopean eye as the mountainous whale glided past him. Panic-stricken, he dived again and swam with frenzied strokes in the direction of the nearest whaleboat. Its crew, however, their hunting zeal momentarily overcome by the bloody spectacle they had just witnessed, was rowing away with all their strength to distance themselves from the bull. Finally, Mr. Maxfield was able to restore order, and the Starboard Boat came about, ready to attack the whale. When Daniel reached it, he was pulled on board, shaken and breathless. He could now see that Isaac and Dugan were safe in Mr. Carringer's Bow Boat.

As though sated, the sperm whale made a final sounding and, after many minutes, spouted nearly a mile away before disappearing completely. A search for the bodies of the three victims was fruitless and, after hunting for nearly an hour, the remaining three boats pulled toward the distant *Ellie*

Mae. Todd stared down at his shaking hands and tried to steady them. He was unsuccessful.

- - -

On the day following the accident, Captain Corbet read a service for the three victims. There was little emotion in his voice as he dutifully droned the words. Just as he started the final prayer, a refreshing breeze suddenly stirred the air. The captain cocked a weather eye at the sails as they filled and, paraphrasing the devotional to make it even more brief, he quickly blurted the words, "We come into this world with nothing and leave it in the same manner. God have mercy on their souls. Amen."

Without missing a beat, Captain Corbet bellowed his orders to the helmsman, "Ready about! Helms alee!"

The great mainsail was the last to fill. As it slowly billowed, the ship began to move, leaving just the trace of a wake.

- - -

Mr. Carringer, the Fourth Mate and boatheader of the Bow Boat was promoted to take Mr. Halbert's post as Third Mate. As expected, Isaac Lawrence was made Fourth Mate. He was left in command of the Larboard Boat, though, and Mr. Carringer stayed in the Bow Boat. Chastain, a boatsteerer from the Waist Boat was made the harpooneer to take Tolliver's place, Dugan became boatsteerer and two Bravas, Andrade and Barros, became the other Larboard Boat oarsmen.

Isaac was not accorded the appellation of "Mr." Lawrence until he moved out of the fo'castle steerage. Apparently, that transfer was being delayed for a few days until a seemly period had passed before he occupied the dead officer's room. He was, however, now the boatheader and in full command of the new Larboard Boat which, in the past, had been the spare and hung in the "tail feathers."

The breeze that had terminated the funeral service grew into a satisfying wind that gradually approached gale force but brought no rain. The *Ellie Mae,* moving southerly with the trade winds, had covered slightly over 200 miles in the last twenty-four hours

Following the evening meal, Todd and Isaac were enjoying the cool wind and stood, bracing themselves against it, on the weather deck. Suddenly, there was movement in the shadows, and a belaying pin struck downward from out of the gathering darkness to deliver a crushing blow to the front of Isaac's head. It swung back in an almost continuous motion to strike a second blow, but with an instinctive movement of his arm, Isaac was able to deflect it even though he was already slumping to the deck.

Trumbull emerged from the shadow, having taken the opportunity to vent his hatred before Isaac would become less accessible by moving to officer's quarters aft. Trumbull had carefully chosen this time for his attack.

"And I've got somethin' here for ye, too, Sea Pussy. Ye'll both be shark bait tonight," he growled, advancing toward Todd with the bloody belaying pin cocked.

Daniel gave ground, wondering briefly if reacting differently in his earlier skirmishes with Trumbull would have made any difference now. No, nothing made any difference now except finding a way to survive. As Daniel retreated, his outstretched hand encountered the barrel of mincing spades Mr. Swan, the Cooper, had been sharpening earlier in the day. They stood, as though at attention, their razor-sharp blades glinting in the fading light as they pointed skyward. Daniel pulled one out and waved it threateningly. It seemed strange; that day, long ago in the blubber parlor, he had fingered such a spade to bluff Trumbull but now, he sincerely wanted to kill the man with it.

Trumbull stalked him and taunted, "Pussy! Pussy! Ye ain't got the balls to use that thing!" He held his left hand out, guarding and set to grasp the handle of Todd's spade, but drawing back the other with its belaying pin as he prepared to strike. The next thing seemed to happen before either man realized it. There was a sudden twitch of Trumbull's belaying pin, and Todd swung the spade with both hands, putting every ounce of his strength into the effort. Trumbull's left hand proved to be no barrier. The knife-edged spade crashed it aside and laid open his belly just below the rib cage. Trumbull looked down in surprise to see his guts spilling out through the bloody rent in his shirt. Slack-mouthed, he slumped to his knees on the deck. The belaying pin clattered from his grasp, and he cradled his bowels in both hands, sprawling full length on the deck.

Todd rushed to Isaac and was grateful to feel a pulse in the man's wrist. He bellowed, "Ahoy the Deck. Two men down. Up forward!"

"Bow lookout! Check it out!" the Officer of the Deck shouted through his voice trumpet.

Zenker, the bow lookout of the starboard watch, noisily raced aft and almost stumbled over Lawrence. He gazed at the bloody spade still in Todd's grasp and then at Trumbull's ineffectual crawling movements. "My God, Todd! What've ye done, lad?"

"Get the Captain," Todd ordered.

In just a moment, Captain Corbet rushed on the scene, fully clothed but in stocking feet. "What've ye done, Todd? Ye gone daft? Unhand that spade!"

Todd pointed at Trumbull as the mincing spade clattered to the deck. "He clubbed Lawrence with that belaying pin, Cap'n, and attacked me—shouted that he'd make us both shark bait tonight. I did for him with that spade."

Captain Corbet silently took in the whole scene and then growled to Zenker, "Throw him in the lazaret," and pointed with a nod of his head in Todd's direction.

"It was self defense, Cap'n. Are you, as the *ship's doctor*," Todd stressed the last two words to emphasize their irony, "going to sew up Trumbull's belly—or treat Lawrence's busted skull?"

The captain cast a cranky eye at Todd, pursed his lips in a quinine-sour pucker of frustration and growled, "Can ye save 'em?"

"I don't know, Cap'n, but that's what I'm trained to do. I think, Lawrence maybe; Trumbull, probably not," Todd replied calmly.

"He's my new Fourth Mate," Corbet barked, stabbing the air between himself and Lawrence with the thrust of his finger. As though that rationalization made his concession permissible, he allowed, "Do what ye can."

"I'll need lamps, a sail-maker's needle, thread from my ditty bag, and hot water. I'll need men to take them down to the fo'castle mess tables. Oh, and I'll need rum," Todd added with authority.

"I'll not have ye besotted at a time like this," Corbet bellowed in his quarterdeck voice.

"Not to drink, Cap'n. To soak the needle and thread in," Todd barked back.

By this time, Zenker had passed the word in the fo'castle and men now streamed from it. "Put Lawrence on a pallet in the fo'castle—not in his hammock. Gently now. Bring Trumbull with me. Carry him belly up so his guts don't spill," Todd ordered. He set off in a rush to clear the mess table.

When the patients were deposited, Lawrence still unconscious and Trumbull mewling his fear and pain, Todd quickly examined Isaac. There was a bloody indentation of his forehead so there was probably a depressed skull fracture. As he moved the left forearm, he could feel the bones grate where they had been broken deflecting the second blow. But with Isaac unconscious for the moment and Trumbull's guts hanging out, Todd's priority seemed clear; he had to work on the man he was least interested in saving. He turned to the challenge he had created for himself in Trumbull's wound. Taking a deep breath that seemed to express his fear and trepidation, he rolled up his sleeves and began putting crude "instruments" into a basin of rum—needle, thread, sheath knife and, after seeing Trumbull's undigested supper issuing from the rent in his stomach, a spoon from the galley. He exposed Trumbull's hairy belly by tearing away his shirt and, unbuckling his belt, said to the groaning patient, "You don't deserve this, you miserable . . ." words failed him. "But I'm going to try to save you. It gives me some pleasure to know that you will feel a great deal of pain in the process. Hold him, men."

CHAPTER EIGHT

Even though Trumbull was still alive when he finished, Daniel was certain that the wounded man would not live more than a day or so. When he had first inspected the wound in the feeble light of the swinging ship's lantern overhead, he found that one lobe of the liver had been nicked and was oozing blood, the falciform ligament was severed, the spleen and gall bladder were intact, the fundus of the stomach was laid wide open and was disgorging Trumbull's supper into the belly cavity along with the blood pumping from the severed gastric artery. He had spooned all of the supper from the wound as best he could and with that, a screaming Trumbull had fainted.

Daniel then took a stitch around the bleeding artery and sewed up the wall of the stomach as though he were closing a sack of grain; the wet tissue was slippery as an eel and hard to grasp because of the blood and stomach fluids. He flushed the blood and the last of the food particles by pouring rum into the wound and then, tipping the patient over to let it run out, had wrapped the lacerated liver and repaired stomach in shreds of omentum and finally, had closed the belly wall.

As he labored, he thought of the cases of puerperal sepsis he had seen—childbirth fever that had followed even uncomplicated deliveries. When he had watched the autopsies on those women, their bellies had all been filled by great pools of pus. Dr. Oliver Wendell Holmes had postulated in a lecture that that inflammation came through contamination by the doctor's dirty hands and that it might be prevented by hand washing in mild carbolic acid. Many doctors had been insulted by such a suggestion but Dr. Channing, the obstetrician who had been Todd's mentor, put great stock in Holme's words and by complying had greatly reduced his complication rate. Rum was probably a poor substitute for carbolic acid; surely, under the present conditions, Trumbull would develop the equivalent of puerperal sepsis and would probably suffer from continued internal bleeding or damage from leaking digestive juices. Tired and thoroughly drained, Daniel felt he had done all that was humanly possible and turned to care for his friend, Isaac, who still was unconscious.

There was fresh blood still oozing from Isaac's nostrils, although no wound was visible on the nose itself. Suddenly, Todd recalled details of the skull he had studied in medical school. He remembered that there had been a large air pocket in the forehead, the frontal sinus, which drains into the nose. Daniel closed his eyes and could visualize that sinus with its posterior wall immediately adjacent to the brain cavity and its anterior wall just under the skin of the forehead. Perhaps—just perhaps—the depression in Isaac's forehead represented a caved-in front skull wall of the sinus and the back wall might still be intact; the bleeding could be entirely from the sinus itself. No depressed skull fracture that endangered the brain! Just the possibility of such a situation lifted a great weight from Todd's mind.

The thought of operating on his friend and trying to elevate a depressed piece of skull off the brain had filled Daniel with dread. He would merely wait for Isaac to regain consciousness and observe him. If he gradually recovered from the shock of the blow itself, that improvement would be fairly good evidence that nothing was pressing on the brain tissue, and Todd wouldn't need to operate. Just observation was the thing now. While his patient was still unconscious, he quickly pulled on Isaac's left arm and molded the fractured bones into place. When the bones were set, he fashioned a splint from barrel staves. Just as he was finishing, Captain Corbet returned to the fo'castle.

"So? So?" he growled.

"The operation is finished, sir. I doubt that Trumbull will survive, but I repaired the damage as well as I could." Turning to Isaac, Todd continued, "Your new Fourth Mate has a broken arm that I have set and splinted. I'm hoping that depression in his forehead is just damage to his frontal sinus and not a true skull fracture. Watching what happens to him over the next hours and days will tell us whether he needs surgery as well. I'm hoping that he will not. He shouldn't be given any rum or laudanum for pain; we need to see how well his brain recovers on its own from the blow it received."

"So, ye're through." Corbet's question was in the form of a statement.

"Yes, Cap'n. That is all that can be done, for the moment."

The Captain nodded in Todd's direction and ordered two of the crewmen standing nearby, "Well, *now* lock him in the lazaret, then."

"But Cap'n, I've told you that Trumbull attacked your Mate and me, and that my blow was self defense. And, how can I watch my patients from the lazaret?"

"Yer blow, yer fault. I'll watch the patients," was Corbet's only response as he stomped up the ladder from the fo'castle.

Stewart and Turner, two of the men who had been holding Trumbull, shrugged their frustration at the order and pointed toward the cramped locker in the extreme bow. "Best get yer blanket, Todd. Ye'll need it up there. Every man-jack here wishes ye'd done for Trumbull long ago," Stewart said.

"Thanks," Daniel replied. "Carefully lift Trumbull down to a pallet on deck and leave Isaac where he is. Splash his face every now and again with sea water. If he doesn't come to by two bells, call the captain."

Daniel entered the dank and stuffy lazaret, and it dispelled any thought he might have had of its being a place to put the sick until they recovered, as suggested by its name. It was a dungeon. The heavy door was swung shut by reluctant hands, and blackness engulfed him as he heard the bolt slide home on the outside.

"And such is my first surgical fee—private lodgings," Dr. Todd muttered ruefully, slamming his angry fist against the dampness of the hull planking. As the bruising pain spread up his arm, Todd began fully to realize that when Trumbull did die, it would be because of a slash made by his hands. Doctors were supposed to save life, not take it. He wondered if any half-measures to repel the attack would have been enough. Supposing he had just hit at Trumbull's hands instead of his body and had knocked the belaying pin away. Would that have saved him and Isaac? He relived it all, panic-filled second by second, and convinced himself that any half-measure could easily have led to a different disaster. If Trumbull had managed to grab the spade handle, Isaac and he himself undoubtedly would be swimming somewhere far astern of the *Ellie Mae* right now, if they were lucky enough still to be alive.

Daniel resolved that he would survive all of this, in spite of Captain Corbet. He hoped Isaac would also.

- - -

Time seemed stationary, each grudging second marked by perhaps two beats of his vaulting heart. Tarry oakum caulk in the seams of the hull saturated the dank air of the lazaret with its pungent odor, but that was not what made it so difficult for Daniel to breathe. It was the impenetrable blackness wrapping him in its suffocating cocoon, and the sensation that the tiny compartment was slowly shrinking smaller and smaller to crush him that constricted his chest as though a steel band twisted tighter and tighter. The black, black air was like a sticky atmosphere of thick tar, and he felt that to fill his lungs with it would be fatal—just like the bottomless black water he had been plunged into by the hurricane.

As a child, Daniel had never been particularly afraid of the dark. It probably held as many imaginary monsters for him as for any other boy or girl, but it was not a thing that filled him with panic. Now, the mounting terror he felt, that the darkness was squeezing the life out of him, had to be the result of his near-drowning, he told himself. Control yourself! Reach out and touch these planks! There's nothing to fear! Think of your patients out there. Has Isaac regained consciousness? Calm yourself. Think about him. You're safe! You're safe!

He knew that exhaustion finally led to sleep because, time and time again, he roused with a start and had to talk himself out of his panic. If only there were a breath of fresh air or even a glimmer of light, it would be so much easier.

In steerage, Isaac Lawrence stirred but wallowed in confusion. He had moved his head as consciousness began to return but immediately froze as a barbed lance of pain seemed to enter the back of his neck and pierce its way out through his forehead. Tenderly, he explored his wounded brow with his right hand and felt the wide depression. Keeping his eyes closed, he searched his memory to determine what had happened and where he was. Vaguely, he saw the image of a club striking out of the darkness and nothing else.

He started to reposition his body using his left hand and again was overcome by nauseating pain. Upon exploring with his other hand, he discovered the splint on his left arm. Groans that bespoke exhaustion and hopelessness issued from a form lying close by; the regular breathing of sleeping men and the faint glow of the ship's lantern over the mess table identified the fo'castle for him. It was all too confusing for Lawrence; he surrendered once again to sleep.

- - -

Suddenly, Daniel heard the bolt thrown on the door and it creaked open. A lantern was thrust into the lazaret, but only when it was moved to one side could Daniel see Dugan's bearded face in its sallow glow. "Ye should see to Lawrence, lad. Quiet, now." He backed out and Daniel bolted upright, rushing to follow the other man.

The others in the fo'castle still slept noisily. As they stood over Isaac, Dugan whispered to Daniel, "He's stirred some, but he's still right adrift. Can't ye do nothin' fer his stove-in skull?"

Todd knelt by Isaac's side. "Isaac. Isaac. Can you hear me?" he asked in a harsh whisper. Lawrence's glazed and unfocused eyes opened but were only slits because of his swollen lids. "Trumbull hit you with a belaying pin. Your forehead is injured, and he broke your arm. Can you hear me?"

"Aye." His voice was raspy and distant.

"Can you move your legs and your right arm?"

Lawrence slowly obliged.

"Very good. Trumbull caved in your forehead, Isaac, but I don't think he fractured your skull. Your head is going to ache and your neck hurt, but you're going to be all right. That arm will take weeks to heal, though."

It was as though Lawrence just needed contact with others to become better oriented, because he now asked in a stronger voice, "Is that Trumbull I hear yonder?"

"Yes. I hit him with a mincing spade. He probably won't make it," Daniel answered. He added ruefully, "The Captain's made me a prisoner because of it. Dugan, here, got me out to look at you."

"I'll tell the Cap'n how he set upon me. He'll free ye," Lawrence reassured him in a voice that sounded more normal with every word.

Daniel wondered how much Isaac actually remembered about last night. "You just rest there, Isaac. Come morning, if your head doesn't ache too much, you can sit up to table and eat. Can we get you anything now?"

"I'm powerful dry," Lawrence said, licking his lips. Dugan hurried up the ladder to get a dipper of water from the scuttlebutt.

"I'm glad you're all right, Isaac. I'll see you again as soon as I can. I best look at Trumbull, now," Daniel said and squeezed Isaac's right hand. In the gloom of the tiny lantern hanging above the mess table, he went and stood over his other patient. Trumbull's eyes were closed and his respirations were labored. Between groans, he panted in obvious pain. His head rolled from side to side in his misery, and Todd almost felt pity for him. He could imagine the burning agony the man must be feeling in his belly if it were filling with pus like those women with childbirth fever. He placed his hand on Trumbull's brow, and it was fiery hot with fever.

Dugan returned with the water and gave it to Lawrence. Turning to Todd, he said, "Sorry, but ye must go back to the lazaret. The Cap'n 'd watch me do a yardarm jig if he know'd I let ye out. Ye think Lawrence'll be fit again, then?" It wasn't a question; he just needed reassurance.

"Yes, I'm sure of it. Trumbull won't, I'm thinking. The Captain should give him so much laudanum that he feels nothing," Todd said, nodding toward his enemy. "I wish there was a way you could tell Corbet that. I will if he lets me out."

"Come, lad," Dugan said, pointing the way with his lantern.

Daniel wanted to ask for a candle so he would not have to endure the misery of total blackness when he was once again shut in his prison, but his pride would not allow him to admit his fear. As the bolt was thrown, he wrapped himself in his blanket and curled up on the deck. He strove to convince himself that he was infinitely better off than either of his patients, even if he was confined in the blackness of this musty dungeon. Or, he thought, I could even be out there on the other side of the cold hull planking where I can hear the surging waves as the ship slices through them. Yes, if Trumbull had had his way, that is where Isaac and I would be at this moment, whether we were still alive to know it or not. He found his situation easier to endure now and tried to think of other things.

Isaac's stories about his sweetheart back in New Bedford led him to thoughts of Elizabeth and hunger for female companionship in his own life. Her rejection of him still hurt but, to a new doctor, Boston undoubtedly would have offered many other new possibilities. Perhaps his decision to go to California was a mistake. Certainly, it had made life far less certain for him. Frustration and fatigue, however, gradually displaced these thoughts and he drifted off into sleep.

- - -

Daniel awakened again to the sound of the heavy door being opened. The feeble light that greeted him was typical of the daytime illumination of the fo'castle. Smithers stuck his head in and said, "Cap'n orders ye to the Deck. Now," he added and offered no explanation.

"I'd like to check on my patients first," Todd replied, blinking at what by comparison was brightness. He could not ignore Trumbull's choked screams.

"Cap'n says 'now'."

The two men went up the ladder to the weather deck. Yesterday's winds had subsided but were still sufficient to fill all sails and send the *Ellie Mae* cleaving the waves. When they reached the poop deck, they found that Mr. Carringer was the Officer of the Deck, but Captain Corbet paced back and forth, prowling impatiently. The Captain cleared his throat and growled, "Mr. Lawrence informs me that he indeed was attacked by the man ye wounded. Sez ye prob'ly saved his life. I'm freeing ye from the Lazaret, but don't mistake my signals. Show any more sign o' troublemakin' an' it's not only back in there fer ye, but ye'll be in chains as well. Now, get ye to work!"

"I've had no chance to see my patients, Cap'n. I don't know how Mr. Lawrence is, but Trumbull was screaming with pain when I came through the fo'castle. I didn't see Mr. Lawrence anywhere," Todd argued. "I would recommend giving Trumbull enough laudanum to make him comfortable. I don't see how he can live, in spite of my operating to repair his belly. But, he should at least be able to die comfortably."

Captain Corbet looked up into his face for a long moment. Finally, he snapped, "If he's goin' to die, I'll not waste laudanum on him. What do ye care for his comfort if he tried to kill the Mate an' ye, as ye claim?"

Daniel could almost hear his father droning the words, "Judge not, lest ye be judged," but he didn't use them in his reply. Instead, he calmly said, "I took the Hippocratic Oath as a doctor to save life and ease the pain of *anyone*, Cap'n."

The Captain impatiently barked, "Then, I judge we must keep a mincin' spade out of yer hands, *doctor*. He'll get no laudanum." With that, Captain Corbet ended the conversation as he turned and resumed his prowling the Deck.

- - -

Todd gratefully returned to his usual duties of watch-standing, caulking, splicing line, and scrubbing. Since no whales were encountered, he was not yet required to be back out in the whaleboat. To finish his recovery, Isaac had already been moved aft to what had been Mr. Halbert's room. Nobody knew if he would be well enough to go out in command of the Larboard Boat on the next hunt. Todd was not allowed by the captain to see him because Isaac now resided in "Officer's Country."

Trumbull's screams were wearing upon the entire fo'castle crew, although the plaintive volume of his suffering weakened as his fever mounted and the hours since his operation slowly dragged by. Finally, on the third night, Trumbull went into a coma and a sludgy flow of pus issued from his belly wound. Daniel had spent many of his off-duty hours at the man's side, just watching him and feeling totally helpless to change the downward course. His hatred of the man was gradually replaced by a measure of pity. Daniel's feelings were a melange of clinical curiosity about the medical aspects of the patient's deterioration, of feeling personal inadequacy as a doctor, of anger at the Captain for not allowing administration of laudanum to ease the man's pain, and of his own guilt at having caused the injury in the first place. He was quite sure that the hours he spent just sitting at the patient's side were mainly an act of penance because he was doing Trumbull no good except to slake his fever thirst from time to time with sips of water. It had been a relief to Todd and everybody in the fo'castle when the former steerage bully had slipped into the coma. By the next morning, he was dead.

Trumbull was sewn into his blanket, along with an old sounding lead for weight, and plunged over the side after a "service" that consisted of less than a hundred words by the Captain. The virtual lack of ceremony in his burial was not considered an insult by any of the crew. They felt he had received his just dues. Trumbull's demise was welcomed by many, accepted by some and mourned by nobody.

CHAPTER NINE

The weather gradually grew colder as the *Ellie Mae* plunged ahead toward the southern tip of South America. She had been briskly swept along by the trade winds until the ship passed beyond about 30 degrees south latitude and then the winds, having been a fairly steady five knots, became much more erratic. Sperm whale harvest became depressingly scanty, but large pods of Humpbacks were encountered. They were not a bad substitute because they were fat, readily approachable, small enough to handle easily and their meat offered a tasty diet. Daniel got so he could identify them even in the far distance because their spout was characteristic—bushy, not as high as a finback, and not angled forward like a Sperm.

In the "River Whaling Grounds", due east of Montevideo and the Rio de la Plata, the ship encountered the largest living being that Todd had ever seen. It was a massive Blue whale, and when all four whaleboats finally succeeded in killing it and then bringing it alongside, Todd noted that the 126-foot-long *Ellie Mae* was scarcely four fathoms longer than the carcass. Late in November, as they edged past 40 degrees south, the so-called "Roaring Forties" and into colder weather, sightings had become less frequent. On several occasions, the boats had been sent out after Right whales which usually were ignored. Their oil was inferior and scanty compared to Sperms, but they yielded quantities of more-or-less valuable baleen. The Bravas on board, even though Portuguese was their native language, all called the Right by its French name, *Baliene Ordinaire*. Isaac, or *Mr. Lawrence* as he was now addressed, was fit enough to command his whaleboat but not able to use the lance because of his splinted left arm. Chastain, the harpooneer, had to take over the lancing duties as well as his regular ones with "the dart". There was conjecture among the older fo'castle hands as to whether the ship would detour to South Georgia Island to hunt Elephant seals for their blubber or would head directly into the Pacific to harvest Gray whales during their calving migration. They surmised that wind and weather conditions around the Horn might well be the deciding factor. Daniel hoped for the earliest possible attempt at the Pacific leg of the cruise.

With the increasing cold, most crew members spent more and more of their off-duty hours in the relative comfort of the fo'castle. There was a cabin stove there for heat, but because of the Captain's intemperate fear of a shipboard fire, it remained unlit. In addition, wet clothing hanging all about the steerage compartment lent the air a chronic dampness. In spite of its defects, however, these latitudes glorified the fo'castle as a protected haven, greatly preferable to the stormy weather deck above. Because of Todd's encounter with Trumbull, he had now become universally accepted by his shipmates and after some had heard him relating an Homeric tale of the Trojan War to Dugan, he was soon besieged nightly with requests to entertain them with similar stories.

During his years at Amherst, Daniel had studied many of the classics and he remembered countless stories from the *Iliad*, the *Odyssey*, many Shakespearean plays, some of *Bulfinch's Mythology*, as well as considerable amounts of Greek and Roman history. When nothing else seemed appropriate, he sometimes even cribbed one or two of Hawthorne's recently published *Twice Told Tales* to entertain his shipmates. He became such a popular storyteller that one night, O'Hara bashfully complained, "Ye must be Irish, boyo—ye're a born *shanachie*. Sure, an' many's the hour I've spent, back in ol' County Monaghan, at the feet of the Old One an' jus' a'listenin' to his wonderful tales of the Little People. But now, e'en though yer stories truly shine like fine silver buckles, I get a kink in me brain from all them gods a'doin' this an' a'doin' that to the lives o' them Greeks. They're some'at like the Little People but 'tis all too confusin' to me, 'tis."

"Well, O'Hara, you're not alone. Most of us don't think like those ancient Greeks did. You see, they believed that their gods all had the same kind of problems that we humans do. So they were certain that various gods would be happy to shed some of their own troubles onto the head of this man or that and just make the god's difficulties or jealousies or hatreds somebody else's problem altogether. That's why the Gods in their stories seem to be moving the men and women around like puppets on a string." Daniel asked, "Now, how would you like to hear a tale about our old friend, Odysseus, on his way home and sailing between this terrible rock and a whirlpool in the Straits of Messina? Remember where Messina is?"

- - -

Mr. Lawrence was the most sympathetic of the officers regarding Lowell's epileptic affliction and had been instrumental in getting him excused from standing any masthead lookout watches. Instead, his post was always that of bow lookout where he performed his duty at deck level and away from the danger of falling many fathoms from a masthead to the deck below in case of a seizure. The only person uncomfortable with this arrangement was Lowell, himself. He felt disgraced and derogated by his handicap and lied that he had had only that one such fit in his entire life and felt he should be considered as able as any man of the crew to do his regular duty.

As the *Ellie Mae* continued toward the Antarctic regions, the weather became so brutal that many men in the fo'castle suffered from the "pip", a disabling cold and sore throat, and were not well enough to stand their usual watches.

One day, when Zenker was to go aloft but lay in his hammock, weak, feverish and unable to stir, Lowell said, "Ne'er fear, Claus. I'll stand yer watch," and was up and gone before anybody thought about the danger.

Nobody knew whether it was the shock of the cold wind, the dizzying effect of the pitching of the ship, or the feel of the icy shrouds themselves, but just before Lowell reached the crosstrees, a seizure struck him. The only witness to the tragedy was Andrade, the Brava lookout that Lowell was climbing to relieve. Afterwards he haltingly described in his "Portugee" English how Lowell "fitted up", seeming just to freeze to the shrouds at first and then breaking away to tumble head over heels backward, all the way downward to the icy deck below. The fall broke his neck and he was dead by the time any of the crew reached him.

All of Lowell's shipmates, particularly Zenker, were profoundly shaken by the accident because of its unusual cause. They were constantly wary of their surroundings, the perils of the hunt, of fire aboard the ship, of all the sharp and dangerous tools they used daily in their work, and of the myriad hazards of the sea itself, but now each realized that even his own body and its frailties might become the agent of his destruction.

The burial service was brief and not unlike those that had taken place previously except that it was snowing. So many of the crew were suffering severe sore throats that the brevity of the funeral was welcome and they started filing back toward the fo'castle immediately after the "Amen" and the sound of Lowell's final plunge into the sea.

Captain Corbet was hastening toward the Quarterdeck when Todd overtook him. "Cap'n, may I have a word with you?"

"Yes, yes, what is it?" Corbet's impatience always seemed to envelop him like a cloak.

"Cap'n, there are many severe cases of the pip among the crew. Some of them have inflamed tonsils larger than any I have ever seen," Todd replied.

"Yes, man. I've got ears, ye know. I hear 'em hackin' an' wheezin' like squally porpoises as they lollop about their work here on deck. My soul an' body, man—what do ye expect me to do about it?" was the callous answer.

"Well, Cap'n, I suspect you have some tincture of iodine among your medicines. If you will let me have the bottle, I'll paint their throats and, I'm sure, it will have a salubrious effect."

"Hunhh!" the Captain snorted. "I'll not waste my medications on any of yer witchdoctor poultices." He wheeled to go, but Todd argued.

"Not a poultice, Cap'n; an actual application of the iodine to the surface of their tonsils. It will reduce the inflammation and give them an opportunity to heal," Todd countered.

"I told ye. I'm the *Ellie Mae's* doctor. Have 'em gargle with hot sea water an' they'll be fit soon enough." Captain Corbet glowered at him for a long moment and then wheeled and strutted aft.

An angry and dejected Todd headed toward the fo'castle but stopped off at the galley to plead with Fishcake to brew a generous amount of tea and heat some sea water for the sick to use as a gargle. Those feeble remedies would be better than nothing.

- - -

The *Ellie Mae* encountered brutally antagonistic winds and, in spite of the most skillful ship handling, could not beat to the southwest for the better part of a week. More Right whales were sighted, but the seas were running too high for the boats to be launched. The futility of a hunt was finally accepted and the masthead lookouts secured from their watches until after the passage around the Horn. The bow lookout was continued, however, and kept extremely vigilant by the frequent ice floes that drifted by, some large enough to dwarf the ship. Any moderation in the weather was dreaded because a squall of freezing rain instead of snow left the sails frozen into rigid sheets of ice and almost impossible to reef or furl; ratlines and spars thickened with their slippery crystalline coating of ice and became even more hazardous as footholds than their plunging and pitching surfaces usually were.

Meals had become distressingly monotonous; the immutable porridge breakfast, other meals of beans, salt horse, ship's biscuit and, very rarely, the treat of dried apple duff. The barrels of sauerkraut had long since been emptied, any fruit was only a memory, and several of the men had early signs of bleeding from the gums. Daniel suspected early scorbutus, or scurvy as his shipmates called it. Through Mr. Lawrence, he had pleaded with the Captain to land and obtain some fresh supplies when he knew they were nearing the Falkland Islands, but to no avail. The only comfort in the unheated fo'castle was hot tea from the galley or when one could wrap into a cocoon by using every available blanket and piece of clothing he owned and then simply hibernate in his hammock. The depressing gloom of the ill-lit steerage and the chorus of coughing and labored breathing all around even detracted from these simple pleasures. Todd was thankful, at least, that they were allowed hot food with a fire in the galley.

It was just after eight bells had faintly sounded from the poop deck when Mr. Lawrence shouted down into the fo'castle, "Dan'l. Dan'l Todd. The Captain wants to see ye."

Todd fumbled his way out of his warm fabric chrysalis, slipped into his boots, and ascended the ladder to the weather deck. The friends exchanged greetings as the frigid wind bit into his flesh and burned his nostrils.

Daniel asked, "Do you know what he wants?"

"Ye'll not believe it, Dan'l, but the Cap'n has a touch o' the pip himself now an' may be a'wantin' some of yer treatment," was Isaac's smiling reply. He was fully aware of the rumored denial by the Captain of Todd's request for medicine for the crew.

Daniel followed his friend along the deck aft to the passageway leading to the Captain's cabin. When they entered, Todd was surprised to find the compartment only slightly less depressing than the fo'castle itself. True, it was much less cramped and was better lighted by stern windows, but it was equally as Spartan and cold since his stove remained unlit just like the one in the fo'castle. There was an oil lamp hanging near the head of the Captain's bed, and its flickering glow illuminated Corbet's flushed face.

"Don't ye go gloatin' o'er me fer orderin' ye here. I'm aground 'cause of this throat, an' I'm sorely needed topside," the Captain croaked. He lay in his bunk, huddled in his heavy grogram bridge coat, swathed in blankets and peering out from under a night cap pulled low on his forehead. He barked a weak cough that was indeed painful to hear.

Todd was tempted to make any number of comments but remained silent. He took down the lamp and held it close so he could look into the Captain's mouth and said, "Let me see your throat, Cap'n."

He peered in at the swollen and purulent tonsils but saw no membrane or abscess formation. He felt for fluctuance, in spite of the Captain's wincing and gagging. The man was obviously feverish and his tongue had a dry coat that was dark brown. Todd wormed his way through the blankets and layers of clothing until he could percuss the chest. It sounded clear.

"Now sit up, if you will, Cap'n." When the patient leaned forward, Todd put his ear to the hot flesh of his back and listened to the sounds of the breath moving into and out of the chest. There were no signs of congestion.

He rendered his diagnosis. "Well Cap'n, you have pharyngitis with inflammation of the tonsils, but no evidence of pneumonia. Where is your chest of medicines?"

Corbet listlessly fell back onto his bunk and merely pointed toward a leather-bound box on a nearby table. He had apparently been searching its contents recently. And meager they were. There was a large bottle of laudanum, a quantity of calomel, a small box of Peruvian bark, a bottle of tincture of iodine, some senna, and a well thumbed copy of Northcote's *Marine Practice*.

"There is not too much here that we can use in your treatment" Daniel observed. "Ordinarily, bloodletting would be in order, but I see no lancet. Leeches applied under the jaw or behind the ears help but, of course, we have none of those, either."

He continued, "Your bowels should be opened, but the calomel here increases salivation and that would be all the more distressing to you because of having to swallow more frequently. To cool your skin, we could use citrate of potash or ammonia, if we had them."

Daniel turned to his patient. "I suggest, Cap'n, that we have you shed some of your clothing in order to cool off your body. I'll paint your tonsils with this iodine, have you drink copious fluids—preferably hot tea—and you should indulge yourself with a gill of rum every four bells. Now then, allow me to search for an applicator for the iodine."

Daniel came back with a quill pen and saturated the feather portion with iodine. He forced the Captain's jaw open and painted one tonsil. Corbet gagged. Dr. Todd painted the other tonsil and Corbet gagged again.

"Now, I'll ask Fishcake to bring you your hot tea. I assume, Cap'n, that you will have no objection if I take the iodine to treat some of the crewmen who are in much the same condition as you."

As though he was afraid Todd might repeat the quill treatment, and still recovering from his violent gagging, the Captain merely motioned him away with a silent wave of his hand.

As he left the cabin, Daniel decided he could put a few drops of this precious iodine in water to treat Flaherty's goiter. The enlargement of that sailor's thyroid gland had been worrisome to Daniel ever since he had come on board. He hurried along the icy and plunging deck toward the galley.

- - -

Just east of the Falklands, the *Ellie Mae* encountered a storm that rekindled Daniel's terror-filled memories of the wreck of the *Southern Cross*. Seas built and built until the mighty waves shed their scud through the tops of the masts when the gale winds tore spindrift from their crests.

"Ain't nearly so high as them North Atlantic rollers," critically observed Chastain, as he squinted out to sea against the wind-whipped spume.

Daniel noted, however, that the massive waves were sufficiently tall to becalm the *Ellie Mae* whenever she lay in a trough between them. Before the sail could be shortened, the wind tore the lower foretopsail away in a great thunderclap of sound and sent it fluttering like a soaring kite across the waves. Now, the ship maintained steerageway under only a storm staysail in an attempt to give her direction and at least some measure of control over her course.

There were still wagers among the crew as to what their next heading might be. Would the Captain veer eastward to South Georgia or would he continue southwest around the Horn, or *Cabo de Hornos*, as the Bravas called it? The majority hoped it would be South Georgia. Clubbing the giant Elephant seals for their blubber would be a welcome change from the normal hunting of whales, although the physical work involved in dragging the huge carcasses to the surf would probably be greater. For his part, Daniel hoped for an early passage up the Pacific coast of South America and on to his destination of California. Now that their diet had become so limited and unappetizing, Daniel especially longed for an early resupply of the *Ellie Mae* at some port not too far up the west coast of Chile. He doubted that many fresh victuals would be available at South Georgia, should that be their destination. He reviewed in his mind what he had been taught about treating scorbutus. It was known clear back in the 1560s that oranges or lemons eliminated it; short of that, esculent fruits, fresh vegetables, undercooked fresh meat, wine instead of spirits were also effective; some alkalescent plants were said to be helpful, even though the acid principle abounding in the citruses and in vinegar seemed more beneficial. That exhausted his memory of the materia medica for scorbutus. At least, the crew could look forward to fresh whale meat in the near future and to the possibility of obtaining some preserved vegetables somewhere along the coast, even if fresh ones were not available.

In spite of this storm, Fishcake did manage to put hot food on the table. Everybody wondered how he could keep kettles on the stove but, at the same time, they railed mercilessly against the dreary meals of beans and salt horse he produced. His invariable rejoinder was a string of the most blasphemous profanity and the challenge, "Catch me a string of leatherjackets an', damn yer eyes, I'll fry 'em fer ye."

He did relent on one occasion and dragged out a jar of pickles he had hidden and gave his curious crewmates nothing but a jaundiced look of silence when asked their identity.

After he had stomped out of the fo'castle and the delicacy had been quickly consumed with great gusto, Calthrop said, "That were *muctuc*, accordin' to the Bering Strait whalemen. Ye take a gob o' Humpback blubber an' pare off all but a half inch o' the whitest, doughy flesh next to the black skin, which is a good half inch thick itself, as ye can see. Ye cut it in squares, mince the blubber part all crisscross-like, bile it 'til soft in seawater, an' pack it away in winegar. 'Tis right tasty, 'tis." Daniel agreed and hungered for more.

Even four days into the storm, the wind and seas continued to mount in their ferocity. The *Ellie Mae* had been blown somewhere off her course, but accurate navigational readings were almost impossible because of poor visibility and an indefinite horizon. Spray had iced masts, spars, and decks to the extent that the ship had become noticeably top heavy as it wallowed in the mountainous seas. The Captain had recovered sufficiently from the pip that he now spent some of his time on the poop deck again.

It was during one of these visits that, with sextant in hand, he was trying to take a reading. With a sudden crash of sound, the main topsail spar snapped under its burden of ice and swung downward, still partially supported by its rigging. Mr. Brewer, the officer of the watch, jumped safely aside, but the boom struck the Captain as he concentrated on peering through his instrument and knocked him to the deck. A fraction of a second later, the rigging gave way and the full weight of the ice-encrusted spar crashed downward to the deck, landing with its full weight on the Captain's left leg. His scream outrivaled the shriek of the storm, and when the wallowing of the ship finally rolled the ice-encrusted timber off of him, his lower leg was a bloody pulp.

Mr. Brewer and Calthrop, the helmsman, blocked the spar before it could roll back over the Captain again and slid him to a safer spot to starboard. The rest of the weather deck was deserted except for the bow lookout.

Brewer barked, "Man the helm again, Calthrop. I'm going to call Todd," and raced toward the fo'castle hatch. He shouted an order down the ladderway and rushed back to the poop deck, skidding to a stop on the icy planking.

The Captain writhed in his own blood and whimpered a mewling groan. Mr. Brewer quickly cut a length of icy line from a coil on a belaying stanchion and used it as a tourniquet on the bleeding limb. Todd slid to a stop on the pitching, icy deck, still buttoning his coat against the freezing wind.

"They tell me ye claim to be a doctor," the officer said. "Look to the Captain."

"You've stopped the bleeding, sir. That's the important step. Now we need to get him to his cabin and out of this weather. I'll get men to help me with that before he goes into shock," Todd said, taking command of the situation with a very professional air.

He hurried back to the fo'castle and recruited several hands to help. They brought a bench with them to use as a stretcher when they returned aft to the poop deck. The transfer was made easier because the Captain had fainted. Even though all aboard ship were inured to the sight of violent trauma, the floppy instability of the crushed limb when Corbet was lifted onto the bench caused several of the hardened crewmen to look away.

When the Captain was laid in his bunk, Todd cut the trouser leg away with his belt knife and, slitting the heavy boot down a side seam, slipped the remnant off the foot. The leg appeared to be hopelessly damaged. It was not a single fracture; the tibia and the fibula undoubtedly were crushed into dozens of pieces, two of which protruded through the skin, and the limb merely seemed to be held together by macerated skin and muscle. The foot appeared intact except it was now pointed a good 100 degrees away from its proper position. Todd noted that his breath, and that of all the others, clouded the cold air of the cabin as they exhaled.

"Build a fire in that cabin stove," he ordered Hiatt and then nodded to Montgomery, "and fetch Mr. Maxfield."

Before either man could respond, the First Mate entered from the passageway. "Mr. Brewer told me. What be his course?" The officer peered down at the patient but directed his question to Todd.

"Not good, sir. His leg is crushed—beyond healing, I would say," Todd replied.

Captain Corbet groaned and began to stir. He peered around as though confused and muttered through clenched teeth, "My soul and body . . ."

"Don't move, Captain. That falling timber has broken your leg. Very, very badly. I'm sorry, but you may lose it," Todd said in a quiet voice.

Corbet raised himself on one elbow and looked down at his left leg, bloody but pale because of the tightly cinched rope around his thigh. "I've faith 'twill heal." His face, however, lacked the conviction of his words; it was pale and sweaty and his eyes were rounded in fearful concern.

Todd insisted. "Cap'n, we have to loosen that rope soon. When we do, you can bleed to death. You've been badly injured."

Corbet responded stubbornly, "I've weathered stormy seas before. Clear the cabin, now. Mr. Maxfield, you stay!"

The First Mate ordered the men out with a wave of his hand but gave Todd a look that bespoke both his awareness of his total incompetence to deal with this situation and his overwhelming desire for it to be Todd's responsibility.

"Aye, Cap'n," was his only response.

CHAPTER TEN

Mr. Swan, the Cooper, had the starboard watch of the crew dealing with the damage from the broken spar even though complete repairs would have to be postponed until after the storm. But meanwhile, the fo'castle was abuzz with rumor and conjecture. How bad is the Captain? Will he die? What does this mean for the cruise? Will we return to New Bedford? Will we continue the hunt, but at South Georgia? Will we go on around the Horn? All turned to Todd for answers, but he could only render the medical opinion that failure to amputate the Captain's crushed limb could cost the man his life.

Daniel had never performed an amputation, although he had observed several. In all but one of those, the surgeons had employed ether for an anesthesia. That agent had been introduced several years earlier at the Massachusetts General Hospital by Dr. Morton. The screaming and pleading during that one horrible exception had so filled Daniel with dismay that the thought of performing such an operation without benefit of anesthesia was almost inconceivable. Prior to introduction of ether, speed had been the surgeon's primary goal in that ordeal and not the more relaxed, meticulous dissection that was possible when the patient was oblivious to pain.

Questions flooded Daniel's brain. Will I be able to tie off the large blood vessels? Can I simply disarticulate the lower leg at the knee joint and not have to saw the bone? If he can have a stump below the knee, the leg will be much more functional. I didn't get to examine him to know if the knee is involved or not. How can I fashion my incision so that I can create a fleshy pad on the stump? There has to be a good blood supply to the stump or it will slough. How can I work on him with all of that screaming, Daniel thought. What if I kill him?

Panic gripped him until he realized that the Captain might not even allow such an operation, anyway. Daniel wondered if he would always feel as inadequate to deal with medical problems as he did with this one now.

It was almost a relief to be plied with all the questions by his shipmates, because it helped to divert his mind from these worries.

- - -

Daniel was bow lookout during the second dog watch. Even though it was mid-December and the Antarctic summer was upon them, the hours of sunlight were still very brief at this latitude, and so he strained his eyes in the inky darkness for the earliest possible sighting of any of the icebergs they had been encountering. The storm was beginning to wane, but the pummeling, icy wind still cut him like a knife, and the enormous swells had not begun to diminish, seeming to argue strongly against the presence of spring. The speed of the ship was negligible because, under only her storm staysail, the *Ellie Mae* was simply maintaining her headway and struggling not to broach in the titanic seas. For that reason, she was not going to crash headlong into any ice that might cross their course, but even making contact with an iceberg could spell disaster in these chafing swells.

His sea boots beat a dull tattoo on the icy deck as Daniel stomped his feet to keep them from freezing. He bundled his muffler around his nose and mouth in an attempt to warm the air he breathed. With visions in his mind's eye of the Captain's crushed limb that he had been allowed to observe only briefly, he visited and revisited his many worries that had been spawned by the accident.

It was not inattentiveness that led to his tardy recognition of the ghostly mass on the larboard bow. It towered so ponderously over the ship and its position relative to the *Ellie Mae* was so constant that it seemed only to cast a slightly grayer shade to the tarry night. It was not until he saw white spray erupt when the huge swells crashed against its wall that he recognized it to be an immense iceberg. Because it was so enormous and as immovable as a rock cliff, it did not appear to have any vertical movement in the giant surf.

"*ICEBERG!*" Daniel screamed into the gale. "ICEBERG, LARBOARD BOW!" He frantically tolled the alarm bell in its bracket on his right. Although he was not supposed to leave his post, he slid and sprinted aft along the icy deck to the poop deck to deliver his warning in person. Mr. Carringer, the Third Mate with the Deck watch, had heard his alarm and immediately began luffing into the wind and attempting to put the staysail aback. The *Ellie Mae* slowly rose and fell like a tiny chip, a total hostage of the mighty seas.

"Fetch Mr. Maxfield," Carringer ordered Todd.

As he raced into Officer's Country, Daniel tried to think what he would do in this situation if it were up to him to prevent the ship from colliding. He had no idea. His imagination was overwhelmed with the horrible image of their ship sinking out from under him and depositing the whole crew in that black and frigid sea. What a terrible death! He pounded on Mr. Maxfield's door.

"Come out on deck, Mr. Maxfield! Iceberg!" The fact that his request came out as an order didn't even register.

Mr. Maxfield flung open the door to his cabin and, hopping on one foot as he pulled on his sea boots, barked, "Report."

"There is a massive iceberg to larboard. It's as huge as a cliff and has become like a lee shore," Todd replied. "Mr. Carringer sent for you."

By this time, the First Mate had pulled on his greatcoat, and he burst past Daniel along the passageway. Todd followed. The icy blast of wind struck them a physical blow from starboard as they reached the Quarterdeck. The gray massif, still indistinct in the darkness, loomed menacingly close to larboard, and the *Ellie Mae* wallowed drunkenly in a trough at its base. In this battering wind, she was totally uncontrollable because she could not regain favorable steerageway, and these seas were threatening to drive her to her destruction. She rose and fell away along the precipitous face of the iceberg.

Then, as though sheared off by the hand of Providence, a gigantic slab of ice calved from the wall of the iceberg and crashed into the sea between its begetter and the ship. The immense tidal wave that resulted caught the *Ellie Mae* just as she was riding up on a swell, lifted her in a mighty surge of black water and spray, and thrust her away from the parent iceberg, spinning her head into the wind. The "calf", itself of colossal size, erupted again from the depths and floated to become a jagged satellite to the glacial "Scylla" in the process, but it had launched the *Ellie Mae* a safer distance away.

"Send the crew aloft an' see to riggin' the boom mainsail, Mr. Carringer," the First Mate barked. "I've got the conn," he added with reassuring calmness.

As the Third Mate slipped along the icy deck toward the fo'castle, Mr. Maxfield observed to nobody in particular, seemingly to be thinking aloud, " 'Tis fortunate the *Ellie Mae* is rigged as a brig, now—we can sail closer to the wind than we could if we was still snow-rigged with just a square mainsail. Methinks she may well edge her way 'round that monstrous an' icy termagant. Todd—d'ye have the bow watch?"

"I do, sir."

"Well, back to yer post then, man. Here, take the trumpet with ye an' sing out loud an' clear everythin' ye see. We're in treacherous seas."

Daniel passed shipmates as they spilled out of the fo'castle to rig the mainsail. He didn't envy them their task in the dark and in this brutal wind, although the latter had slackened a bit just since the beginning of his watch.

The *Ellie Mae* had changed her heading as a result of the vaulting thrust she had received when the iceberg fragmented; she had swung around until the great gray mass was now abaft her starboard beam. Mr. Maxfield would try to sail close to the wind that was now just off her larboard bow. In sidling away from the hazardous ice, they would sail roughly in the direction from which they had just come. The Mate obviously hoped to beat around the eastern edge of the main iceberg. By now, the boom mainsail had been spread and Daniel could feel the bite it gave to the ship as she gathered way.

Separation from the ice was agonizingly slow and every few minutes Daniel called out his report, although Mr. Maxfield's view of the danger astern was now better than his. He was happy to announce, loudly and frequently, that it was, "All clear, ahead." He was no longer conscious of the cold and time seemed to melt away. He was surprised when Zenker appeared to relieve him at the end of his watch. Before he sought the comfort of his hammock, Daniel stopped by the galley on the chance that Fishcake was still there and cooking something, and there would be water heating on the galley stove. He was in luck and wheedled a steaming cup of tea out of the cook. He cradled it in his gloved hands and slid precariously along the rimed deck to the fo'castle. When he shed his heavy garments, he sat at a mess table, enjoying the comfort and relative security as he drank his tea. As he thought about the danger they had just survived, Daniel realized just how fragile the grasp on life any of them really had; how easily the *Ellie Mae* could have been sunk by now and the entire crew drowned. Their tiny ship could be destroyed and disappear from this huge ocean at just any minute, or do it tomorrow, or the day after tomorrow. He marveled at how humans survived, even when they exposed themselves to great danger as they so often did. Why would anyone go to sea? Why would anyone want to hunt whales? Of course, thinking back to Dr. McClure's accident with the runaway horse, Daniel acknowledged to himself that dangers could be encountered in even very ordinary, everyday life. He realized that to keep his sanity when surrounded by these hazards, he could become a fatalist and live the life presented to him or he could simply wrap himself safely in a cocoon of inactivity. He knew that he had been tempting fate immoderately these last months, but if he had tried to be more careful personally, it would not have altered the magnitude of the hazards he had experienced. Considering all the disasters he had survived along with the fortunate events that had seemed to shape his life, he wondered if there might be such a principle as predestination, after all. Was some sort of a central being truly orchestrating all of this? Was he being preserved and groomed to fulfill some destiny in the future? Daniel was too tired to ponder such weighty philosophical questions and, quickly finishing his tea, he retreated to the relative warmth of his hammock.

- - -

The next day, all hands were on deck chipping ice from the davits and boats during the scant hours of daylight although Todd wondered why they bothered; he couldn't imagine a launching into these seas to pursue a whale. Even though the wind had subsided markedly, the ocean still ran in huge swells with combers breaking over the weather deck. The old hands said this was typical "Cape Horn Dirty Weather" and grumbled about any labor that required them to be out on deck where clothing soon became sodden and froze stiff on their bodies. They sighted a number of Right whales, but Mr. Maxfield did not order any boats out to hunt them.

The sea abounded in "growlers", globs of old and worn ice, some almost half the size of the *Ellie Mae*. Several large icebergs were visible, some taller than the mainmast and all white-crowned with greenish-blue sides. The ship delicately picked her way between them, no simple task because ever since they had gotten into the "Roaring Forties", the winds frequently veered drunkenly and could shift to any point of the compass over a period of several hours. At the moment, it was westerly. Daniel could not imagine their staying under sail during the hours of darkness in this profusion of ice, but they had to persist if they were ever to round the Horn.

Just then, Daniel heard a chorus of braying honks and saw his first penguins. He thought they were small porpoises because of the way they swam just underwater and only occasionally breaking the surface and showing just their heads and upright tails.

"Gentoo, or Johnny penguins," Adams observed. "Ye can tell by the white markin's o'er their eyes. I could almost eat their foul, fish-smellin' carcasses, I'm jus' that sick o' salt horse." The other old hands allowed they weren't starved to that extreme yet.

Mr. Lawrence approached and said, "Dan'l, Mr. Maxfield wants you in the Captain's cabin."

Daniel nodded his acknowledgement. As he started to pick his way along the slippery deck, he heard Grover ask, "D'ye know where we head, sir?"

Lawrence replied, "To the Pacific, but we round the Horn an' don't use the Straits of Magellan 'cause of the fickle winds." Grover's response was mostly blown away by that wind but it had something to do with fearing icebergs more.

Todd knocked on the cabin door and then entered. He found Mr. Maxfield sitting beside the Captain's bunk, his haggard face drawn with fatigue and worry. Corbet was unconscious and appeared flushed and feverish. The nearly empty laudanum bottle lay in the loose grasp of his right hand.

"I found him thus when I looked in some hours ago. He ain't woke nor shifted his berth since. What d'ye make of it?" the First Mate asked.

Daniel felt the Captain's brow and it was hot. He checked the pulse and then turned back the blankets to observe the injured leg. He was confronted by an alarming sight. The Captain's entire lower leg was black and swollen to more than double size and was beginning to smell. The toes were just knobby projections from a tightly engorged foot. Daniel held up the laudanum bottle and noted that only a fraction remained of what it had held before.

"I think he was trying to ease his pain, and he has just about killed himself with all the laudanum he drank. If that leg doesn't come off, it will soon finish the job," Daniel rendered his opinion to the First Mate.

Maxfield rubbed his brow, tense and uncertain. "I need not tell ye, I'm a troubled man. Takin' the *Ellie Mae* 'round the Horn, accordin' to his orders; wild ass seas jus' thick with bergs an' mebbe the Cap'n dyin'. An' he'd string me from a yardarm if'n he woke an' found his leg gone, yet ye say he'll die if'n we don't cut it off. I'm against a lee shore, Todd."

"You'll have the same nautical problems whether he lives or dies," Todd replied, "because he won't be able to command the *Ellie Mae* for months, should he even survive. Can you imagine navigating these decks on crutches? Besides, the decision whether or not to take off his leg is the Captain's and mine, as the doctor."

Mr. Maxfield first bristled at Todd's comment, as though he felt his authority was being challenged, but then realized that sharing or completely shedding his responsibility regarding the Captain was greatly to his advantage.

Todd continued, "He's in coma from all of that laudanum, his respirations are shallow and his pulse is very thready. Even though amputating his leg while he's unconscious would be kinder, doing it while he is in shock, as he seems to be right now, could kill him. I'll watch him until he recovers a bit and then discuss the surgery with him. I think you should get some rest, sir."

"I've a ship to run an' ice to shun," the First Mate said as he rose and straightened the fatigue from his back. He shuffled toward the door, obviously very satisfied with this arrangement. "Carry on, Todd."

Todd laid the Captain's leg bare once again and studied the injury. He noted that the bruise and swelling went all the way up to the knee. So I can't leave a stump below the joint, he thought, and supposing that smell is gangrene; is it safe to cut just at the edge of the swelling or will I have to get well above it? It would be easier and faster, he decided, simply to cut the tendons at the knee joint and not cut muscles or saw through the femur above. If I leave it open and do not close a stump of tissue over the end of the bone, I would be able to detect the infection earlier if it does travel on up. Am I just rationalizing the easiest course? I don't think so, he thought. He puzzled and worried over his indecision. Oh well, he thought, perhaps as perverse as the Cap'n is, he won't have any part of my surgery anyway.

He settled in the chair just vacated by Mr. Maxfield and studied the face of his "patient." The man's grizzled beard was more than a week's growth, so he had not shaved for some time before the accident. Daniel wondered if the Captain's ration of fresh water for purposes other than drinking was as restricted as it was for the crew; they were each allowed only one gallon a week to wash clothes. Everything else was done with sea water. The whole crew allowed their beards to grow rather than to shave in cold water hoisted from the sea.

Corbet had deep creases etched around his eyes from years of squinting at watery distances in all kinds of weather. The corners of his mouth drew downward disapprovingly even in his unconscious state. Daniel wondered if the man's autocratic attitude was typical of most ship captains, or if Corbet acted the martinet purely from personal irascibility. Was it due to unhappy marriage, fear of failure, chronic pain; who could know the cause? The term "one-legged bear with a toothache" pretty well described the Captain's past behavior and the thought crossed Daniel's mind that Corbet might indeed be one-legged soon—or dead. He knew he shouldn't be harsh in his judgments of the man. He *had* taken Todd aboard and saved his life and had safely shepherded this craft far and wide over hostile seas. And, he apparently had been a successful sailor for many years. The fact that he refused to accord Todd the respect he felt he deserved professionally should not be that big a thing. After all, it *is* his ship, Dr. Todd conceded. He recalled an incident from medical school days in which Dr. Oliver Wendell Holmes had endured an extremely vicious verbal onslaught by a patient from the nearby asylum and still had examined and dealt with the man in the most gracious, compassionate and thorough manner possible. Daniel recognized that he could not let his personal feelings for the Captain affect his treatment decisions.

As he waited for some sign of consciousness to return, Daniel inspected the cabin. There were only two lonely books on the cribbed shelf hanging on the bulkhead: the *Holy Bible* and Waterton's *Aid to Navigation*. He remembered the volume of Northcote in the medicine chest, but even counting that volume, the Captain's "library" was a very puny affair. The Captain's greatcoat hung from a peg, but no other clothing was in sight. Daniel looked in a small closet above the ship's counter but found only Corbet's personal privy in there. No garments. He assumed that other apparel must be stored in that very large sea chest alongside the privy door but he didn't pry. He returned to the chair near the bunk to wait. Hours dragged slowly by with only the shallow, but noisy, breathing of the Captain and the pounding of the seas against the hull to break the silence.

Daniel didn't realize he was dozing, but he suddenly started awake when Corbet groaned noisily. Darkness had returned and he had to strike a light in the oil lantern.

"Cap'n! Cap'n, are you awake?" he cried, but there was no response.

Daniel felt the patient's pulse and it was stronger, although the entire arm was very feverish. He drew back the blanket to inspect the leg and, even in the dim light, he could see that it was obviously even more congested and black. He could envision the bloody effusion engorging all of that crushed tissue and absolutely knew that the leg was beyond healing. From the smell, he knew that mortification had definitely progressed. Was it gangrenous? Todd couldn't be sure but the man's fever certainly suggested it. He gently shook the Captain's shoulder and finally succeeded in getting him to blink his eyes.

"Captain," he said slowly, "your leg has gotten much worse and unless it is removed, I'm afraid it is going to take your life."

The patient merely blinked his eyes in fevered confusion, looked around him, and then again drifted into unconsciousness.

Todd braved the cold and sought Mr. Maxfield. The deck was dark, but he saw the Mate's face in the glow of the binnacle lantern on the afterdeck. He approached Mr. Maxfield and said, "The Cap'n awoke momentarily but did not seem to grasp his surroundings. He quickly drifted off again. His pulse is stronger, which is good, but his leg is definitely worse. I believe the lower leg must be amputated soon or it may be too late to save the man's life."

"I dunno," Maxfield said. "I wouldna' favor another man makin' that decision if 'twere my limb in question."

"I believe that Mrs. Corbet would be much happier to have part of her husband return home from the sea than to know that all of him lay in the cold, Antarctic deep," Todd replied. "He can blame me for his peg leg if he lives, but I say it must come off." Daniel silently marveled at the words of certainty he heard himself saying while his mind was still so clouded with doubts. Am I rendering a valid medical opinion, he wondered, or am I being swayed by self-importance or some choleric spite I've developed toward the Captain. Daniel didn't think so. I truly believe, he concluded, based on my limited medical experience, that Captain Corbet will die if I don't act, he thought.

"I say the leg must come off," he repeated with reaffirmed conviction.

"So be it. See to what ye need an' I'll be there directly, Dr. Todd," Maxfield said after only a moment of hesitation.

CHAPTER ELEVEN

The preparations had not been elaborate, because Daniel had so little to work with. He had selected two of Fishcake's best knives and Mr. Swan sharpened them to a razor's edge. Having decided to leave the stump open so that the inflammation would be more apparent if it did extend upward, the only ties he planned to use were to ligate bleeding vessels. He had located the heaviest thread on board the *Ellie Mae* and had soaked it and a sailmaker's needle in rum, along with the knives. Just to be safe, he had taken the smallest of the Cooper's saws and soaked its blade also.

They explored the Captain's sea chest, and Mr. Maxfield extracted several shirts to use as bandaging. The First Mate was asked to get several men to hold the patient down; he chose Mr. Brewer and Isaac since Mr. Carringer had the Quarterdeck. He had Todd explain to the other officers the rationale and urgency he felt that made the operation necessary, and that he, Dr. Todd, was accepting responsibility for the decision.

Captain Corbet was awake enough to be able to talk but not coherently, so Todd had him drink the last of the laudanum and then waited until the man slept again. During that time, he carefully cut the patient's trousers off and laid bare the damaged limb. In the light of a number of oil lamps that had been gathered from other officer's cabins, he scrubbed his own hands and the Captain's injured knee in the last of the basin of rum.

Closing his eyes and quickly reviewing in his mind the anatomy he would encounter, he said, "Hold him, if you please, gentlemen."

Mindful of the popliteal vessels at the back of the knee, Todd made a swift cut through the skin at the sides and front of the joint, leaving as long a flap of skin in front as he dared. Even in his obtunded state, the Captain screamed and writhed against the restraining hands of Isaac and Mr. Brewer.

"Steady, now," Todd cautioned as he cut across the patellar ligament and then the insertions of the biceps femoris, the gracilis, and sartorius muscles.

Blood welled into the wound from general congestion of blood in the tissues, and he daubed at it with a tail of one of the Captain's shirts. Brewer turned his head away and appeared faint.

"Breathe deeply, sir," Todd said to him as he sliced through the medial and lateral collateral ligaments and into the menisci. He wrenched the lower leg backward, exposing the cruciate ligaments, which he severed. The Captain had slumped into unconsciousness and no longer offered any resisting movements.

The lower leg was now held on only by the skin and vessels at the back of the knee. Todd swept around the popliteal artery and vein with the sailmaker's needle on which he had mounted the heavy thread and tied the vessels off very tightly. He then cut across the mass of blood vessels, nerves and the skin below the ligature. The amputation was complete and the end of the femur glistened white in the pale lamp light. Blood oozed everywhere from small, congested vessels, but there was no arterial bleeding. Todd laid the flap of skin back up over the femur but didn't place any sutures in it. He then tamponaded the whole area with a wad of shirt cloth. He applied pressure to it with his hand until blood no longer appeared. Brewer vomited on the floor of the Captain's cabin, and Isaac swallowed deeply to keep from doing the same.

"What'll we do with the leg, doctor?" Mr. Maxfield asked, while Todd fashioned a bandage out of the available cloth that remained.

"It's a source of contagion and should go over the side," Todd replied.

"Seems fittin' that we hold some sort o' ceremony—burial like," the First Mate replied.

"Let's pray that no actual burial will be necessary, here," Todd said, as he took a deep breath, overwhelmed with relief that the ordeal was over.

Mr. Maxfield disappeared in the passage to the weather deck with the foul smelling limb. Todd nodded to the other two officers and said, "I'll take care of him now. Thank you both very much."

Lawrence and Brewer both seemed happy to leave the cabin where the stench lingered so heavily. Todd felt limp and drained. He wasn't sure whether his exhaustion related to the burden he felt for his decision to remove the Captain's leg or just to the strain of performing a procedure of this sort for the first time and under these conditions. He poured water into the basin from the Captain's ewer and washed the knives and then the blood from his hands. He had expected to be covered with it from head to toe but had been surprised how little blood had actually been spilled during the operation. Finally, he cleaned up Brewer's vomitus and slumped, spent and drained, into the Captain's chair. He was there when Mr. Maxfield returned.

"I judge yer place to be here wi' the Cap'n, now, 'til he recovers some'at, doctor," the Mate said.

"I agree," Todd replied, thrilling to the appellation of "doctor" used by Mr. Maxfield now for the third time and obviously not spoken by mistake. "I will stay with him night and day, because he must stay abed and will need a great deal of care."

Turning to the First Mate, Dr. Todd asked, "Can you have a bottle of rum sent around since the laudanum is gone now, and he will need something for the pain he is going to experience? Oh, and I don't know what quality beef broth can be made from salt horse, but he should have great amounts of that."

"Aye, I'll do that an' have Fishcake bring vittles fer ye both."

When the First Mate had gone, Todd settled to await the Captain's return to the world of consciousness and dreaded the moment when the man became fully aware that his leg had been taken.

- - -

The hours dragged by slowly, tolled by the distant sound of the ship's bell. Todd maintained his vigil, wrapped in one of the Captain's blankets and braced in a chair to keep from being spilled out by the rolling of the vessel. The fire in the cabin stove had long since died, because nobody had brought more fuel. The Captain remained feverish but slept soundly, his breathing strong and regular. Todd could detect no real change in the manner that the *Ellie Mae* rhythmically rose and fell away as she wallowed through the mountainous swells. It seemed to him that this struggle to round the Horn was interminable, and he wondered just how long the ship, rendered tiny and insignificant by the endless expanse of black, violent, ice-studded ocean he knew surrounded them, could survive. But he decided, throughout life you simply must breathe in and breathe out, one breath at a time, and wait to see what the next minute holds; that certainly is what is required on this voyage. Just have faith and patience—faith and patience. The promised food had never arrived and Daniel longed for a hot cup of tea and even a bowl of Fishcake's porridge but, in their absence, he simply inched deeper in the blanket and tried to sleep.

Rustling movement in the bunk awakened him. He rubbed his eyes and wondered how long he had slept. Feeble daylight now filtered through the stern windows and humbled the even weaker glow of the oil lamp.

"My soul and body, but my foot itches! 'Twill drive me ta Bedlam, 'twill," the Captain mumbled in words so thick that they were barely intelligible.

Todd rose and approached his bedside. "Are you in pain, Cap'n?" he asked.

"What're ye doin' in my cabin?" Corbet challenged. "Get out!"

"You have been very ill, Cap'n, because your leg became so inflamed. Do you remember crushing your leg? It was becoming gangrenous and I had to take it off," Todd reported and braced for the storm of anger.

"Are ye daft, man? My foot itches like sin. It ain't gone," the Captain barked and raised his leg so he could scratch his affliction. The movement undoubtedly caused pain, but the consternation that now flooded his face resulted from his finding nothing there but empty space. He groped with frantic hands to feel his leg but found only the bandaged stump and then vented a maniacal scream. Grunting with animal fury, he struggled to rise and attack Todd.

Todd restrained him with great effort and cautioned, "Be careful, Cap'n, or you'll start it bleeding. Just lie back and relax. You will be fine."

"MAXFIELD!" Corbet bellowed angrily. "MAXFIELD." In his weakened state, his struggling soon faded and the Captain lay limp, panting heavily, to await the appearance of his First Mate.

Apparently, Mr. Maxfield had been asleep in his quarters just next door because he burst into the Captain's cabin only seconds later. "Aye, sir."

"D'ye see what he's done? D'ye see?" Corbet was screaming his anger again.

"Aye, Cap'n. I was here, along with Mr. Brewer an' the new Fourth Mate. Ye were out'n yer head, Cap'n, an' in horrible straits. Dr. Todd here said ye was dyin' the way ye was." Maxfield's calm words had a slightly soothing effect on the weak and still feverish captain who searched the Mate's face with eyes filled with confusion. He slowly turned his face away toward the bulkhead in sad dismay.

"You'll get well, now, Cap'n," Todd added reassuringly.

"Get him from my sight, Mr. Maxfield," Corbet ordered in words weak in volume but brittle in their hatred.

"Ye'll need care, Cap'n, ta do fer ye an' care fer yer stump an' all," the Mate argued.

"Fetch Mr. Swan. The Cooper'll care fer me. Get him outa my sight," the Captain snarled, angrily pointing with a nod in Todd's direction.

Mr. Maxfield replied, "Aye, Cap'n," and ordered Todd with a glance toward the passageway. "I'll fetch Mr. Swan."

Once out of the cabin, the First Mate said to Todd, "I doubt not that he's better an' I'm sure ye did right, Doctor. I'll tell Mr. Swan ta follow yer orders. Get some sleep."

He turned and moved off to seek the Cooper and Daniel headed for the fo'castle. He hoped the Captain's storm of anger would subside with time but he doubted it; he could not help but wonder if the Captain's hatred for him would prevent his reaching California. Right now, all he wanted to do was retreat to the security of his hammock.

CHAPTER TWELVE

For the crew, life resumed its dull rhythm; the same watches, the same finger-numbing making and furling icy sails, the same monotonous meals, the same miseries of the cold. The Captain was absent from the deck, of course, and Mr. Maxfield had taken over the running of the ship. Daniel's worries and concern over the condition of Captain Corbet were only teased and far from relieved by the snippets of information that Isaac Lawrence was able to share with him. All of that was only imprecise rumor, of course, having passed through several mouths before it reached him. Mr. Swan did not report to him on the Captain's condition nor did he ask Todd for advice. And, except for nautical matters directly concerning the ship's voyage, Mr. Maxfield apparently was being shunned by the Captain also.

On two occasions, when the "Cape Horn Dirty Weather" allowed, Mr. Maxfield launched boats to harvest ice from nearby icebergs to augment the ship's fresh water supply. On one of those trips, three sea lions were harpooned and everyone on the *Ellie Mae* enjoyed a meal of fresh meat.

Finally, the ship's prevailing course was north by west and everyone felt that their passage around the Horn had finally been completed. Somehow, Daniel expected meek and peaceful waters once they entered the Pacific, as the name implied, but a violent, terrifying gale assaulted the *Ellie Mae* as the *Cabo de Hornos* exacted its parting toll. The winds mounted, coming out of the northwest as they had quite constantly over the past week or more. The seas built even higher than the mountainous swells to which everyone had become almost accustomed during their recent passage. The ship, still heavily glazed with ice, struggled through the hours of darkness and all hoped for relief to come with the dawn. Early morning's faint light, though, only revealed more clearly to them the threatening size of the waves with their scattering crowns of foam and their spidery streaks of spindrift.

Then, the capricious wind began shifting and hands were called away to work the already shortened and icy sails. Fernando, one of the Bravas, was ordered high on the mainmast to free the girtline block which had fouled. He had almost reached the peak when a comber suddenly heeled the ship far to starboard. Fernando lost his grip on the icy shroud and plunged screaming into the anticipating sea which eagerly consumed him as though it had just been waiting for such a sacrificial offering. He bobbed only briefly in the frigid, surging water and was even then far beyond the reach of the line thrown over the side in a futile attempt to save him. There was absolutely nothing that could be done for the poor man, and the *Ellie Mae's* own struggle for survival continued as the aging O'Hara went aloft to free the block.

The tragedy weighed heavily on everyone and once again emphasized for all that life, especially for a whaleman, was extremely uncertain and could abruptly end at any moment. For Daniel, it became another ill-fitting piece in the philosophical jigsaw puzzle he was trying to put together in an attempt to work out his personal theology. If there were such a thing as Divine guidance of one's affairs in this life, it certainly seemed capricious and short on justice. He thought of his father's frequent affirmation that "God works in mysterious ways" and shook his head at how unsatisfying he found that pronouncement.

The seas gradually became quieter over the next two days and, when pods of Humpbacks were spotted, the business of whaling resumed. Todd enjoyed immersing himself again in the now familiar routines of hunting and the hours of cutting in and trying blubber. Night and day, black smoke from the tryworks furnace streamed off into the otherwise clear sea air. Fresh whale meat or messes of pilot fish caught near the circling sharks that shadowed the ship for castoff whale carrion replaced salt horse in their diet, but signs of scorbutus had grown more prevalent among the crew. Todd was anxious for them to make some port where fresh vegetables might be obtained.

Resumption of whaling required Mr. Swan to leave the Captain's cabin and perform more of his regular duties on deck. This gave Todd an opportunity to question him about the condition of his patient. Swan was very reticent, even hostile toward him at first. Obviously, the canker of Corbet's hatred had sullied the Cooper's opinion of him. "Is there any pus or foul odor when you dress the Captain's wound?" Todd asked him, in spite of the barrier.

Mr. Swan interpreted the question as an indictment of his care as evidenced by his bristled response, "'Course not. I take good care o' him."

"He had gangrene of the lower leg," Todd replied. "That's why the leg had to be removed. He could die if that infection moves on up."

The Cooper silently looked at him more appraisingly and then muttered with obvious apprehension, "Gangrene?"

"Yes."

"Ye didn't just stump him 'cause his leg was bad broken?"

"No. He would have died soon if I hadn't removed it. He could die even yet if the rest of the leg gets gangrene and nothing is done."

"Would ye cut more off?"

"Yes, if I have to, although if it hasn't set in by now, I don't think it will," Todd replied.

"I'll let ye know 'bout anythin' out of ordinary," a more mollified Cooper said as he returned to sharpening a flensing spade.

Just then, the Main masthead lookout sang out, "B-L-L-O-O-O-O-W-S-S, larboard bow!" Everyone on deck cast a practiced eye in that direction and immediately identified Sperm whales. The prospect of once again harvesting the more lucrative Sperms sparked excited activity as line tubs were swung into the whaleboats and everyone awaited orders to "launch boats." After deciding that adequate hours of daylight remained, Mr. Maxfield called away all boats and the hunt began. It was successful and three big Sperms, one a 65-barrel bull, were brought back to the ship as darkness settled around them. The next two nights and days would be busy ones. Daniel worried now that the harvest would suddenly become so rich and their hold so guttled with oil that the *Ellie Mae* would return to New Bedford without ever reaching California.

- - -

The ship worked its way northward with favorable winds and good hunting. The days were getting longer and the labors of long hours of whaling drained the crew. Their health seemed to improve slightly on a diet rich in fresh whale meat, but their vegetables were still restricted to beans and the thick soup made from dried peas. The crew could scarcely remember when they had had potatoes. Fishcake had long ago served up the last of those sliced raw into vinegar in an attempt to satisfy the crew's complaints of lack of variety in their meals.

The *Ellie Mae* was close enough offshore now that the towering, snowcapped Andean peaks were sometimes visible in the far distance to starboard. Finally, after many days, they entered a broad inlet—Seno

Reloncavi, according to the word overheard from the Mates on deck watch—and anchored off a tiny village, Puerto Montt, adjacent to Isla Tenglo. It was a German settlement, in spite of its name, and had a broad agricultural hinterland. The boats were launched and, over the course of two days, filled the storerooms of the *Ellie Mae* with fresh mutton, cured hams and bacon, potatoes, kraut, carrots, turnips, dried fruit, wine, and casks of beer. The crew's enthusiasm in bringing these treasures on board was rewarded at the end of the second day when Mr. Maxfield gave each man half a silver dollar, issued against the future lay of each, and allowed them a few hours of liberty ashore but warned that the ship would sail next morning with the tide.

Daniel joined his shipmates and felt giddy for the first minutes after his feet touched on solid ground. Puerto Montt consisted of a handful of houses built along a single street that led down to the warehouse and tiny pier at the water's edge. The town's economy was obviously a blend of agriculture and maritime re-supply. As part of serving the latter, the house nearest the pier had installed a tiny bar in a side room and most of the crew got no farther than that once they discovered that all of Puerto Montt's female population had been safely sequestered. Daniel indulged in two five-cent steins of German beer and then walked along the narrow street, enjoying the strange sensation of firm earth under his feet.

It was late March, but since Puerto Montt was so deep in the southern hemisphere, the gardens up the valley to the north of the village were being cleared of their late summer foliage. Scattered flocks of sheep dotted the far distance and the towering Andes' peaks jutted high into the sky to the east. It was an idyllic rural landscape and Daniel even toyed with the thought of simply remaining here to start his practice. He felt suffocated, though, in being so tightly embraced between these mountains and the sea. Besides, how much medical care could these few families require? He returned to the bar and found that most of his shipmates had exhausted their meager funds and were now reduced to singing and dancing for entertainment. With what remained of his half dollar, Daniel bought another round of drinks for whatever eight of his friends were still thirsty and then he was ready to return to the *Ellie Mae*.

None of the ship's officers had come ashore and he suspected they were indulging in a few drinks themselves, out of the Captain's sight. The capacity for alcohol by most of the fo'castle crew was tremendous and it was hunger and penury rather than overindulgence that rendered them ready to go back on board ship when darkness began to settle. Their liberty had been remarkably peaceful and all, especially the owner of the bar, were satisfied.

Raucous sea chanteys filled the air as the whaleboats crossed the water to the anchored ship.

Humpbacks, Sperms, and finally Grey whales were the prey as the *Ellie Mae* inched northward and the harvest was prodigious. Their passage, as they sailed up out of the Antarctic summer and late fall, gradually carried them toward the northern spring. As Chilean coastline gave way to Peruvian and the *Ellie Mae* approached the equator again, she was caught up by the westerly trades. Their more or less constant ten-knot to twelve-knot winds and fair weather carried the little ship in a general course toward the Hawaiian Islands. It was good sailing for the whaler.

One evening on deck, Daniel asked his friend, the Fourth Mate, "With a course like this, do you think we will ever reach San Francisco, Isaac?"

"The Cap'n forbids us enter there," was the reply. "Tales be that 'Frisco harbor's chock-ablock wi' ships what can't sail 'cause their crews jumped an' went lookin' fer gold. 'Tis a forest o' idle masts, an' he won't risk losin' crew."

"How am I ever going to get off of the ship, then?" Todd asked, obvious worry infusing his words.

"Mr. Maxfield an' I bin talkin' 'bout that, Dan'l. Ye know that Cap'n Corbet hates yer gizzard an' 'ud keep ye 'board out o' pure spite. The Mate thinks ye did right in operatin' an' will put ye on any 'Frisco-bound ship what we cross courses wi', sorta' on the sly like. This be the sea lanes fer the clippers, ye know—the westerly trades a'givin' them their fastest passage."

Lawrence drew deeply on his curve stem pipe with satisfaction, the "smoking lamp" being lit. "'Course, we mightn't see sech a ship."

"Tell Mr. Maxfield 'thanks'," Daniel replied, his voice now full of anxious hope. He thought about the affair of the Captain's leg many times each day, and Lawrence's reference to the man triggered the process again. His feelings held mixed traces of nagging doubt over his decision to operate, of pride in his work and a good amount of bruised anger at the Captain's attitude. Undoubtedly, he thought, every doctor desires admiration and gratitude bred by success in dealing with his patients—that's only natural—but the Captain's leg continued to be a cloud that dimmed that reward for Daniel. He derived satisfaction, though, in just knowing that the Captain was still alive and well even if he weren't happy. And, it was good to know that the incident might not prevent his getting to California.

The two men silently stared at the magnificent sunset, each picking at his own thoughts.

- - -

The usual "fo'castle tattoo" that always accompanied breakfast, the dull thump as pieces of hard ship's biscuit were pounded on the mess tables to dislodge squirming weevil, was interrupted when Amos Rolfing came down the ladder from the weather deck and said, "Ol' Schvan, der coooper, vants ye in der Cap'ns' cabin, Todd. Schnell!"

The stout German always had trouble making himself understood because his speech was a blend of his native tongue and a confusing overlay of English with a down-Maine accent. He stomped back up the ladder and returned to his watch on deck. Todd drank the last of his cup of tea before he followed, curious and a little apprehensive to know the reason for his summons.

He knocked on the Captain's door and was admitted by Mr. Swan. Without comment, he led Todd across to the bunk where an unconscious Ozias Corbet lay. The sight was shocking. The dumpy figure seemed to have shrunken even smaller, the sleeping face was haggard, the thinning hair tousled and the lengthening beard grizzled and matted.

"He guzzles rum 'til he sinks into such a state," the Cooper said. "He says 'tis the pain. I says 'tis thinkin' he's only half-a-man an' learnin' the ship kin sail without 'im."

Todd nodded in agreement and turned back the blanket to examine Corbet's stump. The bandage was crusted with dried serous discharge, but there was no foul smell. He teased the cloth away so he could see the wound. The flap of skin he had left had a healthy color and was beginning to pucker around the end of the bone. It seemed to be sealing down on a healthy, spreading bed of proud flesh. A small amount of pus surrounded the heavy thread he had used as a ligature on the popliteal vessels but, in all, he felt that the stump was healing nicely. There was no sign of gangrene.

"Do you have a clean cloth that I can use to re-bandage?" he asked.

Swan handed him a large piece of muslin that appeared to be part of a nightshirt and Todd wrapped the stump again. None of this had awakened the Captain.

"His stump may hurt him, but it is healthy," Todd said. "I think you should make him a set of crutches." Actually, he was surprised the Cooper had not done that already. "It will be some time before you can make a peg leg for him and, because the end of the stump is the way it is, almost all of his weight will have to be borne by a leather girdle higher up on his thigh. Once he can get up and around, he can assume command again. I'm sure that will restore his spirits. In the meantime, it would be well for Mr. Maxfield to consult more with him, even on questions that have obvious answers. It will restore the Cap'n's sense of still being in charge of things. And water his rum," Dr. Todd directed.

"I dunno'. The Cap'n 'pears to hate the Mate as much as he hates ye. He curses ye roundly all his wakin' hours."

"I'm sure Mr. Maxfield has skin that is thick enough to withstand that and, with time, the Cap'n will realize that he's lucky to still be alive. Are you able to put up with all of this?"

"Aye, I can," Swan replied, obviously pleased to have his problems recognized.

"Try to get him to shave. Clean him up like a silver buckle and feed him well. He'll look better and feel better. Let me know if the pus from that stump gets worse or begins to smell bad. You're doing a good doctoring job."

Todd wondered how well the Cooper would accept his suggestions since he did issue them more or less as orders. He had decided, though, that Swan desired strong direction and was anxious to share this responsibility. With a nod, he left the cabin and returned to breakfast.

CHAPTER THIRTEEN

Weeks passed and by late June, they were working the seas southeast of Hawaii. Todd had scaled the shrouds to stand the morning watch at the main masthead. He had long since quit using the Lubber's Hole and now swung nimbly on to the platform using the futtock shrouds. As he took over the watch from Harris, he quipped, "You'll be happy to know there's porridge for breakfast, for a change. Have you seen anything this morning?"

"Aye. Cast yer eye astern. A sail's been gainin' on us since daylight."

Sure enough, the smooth line of the southern horizon was interrupted by a definite patch of white peeking over its edge.

"Have you told the officer of the deck?"

"Aye. I told Mr. Carringer soon as I was sure. She's overhaulin' us right smart."

"When you go down, will you tell Mr. Lawrence that I urgently need to talk to him?" Daniel said, trying to keep the excitement out of his voice.

"Aye. I will," Harris replied, giving a quizzical glance and edging his words with curiosity. He disappeared down the shrouds to the deck below.

Daniel had trouble keeping his gaze anywhere but on the following sail and was too excited by the approach of another ship to notice the pod of whales off in the distance. It was the foremast lookout who cried, "Whales, starboard bow. Sperms, they be!" The usual flurry of activity on deck followed. The masthead lookouts were both called down to man their boats and Daniel searched out Isaac Lawrence.

He found the Fourth Mate already at the Larboard Boat, ordering the preparations for launching.

"Have you seen the ship astern?" Daniel asked his friend.

Lawrence obviously had not. He paused and looked in that direction.

"I think she's a topsail schooner and not a whaler," Daniel added excitedly. "This may be my chance to get off the *Ellie Mae*, Isaac."

Lawrence thoughtfully rubbed at his beard for a few seconds and then ordered, "Standby, men." He headed aft toward the poop deck. Mr. Maxfield, in the Captain's absence, had taken over the watch there. His Starboard Boat was temporarily commanded by Adams, the boatsteerer. The First Mate had already shifted his long glass from the whales to study the gradually enlarging sails on the southern horizon.

Lawrence addressed him, "Todd was at the masthead an' allows that ain't a whaler. He's askin' to board her."

"I think he's right," Maxfield replied. "She's a gaff-rigged schooner an' sure to be a clipper. In these waters, she's Californi' bound with cargo, I'm thinkin'."

"You know how Todd wants off the *Ellie Mae*. I say he be let," Lawrence continued.

The First Mate thought for a long moment. "The ol' man's chimney'll be afire when he finds out, ye know."

"Aye, but Todd's done more'n his share while aboard," Lawrence replied. "This may be his only chance ta get to Californi'. I say he be let."

With a nod of his head, Maxfield reached his decision quickly. "Aye, have him fetch his gear an' report to me. Larboard Boat'll take him."

When Lawrence announced the Mate's decision, Daniel scurried to the fo'castle. It didn't take him more than several minutes to stuff his few clothes and his blankets into the sea bag and deliver it back to the Larboard Boat. When he reported to the poop deck, Mr. Maxfield was not there but soon appeared, climbing up the ladder from the passageway below. "Dr. Todd," he said very solemnly, "as actin' Cap'n of the *Ellie Mae*, I release ye from the shippin' papers ye done signed. Ye can quit the ship. I've nae access ta the Cap'n's strongbox, but here's some money o' my own against yer lay."

The Mate handed Todd two $10 gold pieces. "I think ye did right by the Cap'n, Doctor, an' that ye've been ill-used. Good luck an' good winds."

Todd was overwhelmed. With much more emotion than he would have expected, he replied, "Thank you, Mr. Maxfield. I shall always be grateful to you for this. You will make a fine captain."

He shook hands and, with a nod, rushed forward to the waiting Larboard Boat. Its falls had already been cast off. It rose and fell in the choppy water and the crew was in the boat. He and Isaac were the last to enter it by the slide board, and Daniel took his usual place at the stroke oar. As soon as the whaleboat cleared the ship, the mast was stepped and its sail hoisted. Mr. Lawrence set a course to intercept the rapidly approaching clipper.

- - -

"Ahoy! What ship an' where ye bound?" Isaac Lawrence shouted across the watery interval separating the whaleboat from the towering ship which was much larger than the *Ellie Mae*. As they drew closer, the Mate brought his boat to a course ahead of, but parallel to, that of the huge schooner. Sleek and fast as the whaleboat was, though, the ship's massive spread of canvas sped it forward, rapidly closing the gap.

"Make way! We'll swamp ye," was the faint reply shouted across the water.

"I'm Dr. Todd, survivor of the wrecked *Southern Cross*. I must talk to you!" Daniel screamed as loudly as he could.

The clipper plowed past them, its white horse of a bow wave dwarfing the gentle swells of the morning sea. Curious faces lined the rail above, all staring down at them. Finally, one man waved and all of the Larboard Boat crew waved back. Todd shouted his words again.

As the ship seemed to be speeding away on its course and simply ignoring them, orders were shouted from above and the men along the rail scattered. The clipper swung out of the wind, her billowing sails collapsing to shed their wing-like appearance and the ship rapidly lost way. Mr. Lawrence did the same with the whaleboat and eased up alongside.

An officer appeared at the gunwale above and shouted through his voice trumpet, "*Southern Cross*, did ye say?"

"Yes," Todd shouted back. "I am Dr. Todd and I was a passenger on her, bound for San Francisco. She sank. If you are headed for the west coast, I would like to come on board."

There was an anxious moment while the lapping of the wavelets against the hull of the big ship was the only sound. Then, a rope ship's ladder snaked over the side and unrolled to the water below, its wooden rungs clattering against the ship's hull.

Lawrence stepped over the thwarts toward him and Daniel shook his hand with both of his. "Isaac," he said, faltering with emotion, "you've been more than a friend. Thank you for everything. I sincerely hope we meet again."

"Aye. Likewise." Lawrence's words were halting, also. He ducked his head and stroked across the depression in his forehead, as he had grown in the custom of doing when he was perplexed. He would obviously like to say more but couldn't.

Daniel silently nodded farewell to Dugan, Barros, Andrade, and Calthrop, the other Larboard Boat crewmen, and scaled the ship's ladder.

Dugan bent a line on Daniel's sea bag and heaved the rope upward so the baggage could be hoisted.

With a deep sadness that surprised him, Daniel looked over the rail at the five upturned faces below. Finally, with a slight quiver to his chin, he waved farewell and shouted, "Good sailing and give my love to Captain Corbet." He turned from the gunwale and came face to face with an officer.

"I'm Captain Winthrop. Tell me about the *Southern Cross.*"

"She sank in a hurricane off the Carolinas, a little more than a week out of Boston," Todd replied.

The Captain bit his lip and shook his head sadly. "We're the *Calliope.* She was one of our sister ships—all owned by Mr. Cabot of Salem, ye know. Eli Trover an' I shipped together as lads, years gone by. Fine captain."

Daniel briefly described the storm and the splintery destruction of the *Southern Cross.*

Captain Winthrop shook his head. "I feared as much. She were long o'erdue back to Boston e'en when I sailed an' we wondered at it. No other survivors, ye say?"

"None," Todd replied. "We were not long underway when that storm struck. It was unbelievable. The ship simply floundered and was completely destroyed in just an instant. It was truly a miracle that I lived through it all. I was finally picked up by the *Ellie Mae*, a New Bedford whaler, and I've been on her for the better part of a year. I would welcome passage to whatever west coast port you're bound for. I can work for my board."

As he watched Winthrop struggle to digest the news of the loss, the thought flitted through Daniel's mind that Calliope was the mythological Muse of epic poetry, and he wondered at the significance of this name.

Finally, Captain Winthrop shook his head and emerged from his reverie. "Did I hear ye say ye're a doctor an' a paid passenger on Eli's ship?" He suspiciously appraised Todd's bearded appearance and crewman's clothes.

"Yes. I was bound for San Francisco to start my medical practice. I lost everything in the shipwreck and I've been an oarsman on a whaleboat ever since."

"I reckon Mr. Cabot has got his passage money out'n ye already, then. I'll not charge ye more. We'll find 'commodations fer ye, Doctor. Might have to put ye 'fore the mast, though."

"I'm grateful for any berth, Captain. What is your destination?" Todd replied.

"Our cargo be sail cloth. An' San Francisco be our course."

"I've heard that ships lose their crews to the gold fever there. How will you manage to avoid that?" Todd asked.

"My crew be loyal men o' the sea. I pay 'em well an' feed 'em prime. They'll stick."

"I can't tell you how grateful I am for passage on the *Calliope*. Thank you, Captain Winthrop." Todd shook the officer's hand.

Winthrop acknowledged this with a nod but was silent and seemed preoccupied with the sad news of the *Southern Cross*.

Daniel looked across the water at the shrinking Larboard Boat as it neatly sliced the chopping waves and sped toward the other three whaleboats in the far distance. A barely discernible "waif" was hoisted there indicating at least one kill by the group. A touch of sadness clouded Daniel's elation at finally being California-bound. He knew he would always miss the *Ellie Mae* and the friends he had made there.

PART TWO

SAN FRANCISCO

August, 1850

CHAPTER FOURTEEN

The San Francisco harbor was a forest of masts, naked and stark, all pointing like skeletal fingers toward an overcast sky. The ships crowded one another and seemed to swing on their anchor chains in unison like some careening flight of birds. Most rode high in the water, having been unburdened of their cargo, but they floundered as though run aground, because they had been forsaken by crews inflamed by the lure of gold. Some hulks had even been hauled ashore as an answer to the severe lumber shortage caused by the building boom and now were set up as storeships, marketing a variety of wares ranging from the fiery local liquor, *Californio aguardiente*, to beds or bawds.

The sailor wandering the dusty, manure-strewn streets with his seabag on his shoulder and surveying the crude, hastily-built "city" bore no resemblance to a recent graduate of the Massachusetts Medical College of Harvard University. Daniel Locke Todd, M.D., had a ragged beard and wore the watch cap and clothing of the *Ellie Mae's* slop chest. He had no diploma, no instruments, no stock of pharmaceuticals; he had only his store of knowledge, the few clothes he carried in his seabag and the two gold Eagles in his pocket that Mr. Maxfield had given him.

This alien crowd and all of the bustle of activity ashore was unnerving compared to the relative tranquility of the recent months at sea, and Daniel soon returned to the waterfront for security and to ponder his immediate future. He walked along the wharf and finally sat on a wooden bitt. The onshore breeze that had just cleared the harbor of fog was redolent with sea smell and filled with the raucous cry of the gulls. A seal honked and flopped awkwardly out of the water and up into a dory that was tied to the pier.

Daniel knew that he must make himself presentable and find a place to stay. Was that possible on twenty dollars, he wondered? Next, he had to choose between trying to practice medicine on his own or attempting to associate and work for another doctor until he could get established. He decided that, realistically, there was just no way he could start his own practice in his present circumstance. Could he possibly find some doctor willing to take him in? He rubbed his bearded face and looked down at himself. No doctor will ever believe me when I tell him of my training and that I have actually operated on patients. These thoughts had filled his mind ever since he had boarded the *Calliope,* but now they took on a frantic urgency; the time for action was upon him. Starting a practice out here seemed so simple when I was back in Boston and just imagining life in California, he thought. Not in his wildest dreams could he have foreseen all that he would encounter in his journey west.

He heard movement at his back. Turning to look, he saw a neatly corded stack of large pipe. Staring out at him from one of those at shoulder level was a rat, larger than a house cat, its ravening eyes fixed on him in the most aggressive manner. The creature seemed the embodiment of this hostile world that Daniel felt he had stepped into. Shaking his head, he pushed that depressing thought from his mind and remembered what the *Ellie Mae's* little Irishman, O'Hara, used to say: "Ye can't plow a field by just a'turnin' it o'er in yer mind."

Daniel hoisted his seabag onto his shoulder, took a deep, resolute breath and turned away from the crowded bay and toward the bustling town.

He remembered having passed the Astor House earlier and, although it was a far cry from even the most modest Boston hotel, he was certain it was beyond his means. He walked past three "hotels" of similar appearance and finally entered a doorway cut through the bow planking of a beached storeship. He asked the price of hammock space and the weasel-faced man who seemed to be in charge said, "Two dollars a night. Ye can have the Cap'n's cabin fer ten or with fifteen ye also git a visit from Sadie or one o' her gals."

"Just a hammock. One night," Daniel replied and handed over one of his Eagles.

The weasel took the coin and bit it, casting a covetous eye at his customer to check the possibility of there being more of those. Daniel simply rested his hand on his sheathed belt knife and stared at the assortment offered to him in change; three small Spanish silver pieces and a tiny, amorphous blob of gold.

"What is this?" he asked suspiciously.

The weasel replied, "'Tis a five dollar slug. A feller here melts gol' dust an' stamps these slugs. Ye'll find 'em used all o'er 'Frisco. 'Tis handier than wrasslin' dust."

Daniel chose a hammock at the far end of the compartment and placed his bag in it. "I'll be looking for you if that is disturbed while I'm gone," he warned the proprietor.

The weasel glared a wordless reply.

Daniel got a haircut, a beard trim and a bath for three dollars at a little shop run by an old *Californio* who spoke no English. He then set out to look for new clothes but found them all to be outrageously expensive. Shirts were $15 apiece and the roughest pantaloons $25. The simplest suit, such as he had worn in Boston, was $125. He would just have to make do with what he owned. At least, his boots didn't look out of place. The manure-strewn streets, with their alternating stretches of dust or loblollies of mud, were a great equalizer for the condition of everybody's shoes. The eating establishments he passed tempted him with their assortment of aromas, but he knew that he had to carefully marshal his rapidly disappearing funds and decided to wait until later in the day to eat. He began walking the streets, looking for any doctor's office.

- - -

It was a tired and dejected Dr. Daniel Todd who finally bellied up to a rough wooden counter and hungrily consumed a plate of mutton stew. The place was small and accommodated only four other men besides himself at the sideboard-like table, but it seemed popular and any vacant spot was quickly filled. The sign in the dingy window simply read "EATS" and the single-item menu was scrawled on the wall in chalk: "Stew—$2". Outside, the day's failing light was further muted by a fog bank that slowly crept in from the bay. He thought wistfully of his friends back on the *Ellie Mae*; of Isaac and Dugan and O'Hara and even the perverse old Fishcake with his porridge and *muctuc*. Right now, Daniel thought, he would gladly trade the life of an impoverished, unemployed San Francisco doctor for once again being a stroke oarsman on a New Bedford whaler.

He was certain that he had walked every street in the fledgling city, and he had discovered only nine doctors' offices. Like most business establishments in the burgeoning boomtown, the priorities of availability, price and location seemed to take precedence over elegant appearance. Five of these offices were little more than holes-in-the-wall, two were at the top of outside stairways, both with a pointing-finger sign at the bottom indicating "Doctor", one was at the rear of a saloon and only the ninth was an accommodation of any size or of reassuring aspect. But the response he had received at all of them had been universal rejection. Each doctor seemed to be jealously guarding his own turf.

Daniel had known immediately that he wouldn't wish to associate with any of the first eight. He was certain that none of them had gone to medical school and, from the filthy, unhealthy appearance of their "offices", he doubted that any of them had even apprenticed. The ninth, Dr. Abbott, was affable and had a very professional bearing which seemed in accord with his office. But he had complained, in smug earnestness, that the community didn't seem in need of additional doctors, judging by how infrequently patients crossed his threshold. It was during this exchange that Daniel, gazing about the room, noted a diploma, in Latin, from Yale University.

"Ah," he had said when the opportunity presented itself, "you graduated from medical school at Yale."

"Yes," the good doctor replied, "as you can readily see by my diploma there on the wall."

Then, Daniel saw that the document read "*Artis Baccalaureatus admiserunt eique dederunt...*"instead of "*Medicinae Doctoris...*"The diploma conferred a *Bachelor's degree* and not that of a Doctor of Medicine! It was a college diploma and not one from a medical school! Daniel marveled at the brazen audacity with which the man so falsely presented himself to the world. The thought crossed his mind that perhaps he could be of considerable assistance to "Dr." Abbott in really treating patients correctly with the result that more of them might begin to enter through his door. On the other hand, Daniel didn't wish to begin building a reputation of being associated with a charlatan like this man, and he had quickly returned to the street.

San Francisco seemed like a swarming midden of humanity to Daniel. After his months at sea, he felt suffocated by the shoulder-to-shoulder seething of rough-clad men crowding around him. Boston had struck him somewhat that same way when he had first moved there from the comfortable, tree-lined streets of Hadley, but even Boston had exhibited a sedate orderliness and was almost languorous in its pace of life, the behavior of its people, and the permanence of its buildings. Here, the impatient pace of the pressing crowds and the patchwork construction of the "city" emphasized the fluid nature and frenzy of life in this new West. Daniel found it overwhelming.

Exhausted from his day's walk and depressed over the apparent bleakness of his future, he slogged through the sloppy street to his "home" at the storeship barracks. The weasel was still there, perched on his high stool like a brooding raven, and Daniel found his seabag undisturbed. He placed his coat in it and extracted his blankets. Just three of the crowded hammocks were occupied by snoring bodies at the moment but most of the others had gear slung in them; obviously the compartment would be crowded later. The only light came from a single gimbaled ship's lantern on the bulkhead above the weasel's head.

Daniel swung into his hammock and took stock of his situation. His worldly possessions consisted of only $13 and the contents of his seabag. With his grooming today, he was relatively presentable but certainly no jack-a-dandy. He couldn't believe how expensive everything was in San Francisco and shuddered at the cost of trying to establish a practice here. Even staying in this place and eating only a single meal each day, he would be destitute in half a week. In order to practice anywhere, he would have to get instruments and pharmaceuticals. With the apparent lack of any regulation of medical practice in California, his not having a diploma to prove his graduation and qualifications appeared to present no great problem, although he felt he must get a copy of that document soon for his own affirmation and peace of mind, if nothing else. Perhaps he should just head out to a mining camp somewhere and fill whatever medical needs he found there—simply "make-do" medically as he had done on occasion aboard the *Ellie Mae*. Although he had not seen an apothecary in his wandering today, surely there must be *some* place in San Francisco where he could purchase the basic medications he would need if he chose that course.

Money was the problem and he had the fleeting thought that perhaps a bank might lend him the necessary funds to make his start but decided that was an unlikely possibility without some sort of "sheepskin" as a *bona fide*. Perhaps he should try his hand at gold mining and make a stake that way. Perhaps he should go back to sea; he was now an experienced whaleman and certainly seamen were scarce in this port. Maybe he could find a job as a clerk in a store or business here in town until he could accumulate what he needed for his medical practice.

With these worries niggling his brain and the mutton stew lying heavy in his stomach, sleep did not come easily. He would have sworn he had just been lying there with his eyes closed, but when the woman's screaming string of shrieks and curses ripped the air and brought him to his feet on the deck, he realized he had been sound asleep. Over a dozen other men were now occupying the dimly-lit compartment, and they bolted from their hammocks as did Todd. The wailing reached a new pitch, and most of the men rushed as a group toward the after part of the old ship. When they burst into a small cabin, the darting figure of a man swept out and past them before they could stop him. A caterwauling, cursing woman lay sprawled on a narrow bunk, nude except for a thin shift bunched high on her sagging breasts. She cradled her left arm gingerly and made no attempt to cover her nakedness.

"Catch that miserable sonuvabitch! He took his poke an' then done runned off wi' all my money!" she screeched with the shrillness of a seagull. "Catch the bastard!"

Daniel decided this must be Sadie but just then, three other women who were just as scantily attired muscled their way through the crowd. They clustered around the noisy one to comfort her.

One turned to the men and, with an angry crispness in her voice, ordered, "Ye've all had yer cheap look. Now git the hell out'a here! Cain't ye see she's been hurt.?

The men mumbled and turned to leave as the sounds subsided to just a mewling groan, accompanied by the sympathetic clucking of the other women.

Daniel edged forward against the flow of the emerging crowd and said, "Can I help? I'm a doctor."

"Ha!" the authoritative one scoffed, taking in his seedy appearance with a glance. "If'n ye're a doctor man, I'm the goddamned Queen of Sheba."

Ignoring her, Daniel insinuated his way between the women and stood in front of the injured one. "My appearance notwithstanding, I *am* a Doctor of Medicine and will help if you wish."

"Well, don't he talk purty?" sneered the spokeswoman.

"Goddamn it, Lottie Jo, it's *my* arm what's hurt. Go peddle yer goddamn papers somewheres else. I'm Sadie, mister," she said, looking up at Todd. "Give 'er a go at fixin' the damn thing, if'n ye can. I think she's busted. That sonuvabitch liked to twist the goddamn thing off, he did."

The woman still made no move to cover herself and Daniel could not help noting a cluster of venereal warts between her legs. He tenderly examined her left arm and found that there was a fracture of the radial bone, high in the wrist.

"Yes, Sadie, it's broken. I'll have to set it and put a splint on it." Looking around at the other three women, none of whom had made a move to leave the cabin, Daniel said, "I'll need some wooden slats and some cloth that we can tear into strips. Can any of you ladies bring that to me?"

A surprised look appeared on all three faces at being addressed in such a gentlemanly fashion. One said, "I'm usin' a packin' crate what to stan' my lamp on in my room. I s'pect it can spare some pieces an' still hol' together."

Another said, "I got a clean mattress cover. I'll git it."

The authoritative one simply glared her doubts in silence.

When the other two reappeared with their "supplies", Daniel said, "This will hurt, Sadie. Are you ready?"

She nodded, closed her eyes and turned her head to one side.

"Hold her shoulder, please," Daniel said to the woman who had brought the mattress cover. He proceeded to pull with a slow, steady traction on Sadie's hand with his left while gently rotating it as he molded the bone into alignment through the skin with his right.

Sadie was one tough customer. She made no response except for an initial wince and then, when it was all over, hissed through clamped teeth, "Goddamit. That hurt."

"You did very well, Sadie. Don't move and I'll splint it. Do you feel faint?"

"Hell no, I ain't goin' to faint," she scoffed her dissonant response as she glowered at such a question. "But I could sure as hell use a shot o' 'guardiente."

One of her companions produced a bottle from a bureau while Todd wrapped padding around her forearm and then tied on a splint which immobilized Sadie's hand as well as her arm. He made a sling out of the last of the mattress cover and eased Sadie's arm into it.

"There. Try not to twist that and you'll be as good as new in a couple of months. I'll look in on you tomorrow," he said as he moved toward the door.

"Thanks, Doc," Sadie said and waved the half empty bottle at his retreating figure.

- - -

There were no ship's bells to toll the hour nor any clock to chime the time, but Daniel was awakened by the stirring around him and the usual sounds of men turning out—phlegmy coughs, shuffling feet on the deck, murmured conversation. He looked about and drew his blankets closer against the dank chill that filled the compartment. It felt as though cold fog must enshroud the city outside and had even crept in to suffuse the dimly lit berthing space. He could think of no reason why he should stir. His prospects were just as bleak this morning as they were last night when he went to bed. Well, he thought, at least I do have a patient now; checking on her condition was his only inducement to getting up.

He dozed and sorted through memories of the whaler. Even standing a masthead watch would be welcome compared to the frustrations he was encountering at the moment. With just a few instruments and medications, he thought, I could do what I have been trained to do! Why should that be such a problem?

He must have gone back to sleep because suddenly the weasel was shaking him and saying, "Ye be the one what fixed Sadie's arm? She wants to see ye."

Daniel swung out of his hammock and drew on his boots. Rolling his blankets and stowing them in his seabag, he ducked through the jumble of lashings and made his way to the cabin where he had treated his patient the previous night.

He saw Sadie there, but she appeared much different than when he had last seen her. She wore a robe that was draped to leave the left arm, which was still suspended in the sling, free of the garment. Her hair was combed and drawn up in a bun on the back of her head. A coffee pot was on the crate at her bedside, and there was a spare cup in addition to the one from which she drank.

"How is the arm this morning, Sadie?" Daniel asked as he approached her bedside.

"Hurt like hell las' night 'til I drowned the damn thing in '*guardiente*. Feels tol'able this mornin'. Thank ye, Doc. Charlie tells me ye only stood fer one night here. 'Zat right? Gol' fever got ye by the balls like ever'body else in this goddamn town?"

"No," Daniel replied simply. "Let me loosen that splint and make sure your arm isn't swelling too much."

As he unknotted the strips of cloth to free some of the slats of her splint, Sadie continued, "I guess a doc like ye is inter'sted only in the ague an' busted bones an' the work o' six guns an' knives an' sech. Right? The yaller stuff don't tickle yer fancy, huh? Jus' as well. I were out there all las' year an' when the surface stuff played out, mos' them bastards couldn't pay fer their grub wi' what they found, let 'lone come up with the price of a poke. I done brought my gals back to town—don't pay as well here, but 'tis reg'lar. 'Spect ye want a poke as yer fee fer las' night. Right?"

"No, thank you, Sadie. Your arm looks very good. It's a little bruised where the man grabbed you, but there's no bleeding inside. This arm will heal as good as new. Just keep it splinted for six or eight weeks so you don't rotate your hand," he said as he demonstrated. "You'll have to accept your money with your right hand, I suppose," he joked, showing what he meant by turning the palm of that hand up.

"Have some coffee, goddamn it. Ye're a doodle, ye know that, Doc? Ere ye goin' to do yer doctorin' here in town?"

He refilled her coffee cup and gratefully poured one for himself. He shook his head and said, "I don't think so, Sadie. Just as soon as I can get enough money together to buy the supplies I need, I think I'll find some gold camp and set up an office there."

"Christ a'mighty!" she howled. "What fer? Prices is as high out there as a cat's back on stilts. Flour is $400 a barrel, brown sugar what's half sand is $6 a pound—same fer coffee what's half sawdust. Hell, laud'num cost a dollar a *drop*. I had to charge $10 a poke, but what digger cud 'ford it? 'Tis crazy out there, I tell ya. Hell, e'en to take a dory 'crost the bay 'ud run ye a hunnert or sometimes two hunnert dollar. Else ye had to walk forty goddamn miles jus' to get 'round the bay 'fore ye cud start up the river."

Sadie took a long drink of coffee and said, "Stay in town here, Doc. I kin prob'ly steer some bizness yer way—either some o' the gals in town what's got one o' the fevers o' the trade or one o' them sports what went in fer a poke an' got more'n he bargained fer."

"Well," Daniel said as he eagerly refilled his cup, even though she had not invited him, "I'm here for a short while anyway. I guess I'll give what's his name—Charlie?—the price of another night's stay. If you need me, I'll be around. Thank you, Sadie, for the coffee." He quickly drained the now tepid contents.

"Ye're al'right, Doc. Come back an' meet my gals t'night, e'en if ye ain't buyin' their wares."

"Take care," Daniel chuckled as he put down his cup and took his leave.

CHAPTER FIFTEEN

The cold afternoon fog clutched at Daniel, and he felt its clammy moisture creep deep into his lungs with each breath. He wanted to postpone his single meal of the day as long as he could, but the emptiness of his stomach was growing almost painful. Sadie's coffee this morning had been an unexpected treat. He decided he would have to make his rounds to check on her condition again tomorrow. His conscience scolded him for the beggarly thought. But thinking about Sadie brought Charlie to mind and how much friendlier the man had been when Todd purchased another night's lodging. I suppose he has some relationship with her, business or otherwise, he speculated. Daniel wondered if he has venereal warts, also.

He hunched deeper in his coat and bundled the collar tighter around his neck. He didn't remember Cape Horn weather as being any colder than this San Francisco fog. He had roamed the streets of San Francisco most of the day to see if he could discover another doctor's office somewhere and perhaps a physician sorely in need of even a ragged associate. He had found none. Either the population of this city was very healthy or the people had discovered the futility of visiting the "healers" Daniel had met. He was walking along the board sidewalk in front of the Astor House when he almost collided with Captain Winthrop of the *Calliope*. Both men had their heads bent and were not as attentive as they should have been.

"Excuse me," Daniel said and then realized the other man's identity. "Ah, Captain Winthrop. How are you, sir?"

It took the Captain a second or two to recognize Daniel and then he said, "Well, well. Doctor Todd. I'm surprised to see ye here on the street. I'd expect ye to be long gone to the gold fields, like all else here in this miserable port."

"No, not quite," Todd replied with an acerbic grin. "When do you sail, sir?"

"I'm still loaded chock a'block wi' cargo—no market for my sail cloth here wi' all these idle ships. I've had tide an' favorable wind to sail an' peddle it elsewhere but not e'en half a crew. I might as well be aground. Some beggarly mucker flashed a fist-sized pouch o' gold an' most o' my men just took off after him like the bastard was the Pied Piper."

The frustrated captain shook his head in disgust. "I was searchin' today for some gullible buyer for my canvas—somebody wi' more money than brains—but findin' none, I decided to eat ashore. Will ye join me for supper?"

Daniel struggled to suppress his eagerness. "I would be honored, sir."

The two men entered the Astor House and were shown to a table by a waiter who looked disapprovingly at Todd's garments. Captain Winthrop ignored his attitude and promptly ordered two whiskeys as well as a pair of steaks.

"What be yer plans?" he asked as they sipped their drinks.

The whiskey burned his empty stomach and Daniel made the one last while he briefly recounted his problem and Winthrop drank several glasses. The waiter brought their steaks and both men attacked them with enthusiasm. So enjoyable was the meal that the conversation was limited, although as the tally of Captain Winthrop's whiskeys increased, so did his mellowness. In the wake of his disappearing food, he became almost maudlin over his professional and financial plight.

Daniel was not eager to leave the comfortable warmth of the restaurant and when long periods of melancholy silence on the Captain's side of the table hinted that the evening was almost over, he said casually, "You know, Captain, a thought just came to mind about what you might do with your cargo of canvas."

"Oh, yes?" Winthrop replied.

Daniel continued, "When I was a whaleman, our labors were very destructive of our clothing, particularly our pantaloons. We were constantly mending and patching. I'm sure that miners are even harder on theirs. I find that they charge $25 for the roughest sort of trousers here in San Francisco and, from what I hear about prices out there in the camps, they probably sell for double that amount or more. Why not use your canvas to make work pantaloons and sell those instead of a whole cargo of sailcloth? Did your sailmaker jump ship with the rest of the crew?"

"He's too crippled to flee," Winthrop replied flatly. The Captain did not change his expression and Todd thought the man was perhaps too obtunded by drink to grasp the possibilities of his suggestion. But slowly, like a ship gaining way as its sails slowly fill, Winthrop stirred from his apparent stupor and said, "An' there be prob'ly a handful of tailors here in town that a man could hire, as well." He rubbed his grizzled beard thoughtfully. "Could sell 'em for $50 or more, ye say?"

"Yes. I'm told that even a barrel of flour sells for $400 out there."

Winthrop hailed the waiter and said, "Two more whiskeys."

"I think I'll just have coffee instead, sir," Daniel interjected.

"Whiskey and a coffee, then," Winthrop amended his order and then pondered in silence. Finally, he said, "If I had me a crew, I'd simply stow my cargo in a warehouse here, an' jus' make sail for Boston ag'in. Don't have no crew, though, so as 'tis, yer course has merit. The fo'castle's 'bout empty. We could put what crew's left to work up there with extra lamps an' all. As long as *Calliope's* gatherin' barnacles anyway, might as well use her."

After a thoughtful pause, he added, "Since ye ain't doctorin' right now, kin ye use a needle?"

"I'm no tailor, but I suspect I can use a needle better than some," Daniel replied.

"Be company for my Mate in this enterprise, then. Impress any tailors ye might find adrift an' have 'em dockside by noon tomorra'. I'll cal'clate terms for any o' 'em ye find an' for ye also. An' ye might as well move back aboard *Calliope* yerself, Doctor."

Captain Winthrop downed the last of his whiskey with a gulp and stirred to leave. Daniel would have liked to finish his coffee, but he was so grateful for the elegant meal he had just finished and for the Captain's offer of employment that he felt it more appropriate to leave at the same time.

He rose and shook Winthrop's hand. "Thank you for everything, Captain. We will hope that this becomes a very profitable arrangement for all."

Winthrop nodded his agreement and moved toward the door. Daniel wondered if the other man would be of the same mind in the morning when all of his whiskeys had worn off.

They reached the street and parted in the foggy darkness. As he turned his steps toward the barracks ship and his bunk, Daniel's frame of mind was markedly better than it had been earlier in the day. The fog didn't seem nearly as cold or dense.

- - -

Charlie was the one who wakened him once again. "Sadie wants ye, mate."

Daniel roused, yawned, and sleepily looked about him. At least half of his fellow lodgers were already up or in the process. He nodded and, swinging out of his hammock, prepared to visit the "queen bee". He found her much as she had been the previous morning.

"Pour yerself some coffee," she offered with a sweep of her hand toward the pot.

"How are you this morning, Sadie?" he asked as he gratefully poured a cup for himself after filling hers.

"Top of the heap. The ol' wing don' hurt me none," she replied, flopping her left arm in its sling.

Daniel took a sip of the hot coffee and said, "Let me loosen that splint and see how the arm itself looks."

While he was doing this, Sadie looked up at him and said, "I skeered up some more biz'ness fer ye, Doc. Lottie Jo's got a bellyache."

"Oh? I'll be happy to examine her. Your arm looks fine. No swelling at all; just that same bruising." He tied the splint back on. "Lottie Jo? As I recall, she didn't approve of me very much the other night."

"Yeah. She's always sour as a green 'simmon, but she's hurtin'. E'en axt to see ye. Her crib's next door," Sadie replied.

"I'll look in on her and then come back here before I go." Daniel finished his coffee quickly and then went down the passageway to the next room. A grumbly voice answered his knock, "Yeah?"

"It's Doctor Todd. Sadie said you wanted me to check your stomach," Daniel replied.

"Come on in."

The tousled woman lay on her side in the fetal position with her arms clutched around her abdomen. The room was quite dark and Daniel struck a match to the coal oil lamp by her bedside. The chimney was so blackened that little light showed through, so Todd removed it.

"When did this start, Lottie Jo?" he asked her.

"It's ailed off an' on fer weeks. Worse wi' my monthly. Been bad, though, last two day," she complained as she rolled on to her back.

She wore the same thin shift as the other night, and in the dim light, the bedding looked particularly dirty. A rancid body stench hung in the tiny room like a vapor. Daniel wondered how Lottie imagined she could successfully market her wares in such surroundings. He gingerly palpated her abdomen. The upper portion was doughy soft and only mildly guarded. As he touched the lower abdomen, though, she winced, bit her lower lip and tightened her abdominal muscles against any further pressure.

"Damn! That hurt," she hissed.

Daniel persevered. There seemed to be no difference in her response between pressure on one side or the other, and the most acute tenderness seemed to be just above her pubic bone.

"I must examine you down below, Lottie Jo," he said.

Without hesitation, she pulled up her shift and spread her flexed legs as though preparing to service him. He held the lamp in place and his examination showed what he first thought was severe leucorrhea, a white vaginal discharge, but on moving the flickering lamp closer, he could see that the excretion bore the pale yellow color of pus. Putting the lamp down, he carefully spread her labia with his thumbs and could see that the pus issued from the vagina and not the urethra.

"Your whole pelvis is undoubtedly infected, Lottie Jo. It seems to be located around your vagina and uterus rather than your bladder. It could spread to cause a generalized peritonitis—that's an infection of everything in your belly. I think you have an acute attack of chronic gonorrhea, Lottie Jo," he said, moving back.

"Ain't that the clap?" she asked. When he nodded agreement, she argued, "I had that a'fore an' this ain't nothin' like it."

"This has spread up into your insides and that's why your belly hurts." He pulled her shift down and went around to her side. "This could be very serious. You could even die from it if it spread widely in your belly. For the present, you must stop your professional activities, douche hourly, alternating between diluted vinegar and a solution of nitrate of silver, and sit frequently in a bath of very warm water. Warm compresses held against your lower belly will give you some comfort also. I don't have any silver nitrate, but I'll write it down for Sadie to get for you. In the long run, if you value your health and your life, you must give up the sort of life that you have been leading."

Daniel turned to leave, feeling the need to wash his hands, but he saw no basin in Lottie's room. He wondered how she could follow his orders with the limited facilities available in this old hulk. He stopped and further advised, "If you don't get better by tomorrow night, you should present yourself to that new hospital I saw. I think it was on Kearny Street, or some such name."

Lottie Jo's only response was a snort, scoffing the likelihood of being able to find the help there that he suggested.

"I'll look in on you tomorrow," Daniel promised.

"Thank ye, Doc," she reluctantly ceded as he was leaving the tiny room.

Todd told Sadie of his findings and admitted that, being the stranger he was to San Francisco, he did not know where she could obtain the nitrate of silver, but he wrote down a prescription on a scrap of paper that she produced. She promised to find it that morning.

After describing to Sadie the same treatment regimen he had outlined for Lottie Jo, he left to visit the seldom-used wash stand and community towel at the rear of the berthing compartment. He felt that this incident with Lottie Jo had not been a very satisfying employment of his medical skills. He was afraid that the prostitute's condition would persist "off and on", in her words, for a long time into the future and would probably mark a good many men along the way.

Putting his frustration aside, he felt the need for breakfast before he set out to find any available tailors. After all, if he were now going to reside aboard the *Calliope*, he could afford to indulge his appetite this morning.

- - -

At noon, Daniel and only one other man waited at the end of Long Wharf for the *Calliope* dinghy. His companion was a stooped comma of a man who had a full beard and appeared in chronic need of a good meal. His name was Stefanovich and he spoke with a thick foreign accent. Daniel gathered that he had come to San Francisco when the Russians departed nearby Fort Ross, but he could only understand a word here and there when the man spoke. The language barrier was probably the reason the man's tiny tailor shop had not been more prosperous than it appeared to be. Unlike the five other tailors Daniel had visited, Stefanovich readily agreed to come out to the ship when he finally understood the job that was being offered. His availability was welcome, but Todd wondered if it might be an ill omen and a bad indicator of the man's tailoring skills.

The two men stood silent in the weak sunlight, Daniel with his hands deep in his pockets and Stefanovich hugging his thin and worn coat close around his body. Conversation was limited because of the language problem, and it was a relief to Daniel when the white dory from the *Calliope* was very smartly rowed up to the wharf by three of her sailors.

"Ye Todd?" the one who seemed to be in charge asked.

"Yes," he replied. He was very pleased that Captain Winthrop had apparently not had second thoughts about the venture. Todd helped Stefanovich into the boat and then threw his own seabag in after him. The party was soon skimming across the glassy surface of the harbor toward the anchored clipper ship.

- - -

Captain Winthrop was disappointed that Todd had found only one tailor. He had prepared the fo'castle for more by having many of the hammocks stowed, had connected the mess tables by planking to form a sizable cutting table, and had had several huge bolts of sailcloth brought up from the hold. Daniel was introduced to Chigger Lane, the crippled sailmaker, and then, while the Captain looked on, the two of them tried to explain to Stefanovich what was expected of him. This arduous task was undertaken by using pantomime, sign language, demonstrations with a pair of pantaloons from Todd's seabag and with many words spoken overly loud in the vain hope of making them better understood. Finally, Winthrop remembered Olav, the Bering Strait sailor, who had shipped on the *Calliope's* recent voyage and who was still aboard. He sent for him as interpreter.

The little tailor probably comprehended the task ahead better than they suspected and much of his response was soon directed toward determining the wage he would be paid. Daniel was not certain, but he believed that the final agreement was that Stefanovich would get twenty-five cents for simply cutting out the pieces for a pair of pantaloons, $1.50 for cutting and sewing one pair that had one pocket and a codpiece or $1.75 if the garment had a two-button fly instead. Captain Winthrop was a raspy trader and drove a hard bargain but agreed to the terms and also that Stefanovich could live on board with his bed and found being free.

The Russian finally made it understood that he had a sewing machine that must be moved from his shop, that he would get it along with his gear and start work the next morning. Winthrop insisted, though, that a pattern for the panels of the pantaloons be scribed before the tailor left the ship and that he return with his things today and not tomorrow.

Daniel's concern about the little garment-maker's tailoring skills was quickly allayed as Stefanovich drew a pattern with swift and expert strokes of a pen on a spread of canvas. In five simple drawings, he had fashioned the front and back panels that would become pant legs, each with long enough tops to be doubled over for a waist band, a separate pocket, the fly insert, and belt loops. As soon as he left to fetch his things, Todd, Chigger Lane and two crewmen started cutting canvas. Only one pair of scissors heavy enough to cut the stiff and rugged sailcloth was available so a pair of tin snips was honed to an appropriate sharpness; even two belt knives were employed.

By the time Stefanovich returned with his sewing machine, tailoring tools, skeins of heavy thread and his few clothes, he was confronted by stacks of pantaloon parts. His eyes shone with eagerness as visions of unprecedented wealth swept through his brain. Within minutes, he had set about sewing his first garment. As he trod on the foot cradle and moved the cloth first one way and then another to double stitch the seams, the pantaloons began to take shape. Todd, Captain Winthrop and, especially, the sailmaker watched with fascination. Chigger Lane could only think of the many hours of his work on sails and other sewing tasks that could have been saved with a machine such as the little tailor used.

The Captain tallied the elapsed time by frequently checking his large pocket watch; even with Stefanovich's skilled and swift sewing, it took him 64 minutes to complete one pair of pants from pieces of cloth that had already been cut. He had produced a very satisfactory product. Hand sewing by Todd, Lane and members of the crew would be much, much slower so it was obvious that other help would be required.

Winthrop again conversed with the tailor through Olav over the possibility of recruiting more tailors. Stefanovich agreed to take cut material ashore and try to place it as job work with some of his acquaintances as long as he continued to get the agreed upon rate for each garment. Judging by the shrewd look in the man's eyes, Daniel was certain such a practice would still put considerable money in the little tailor's pocket. Even though Winthrop was unhappy over these other tailors possibly leaking news of his venture and the likely competition from other ship's captains who couldn't market their sail cloth, he agreed to let Stefanovich try.

Four bells sounded from the quarterdeck and so the afternoon's desultory efforts toward garment manufacture came to an end. Stefanovich bundled the pieces of sail cloth that had already been cut and was rowed ashore once again in the ship's dinghy with his promises to be back at the wharf at first light the next morning.

- - -

Captain Winthrop invited Todd to dine with him in his cabin and fretted through the entire meal about all that might go wrong with the garment-making plan: suppose the pants fail to sell; what if production turns out to be too slow; how could he finance the job work if Stefanovich were successful in recruiting other tailors and they insisted on daily payments? On the other hand, what would they do if the Russian couldn't find any other help; what would Mr. Cabot, the owner of the shipping line, think of this wholesale shredding of his cargo? Todd didn't suppose that the captain of a vessel ever had these doubts about his decisions and was relieved when Winthrop's third whiskey following the meal gradually seemed to ease the man's concerns.

"I am certainly no businessman," the doctor finally ventured as he sipped sparingly at his single glass of whiskey, "but it would seem to me that the way to obtain operating funds would be through securing a bank loan on a portion of your cargo of canvas. I am sure any banker would insist on greatly discounting its value under the circumstance of all of these stranded ships, but I would think the loan could still be large enough to finance a reasonable number of garments." Captain Winthrop sat quietly, listening to Dr. Todd.

"Then, it would seem prudent to have some person whom you trust—perhaps one of your Mates, if any are still on board—to take the pantaloons to a mining camp or two out there and just sell them on the spot for the same price that is being charged here in San Francisco. Such a bargain should certainly result in the sales being swift and enthusiastically supported. You would be creating demand for your product and, at the same time, obtaining further operating funds. Who knows but what a number of peddlers might then realize the market is out there and buy your pants right here at dockside, so you wouldn't have to even worry about selling to the miners yourself."

Winthrop poured another whiskey for himself and rubbed thoughtfully at his beard. Todd was proud of the solution he had offered to the Captain's problems but was taken aback when the man squinted a pawky eye and said, "Why don't *ye* go sell 'em? 'Twas yer idea."

"I'm a doctor, Captain, not a salesman. I would hardly know where to start."

"Ye're not a doctor, at present. Ye're a pauper who *wants* to be a doctor," the captain challenged with a gloating and slightly inebriated look.

As Winthrop poured himself yet another whiskey, Todd had a moment to consider the offer. After all, he thought, I'm not doing anything else, and it would give me an opportunity to see some of the mining camps. Perhaps I could choose where I might like to practice, when I can. The alternative is to sit on the *Calliope* and sew pantaloons. What do I have to lose?

"All right," he finally said. "If you still want me to peddle the pants when there are enough of them to matter, I'll do it. You will have to give me funds to operate with, however, and I also want you to advance me enough money to buy a supply of medicines. If I should encounter a prospective patient out there, I would want to be able to treat him."

Winthrop's face had become flushed from drink, and he rose to the bargaining challenge with vigor. "Ha! An' ye'll sell my pants, skedaddle elsewhere an' set 'bout yer doctorin', all wi' my money! Won't ye, now? I'll have none of it."

"No, I'm a man of my word, Captain," Todd replied evenly. "I pledge that I will bring back every cent from the sales and whatever is left unspent of the operating funds. But, don't make up your mind yet. You have only one completed pair of pantaloons. I'll work right along with the others to make as many pairs as possible and perhaps during that time, one of your officers will return to the ship, and you can send him. Let's both sleep on it."

The evening drew to a rather abrupt close with Winthrop pouring yet another drink for himself. Daniel thanked him for the meal and made his way forward to his hammock, thinking that judging from the Captain's gargantuan consumption of alcohol tonight, the man was sorely worried about gambling the ship's cargo on such a potentially profitable, but still risky, venture.

CHAPTER SIXTEEN

The chill evening fog spread off the bay and caused Daniel to hunch his coat collar high on his neck, but the dampness did little to settle the dust of the street. He stepped around piles of manure and picked his way toward the barracks ship. He felt guilty that he had not been back to check on Lottie Jo earlier, as he had promised. Captain Winthrop had kept every available man busy from dawn until long after dark for over a week with cutting and sewing, and it was only this evening that Todd had been able to borrow the *Calliope's* dory and row ashore to make his rounds.

All things considered, the garment-making was progressing very well. Stefanovich had been able to interest two more tailors in the sewing of the pants, and he had found a little Jewish backpack peddler who had haggled with Winthrop all of the day today for purchase of the pants right at the ship. He planned to pack them to the mining camps and sell the garments there himself. The shrewd little fellow was not willing to pay as much for the ones sewn by the *Calliope* crewmen as those done by the tailors, but Todd had to admit that the difference in quality really did justify a lower price.

As a result of the deal, if it came about, Winthrop would get the money for his product immediately, the manufacturing could continue, and nobody from the ship would have to travel out into the countryside. Daniel was quite certain his employment would come to an end in the near future as, no doubt, the Captain would soon insist that all of the sewing be done by the tailors. But, if he were able to purchase some medical supplies as a result of all of this, Dr. Daniel Todd was satisfied.

When Daniel entered the canvas-covered doorway of the barracks ship, he found Charlie just inside, perched precariously on his stool, drowsing in the feeble light spilling down from the gimbaled ship's lantern. The weasel face gaped slack-jawed as half snores escaped it.

Daniel awakened him and asked, "Is anybody back there with Sadie or Lottie Jo? I've come to check on their condition."

Charlie had a confused look as he gazed about him and then yawned. "I guess Sadie's busy," he growled and then complained testily, "but Lottie sez ye tol' her to keep her goddamn legs crossed tight. Won't even see a man but still 'spects a bed an' to be fed, howsomever. Go on back an' tell 'er to get her butt back to work, why don't ye?"

Daniel shook his head in disgust and made his way aft through the jumble of hammocks. Most of them were unoccupied and that was probably the main reason for Charlie's crankiness. When he arrived at Lottie Jo's door, he knocked and said, "Lottie Jo, it's Dr. Todd. May I come in?"

There was an audible scurry of activity inside and then her voice. "Yeah. Come on in." The vinegarish tone of voice that he had heard before was missing.

He opened the door and stepped inside. "Hello, Lottie Jo. I'm sorry that I'm a few days late in getting back to you. I was detained on a ship in the harbor."

Daniel was pleasantly surprised by what he saw. Lottie Jo no longer had the slatternly appearance he had seen before. Her hair was drawn back into a neat bun at the back of her head and, although barefoot, she was clothed in a gingham dress that was clean and not immodest. Even the tiny room was neat.

"Ah," he said, "it looks as though you are feeling better."

"Yeah. Don't know when I've felt this good. The pit o' my belly's still sore, but I'm fit as a fiddle otherwise."

"Charlie, out there, seems anxious to put you back on the job," Todd replied. "I really think it would be best if you tried to find some other line of work."

"Yeah, I've had me some pause 'bout all this here fer a long time, now," she agreed. "They's things that gnaw on a woman worse'n a bad sore bellyache. I ain't tol' Sadie yet, but I'm goin' to leave. Done made up my mind."

Daniel was gratified but felt that he had to discuss reality with her. "What type of work would you plan on getting?"

"I was next oldest in a big passel o' kids, so's I had to do a heap o' cookin' back then. I think I'll mebbe amble up Angel's Camp way—that's where Sadie had us 'fore—an' get me a job burnin' hash somewheres an' try an' put all these bad times behind me."

"I think that would be a marvelous idea, Lottie," Daniel replied. "Perhaps, among all of those miners, you might even find the right man and take him as a husband."

"Well, ye might say, Doc, I've had me a bellyful o' men already. I jus' want to make me a livin' out there an' get away from all o' this. I'm 'bliged, Doc, fer ye takin' care o' my bellyache an' aimin' me right. I'll pay ye sometime."

"Don't worry about that, Lottie. I'm sure you were on the brink of changing the course of your life anyway, but I'm happy with the way things have turned out. Your medical problem may come back from time to time, but if it does, just treat it like you did before."

Daniel started to take his leave. "I think I'll look in on Sadie before I leave and see how her arm is healing. Goodbye and good luck."

He wondered if Lottie's resolve would last through the hard times that she would undoubtedly encounter. He was sure that Sadie and Charlie wouldn't be happy about it. Lottie reached out and put her hand on his arm and just gave him a reassuring nod. The strong resolve in her eyes made him feel more confident about her future. Daniel patted her hand and went out into the passageway.

Just as he turned toward it, a man came out of Sadie's door. He was tucking his shirt into his pants and paused to glance back at Todd. "She's all yours, mate. Sure as hell, ain't worth the money, though."

Daniel waited a few minutes and then knocked on the door. " Sadie?" he called.

"G'wan down the hall to Squirrel Tooth's. I'm bathin'."

"It's Dr. Todd, Sadie. I've come to check your arm," he replied.

"Oh, Doc. I'm glad ye come," she hollered in a loud voice. "C'mon in."

When he entered, Sadie was indelicately squatting over a basin and washing herself with her good right hand. He turned away and she said, "Ah, c'mon in, Doc. Ye've seen more o' me than that already."

"I can come back."

"Ah, hell. Ye're so goddamn delicate." In just a minute, she said, "There, I'm decent. Have a seat. Want some 'guardiente?"

"No, I'm fine. How does your arm feel?" he asked.

"Don't hol' me back none. Feels fine. But, I got other fish to fry with ye, Doc. Sit fer a minute."

Todd sat on the only available chair and Sadie shuffled her skirt down over her hips before she sat down on the narrow bed.

"Lillie's my newest gal. She's gone an' got herself knocked up, Doc. I tol' her she can't work here when she starts showin' an' she's beside herself 'cause she ain't got no other place to go. She's already tried gallopin' horseback, eatin' juniper berries, an' done shit herself silly with all sorts o' them physics, but she ain't lost the damn thing an' she's startin' to git a big belly. I want ye to help her get rid o' it. Ye got ways to do that. I know ye have."

"Oh—wait a *minute*, Sadie! Causing an abortion like that would be totally against the Hippocratic Oath that I took. I could not take a life!" The memory of Trumbull flashed through his mind. "Especially, just to convenience her and you." Todd looked Sadie up and down with great severity, incensed that she would even suggest such a thing.

"And even if I could find justification for doing an abortion, such as the pregnancy putting the girl's life in danger, I don't have the proper instruments or medicines. I'll talk to her and give her my counsel. After all, Lottie Jo is going to find other things to do with her life. There's no reason this girl can't do the same thing and raise the baby."

Sadie exploded. "Lottie Jo's leavin'? Goddamn ye, Doc, ye're hell bent on puttin' me outta business, ain't ye!" She rose from the bed and stomped about the room. "Jesus H. Christ! Ye're goin' to ruin me 'fore ye're through."

"Calm down, Sadie. After all, I didn't get Lillie pregnant. And Lottie Jo has inflammation of her pelvis and will keep having it from time to time, especially with frequent 'animal contact'. You don't want to get the reputation for your girls spreading the gleet around town, do you?" He could hardly suppress a smile when he said this because he was certain that preventing the spread of venereal disease was not one of Sadie's concerns.

When Sadie had finally calmed down, she said, "Naw, I don't want ye to go talkin' to Lillie. I'll tell her what ye said myself. Now, git the hell outta here." Without having poured any, she re-corked the bottle of *Aguardiente* that she had been carrying and slammed it down on the nightstand with a finality that definitely signaled to Todd that he was no longer welcome.

He said, "Well, I'm aboard the *Calliope*, out in the harbor. Get word to me in case you need my services." He felt as though he should thank her for her referrals to the only medical practice he had enjoyed so far in San Francisco but it didn't seem appropriate. He finally just said, "Goodbye for now, Sadie," and left.

He made his way out past the hammocks, which were still vacant, and past Charlie, whose eyes followed him with a questioning gaze. Finally, just before Todd's departure through the canvas-covered doorway, the weasel shouted "Well didja tell her to get her ass back to work?" Todd ignored him and strode out into the foggy night.

He had not gone even a block when he heard a shuffling movement in the alley he had just passed. Before he could turn to investigate, he experienced a massive explosion of light and heard the echoing sound of a gong in his head. A flood of paralyzing pain barely preceded the bottomless plunge he took into a black but blissful sea of unconsciousness.

- - -

The man stumbled over the body in the darkness and cursed the "damned drunk" for nearly causing him to fall. It was only when the faint lamplight spilling from the nearby storefront reflected off the bleeding scalp that he looked closer. He rolled the body over and thought that he recognized the face as one that he had seen at the barracks ship where he had been staying since arriving in San Francisco. He stooped and studied the features more closely. When he was certain, he knelt to where he could place his ear close to the half-open mouth and was quite sure that he could hear faint breathing. Without hesitation, he dragged the limp body in the direction of his quarters, leaving a bloody trail behind.

- - -

Gradually emerging sounds; unintelligible babble; noise suddenly there but fading gradually and then totally drifting away into silence; explosive headache; crazily spinning dizziness so violent that Daniel thought he couldn't help retching but hazily remembered vomiting before and how that made the trip-hammer pain in his head worse; DON'T RETCH! Am I in the black maelstrom of the sea, being tumbled about and spun so that I can't breathe, he wondered. Am I drowning? At times he became aware of warm body pressure against him, but when he reached to grasp it, his arms closed around emptiness. Vomiting; violent, violent pain in his head; faint sounds from time to time; darkness; warm body; confusion. What's happening to me? Where am I? Darkness; spinning dizziness; retching. Oh my God, pain in my head, darkness again.

- - -

"What's it been now?" Sadie asked. "Four days? Five days? I tell ye this, Lottie Jo, less'n he snaps outta this damn soon, he's gotta go!"

"Gotta go? What the hell ye be fixin' to do? Throw him out in the street? Christ a'mighty, Sadie, he done set yer busted arm, didn't he? He cured my bellyache what was fixin' to kill me, an' he ne'er axt either o' us fer a red cent, did he?"

Lottie cocked her hands defiantly on her hips and challenged Sadie. "I bound up his head *myself* an' put him in *my* bed. He ain't takin' up any extry o' yore precious goddamn space. Sure, he thrashes 'round some an' pukes an' don't make no sense any o' the time, but he's better. I *know* he's better'n he was. He done quit bleeding an' when he opens up his eyes, they ain't e'en crossed no more. Damn it all, he's better, I tell ye, e'en though he don't seem to know where the hell he be."

"Well, Miss Fancy, he be *here*, that's where he be! So long as ye an' him are takin' up that bed an' ye're not makin' me any money usin' the damn thing, ye're both dead weight," Sadie countered in her discordant voice. "Jus' dead weight, an' with Lillie gone, I'm getting' powerful short-handed."

"Dead weight! I'm carryin' *my* weight doin' all the cookin' in the galley fer ye an' that goddamn Charlie an' the other girls. Ye ain't short o' beds 'til ye find a warm body to take Lillie's place."

"Soon's he be all right," she challenged, nodding in Todd's direction, "him an' me'll both clear the hell out o' here an' be happy to do it."

The argument ended in a truce, and Sadie stomped her way down the passageway and back to her room.

CHAPTER SEVENTEEN

Daniel's awareness of things around him returned slowly; brief waves of reality were interspersed with long periods of sleep and confusion. He noticed that when he sat up, he felt much better than when he lay flat. Bending over or coughing or retching produced explosive pain in his head. Although he could remember nothing after leaving the *Calliope* in the dory, the matted blood on his scalp and the unmistakable evidence that the pressure was up inside his head made him certain, during his brief periods of alertness and in command of his medical training, that he had received a blow on the skull that had produced severe traumatic cerebritis. In a panic, he clutched at his pocket to assure himself that his canvas purse with its two gold slugs had not been stolen during some attack. Only the skin of his legs greeted him. Under the thick comforter, he was naked.

When Lottie Jo held up a little mirror, he could see that his pupils were dilated, but equal in size. He was quite certain that when he moved his head and a bout of dizziness overtook him, his eyes swung back and forth in nystagmoid movements. He marveled that, in spite of the confusion he felt, he could put the signs of nystagmus and vertigo together and remember enough Medicine to conclude that he must have sustained some sort of damage to the medullary portion of his brain to cause this cerebritis. Even though the details leading to his self-diagnosis seemed to fade in and out of his awareness, the hope that he would eventually regain normal brain function was constant.

An entire week had passed before he awoke feeling relatively normal and without confusion. He swung his legs out of the bed and sat on its edge. This movement awakened Lottie who had been lying beside him.

"Well, look at ye. Feelin' better?"

"I guess I do. What happened?" Todd asked.

"Somebody 'bout took yer head off a week ago. Some feller from up for'ard recognized ye an' drug ye back here. Ye bled like a stuck pig an' looked like ye'd been pulled through a knothole back'ards. Ye mostly been outta yer skull since. Don't ye 'member?"

"No. I can't even imagine how I got here off the ship I was on. Did you take care of me?" he asked.

"Yep."

"Apparently, I wasn't very well dressed when I arrived," he said and nodded down at his nakedness which was covered by the quilt he had pulled up around him. The nod produced pain in his head and he winced.

"Well . . ." Lottie hesitated. "Ye weren't able to use no chamber pot in yer condition so's I sorta had to—ye know . . ."

The prostitute appeared as embarrassed as he was and Daniel thought it quite touching. He said, "Well, Lottie, I sincerely thank you for your care, and I will try to make it right with you when I can."

"Happy to do it, Doc. After all, I figger I owe ye." She got up and crossed the little room to where she had placed his clothes. They were laundered and neatly stacked. "They was 'bout as big a mess as ye were," she said as she handed them to him. His canvas purse was not there, but he feared that any mention of it would seem to indict Lottie and he couldn't believe she was guilty of that. He had undoubtedly been robbed in the attack.

He expected her to turn away while he dressed but she didn't. He finally decided that she had seen about all of him there was to see, and he gingerly proceeded to don his garments. In the process, he asked, "What did Sadie have to say about all of this?"

"She were some galled 'bout it all an' wanted ye outta here. Said she needed this crib for her business. Hell, since Lillie died though, Sadie's got more cribs than girls. But then, Sadie's Sadie, ye know," Lottie replied.

Daniel appeared puzzled. "Lillie. Why does that name sound familiar?"

"She were pregnant an' I guess Sadie wanted ye to make her lose it. Sadie tol' her ye said 'no', an' that night Lillie tried to do it by herself with a knittin' needle. Sadie found her the nex' mornin' in a big puddle o' blood. Dead. I tell ye, 'twixt Lil an' ye, we had more blood 'round here last week that I ever did see 'fore."

Lottie rambled on, but Daniel no longer heard her. He struggled to remember when he had last talked to Sadie and what he might have said to her. Apparently, he had refused to do an abortion on Lillie and she was dead because she tried to do it herself. As his sluggish brain tried to process these thoughts, Daniel stood to pull up his pants and dizziness sent him crashing back on to the bed. He lay there panting and hugging the mattress to keep from falling off. As he struggled to keep from vomiting, Lottie rushed to his side.

"Reckon ye ain't ready to ship out jus' yet, are ye, Doc? Jus' lay there an' I'll round up some vittles fer ye."

She left the tiny room and Daniel's dizziness gradually disappeared. Amidst the fear and worry about the condition of his brain, he agonized over the devastating news of the pregnant girl's death.

I was right not to abort her, he reassured himself. How could a doctor destroy a healthy, developing little human being? How could he dislodge from its Mother's body the life that was innocently and safely forming there into a person whose potential could only be imagined—perhaps genius, perhaps idiot. Who could know? To be asked to rip out that life and kill it for no other reason than that it just is *there* and that it is *inconvenient* seemed horrifying to Daniel. It's murder, he thought. Yet, not only is that tiny life dead now, but so is the mother. Daniel's thoughts drifted back to consider the concept of predestination that had seemed to be germinating in his mind. Perhaps this fetus was never destined to be born; that it was a misfit. If that were the case, why didn't it just miscarry naturally? Perhaps it was meant to be the instrument of the girl's death—Lillie, they called her. If that were so, then my refusal to do an abortion would be one element of the plan. Can there possibly be such convoluted and intricate plans put in motion by some superior intelligence—some god—in the lives and actions of people. Heavens, we humans number in the *millions,* he thought. It would have to be a chess game of unbelievable complexity to weave all of these lives toward some final conclusion. All of this was more than his muddled brain could treat. He simply surrendered to the suspicion that if he ever got to practice medicine like a real doctor and was asked to do an abortion, he would have to consider the resolve and mental state of the mother and the dangers she might encounter if she resorted to self-treatment.

He drifted back to sleep and was startled awake when Lottie returned with broth, bread and coffee. He slowly sat up to receive it. "This tastes very good to me. If I've been here a week, you must have had to feed me before," he observed.

"Ye've had a bucket of broth o'er the past week. Most of it, a spoonful at a time."

"Well, thanks again for all of your trouble, Lottie. I've got to get back to the *Calliope*. They'll think I've skipped the country," he said.

Gradually, as awareness crept into his mind, he remembered that he had rowed the ship's dory to get ashore; *they have been without it all this time,* he thought. *Supposing somebody has stolen it from dockside?*

"Best take 'nother day to get yer sea legs under ye, Doc. I'm ready to pull up stakes an' I'll haul outta here tomorrow with ye. Jus' in case ye stumble, ye know. In the meantime, ye can wrap 'round some solid food an' get yer strength back." Lottie was convincing, and Daniel lay back down when he finished eating.

- - -

Daniel and Lottie left the barracks ship without ceremony, she with her meager belongings bundled in a bedsheet-wrapped pack, and he in the clothes he had arrived in sans watch cap, which apparently had been lost in his attack. Sadie didn't appear on the scene to see them off, and Charlie simply sneered his disdain silently until they were out of the door and then he shouted, "Ye'll be back, Lottie Jo. Ye're worth *nothin'* 'cept as a whore!"

Once on the street, Daniel said, "I'm going to head down to the wharf and try to catch a boat out to the *Calliope*, Lottie. I wish I had some money to help you along your way but apparently my assailant took all I had. I wish you the best of luck, and I know you'll do well as a cook." He reached out and shook her hand.

"I owe ye a lot, Doc. I'll get by," she said and nodded her head, but the fear and uncertainty in her eyes belied her confident words.

"I owe you even more, Lottie. I'll be on the *Calliope* but I don't know for how long. If you need anything, contact me there," he said. She nodded and then strode resolutely down the street with her bundle of belongings on her shoulder as he watched. Daniel realized that he feared for Lottie Jo's future more than for his own, but he was all too painfully aware of his inability to help. Slowly he turned and gingerly picked his way along toward the waterfront. Any incautious step jarred his head and sent a stab of pain into his brain.

- - -

"Where in the name o' sweet Jesus ye been?" Captain Winthrop shouted. He shook his head in anger and then turned back to his attack. "We was without our dory 'til I hired a boat an' went lookin' fer it. Ye can't up an' go on a weeklong drunk an' 'spect me to welcome ye back. What in God's name was ye thinkin'?"

Daniel simply pointed to the crusted wound on the back of his scalp and said, "I didn't have much choice in the matter, Captain. I was attacked and robbed. I didn't regain consciousness until yesterday and I'm not feeling very well even yet."

"Humphhh," Winthrop growled and casually inspected the dry, matted wound on Todd's head. He growled again and paced back and forth as he wound down from his fret. "Well, I reckon ye couldn't help it." More pacing. "Well, ye best set down then 'fore ye fall down. Humpfff."

As he continued to pace, the Captain brought Todd up to date. "I s'pose I must tell ye that that Jew, Strauss, bought up all the pants an' wants e'en more. 'Pears as though the bizness ye suggested is sound. I've fetched up some bank money an' leased space ashore to set up a factory. The Russian's goin' to ship in more machines fer sewin' an' train some *Californios* to run 'em. I bought up two more shiploads o' sail cloth an' I may not e'en go back to sea. The *Calliope*, if Heaven e'er sees fit for her to sail 'gain may very well hoist anchor without me."

Not yet quite willing to give Todd any more of the credit than he already had, Winthrop paced up and down some more. "Are ye goin' to be all right?"

"Yes, I hope so. I still have quite a bit of dizziness and frequent headaches," Todd replied.

"An' I 'spect ye figger ye're a partner in this here bizness," Winthrop offered reluctantly. "Bein's as ye . . . well . . . as 'twas yer idea in the first place."

After a moment of thought, Todd replied, "No, Captain, I don't. It was your cargo of canvas, your ship, and you have not only given me food and lodging, but you have paid all of the other expenses in this venture thus far. It's *your* business."

Seeing the expression of relief spread over Winthrop's face was almost payment enough for having suggested the plan in the beginning; but, not quite. Todd added, "But, if you feel that you owe me something, Captain . . ." A worried expression flooded back over Winthrop's face. "I would consider a very short-term loan of money to start my practice to be a Godsend and more than payment in full. The pantaloon business would be yours without legal or moral encumbrance. I could buy medical supplies, depart the *Calliope*, and get started practicing Medicine. The loan would be repaid very soon."

"Loan ye money! Great Jehoshaphat, I'm havin' to borrow it *myself*. How in God's name do ye 'spect me to loan ye money?" The Captain glowered his displeasure.

"Obviously, you feel some obligation to me or you wouldn't have mentioned it in the first place. The thing is, Captain Winthrop, as you have already indicated, you have the ability to borrow from a bank and I do not. If you would advance enough money to me to buy instruments, a stock of medications, and basic supplies to support me for a week or two, I can start doing the things I have been trained to do. I graduated from the Medical College of Harvard University, a very reputable institution, and I am a good doctor. Give me a start, and I am certain that I can repay you very, very quickly."

Winthrop clasped his hands behind his back and paced back and forth, much as though he were striding his Quarterdeck. Finally, he growled, "And ye'd sign a paper that ye have no claim on the pantaloon business?"

"Of course."

"Well, if it didn't have prospects, I'd tell ye to go to Hell. And it seems I ain't paid ye anythin' for your labors here on the *Calliope* so far." After a long pause that marked his painful indecision, he asked, "How much would ye need?"

Hope flared in Daniel's aching brain, but he realized that he had no idea how much it would cost to do the things he had mentioned or even where he could find the items he would need. But, one thing at a time. How much would the Captain be willing to lend, he puzzled.

"Three hundred dollars, Captain," Daniel said with apparent certainty. "I'm positive that three hundred dollars will get me started in practice."

"*Three hundred dollars!*" Winthrop exploded. "Three hundred dollars! Jehoshaphat man, I can buy a whole ship's cargo o' canvas for scarcely more," the Captain exaggerated.

"You know how expensive everything is here, Captain. I'll pay you double the interest that the bank is charging you. And I'll wager that when that Jewish peddler sees the market that is available for those pantaloons, you'll be able to charge him a great deal more than you received for the last consignment," Todd argued.

Winthrop's bluster waned and greed surged as he pondered this last. Finally, he surrendered and said, "I'll draw up the contract."

"One final thing I would ask, Captain Winthrop. When I get my supplies, I will need one of your crew to take me across the bay in the *Calliope's* dory."

"Are ye certain sure ye don't want me to row ye there *myself?*" Winthrop asked with heavy sarcasm.

Pain was lancing through Todd's head from all of this haggling, but he could not suppress the wave of elation he felt. At last, the door to his medical practice was opening a crack.

- - -

The next day, when the dory transported sail cloth to Stefanovich at the waterfront, Daniel felt better and he went ashore, the money in hand that Captain Winthrop had so reluctantly loaned him. He returned to "Dr." Abbott's office to seek out a possible source where he could purchase medications. The charade being performed by the bogus physician was very quickly made more apparent when Todd found that the man's supply of pharmaceuticals consisted of only a few emetics, laxatives, and alcoholic tonics. He had no chemicals from which to compound a medication, even if he knew what to mix, but he did direct Todd to an apothecary near the new hospital on Kearny Street where he said various drugs were available.

When Daniel found the place, he purchased balsam copaiba, gum camphor, Glauber's salts, laudanum, oil of cantharides, Jalap, ipecacuan, mercury ointment, Peruvian bark, tragacanth, zinc sulfate, tincture of iodine, an assortment of bottles and several packs of lint. The items filled a bulky sack, but the list of medications that were not available was long and when Daniel asked about medical instruments, he was told that he could order a set but that it would probably take eight to ten months for them to come around the Horn. The pharmacist did have a used pair of stout dental forceps and a pair of tweezers whose tips had been bent so they could be used as toothed thumb forceps to pick up tissue. Todd purchased those two items but would have to get by with a common knife and saw instead of scalpels and more refined amputation gear, because the proprietor refused to order the set of medical instruments unless they were paid for in advance. Daniel had no idea what he would use to catheterize a patient, or crush a bladder stone, or to employ as forceps for the delivery of an oversized baby. He had no probes or long forceps for the extraction of a bullet, and he would have to use common sewing thread to close any wounds. The pharmacist had not heard about ether so narcotics such as opium, henbane, or nightshade would have to do in place of an anesthetic when one became necessary.

Daniel made his purchases and, as he headed back to the *Calliope*, decided that he would write to Dr. Channing, his old Professor of Obstetrics at the Boston Lying-In Hospital, and describe his situation. He thought that his relationship with Dr. Channing had been close enough and that the good doctor's philanthropic nature was such that he might be willing to send a set of instruments and a supply of ether and other medications. Daniel would promise to forward payment for these items as quickly as he earned some fees. The shipment would probably take months to arrive, but the delay would not be as long as if he waited to order until he had the money in hand.

Daniel cringed at the thought of such an imposition on his old teacher in calling upon their close professional relationship in this manner, but he felt desperate. He thought back to the far less than satisfactory level of Medicine he had been forced to practice on the *Ellie Mae* when he was simply "making do" with what he had and was equally uncomfortable about the Medicine he would undoubtedly be practicing in the immediate future until he had proper instruments.

The *Calliope* dory was long gone from dockside and Todd hired a boy to row him out to the ship to begin packing his gear so he could leave. He obtained some writing materials from Captain Winthrop and carefully composed his letter to Dr. Channing, emphasizing the fact that after Fate had delayed him for over a year and a half, he would finally be able to start his practice, hampered though he was by the things he did not have in this frontier setting.

Daniel fully recognized the tremendous help Captain Winthrop had been and, when he was ready to leave the ship, thanked him profusely. "On every possible occasion, I shall extol all the admirable qualities of Winthrop work pants. I wish you great success in your new business, and you have my solemn word that I will pay off my debt to you just as quickly as possible. You have been . . ."

Overcome by his great sense of obligation, all he could do was hang his head and extend his hand. "Thank you, sir. I can't tell you how much I appreciate what you have done for me."

- - -

Daniel shared the oars with Kruger, the burly seaman Winthrop had ordered to row him across the bay, and was grateful that the man was so taciturn. He himself did not feel like talking: his head was still quite painful whenever he made sudden movements and he felt depressed. Although he was grateful to be leaving the teeming and inhospitable congestion of San

Francisco and thrilled with anticipation at the thought of finally starting his medical practice, he hated to feel obligated. He owed Captain Winthrop so much and certainly the list of those who had helped him in the last several weeks was long: Lottie Jo, Stefanovich, the man who had found him after the attack—even Charlie and Sadie had contributed, in their own way. He thought back to his days on the *Ellie Mae* when he could take pride in fulfilling his share of any duty, of being able to do what was expected of him, of feeling himself a man among men. Oh, how he missed those shipmates; Isaac Lawrence, Dugan, Calthrop, even the dead Pinchot and Mr. Halbert. In truth, he had to admit that he now felt buffeted, adrift and longing for those whaling days when his duties were so well defined and how, over the months, he had grown capable of dealing with them.

He was uncertain of his immediate destination and, although he claimed to be eager finally to start his practice, Daniel found himself wondering if, after all of this time, he could really be the doctor that he had always expected himself to be. Struggling to put these secret self-doubts out of his mind, he was buoyed by the liberated feeling he experienced in leaving the inhospitable city of San Francisco, and he bent his back to the oar.

"Know where ye want to go?" Kruger asked.

Todd looked back over his shoulder and saw a small pier and a rude cluster of shacks on the eastern shore, a little north of their heading. "I suppose that spot, a little to larboard," he said with a nod of his head. "They say that any journey begins with the first step and that place looks as good as any to take it."

CHAPTER EIGHTEEN

Daniel Locke Todd, M.D. paused and straightened his back while wiping the sweat from his forehead. Pushing the wheelbarrow was difficult at best, but the road veered away from the river to climb around a marsh, and even the slight incline of the hill was a punishing obstacle this late in the day. He was tempted to stop and make camp and struggle on toward the top in the morning. But what if the road only climbs higher and higher and I'm confronted with that tomorrow, he wondered. I would rather know about it tonight and then face it fresh tomorrow morning. He lifted the handles and set the heavy load in motion once again.

The wheelbarrow held everything he owned; his seabag filled with clothes and blankets, the wooden box containing all the medications he had been able to purchase in San Francisco, and the burlap sack that held the food supplies and Spartan collection of utensils that had cost him the last of his money at the trading post where the *Calliope* dory had deposited him on the east side of the bay. The proprietor had thrown in the dilapidated wheelbarrow at no charge when Todd mixed a solution of lead acetate eye wash and gave it to him for his pink eye. Without the disintegrating vehicle, transporting his belongings into the mountains would be impossible. He just hoped that the wobbling wheel did not come off before he reached his destination.

On either side of the well-used freight road that roughly followed the Sacramento River, rolling hills spilled off and climbed toward the mountains in the distance. 1850 had been a dry year and the grass spreading over the rolling countryside had burned brown in the late summer heat, but the clumps of oak trees scattering across the low hills as far as the eye could see lent some color to the landscape. Clusters of cattle grazed here and there. Daniel wondered how they had escaped the clutches of the hungry men on their way to or from the gold fields. His own stomach cramped with hunger and, even though his evening meal would be a simple one of cheese and a small pan of boiled beans and bacon, he could barely wait to partake. Of course, the beans would take several hours to cook but as hungry as he felt now, he was certain he would eat them while they were still very, very crunchy.

He topped the long rise and was delighted to see the wagon tracks stretch on for at least a mile on the level ahead. Daniel wheeled his load over toward a spreading oak and collapsed in fatigue. He lay there and wondered how far he had come today and how far it still was to Sacramento City. On questioning the man at the trading post, he had been told that earlier almost everyone had taken advantage of Captain Sutter's hospitality and that his fort had been the activity center of the Sacramento Valley. When gold had been discovered on up the American River and the rush had started, a chain of events transpired that now left Sutter virtually penniless. He had to sell his fort with its tannery, still, blacksmith shop and grist mill as he watched Sacramento City grow to flourish nearby. At least, while in that city, Daniel could learn the latest news about the surrounding mining camps.

He fashioned a fire ring and started a small cooking fire. With water from his canvas canteen, he put a pan on to boil for tea and rationed out a handful of beans to add after his tea was made. He spread on the ground a square of canvas that he had brought from the *Calliope*. It would serve as a ground cloth tonight but could be used as a simple shelter tent when necessary. He knew he looked like a true vagabond—his scanty belongings, the rude conveyance transporting them, just the sky for his roof—but he finally felt some measure of independence and enjoyed it by stretching out to rest his aching muscles. The setting sun streaked the low clouds in the west with red and gold and gave the surrounding hills the appearance of soft velvet.

How marvelous it felt to be free of the hurly-burly of San Francisco. He thought it inconsistent, though, since he was dedicated to curing the ills of mankind, that he found Nature as satisfying as in those bucolic scenes described by Washington Irving in his tales of the Hudson River country and the seething of crowded humanity in cities so repugnant. Perhaps the attack on him and the rap he had received on his head had been a factor in this recent antisocial attitude. That thought reminded him that his head had not hurt all day, in spite of his exertions. Satisfied with that bit of comfort, he stretched out to wait for his tea water to boil.

- - -

Sacramento City was more of a tent and lean-to affair than San Francisco had been. It had the same sprawling jumble of would-be merchants trying to hawk their wares out of rude, temporary "stores" or tents, the same dusty streets that were churned to mud in places by an admixture of manure or discharges of water of questionable origin, and the same stench of humanity that Daniel now associated with frontier towns. Only in the central few blocks were there buildings of permanent construction, although many of those had fronts more grandiose than the structure back of them. Even so, Daniel was happy finally to reach this settlement after the days of pushing his wheelbarrow. He wished that he had the price of a mug of beer but since he did not possess even that, he decided that he should pick a vacant spot, set up his shelter and try to market his skills as a Doctor of Medicine.

Tents were pitched helter-skelter back off the street, but he felt that he had to establish himself in a more visible and accessible spot and that decision took him toward the outskirts. He finally parked his load on a bare spot near a patched combination of wood and canvas and sought out the owner of that shelter to see if there were any objection to his setting up next door.

"Hello," he called at the closed flap. "Anyone home?" There was no answer and he repeated his inquiry. He was about to turn away when he heard violent retching inside the tent. It sounded as though somebody had a horrible hangover but when he heard weak and pitiful groans, he decided he should investigate.

Drawing aside the flap, he looked in and asked, "Do you need any help?"

He was met by the wretched sight of a very pale man who apparently was so weak that he couldn't stand but had managed to roll to one side and had tried unsuccessfully to vomit beyond the edge of his blankets. The old vomitus from previous attempts had a bilious green color. The man didn't even try to answer but simply collapsed back onto his bed with a groan.

Daniel bent near to him and said, "I'm a doctor. Perhaps I can be of help."

The man merely closed his eyes and breathed deeply, apparently drained of even the energy to answer, but he obviously was trying to avoid more retching. Daniel noted that his skin appeared very dry and, as he drew down the slack jaw and looked in the man's mouth, he saw that the tongue was terribly desiccated and had dense brown "fur" on it. When he touched the man's belly through the blankets, the response was a wincing movement.

"Water. Please—water." The words were almost inaudible, softly whispered and garbled because of the dryness of his tongue. "Careful where you touch, mister—'fraid I shit all o'er the dashboard."

Drawing down the blanket, Daniel saw that the almost clear, liquid stool was smeared everywhere. The man had obviously been too sick or too weak to move from his bed to defecate. The stench of the sick room was overpowering. Looking around for some drinking water, Daniel found only a pan half filled with brownish water so dirty that a layer of soil had settled in the bottom. He took the cup that he found next to the pan and went outside to his wheelbarrow to fill it from his own canteen. Returning to the sick man, he helped him drink the clean water. The patient licked his lips to moisten them and muttered, "Wonderful." Daniel checked his pulse and found it to be rapid and thready. The skin was very hot to the touch.

Daniel tied back the flap of the hovel's "door" to air the place out and pondered the plight of the feverish man. Gastroenteritis? Food poisoning? He doubted it because this condition had apparently persisted for some time. He'd heard that malaria could sometimes act this way. It seemed to him, though, that the bile in the vomitus and the almost clear, liquid stool, the abdominal tenderness and the severe dehydration of the body meant some sort of severe enteric inflammation. Its extreme severity made one possible diagnosis stand out for him above all others.

As Daniel stood considering the diagnosis, a burly man stepped into the structure and challenged him with hand on belt knife. "What the hell you doin' in here?"

"I was passing by and heard this man in distress. I'm a doctor and I came in to help," Todd replied.

"Well, get the hell out. We don't need you nosin' 'round our things. He's jus' got a touch of the ague,"

"I think your friend has cholera," Daniel replied calmly. "He needs great quantities of weak tea and all the beef broth that he can manage to keep . . ."

"*Cholera!*" The man recoiled.

"Yes, that is my diagnosis. I will be happy to help him, if he wishes, but I won't force myself on either of you."

The intruder, still backing to safety, was already through the doorway.

Todd became authoritative. "I'll need for you to get a fire started, fetch great quantities of fresh water and purchase some fresh beef, if you can find any. And, he'll need salt if you don't have much here. In the meantime, I'll try to get him cleaned up and get this . . . this pig sty aired out a little bit."

The other man stopped and stood his ground, seeming to reconsider what he had been told. "Cain't be cholera. Must be a dozen or so men right nearby what got the ague, jus' like Charlie there."

"That doesn't surprise me. Cholera comes on in the heat of August and usually afflicts epidemic numbers before it goes away. Are you going to get that water and beef?" Todd pressed in a stern tone.

"Yeah. Yeah, anythin' fer Charlie. Me an' him is partners." The man turned to rush away but paused and reached back inside to get a bucket.

Partners, Daniel thought. Partners at what? What are they doing here in Sacramento City? I would expect them both to be out in one of the mining towns or other. That seems to be everybody's compulsion. While he puzzled over this, he started a fire in the circular pit in front of the hovel since the partner had departed without doing that chore and searched for the means to begin cleaning up the patient. He used the remaining water from the pan for that purpose but gave Charlie repeated drinks from the contents of his own canteen.

He stripped and cleaned the patient as best he could and wrapped him in a relatively clean blanket that he found, suspecting it probably belonged to Charlie's partner. He was just pondering how the soiled clothes and bedding could be washed when the burly man returned. His pail of "fresh" water had the same muddy appearance as what Daniel had found earlier in the pan. When asked, Charlie's partner said that it came from the river. Daniel put some to boil in the coffee pot for tea as well as for cooking the slab of grayish beef that the man had found.

"I'm Dr. Todd, by the way," he said to the partner and extended his hand.

"Clay Jackson," the burly one replied and shook Todd's hand. "Me an' Charlie have been doin' carpenterin' here 'bouts. Tried our hands at minin' but couldn't make a go outta her."

Charlie's retching interrupted the conversation.

Todd held the patient up so that he vomited into the chamber pot. It seemed as though the tea he drank caused him to be more nauseated, but his thirst was so great that he eagerly accepted cup after cup. When the beef broth was ready and administered, it also produced abdominal cramping in the patient. His diarrhea was so bad that Todd started giving him laudanum. Gradually, the patient seemed to gain strength and, with the help of Daniel and Clay, could feebly rise to use the chamber pot when it became necessary.

"My God, Doc, how d'ya keep from pukin' yerself silly doin' this sort o' work?" Clay asked, swallowing hard and drawing back as far as possible while still supporting the patient as he used the pot. "Charlie's my partner, but he's a stranger to you."

Todd merely shrugged. "I'm a doctor."

- - -

Evening, with its lengthening shadows, came and with it, some measure of normalcy returned to the hovel. Daniel had succeeded in getting it much cleaner and had managed to air it out. He had put Clay to the task of washing the fouled bedding and, with great quantities of liquids and administration of Dr. Todd's laudanum, Charlie was resting easier.

Daniel took this opportunity to have Clay Jackson accompany him down the dusty street to check on his acquaintances thought to be suffering from the same disorder. They found many in the scattered rude shelters and Todd advised the companions of these men on the care they should administer. Three of the sick were suffering in solitude so Todd went back to where he had left his things and, after depositing most of them with Clay for safekeeping, brought only the essentials with him as he returned to care for the sick.

It was a long night and by dawn Daniel was exhausted; two of his patients had died so he set out to find a mayor or some other leader of Sacramento City. He felt there must be some hall or structure that could be turned into a hospital, and he wished to learn if there were other doctors in town who were encountering the same problems. There was no way that he could spread himself among so many afflicted and give adequate care. He was disappointed when he was told by the man who claimed to be more or less the leader of the town that Sacramento City had no facility nor any funds that he knew of that could help.

"The ruddy buggers knew this warn't no Boston or Philadelphie when they came west. They jus' has to take their chances," were the words of the nominal *mayor*. Nor did Daniel find any other doctors in the area.

He was retracing his steps to make rounds on his patients when he noticed a false-fronted structure under construction that had a moderate-sized tent at its rear. That in itself was not unusual, but the sign that caught his attention read "Grace Evangelical Church—Reverend Simon Edwards, Pastor." A heavily-muscled man with a long beard was sawing on a board out in front.

Inspired, Dr. Todd went over and asked, "Are you Reverend Edwards?"

"Verily, I am he," the deep basso voice of the giant proclaimed.

"I am Dr. Todd and I am delighted to make your acquaintance," Daniel answered and extended his hand.

"Are you feeling the need for salvation, Doctor, or have you come to join the long and multitudinous line of my detractors and scoff at my venture?" Edwards boomed as he shook hands.

"Well, neither, Reverend. You seem to be in the business of saving souls much the same as I strive to keep soul and body together for as long as possible. I take it from your comment that neither of us is having resounding success at the moment."

"What do you mean?" Edwards asked.

"I arrived in town yesterday and found myself in the midst of what seems to be a cholera epidemic. Sacramento City has no hospital and so the cases are scattered from one end of this community to the other. Two of the patients died during the night because consistent, centralized care couldn't be given them. I note your large tent back there. What would you think about temporarily turning it into a hospital?" Todd asked.

"A Lazaretto, eh? Bring us your poor and your sick and your lepers and we shall restore them to their healthy but sinful ways." Daniel wondered if the man ever spoke *soto voce*. "My initial reaction is negative, sir, but I fear that a hint of pique colors that inclination—resentment at the derision that I have received from these canting Pharisees. On the other hand, my 'temple of worship' is practically virginal and unused. God's work perhaps needs to assume some other guise. Follow me, Dr. Todd, and join me in a cup of freshly brewed coffee whilst we discuss this matter."

The tent was filled with rows of crude benches. The far end was screened from the rest by a drapery hanging from a rope that completely spanned the interior and, behind the curtain, Edwards' living quarters were located. His space was opulent by frontier standards with a bed and mattress, a coal oil stove for cooking, a brimming bookcase, lamps, an easy chair, and a table surrounded by several straight chairs.

"Have a seat, Dr. Todd," the giant boomed and proceeded to pour two cups of coffee that was still hot enough to steam.

"Well, Reverend, I am very impressed. From appearances, I would surmise that your church is quite successful, in spite of what you said earlier."

"This?" thundered Edwards, with a sweep of his hand. "On the contrary, my success was in mining and everything that you see surrounding us is the result of the fortune that I reaped thereby. I came to California in '48 to preach the gospel and, by chance or fate, found myself at Coloma on the American River. In those halcyon days for the greedy, the streambeds were veritable streets of gold, there for the mere plucking. To my eternal shame, I eagerly plucked with all the rest of the horde."

Reverend Edwards waved his hand and said, "What you see here is my feeble attempt to return to the ways of the Lord. I am attempting to lead others on the Pathway of God, but I am finding few followers willing to journey along with me. We are surrounded, my good doctor, by the flock of the Devil, by the sinful host, by the multitude of the unrepentant. My labors are destined to be arduous and long, but I shall persevere."

"What you are surrounded by, Reverend Edwards, is a host of sick miners with cholera who will go to their eternal reward prematurely without your help," Daniel replied.

"What would you have me do?"

"We could arrange those benches out there into pallets for the sick; we would have to create a latrine because that will be the most utilized facility here; we will need great quantities of hot tea and beef broth that could be cooked on this stove. We could thereby have the patients grouped together for easier care. The two who died last night were the most desiccated of all that I have seen and so our main treatment will have to be directed toward getting fluids into the survivors to keep them hydrated. I think that many can be saved. Donation of money for food will be necessary, of course, because I don't have a penny to help in that regard."

Daniel was willing to plead, if necessary, to convince Edwards that he should do this.

The minister sipped his coffee in silence.

"I would wager that every survivor from all of this will be extremely grateful and will become a very vocal advocate for your religious efforts here in Sacramento City," Daniel continued. He didn't wish to appear overly aggressive in his persuasion, but he couldn't think of a more "Christian" effort for the preacher to pursue.

He was just preparing to challenge Edwards further along this line when the man said, "Money for supplies would be no problem. I would contribute that myself." Another pause, then, "But I don't want to take advantage of any man's illness in order to win him over to Christ. I would consider that to be poor form."

Daniel chuckled. "You don't hesitate to invoke the horror of an eternity in Hell's fire nor cataloging some man's sins that will surely condemn him to such a fate, do you? If you don't, you're different from any preacher I have ever encountered," he challenged. "What's wrong with obligating him just a tiny bit by saving his mortal body?"

After another pause, Edwards said, "Very well, I'll do it. This will become the Grace Lazaretto. I'll house them, Doctor, I'll help nurse them, I'll feed them, and I shall even carry their night soil. Just don't chide me if I try to convert them in the process."

"We have a deal, Reverend. And thank you, sir. You are joining in a noble effort, and I think that you can consider them fair game. I shall start directing the sick here immediately and spreading the word for any who might become sick in the future that this is the place to come."

Daniel savored the last of his cup of coffee, straightened the fatigue from his back and set out through the worship area of the church, first to bring Charlie to the tent hospital and then to start gathering the rest of his newly-found flock of patients.

He called back over his shoulder, "Better start preparing tubs of that beef broth, Reverend."

CHAPTER NINETEEN

The number of sick swelled for over a week before the numbers began to diminish. Dr. Todd and Rev. Edwards worked night and day, cleaning up after the vomiting and diarrhea of their patients. The number of those afflicted grew to be several dozen at the peak of the epidemic. Daniel and Simon recruited as many companions of the sick as possible to help with their care. Four or five volunteered, but that was never enough. The coal oil cooking stove was kept going around the clock preparing tea and beef broth for the sick; the caregivers scarcely had time to take in nourishment themselves. The supply of laudanum was exhausted by the end of the fourth day. Five men died, but Todd was gratified to know that they were among those who had been in the worst shape when they were brought to the "hospital". Charlie, his first patient, had survived. Early and vigorous efforts to hydrate the patients and keep them from getting too "dried out" seemed to have been the best treatment. This therapy was surprisingly effective in most of the cases; Todd bled very few of the patients.

On the fifth or sixth day, a non-cholera patient was brought in, so it appeared as though the "Grace Lazaretto" actually was gaining local fame as a medical center. The man had been shot in the thigh. The wound was a clean through and through injury with no embedded bullet or bone damage, so when Todd determined that the bleeding was not from any major vessels, he simply worked a strip of iodine-soaked cloth into and through the wound with the long tweezers, one of the only two instruments he currently owned, and sawed it back and forth to the loud complaints of the patient. With the doctor's reassurance that his wound would only be sore and not crippling nor dangerous, the man quickly left. Without paying, Todd noticed.

The epidemic finally waned and when the last patient was discharged, Edwards and Todd nearly collapsed in their exhaustion. Both men slept and lounged for several days as they attempted to restore themselves. Even in their wasted state, they were exuberant. Todd, because he felt that they had saved a number of lives through their efforts, they had defeated the epidemic, and he had gathered enough money in gratuities given by grateful patients to purchase additional supplies and to acquire an actual tent where he could set up his practice; Rev. Edwards, because he realized how helpful he had been through his many, many hours of work, the use of his facility, and the food he had provided for everyone. In addition, he was certain that he had gained the nucleus of a congregation from among those who had been treated, as well as from those who had helped to care for their sick comrades.

The robust and sociable Reverend Edwards had taken a genuine liking to Todd. As the doctor was placing the last of his belongings on his disintegrating wheelbarrow, Edwards said, "Daniel, there is more than adequate space next to the church for you to set up your establishment there. Why not be my guest and we can continue our collaboration?"

"Well, Reverend, you have not tried once to proselytize me so I accept your generous offer," Todd replied. His wheelbarrow journey was a very short one.

- - -

The weeks passed quickly. Edwards returned to the construction of his church and Todd's practice grew very rapidly. He learned that there were only two other professed doctors in the community and the fact that they had not come forward to help during the epidemic was widely known. Todd treated fractures, boils, sore throats, diarrhea that was feared by his patients to be another flare-up of the epidemic, a few gunshots and knife wounds, and even delivered a baby who was claimed by some to be the first child born in Sacramento City. By practicing great frugality, Daniel was able to repay Captain Winthrop's loan and even sent some money to the good skipper with the request that he forward it to Dr. Channing in Boston. This was no small task since it required the sending of actual gold; there was no bank in San Francisco yet whose draft was certain to be recognized on the east coast.

A magnificent autumn reached its perfection and then the fogs began to enshroud the city with their cold dampness. Still, it was very moderate compared to the winter weather that already was besetting the Sierras to the east.

Several times each week, Todd and Edwards dined together and, as though he could contain himself no longer, the preacher finally said, "You know, Daniel

I have not pressed you on the subject, but your absence from my services has been most conspicuous. Are you of the Catholic faith, perhaps?"

"No, Simon, I'm not. I suffered an estrangement from my own father over religion. He is a Congregational minister in Massachusetts and when I announced that I had become an agnostic, he disowned me in his wrath. That was a long time ago and I have had many significant experiences in my life since then that have caused me to ponder over it all. I've still not arrived at any conclusion in my mind about the ultimate purpose in our lives."

"So, you are not an atheist. You *do* believe there is a God," Edwards pressed aggressively.

"Oh, yes. I feel that life, as we see it all around us, is far too complex merely to have happened by chance—the complicated relationships of the stars, the miraculous abstruseness of the human body or even that of the lowest insect, for that matter; it all fits together too neatly to have occurred by accident. Just think of how marvelous is the human brain with its ability to perceive or remember or to direct very precise movement—how complicated just the sense of sight or hearing or touch is."

Daniel hesitated, then he said, "But to believe that this Universe was created for us humans—'man, created in God's image'—that the Bible is God's own word, that man is to be the sole entrant into some mythical hereafter, that there is an easy entrance into that Heaven through acceptance of the sacrifice of 'God's Only Begotten Son', or the concept of eternal damnation based on whether or not man yields to primal urges that are basic to the existence of all animals in general—I just simply can't believe all of that.

He turned to his friend and said, "Perhaps one day I will find the answer in my mind but, in the meantime, attending your services would be hypocritical of me and would be denying the power of reason that whoever created me has seen fit to place in my brain. Nothing against you, Simon, but I can't substitute faith for reason"

"No offense taken, Daniel," Edwards said with remarkable grace. He savored the fine wine that he had purchased for their dinner and, looking long at his companion with eyes that seemed to penetrate deep into Todd's soul, said, "I hope, for your sake, that you are able to find your answers. I shall not press you, my friend. I will say only that I, too, did not have an uneventful epiphany. In God's good time, I pray faith will come to you also."

CHAPTER TWENTY

Dr. Channing did not disappoint Todd. Much sooner than expected, a fine set of instruments arrived that consisted of a complete kit necessary for amputation—three long-bladed scalpels, a ratchet tourniquet, two saws, and three sets of thumb forceps, all encased in a fine mahogany chest—other scalpels, forceps, probes, surgical clamps, a set of lithotomy clamps, hemostats, needles and suture, two sets of obstetrical forceps, a cervical tenaculum, uterine curettes, and two dental forceps. It was all much more than could be contained in the impressive black bag to be carried on house calls and was everything that a Boston surgeon could ever desire.

The array of pharmaceuticals was breathtaking. Some were so alien to Todd that he knew he would have to study to learn their usage, but as though anticipating such to be the case, a copy of the new book "The Complete Herbalist" had been included. And *ETHER*! Since that had been favored so early on by Dr. Channing, he had included four cans in the shipment.

The note that accompanied the shipment implied that this all was a gift and simply read, "I am proud of you for taking top quality Medicine to the frontier. Use this paltry gift of supplies for the benefit of those people out there."

Todd, of course, intended to continue sending money to Dr. Channing, but he calculated that it would take him months and months to repay his benefactor for everything he had sent. What a mentor! What a friend! Finally, Daniel felt like a real doctor!

- - -

With the passing seasons, Todd's practice thrived. Although his friendship with Edwards continued to be cordial and harmonious, he rented space on the second floor of a permanent building on Front Street in the autumn of 1851 and moved his practice out of the tent next to the Grace Church. Affording him comfortable living space, the three rooms provided one to become his general living area in which he placed a desk, reading lamp and several chairs so that he could receive patients there as well as using it for his parlor. A second cubicle served as his treatment room where he kept his medications, instruments, and was complete with an examining table that could double as an operating bench. He also placed a cot there for the occasional patient who was too ill for him to leave at home. A third room was his bedroom that housed a genuine bed and mattress, an armoire for his two suits of clothes and linens, and a washstand.

It was a remarkable contrast to the tent in which he had started his practice in Sacramento City just one year ago. Of course, he furnished the rooms in the most frugal manner with used items that he purchased at the cheapest possible price. He took his meals at a small nearby restaurant and did not keep a horse or buggy; he visited patients by walking or, on the less frequent visits he had to make to nearby ranches, he hired a horse from the livery. On one occasion, he was called to the Hock Farm where Captain Sutter—now called Colonel Sutter—lived with his family on the last remnant of what had been his vast empire. Dr. Todd treated the Swiss Mrs. Sutter's gout and visited with the Colonel, finding that man to be gracious and outgoing and not nearly as embittered as might be expected by the gold rush that had led to his massive financial losses.

Todd's reputation grew rapidly although he knew, as did doctors even much more egotistical than he, that many of his patients often would have recovered on their own and that his intervention, in those cases, probably did little more than comfort them. He did, however, repair lacerations, set broken bones, lance boils, probe a number of non-fatal bullet wounds and cared for other gunshot victims as well as he could until they died; he treated a great deal of venereal disease and its complications, delivered a surprising number of babies, cared for catarrh, sore throats, extracted painful teeth, lanced aching ear drums, treated skin eruptions—the list went on and on. It seemed that the needs of his patients were varied and endless. More frequently than he would have wished, though, he encountered cases that humbled him and made him painfully aware of how little he did know and how limited his "cures" seemed to be. Those patients died. He acquired several medical texts to refresh and expand his knowledge and, when he was financially able, subscribed to the British medical periodical *Lancet*, although its arrival was fitful and always delayed many months.

Daniel finally became totally debt-free in the summer of 1852, but he had not been able to replace his lost diploma and he still felt diminished by its absence. All in all, he was thoroughly enjoying life and had virtually lost the adventurous desire he once had felt to reside and practice among the gold miners at the raw edge of the frontier. This change in him had happened so gradually that he didn't realize how settled and domesticated he was becoming.

From time to time, in the bits of news that drifted eastward about events in San Francisco, he learned that Eli Winthrop, former captain of the *Calliope*, had become a very successful bay area clothier, but that fact did not dismay him or cause jealousy. He was very satisfied with the life that he was establishing for himself here in Sacramento City; the very thought of overgrown San Francisco, with its seething congestion of people and the resulting tumult, grated on his nerves. Of course, even in these pleasant and quieter surroundings, he frequently recalled with fondness those days on the *Ellie Mae* and the free, uncomplicated life of simply being a hard-working whaleman.

- - -

Perhaps the two cases that he found so disturbing and so shattering to his self confidence came at a bad time; perhaps he was merely at the nadir of mood swings that affect everybody from time to time. In any case, the results of these two were devastating to him.

An extremely pale young man, about Todd's age, came to his office with an abscessed tooth. As he prepared to extract it, Daniel noticed that the man had many tiny petechial hemorrhages on the mucous membranes of his mouth and that his gums were swollen everywhere, not just in the area of the abscessed tooth. Further inspection revealed scattered bruises on the man's limbs. The extraction was unremarkable, but the bloody aftermath was alarming. The hemorrhage was not simply oozing of blood from the distended tissue. It pulsated and was arterial. Having the patient bite firmly on a pack of lint was ineffective and, finally, Todd was obliged to heat a probe in his alcohol lamp and cauterize the base of the yawning socket.

While the patient continued to apply pressure, Todd had him lie down so he could examine him more completely. In addition to bruising even on the trunk, he found some palpable lymph nodes in the axilla and groin; the liver and spleen were enlarged and the man had marked sternal tenderness. He was not feverish but his pallor indicated a severe anemia. Todd gave him a tonic, more lint for a pack in case the bleeding started up again, and suggested that he come back the following day.

Continuing to be puzzled and unsure of the diagnosis even then, Todd had the patient return daily and noted a rapid deterioration in his appearance and well-being. Severe nosebleeds, alarming collections of blood under the conjunctiva of his eyes and increasing evidence of bleeding into the mucous membranes of his mouth made Todd suspect some sort of a cancer of the bloodstream; the onset of high fever and congestion in the patient's lungs made him more certain of it. He put the patient to bed in the examining room in order to treat his pneumonia. Since the young man had suffered so much bleeding already, Todd did not believe that bloodletting was indicated. Day after day, he dosed the young man liberally with tartar emetic while filling the room with fumes created by burning tincture of benzoin in an alcohol lamp. The pneumonia did not respond and when the patient began vomiting; his emesis contained great quantities of blood. In a sudden fit of apoplexy, he simply collapsed and died. Todd could not help but blame his own lack of knowledge and the inadequacy of the treatment for this sudden and sad result.

- - -

As he finished cleaning up the office after the undertaker had removed the unfortunate young man's body, Daniel was anticipating a refreshing stroll through the city to rejuvenate himself after the exhausting ordeal of the past week's treatment. Just then, a woman came through the door. It took a moment before Daniel recognized her. Instead of the vigorous young woman he had last seen in San Francisco two years before, Lottie Jo was now extremely pale and wasted. Climbing the stairs to his office had obviously been almost too great an effort for her. Strands of her hair strayed from the bun on the back of her head, as though she was too weak to control it. Her thin face mirrored the pain and fear that even the dullness of her eyes could not mask. She bent forward in her shuffling gait, her thin body too frail to keep her comma-shaped back in an upright position.

"I need your help, Dr. Todd," she wheezed. Just the effort of speaking these few words sent her into a spasm of coughing and Daniel noticed that the sputum she hacked into a rag was bloody.

"Come and sit down, Lottie," he invited her gently. Taking her arm, he supported her as they moved toward a chair. "Tell me what has happened to you." He poured a small amount of brandy into a glass and gave it to her.

She closed her eyes and took a deep breath after drinking the liquid. "I don't know where to start, Doctor," she allowed in a very weak voice. "I cooked in Sonora fer a while after I left 'Frisco an' then I married Will. He mined there a spell but d'int have much luck. We drifted on to Shingle Springs, Fiddletown, Whiskey Hill, an' finally to New Jerusalem, but t'was allays the same. I made more keepin' a hash tent than Will did minin'. I began feelin' poorly an' then he got kilt loggin' to build a flume. I stuck it out cookin' 'til I could barely stan' up an' then somebody tol't me ye was doctorin' here in Sacramento. I come to see if'n ye can hep me."

Talking seemed to have drained her of what little strength she had left, and Daniel gave her a larger glass of brandy. Drinking it resulted in more coughing.

When she seemed somewhat recovered, Daniel said, "Why don't you let me examine you, Lottie, and let's try to get to the bottom of your troubles?" She nodded and he assisted her to rise and move to his examining room. "I'll need you to loosen the upper part of your dress so that I can listen to your chest."

Lottie Jo unbuttoned her dress down to her waist from where it had been fastened high on her throat. The garment hung in loose folds because of her weight loss and fell away easily. As it draped down around her hips, Daniel was able to observe the cachectic condition that led to an emaciated drooping of her breasts.

With a finger, Todd tapped his other hand as he placed it first in one place and then another on Lottie's back. The result was a dull, thudding sound in her upper chest on the right and only slight resonance elsewhere. Even this gentle stimulation set her to coughing again. Daniel was certain what he would hear when he placed his tubular wooden stethoscope on her chest and he was right; the breath sounds to be heard everywhere were very distant and accompanied by a moist rattle except over the right upper lobe where there was no sound at all. Elsewhere, the rattle cleared somewhat whenever she coughed but returned almost immediately. The rag Lottie was using became bloodier with each coughing fit.

"That's all for now. Why don't you get dressed again, Lottie, while I make a pot of tea for both of us?" Todd said. "We'll talk it all over then."

He went to the back room and put the long-spouted metal teapot on the small coal oil stove he kept there and pondered what he was going to say to the woman. She undoubtedly had tubercular phthisis of the mucous membranes. Her wasting probably indicated intestinal involvement as well—perhaps even the liver had tubercles. He recalled the pelvic inflammation she'd had two years ago and wondered if she had had Fallopian tube involvement even at that time. Certainly, her horribly stooped back indicated that the disease had spread into her spine.

Daniel had never seen a patient at this very late stage of what was often called "consumption". He had observed many who were in the earlier phases of the slow-moving, chronic form of the disease and he had also seen the autopsies of some who had died of the affliction. He had never seen anyone so far advanced in the disease as Lottie, who could only be described now as the walking dead. How many days or weeks does she have to live, Daniel wondered. Is there *any* treatment that might save her at this late stage? What is the best way to tell her all of this? His reverie was interrupted by the steaming teapot. Daniel added a large pinch of tea leaves and carried the teapot and two mugs into the next room. Lottie was dressed and sitting beside the examining table.

"A good cup of tea will make both of us feel better," Daniel said cheerfully.

"Ere ye ailin', too?" Lottie asked.

"I'm fine. That was just a manner of speaking." He poured tea and handed a mug to her. He faltered a moment before he began his discussion. "I'm afraid that you have quite a bad case of tubercular phthisis, Lottie. There are medicines I can give you and I will start giving them to you right away. It . . . it might possibly be that you have waited . . . that the course of treatment will be very long. Without a doubt, you have an uphill road to climb."

"Ere this consumption?" she asked. "Two o' my sisters died of consumption."

"Yes, it is consumption, but don't feel defeated just because your sisters died of it. Many people, with time, recover from the disease." Daniel couldn't bear to tell her his true feelings. "As I said, I shall start you on some very potent medicines and we shall get lots of good, nourishing food into you. Of course, you will stay right here until you are well. That will give us an opportunity to catch up on the news of each other's lives."

Tears trickled down Lottie's face. Daniel wasn't sure whether or not she really understood the truth and was surrendering to the certainty of death, or if she simply was weeping in relief at finding hope and a helping hand.

"I'm down to nothin', Doc. I cain't pay ye. Ye'll have to wait fer money 'til I git on my feet ag'in," she said and hung her head.

"You're a doodle, Lottie," he said with a chuckle. "Worrying over such things right now. Don't fret yourself over the bill and I won't either. Now, you will use that cot over there. You get yourself settled and I will go down the street to the restaurant and get a tray of supper for both of us. How would some roast beef taste?" he asked.

"That'd be fine, Doc. Don't get too much. I ain't much hungry of late."

"It's important that you build up your strength. Now, I'll be back in just a little while," Todd replied and went to the door. He hoped that the fact that he was fleeing was not too obvious. The certainty of the outcome for Lottie, his feeling of complete impotence in the matter, his tender feelings and gratitude for the way the woman had nursed him two years ago, the need to appear optimistic for the sake of the patient; it was all overpowering. He needed to get out on the street and think.

- - -

Daniel puzzled over what treatment he should employ. Lottie's wasted state undoubtedly indicated *Strumous Dyspepsia* from congestion of the abdominal venous system with the disease, he thought. Letting six ounces or so of blood each of the next half dozen days should help that problem and then he would start her on daily emetics—ipecacuan medication along with sulfate of copper every day. With *Strumous Dyspepsia,* Daniel decided, he should treat her liver also—pilula hydrargyri was as good a form of mercury as he knew to give her for that purpose. As effective as iodine was in the scrofulous form, Daniel knew it should certainly be employed as an alterative here. He would have to add some tincture of conium, though, to subdue the iodine's irritating qualities. Camphorated spirits would be a milder rubefacient than cantharides or tartar emetic, but he thought it should be sufficient to excite the cutaneous vessels of the chest. He would get her to inhaling steam impregnated with opium as well as giving her muriate of morphia by mouth to alleviate that cough. Wrack his brain as he would, Todd could think of no other treatments that would be of more benefit to Lottie than all of these.

- - -

When Daniel returned with the tray of food, Lottie was asleep on the cot. It was as though she had driven herself to reach the sanctuary of his care and then, completely spent, simply collapsed. He wakened her and helped her eat the dinner but she picked at it very mincingly and he did not persevere.

He gave her another generous shot of brandy and helped her back on to the cot. She fell asleep again almost immediately. Looking down at her sleeping form, Daniel suddenly felt guilty for not offering her the use of his bed and for him to take the cot. After all, she had actually shared her bed with him when he was recovering from the blow on his head.

He decided to let her sleep and he would start her medications when she woke up.

CHAPTER TWENTY-ONE

It was almost morning and Daniel dozed in a chair near Lottie's bed. The first two days of his treatments had seemed to help her. Although she complained about how unpleasant they were, she gained strength and was much more alert. Her cough was quieted by doses of laudanum but by not bringing up sputum, the breath sounds in her chest were reduced because of the congestion there. On the third day, she worsened and it had been a downhill course since. Her night sweats left her soaking wet and she became so averse to food that Todd discontinued giving her emetics. Her kidneys had stopped working and she had passed no urine for over 24 hours. She had been unconscious since late the previous afternoon and Daniel had expected the end to come at any time since.

He had studied his patient's face, so pale in the dim lamp light, through the long hours of the night and pondered many things. He chastised himself for his inability as a doctor to prevent her death; he wondered if, at any time in her life, she had been pleasured to the point of giggling or had enjoyed teasing or had she ever been truly grateful to be alive; he mused over the purpose of Lottie's life, of what was in store for her after death, of what her religious beliefs were, and whether or not she thought there really was a God, a Heaven, a Hell. Other than my being male and her being female, pondered Daniel, what makes her any different from me? What takes her down one path of life and me down another? Was there some tiny, *tiny* element in the composition of the body of Lottie Jo Jacobs that made her different than Daniel Locke Todd—different thoughts, different skills, different purpose in life? Was it something in that *tiny* element, placed there by God or whoever launched this whole world in motion, to direct her in her actions, to steer her on some predetermined course and who also directed something in my element that guided me on my path? Is that how that Supreme Intelligence, or God, or whatever it is, moves us all to some predetermined destination, to play some particular role in order to fulfill a divine purpose?

Unable to keep himself out of the equation, Daniel wondered if Lottie's role had been to save his own life back when he had been attacked. He chastised himself for considering such an egotistical possibility, but not before wondering how he was to achieve that goal toward which he had been directed, if any such plan really existed in the design of his Creator. Perhaps, he thought, if I had been out there in the mining camp when Lottie's disease first manifested itself, I could have saved her. Maybe I'm in the wrong place and not supposed to be sequestered here where there are other doctors to furnish medical care. Perhaps I should be out there where I am more acutely needed. Maybe . . .

Daniel drowsed in his exhaustion but was suddenly startled awake by Lottie's violent fit of coughing. Her apoplectic spasm was so massive that her eyes bugged wide with fear; then, a torrent of blood exploded from her mouth and nostrils. She choked as the ruptured vessel . . . it must have been a major branch of the pulmonary artery . . . flooded her throat. She hemorrhaged so uncontrollably that she was dead in less than a minute, her only sound a gurgling moan that was throttled by her own blood.

The eruptive suddenness of Lottie's death overwhelmed Todd. He eased her body back down onto the bed and sat for several minutes, just studying the sad, wasted remains of what had been Lottie Jo. He considered it a terrible, terrible defeat once again to have to summon the undertaker. Silent tears coursed down his cheeks; some for this woman for whom he had such a special place in his heart, some for his own failure as a doctor.

- - -

After Lottie's body had been removed and Daniel had made arrangements for her funeral, he cleaned up the gory scene that marked her passing. Then he sought out Simon Edwards for consolation. Or was it absolution?

The pastor kept only an office at his church now; his own living quarters were "downtown" also. Since it was early morning, Daniel found him in his sanctuary. Over the past three years, the Grace Evangelical Church gradually had taken on the mature appearance of permanency. The rough benches under the canvas roof had given way to finished pews in a building of reassuring solidity. The nave was not of cathedral proportions, but it echoed any sound as though it were. Daniel found Simon doing some light janitorial work there.

"I'm troubled, Simon, and desperately need to talk to you," Daniel said as he walked down the aisle.

"Well, Daniel, halleluiah!" Edwards boomed. "I have finally lured you into the sanctum sanctorum." As always with Simon, there was this initial bombast, but whenever he was around Todd now, it quickly faded and the two men related to one another in a much less formal manner.

"Not exactly, Simon. I come to you as a friend. I have lost my last two patients; a very pleasant young man a week ago and just this morning, a woman to whom I was greatly indebted. And I find it all terribly depressing," Daniel replied.

"Surely, these are not the first failures you have encountered as a doctor. Even though it is very early in the day, let's share a glass of sacramental wine and you can tell me about it." Simon beckoned Daniel toward his office where he poured two large glasses of wine, handing one to his friend while gesturing toward a chair with a nod of his head.

"No, you're correct. I have had my share of medical failures. This man, though, was even younger than I and he died . . . I don't know . . . he just died very suddenly and I am mystified as to the cause. I suspect he had some sort of a cancer of the blood but I don't know. He was unable to form clots whenever he hemorrhaged and he died so quickly from his pneumonia that he seemed totally incapable of fighting it. The woman had very far advanced tubercular phthisis. Her death, also, was alarmingly sudden."

"And you feel guilty?" Edwards asked.

"I feel stupid; too stupid to deal adequately with disease."

After several thoughtful sips of his wine, the Reverend replied, "You treated them both the best you knew how, I'm certain, and that was not enough. Perhaps nothing could have saved either of them. Have you considered that?"

Daniel simply hung his head, not willing to accept that as an excuse.

Edwards continued after a silent moment of thought, "All right. Imagine you are on the rim of a canyon that is certain to become flooded because of a cloudburst upstream. A dozen men are scattered on ledges below and you have only one rope. You lower it to first one and then another, drawing them up to safety, one by one. Alas, your rope is too short to reach the twelfth man and he is swept away to his death by the flood. You wouldn't blame yourself just because your rope was too short or that the flood came before you could somehow devise a better means of saving him, would you? We all simply die when our time comes, Daniel."

"So you feel that things are predestined to happen?" Daniel asked. "You know, if you carry that thought to its logical conclusion, none of us can ever be guilty of sin. We are simply fulfilling roles that have already been cast for us and you, Reverend Edwards, are then out of the salvation business."

Edwards made a surprising confession. "I don't know what I truly believe, Daniel. I really don't. I know what I would like to believe and I preach that. But after all is said and done, who really *knows* the answer?"

"I should know more Medicine; *that* is certain! We should have more effective treatments," Todd growled angrily, making a fist and striking his other hand vehemently.

Edwards countered, "You're like a clock maker, Daniel. You know what makes many of the clocks tick and, given adequate parts, you feel that you can repair most of the broken ones. But, in hunching over that dimly-lit workbench that is your life and tinkering away, aren't you losing sight of *time*, the very thing of which you are trying to allow your charges to enjoy longer or with greater comfort? You are frozen in one period of time, as are your clocks, your patients. You must carry on your work with the tools that are available to you at this moment in time.

"Of course," Simon continued, "my metaphor is a poor one, referring to mankind. You repair the broken clocks. The skill required to repair them is not a reflex or an inherited thing. It's learned and imperfect, but you do it better than a doctor did a hundred years ago. Your counterpart a hundred years in the future almost certainly will do it better than you, as more things are gradually learned. Accept that fact and repair clocks the very best you can right now. There will be some that you simply don't have the parts for. That may well limit how much time those clocks will record but, perhaps, that is not meant to be subject to your tools—or in this case, your expertise."

With this, Reverend Edwards drained his wine glass.

Daniel was silent for a long moment. "Well, Simon, I probably don't understand what you are trying to tell me, but I think perhaps I should move my shop and repair clocks out where I'm needed more; imperfect as my skills are. I decided this morning, while I watched my last patient just before her death. I'm going to leave Sacramento City. I'll find a place that needs me more."

"Ah," Simon said, pouring more wine in his own glass and topping off Daniel's that was almost untouched, "you are going to become a missionary, out among the great unwashed? Well, my friend, you are picking a very rocky row to hoe. I've been there, and I know whereof I speak."

After an appreciative sip of his wine, Simon asked, "Are you certain that you are not just running away?"

"No, Simon, I'm not sure. I can't help but believe, though, that if I had started treating this last patient when she first noted her symptoms, the result would be different. It almost killed her to make the journey to avail herself of my care—all the way from Fiddletown or New Jerusalem or someplace. The more I think about it, the more certain I become that this is what I should do. Maybe even what I am supposed to do."

"Give yourself a few days to really consider this kind of move," Simon advised.

Daniel felt better for having talked to his friend, although Edwards' philosophic metaphors didn't relieve his own certainty that his simply knowing more would benefit his patients tremendously, and that he was obliged to try to acquire that knowledge. He was grateful, though, for Simon's efforts to relieve his anguish.

"Perhaps a few days delay will allow me even to attend one or two of your sermons, Simon. I didn't realize that you were such a philosopher." Todd chuckled and relaxed, able now to enjoy the wine as much as the Reverend obviously did.

CHAPTER TWENTY-TWO

The next two weeks were busy ones for Daniel. He started by asking as many sources as he could about possible sites where he might settle. Most advised Jacksonville in Oregon Territory, a boom-town in Rich Gulch, north of the California border near the Applegate River, a branch of the Rogue. It was the location of a new strike that had been made the previous year, and the town now was a magnet that was drawing miners from the California gold camps that already had yielded up their most accessible riches. Daniel felt certain that he would be needed there.

A stage road was being built up the Sacramento Valley that eventually would accommodate stagecoaches to and from faraway Portland City, so Daniel purchased a wagon and a team to transport all of his possessions and his supply of pharmaceuticals as far as he could. He even purchased another large tent in which to live and practice, feeling quite certain that Jacksonville would be just as primitive as he had found Sacramento City, in the beginning. He boarded his team at the livery barn down the street from his office and began packing his things.

Daniel dined almost nightly with Simon and even attended several of the man's sermons. Although he could not agree with the content of them, he was amazed at the role Edwards assumed during their delivery—boisterous and coarse, commanding those attending to follow the gospel or suffer Hell's fire and delivering all of his threats in that booming voice inflected with such educated grandeur. He was impressive but so different from the Simon Edwards that Daniel had come to know that it convinced him how much showmanship and theater was involved in at least some aspects of religion.

When his wagon was packed and Todd had placed a placard outside his office door that read "Gone to Oregon," he stood and surveyed his possessions. His present situation was considerably different from what it had been when he arrived in town so long ago. He even had money in his pocket now.

"Maybe I'm foolish to be moving," he muttered, but then he pictured in his mind the wasted wreck of Lottie Jo and was reconfirmed in his intent to take medical care out to where it was so lacking. And, though he would be the last to admit to the childish impulse, he was a little excited at the prospect of being in an actual gold camp.

Although he had said goodbye to Simon when they dined the previous night, he drove past the Grace Evangelical Church for a final handshake on his way out of town. He found the Pastor again performing janitorial duties and said to him, "I'm on my way, Simon. You had better come along with me and put on your show in Jacksonville."

"When you've seen one gold camp, Daniel, you've seen them all. I'm up to my armpits in sinners right where I am. Perhaps you'll come back here when you get this missionary nonsense out of your system."

They both chuckled at the friendly exchange and Daniel left with a wave. He knew he would miss the mercurial man in the same way as he did his friends back on the *Ellie Mae,* particularly Isaac. Within half an hour, Dr. Todd had his slow-moving team headed northwestward on the coach road.

Sacramento City was history, but it had served him well, both financially and in valuable experience.

- - -

Traveling up the coach road through the long Sacramento Valley was relatively easy, but it was a long way. Camping out was like a vacation for Daniel. It took him two weeks to reach the northern end of the valley and, when he was confronted by the Cascade Mountains that lay between him and the little town of Yreka which he had heard was near the border of Oregon Territory, he considered hiring the services of a professional freighter. He was convinced that this was his only choice when he began to hear tales of army escorts being necessary to guard mail shipments from marauding bands of Karoks or Okwanuchu Indians in those mountains. He didn't even own a gun: what chance would an unarmed and solitary traveler have against violent savages?

Daniel was fortunate to encounter a freighter, Sam Leonard, who had more horse power than he needed for the two wagons his animals were currently pulling. When Daniel and Sam agreed on a price, they hooked

Todd's wagon in line and waited for other teamsters to join them so they could form up a train. When their numbers were sufficient for mutual protection, the string of freighters headed up over the Cascades. Daniel rode one of his team horses bareback and led the other.

He was fascinated by the almost artistic movements of the many horses and the expertise of their drivers. It seemed that nearly all of the outfits consisted of two or three heavy wagons hooked together like railroad cars. A long chain was attached to the lead wagon of each group and as many as two dozen horses were hooked in pairs to the chain. The driver rode one of the horses nearest the lead wagon. He controlled the string of teams by a stout line that went all the way up to the lead horses—drivers called it a "jerk line"—and directed them by a steady pull for "gee" or a sharp jerk for "haw." The horseflesh ballet was so coordinated that when the lead team was being steered in one direction, the "pointer team," the second from the lead wagon, would step over the chain and pull in the opposite direction in order to keep the freight wagons from turning too sharply and going off the rude roadway. The deep ruts cut in the road by the wheels of the wagons attested to the heavy loads of flour, various foodstuffs, dry goods, or heavy equipment that each outfit carried. Daniel was very happy that it was these professionals, and not he, who were negotiating the steep hills, moving along precipitous cliffs and around sharp curves.

Daniel and Sam camped together each night and shared their food. The old freighter never seemed to tire of spinning his tall tales and entertained Todd with them far into the night. Sam was only going as far as Yreka, but he agreed to find a freighter who would take Todd's things on to Jacksonville.

"Ye may have to settle fer a string o' mules. I ain't e'er been on up to Jack'ville, but I hear 'tis too rough a country fer wagons. I'll buy yer rig; horses an' harness an' the whole shiteree if'n we can reach a fair price."

"I'm certain that we can," Daniel replied as he settled back to enjoy his coffee, the blazing fire and another of Sam's endless stories.

As they ascended the Cascades, there was a nip in the evening air and it was a reminder that autumn was rapidly approaching. Except that he helped Sam harness and un-harness his many horses each morning and night, Daniel had been merely an accompanying tourist over these past several days. He had been able to impress the freighters by showing them how to tie some of the knots he had learned in his whaling days, and he also supplied professional services on one occasion when the jerking of an unmanageable horse had dislocated the shoulder of one of the freighters.

Todd had put it back in place by taking off his own boot, applying the heel of his foot to the freighter's armpit and pushing there while he pulled on the arm. The man had to accept the help of fellow freighters in harnessing his horses after that because Todd bound the injured arm to his body to stabilize the joint.

When they finally reached Yreka, it was as Sam had predicted and Daniel's possessions had to be expertly packed on mules for the remainder of the trip. Sam Leonard bought his rig for enough money to enable him to purchase a saddle horse and tack and to pay for his entire move from Sacramento to Jacksonville.

As the days of the next week-long segment of his trip slowly passed, Daniel was to learn much about the irascibility of mules. Several times, when the bucking, cavorting, lying-down-and-rolling mules performed what the *Californio* packer called a *rodeo*, Daniel feared for the survival of his possessions and was delighted when, after a tiresomely long week, the string of *bandidoes* finally plodded into the rude tent town of Jacksonville.

PART THREE

1853-1864

CORDELIA

CHAPTER TWENTY-THREE

Jacksonville could hardly be called a town. It was more like an anthill with its occupants crawling and seething over one another. Jackson Creek, still vigorous in spite of the October date because the entire year of 1853 had been so wet, was nothing but a flow of thin liquid mud since miners with gold pans and every imaginable mining contrivance were using its water to flush gold from the soil of its banks. The stream flowed out into a wide valley, almost what Todd would consider a caldera, a broad basin with a surrounding crown of jutting mountain peaks. The few buildings that comprised the town were crowded along the one muddy street that issued down the tight canyon cut in the hills from the west. These structures, being built from sawed boards, were in varying stages of construction. A scattering of log cabins stretched up the hillsides on the north and south but otherwise, the community was simply a sea of white tents. Once again, Daniel found himself searching for some vacant spot he could claim to erect his own living quarters.

At some time in the past, the people of the emerging town of Jacksonville had had the foresight to dig a small ditch along the hillside above the town on the south. Part of Jackson Creek had been diverted far enough upstream that it still ran clean, not yet fouled by mining, to provide the fresh water supply for the community. Daniel found a site for his tent near where this ditch brought its water tumbling back down into Jackson Creek. He felt fortunate in his location but wondered how long it would be before the mining operations either moved upstream to begin working more new claims and commandeer this water or out into the broad valley to the east and displace him.

Night fell before he had time to do more than just pitch his tent. He stowed his possessions inside and set out to find a place to board his horse. There was no livery stable but he did find a pole corral where José, the

Californio mule skinner, had lodged the animals of his pack string. The man who seemed to be the proprietor sat at the opening of his nearby tent.

"Is this your corral?" Daniel asked.

"Yep."

"Can you board my mare also?"

"Them damn mules'd kill any hoss you put in there," the man replied. "Can tie her up outside. Cost ye $25 a day."

"*Twenty-five dollars*. That's outrageous!" Todd exploded.

"I'll grant ye that. Grass hay's twenty-five cents a pound, howsomever. Advise ye to sell that hoss."

"Oh, and I suppose *you* might buy her?" was Daniel's sarcastic answer.

"Yep. I'll give ye $25 fer the mare."

Todd laughed ruefully. "You would give me just one day's board bill for my horse?"

"Yep. Ain't much call for 'em up here, hay bein' what 'tis. Hell, I'd prob'ly have to send her all the way back down to Yreka with José to get my money outta her."

"That's where I bought her," Daniel snorted.

"Yep, I know. I done bought an' sold that there mare three times a'ready."

Todd merely shook his head in defeat and handed over his mare's lead rope to the man. This was not a propitious introduction to a Jacksonville career.

- - -

Todd awoke in a better frame of mind. After the horse debacle, he had returned to his tent, cooked up some bacon and potatoes, and gone to sleep. Gunfire awakened him twice, but the night had been otherwise uneventful. Now, he would get settled, display his shingle on the front of his tent and circulate around town to acquaint himself with it and allow it to become acquainted with him.

Carpenters were hard at work on the new buildings, but a fire burned at each site and the frosty morning air forced the workers to gather round from time to time to warm their hands.

Many miners were already at work on their claims; digging with shovels, hunkering down at creek side and swirling water in simple gold pans, sinking vertical shafts and winching up buckets of dirt by using crude windlasses, piling dirt into Long Toms or even short cradles and then washing it with buckets of water that splashed back down into Jackson Creek again as a muddy slurry. Some men were wheeling larger rocks in wheelbarrows to be crushed in a horse-powered arrasta, a giant coffee grinder affair, south of the creek; the poor beast powering it was walking its endless circle even this early in the morning.

Daniel stopped at many solitary miners and at every small group of men, greeting all of them with, "Good morning. I'm Dr. Todd and I have set up my office in a tent at the end of the street. I treat any affliction or injury."

Some responded with a friendly nod or an "I'm so-and-so. I'll try not to see ye, Doc." Some glowered as though angry at being interrupted. Some just ignored him entirely.

One leaned on his shovel and said, "Are ye a real God-fer-certain doctor? My partner has a helluva bellyache an' has been takin' a bunch o' weeds from that goddamn Chink what calls himself a medicine man. Mebbe ye can have a look at him."

"Yes, sir. I would be happy to examine him. Can he come by my tent or do you wish me to come to his place?" Todd replied.

"Hell, he ain't in no shape to even git outta bed. Come on; I'll take ye to him."

The miner was late middle-aged and walked with slope shoulders from years of heavy manual labor. "I'm Zeke McBride," he said over his shoulder as he strode away from the creek. "Tuck Gimbel's my partner."

Todd followed him partway up the hill to one of clusters of tents that jostled each other up there. Zeke held the tent flap back and said, "Here he be. Hope ye can hep him."

Todd bent and entered. Stale sickroom air filled the tent where a man lay groaning on a pallet. "Tuck, this here's Doc Todd an' he's come to look at ye," Zeke said as introduction.

"How long have you been sick?" Todd asked. Tuck just rolled his head from side to side in his misery and didn't answer.

"Been four-five days," Zeke volunteered. "That Celestial, Gung Pi, give him all sorts o' herbs an' frog legs an' sech but he's jus' got worse an' worse. I couldn't do nothin' fer him so's I been out there diggin' an' trying to keep us in grub."

Todd knelt and drew back the blanket far enough to expose Tuck's bare belly. Its musculature was rigid and a touch any place on its surface caused the man to wince. Todd gingerly pressed everywhere; it seemed to him the greatest tenderness was low in the right abdomen. Suddenly releasing the pressure of his hand there caused the patient to jump and loudly exclaim,

"*Goddamit man*, ye trying to kill me?" Tuck's skin was warmer than normal so he was feverish. Todd put his ear to the man's belly and could hear no sounds coming from the bowel.

"Has he been vomiting or having the runs?" Todd asked Zeke.

"No pukin'—had the shits in the beginnin' but none last day or two."

Todd rubbed his chin thoughtfully and then covered Tuck again with the blanket. He invited Zeke outside with a gesture of his head and then followed after him.

"I think your partner has an abscess in his belly," Todd said. "Judging from the tenderness, it seems to be down where the small bowel empties into the large one. His guts are simply not working and that probably means that the abscess has ruptured and his belly is full of pus. We call that peritonitis—it probably came from a ruptured appendix—so his chances of living through this are almost zero." Todd continued, "I did see an autopsy one time where this had happened to a man who lived through it, but then he died several weeks later from another cause. The area of his abscess was walled off because a blanket of fat that we call the *omentum*, had wrapped itself around the perforated gut. If that can happen here, we might have the possibility of saving him but that's his only chance . . . and a very slim one at that."

Todd didn't believe Zeke understood much of what he had said but was surprised when the man asked, "How can we make that happen, Doc? Some other kind o' weeds or somethin'?"

"No, no medicine will do it and I'm not sure we can even help it along, Zeke. I think his only chance is if we can somehow keep that pus pocketed down near his abscess. I'll bring over a cot and we'll prop him up on it to keep things drained down into what we call his gutter. You'll have to keep him very quiet. I'll help."

"Lord bless ye, Doc. I'll fix some vittles fer him. He'll need his strength."

"No. We'll only give him hot tea and as little laudanum as possible to ease his pain a bit. No food," Todd emphasized. "I'll go get the cot."

By late afternoon, Tuck was quiet, sedated somewhat by the laudanum. Todd and Zeke McBride had placed objects on the cot so that Tuck lay on his back, tipped slightly on his right side but in an almost sitting position. His torso was nearly upright, and his knees rested on a pile of clothing so that his thighs made a right angle with his body. Whenever he awakened and needed to urinate, Todd had him use a pan so that he did not have to stir from his position in bed.

When Todd had gone to fetch the cot, Zeke rebuilt the fire and a pot of beans had been cooking since. By evening, they were soft and the two men ate. Todd consumed bowl after bowl with gusto because he had taken his morning excursion around Jacksonville before preparing any breakfast for himself, and he was starved by night.

From time to time, he touched Tuck's brow but could note no change in his fever. When darkness required the lighting of a lantern, he thought the patient might be feeling more comfortable but had to attribute most of that to the laudanum. His offer to get his bedroll and sleep near the patient was welcomed by Zeke.

Over the next several days, Tuck's course was erratic although by the fourth day, he was definitely better and Todd discontinued the daily bloodletting. He now required virtually no laudanum and complained of hunger, especially since he was still being given nothing but tea and meat broth. After two weeks, Todd let Tuck get up but he moved about very little and then only in a very slow and stooped gait. His belly was still tender.

Todd took his leave and had returned to his own tent when he felt that Zeke could manage the care of his partner. News of Tuck McBride's remarkable return from death's door spread rapidly throughout the camp and when Todd moved about town now, he was greeted by many more friendly faces and nods than in the beginning.

There was one unqualified exception and that was a short-figured man whose glowering gaze followed Todd as he walked by. He could not help but notice the face that effused such hostility—dark eyes set deeply in a pock-scarred, oriental face surmounted by a high, sloping forehead. The man wore loose-fitting trousers and tunic. Todd suspected this must be Gung Pi, the oriental who had tried to treat peritonitis with "weeds" and that the little man's obvious hatred, which emanated from him like a miasmic cloud, was probably caused by Todd's taking over Tuck Gimbel as a patient. He tore his eyes away from the Chinese man and continued down the muddy street, but his stroll was no longer as gratifying as it had been just moments before.

CHAPTER TWENTY-FOUR

Dr. Todd settled quickly into life in Jacksonville, and he soon had a steady flow of patients. He was certain that Zeke McBride's and Tuck Gimbel's lavish praise was the cause. The cases were quite mundane for the most part—catarrh, hernias, piles, dyspepsia—complaints common to men doing heavy work in the elements and mostly cooking for themselves. Todd had started taking his meals at a café tent that Zeke had recommended. It was frequented by many miners and he usually had to wait for a place to sit but the food was tolerable and, by Jacksonville standards, not that expensive.

During the meals there, much of the conversation berated the fare and compared it unfavorably to the glorious meals said to be served at the fabled "Del's Kitchen". Gossipers said that Lukas Evans had brought his wife, Cordelia, out from the east to join him in his mining adventure. She had no more than arrived when Lukas had chopped his foot with an axe and proceeded to die from blood poisoning. His mining claim was not a good one and Cordelia was left with insufficient money to return home, so she set up a cook tent and served meals to support herself. She was such a fabulous cook that her board list filled immediately; very soon, almost every miner in camp had added his name to her waiting roster, biding his time until those ahead of him on the list either died or left Jacksonville. Daniel followed suit and placed his name at the bottom of the long column. He doubted that he would live long enough to get to Del's table.

One day, a group of miners brought one of their companions in a wheelbarrow to Dr. Todd's tent office. The man had been injured when a section of flume gave way and fell on him, fracturing his right femur. He was in agony and this was made worse by his dog who was so concerned about his injured master that he kept trying to jump up onto the wheelbarrow and on top of him. The other miners finally tied the burly bulldog—Champ, they called him—by a section of rope to one of Todd's tent stakes while he examined the injured man.

Todd thought the break was a clean one and that it should easily heal if properly set and splinted. He gave the patient a stiff dose of laudanum and the man's companions helped move him to the cot. They said his name was Warp Stevens and after the drug took effect, they watched as Dr. Todd set the leg. He then applied splints that spanned the fracture and kept the knee straight. Stevens should not be moved so Todd asked the men to watch their friend while he went down the street to obtain additional food supplies. He assumed there would be two mouths to feed for some period of time.

When he returned, he found the small gathering stunned, shocked by what had just happened. One man uttered in disbelief, "My God, he were jus' lyin' there an' suddenly he sat up an' gasped like he couldn't breathe. Then . . . then he jus' fell back down dead . . . deader'n a weasel. Were it that there medicine ye give 'im, Doc?"

Todd quickly grabbed his wooden tube stethoscope and bared the chest of the patient. He was indeed dead. Standing up, he turned to the other men and said, "We use that laudanum almost every day and it renders nothing but relief. I think that Mr. Stevens either had a heart seizure from the shock of his injury or what we call a blood clot that moved to his heart. There was nothing that anyone could have done to save him. I'm sorry."

The men milled about, uncertain what they should do next. Todd volunteered, "Do you wish for me to make arrangements for his burial?"

"Naw, weans'll care fer him. Warp'd want to be planted on his claim, seein's as there ain't no reg'lar buryin' ground here yet. Can we leave 'im be whilst we dig a grave?"

"Of course," Todd replied. The men filed away but Champ sat at the side of the cot and stared patiently at his master.

It was late afternoon when Stevens' friends returned to claim the body. They had brought a plank to use as a litter and wrapped the body in a blanket before they carried it away. Todd followed the tiny procession up the creek to pay his respects at the burial. Champ lumbered alongside the body and watched attentively as it was lowered into the grave.

The miner who had been the spokesman reporting the death to Todd bowed his head and said, "As ye know, Lord, Warp Stevens were a good man. His word were oak solid an' he hardly e'er got drunk. Have mercy on his soul, Lord. Amen."

There were mumbled "amens" among the other four who then picked up their shovels and began to fill in the grave. As Todd nodded to the others and turned to leave, he noticed that Champ sat, still staring down at the mound of earth. He supposed that Stevens' companions would claim and care for the animal.

The late autumn sun had set by the time he had walked back as far as the café tent, and he went in for his supper. The meal was dumplings tonight in a sea of gravy made from sparse and unidentifiable pieces of meat. Along with well-cooked beans, though, it was better than Daniel would have prepared for himself, so he was quite satisfied. When he arrived back at his tent office, he was surprised to find Champ there, sitting quietly and staring at the empty cot. It was as though the animal, when his master did not emerge from the mound of earth that had been placed over him, expected him to be on the cot. Daniel could not imagine why the dog hadn't stayed with Stevens' friends or returned to the tent of the deceased.

"Come on, Champ. Come on out of there, boy," Daniel coaxed. He repeated the words several times but to no avail. The dog was not going to budge. Todd built a fire and made a pot of coffee, but the dog remained where he was. He was still there even after Daniel had finished his second cup of coffee.

"Come on, boy," he said finally as he tied a length of rope around Champ's massive neck and tried to lead him away. "I'll take him back to Stevens' friends; they'll care for him," he muttered.

The dog sat, as solid as a rock, and merely ducked his stubby head and allowed the rope to slip off. After several more unsuccessful attempts, Daniel foolishly decided to get a plate of leftovers from the café; after all, he couldn't let such a loyal animal go unfed for the night. He got the food for the dog and thereby permanently acquired ownership of Champ. The burly beast made several pilgrimages to the grave over the next several days as though he was puzzled as to what had happened to his former master. He finally dug down to the corpse and, when he was satisfied that his master was dead, he abandoned the site and took up permanent residence at Todd's tent

CHAPTER TWENTY-FIVE

Jacksonville's winter of 1853-54 was a remarkably bitter one, starting with a windswept blizzard in early November. Most of the freight and supplies formerly had been coming into town from Portland by a freight road that linked the mining camp with the Willamette River traffic. When snow blocked this road to freight wagons, supplies came by mule train but these could not keep up with demand and prices soon went sky high. As the violent winter raged on, flour sold for a dollar a pound, tobacco for a dollar an ounce, and salt for its weight of gold dust. Meat was almost as dear and consisted more of wild game from elk herds inhabiting the surrounding mountains than from domestic animals herded through the drifts.

Todd had been fortunate. With the money he had been able to bring with him from Sacramento and that which he had earned since coming to Jacksonville, he was able to buy a rude log cabin when the miner who built it decided to look for richer diggings in some other camp. He then had sufficient storage space and enough spare money to lay in a supply of pharmaceuticals, beans, bacon, salt, tea, coffee, sugar and flour before the snows hit. Whimsically, and on the possible chance that he might once again purchase a horse, he had even bought two gunnysacks of rolled oats. He was probably the best prepared of any Jacksonville resident for the wintry blasts.

He began cooking more of his meals himself at home and taking only the occasional one at the old café tent; this practice allowed him to provide table scraps for Champ. The squat bulldog proved to be a bottomless food pit but was the very best of companions.

- - -

The messenger waded through the drifts and asked, "Can you come down to Del's Kitchen, Doc? Miz Del got bad burned."

Todd donned his old whaling coat and followed the man. The bitter cold had brought mining to a halt and even the street had been surrendered to King Winter. Most miners were enjoying the warmth afforded by the two new buildings that now housed popular saloons. The snow path to Del's Kitchen was well traveled; so her fare apparently had not suffered from the shortages that now gripped the town.

When Todd entered, he saw that a figure was seated beside a table and surrounded by concerned men. A large, black cooking range took up much of the back of the tent and was undoubtedly the only cook stove of its size in this part of the territory. He worked his way through the tight cluster and to a woman whose bun of black hair was tousled. Her eyes were swollen shut and the surrounding flesh had a greasy, angry red color. She panted through parted lips; Todd wasn't sure whether this was because of the pain or that she was close to a panic because of the accident.

"Doc's here, Del," several voices chorused.

"I can't see," were her first words. "I can't see a thing." Her voice was calm and, even under these circumstances, had a melodious ring. Her panting was from pain, Daniel concluded.

"Your lids are swollen shut, madam. That is why you can't see. What happened?" Todd asked.

"I was making a batch of doughnuts for these gentlemen and something tumbled into the hot grease. It splashed into my eyes." Her diction was measured and precise and indicated a background far removed from mining camps.

"Let me see." He inspected her neck and hands. "Were you burned anywhere else?"

"No. It's just my face," she replied.

"I don't want to force your lids apart to look at your eyes, so we will wait for the swelling to subside a bit before I examine them; I would hazard a guess that they will heal nicely. I'm going to go back to my place to get some medicine but first, I'm going to put some snow in a clean dishtowel and have you hold that to your face. Where do you keep your dishtowels, madam?"

"I know," one of the men offered. Even with her red, swollen face, Del appeared to be young and attractive; Todd was sure that she had many volunteers to help her with her dishwashing.

He took the towel, went outside the tent and gathered several handfuls of clean snow. Wrapping it into a bundle, he returned and gently placed this on Del's face. She held it there and Daniel headed back to his own cabin.

"Let's see," he mumbled, "I'll make a 5% solution of aluminum subacetate and moisten a cloth to place over those swollen lids. When I can see the eyes themselves, I'll know but I'm reasonably sure that she will be sloughing the covering of the corneas. I'll need a solution of belladonna and one of lead acetate as an eye wash."

He decided a cream consisting of lard and tragacanth would be good for the burned skin, and wondered if it would also help if he put it in the eyes, too? "I'll try it on myself first," he muttered half-aloud.

Daniel had never treated burns to the eyes before but he thought that it should be pretty straightforward.

When Daniel arrived at his cabin, he found Champ distressed at having been shut inside and prevented from accompanying Todd. He pacified the dog with a few pats on the head and set about preparing his treatments. When they were completed, he ladled some supper stew into the dog's dish and again left Champ to occupy himself inside while he returned to Del's Kitchen.

He reassured the crowd of men that she was going to be all right and then moved her to her sleeping tent which was located behind her "kitchen". She lay down on her pallet and, covering her with a blanket, Todd placed the cloth moistened with aluminum subacetate over her eyelids.

"I'm quite certain that your eyes themselves will heal well after all of this. Don't fear for your vision, madam. Here, take this laudanum for your pain."

"Please call me Del, Doctor. We're not formal around here," she replied and searched with her hands for the glass of medicine he held out to her.

"Where did you come from originally . . . Del," he asked, partly to pass the time while the swelling diminished and partly, because he was fascinated by this attractive, cultured young woman.

"I was raised in western New York state, and I married Lukas Evans there. He was an adventurous one and headed west shortly after they discovered gold in California. Lukas never was successful in finding any great amount of gold in California, but he was very sanguine about his prospects here in Oregon Territory. He sent for me to join him, and I came out with a wagon train to the Willamette Valley. When I arrived, he came north to find me and brought me here. Sadly, poor Lukas was taken from me shortly after that, and I started Del's Kitchen."

"And from what I understand, madam . . . Del . . . your culinary skills have bewitched all of Jacksonville," Todd replied. He found it very easy to talk to Del and couldn't resist complimenting her. "Here, let me moisten that towel again."

"Thank you, Doctor," she replied.

"That's very formal. If I'm to call you Del, please call me Daniel."

"Very well."

"You're from New York. I was raised in Massachusetts and trained in Boston," Daniel ventured. "We were practically neighbors."

"Yes."

He wished she would pick up the conversation. She didn't and finally he said, "You speak so well . . . Del . . . that I know you have had formal training. Where was that?"

"I went to Binghamton Academy and was going to be a teacher before I met Lukas. He swept me off my feet, and we seemed star-crossed. I sometimes wonder where I would be at this moment if I had become a teacher instead of marrying."

The laudanum began to inflict its opiate effect, and she drowsed. Todd felt that was the best thing for her and simply sat back and feasted his eyes on what he could see of her. Under the blanket, her slight form scarcely mounded the pallet. Her raven hair was even more night-mantled in the subdued light of her tent. The medicated cloth covered all of her face except her nose, youthful and provocative, and her mouth, firm but with sensuously parted lips.

Daniel conjured an image of how her face might appear when the swelling was gone and halfway expected to see that appearance when he removed the cloth. Del's lids were still swollen shut, though, when he did pick up the towel to moisten it again, and he had to remind himself that his purpose here was to treat her. Daniel continued with the applications until he had to go into her cook tent to find a lantern to produce sufficient light. When he got back, his patient was fast asleep. He would have liked to rouse her so they could talk some more, but he decided it was best not to disturb her. He was about to leave and return to his cabin when he thought how terrified she might be if she awakened and still could not open her eyes. He searched and found a blanket to keep him warm enough to doze in a nearby chair, and he continued his vigil with only the slightest illumination from a barely flickering lantern. Champ would have to fare on his own.

- - -

Cordelia Evans stirred and awakened Daniel. His first thought, when he saw the faint hint of dawn casting the slightest grayness to the walls of the tent, was that he might have compromised Mrs. Evans' reputation by having spent the night here with her, and he wanted to flee before she could discover him. Instead, she sat up and looked about. He could not see her clearly but it appeared that her eyes were open, although still not completely back to normal.

She said, "Dr. Todd. Did you spend the night here?"

His guilt established, he was only able to stammer, "Why, yes, Mrs. Evans. I applied applications until you fell asleep, and I was afraid you might panic if you awakened and still could not see. I hope you will accept my apologies if that seemed inappropriate."

"Oh, no. I'm grateful for your concern. Things are still a bit blurry, but I can see!" she exclaimed.

"Well, I'll be going, then," he said. "I'll leave a bottle of drops for you in the cook tent, and you should put those in your eyes every hour. I shall return this afternoon to see about your condition." He rose and rearranged his coat before he took his leave.

Another storm had moved in during the night and a fresh blanket of snow was falling on the already deep drifts. As Daniel trudged toward his cabin, he experienced a new and thrilling excitement in thinking that he had slept not more than ten feet from Cordelia Evans all through the night. He scolded himself for such base thoughts and pondered what he might do if, under his care, her eyes did not heal as quickly as he had earlier anticipated.

– – –

Cordelia's recovery was complete, but Dr. Todd continued to make frequent, though perhaps unnecessary, visits to her cook tent to assure himself that no relapse occurred. In his heart, he realized that he was just finding an excuse to return, but he was powerless to control himself. Her image was beginning to flash through his mind time and time and time again throughout the day. He had even begun trying to see more of himself in his tiny shaving mirror, wondering how he might appear to Cordelia. He suddenly found himself wondering what she was doing at that particular moment, what she thought about this or that, whether she found his overly solicitous care offensive, or humorous, or ridiculous or perhaps, pleasant. Should he stop? He couldn't bring himself to stay away from her. Should he perhaps ask her to take a stroll with him? What would she think of a person who would ask her for a walk in all of this snow? Surely there were dozens of other men in Jacksonville who had these same thoughts about her.

Daniel was miserable. But, life had definitely taken on a new dimension for him. He had not even felt this strongly about Elizabeth so very long ago.

Every day, such thoughts continued to pummel his brain and rendered Daniel barely able to function. He realized that he must do something about it and finally resolved to ask Cordelia out; but where? It would not be appropriate to invite her to his cabin. Certainly, he could not ask her to accompany him to one of the saloons. There was no church or school or opera house—no entertainment of any sort. He couldn't invite her to eat at the café; the cuisine there was undoubtedly far inferior to hers and, after all, who would serve that meal to her charges in her absence. Finally, he decided simply to invite her for an evening stroll to look at the stars. Ever since he had arrived in Jacksonville, whenever the clouds separated enough to reveal them, Daniel had been mightily impressed by their radiance and apparent nearness. But, what if she turns me down? Rejects me, out of hand? What would I do then?

- - -

They carried the man into Todd's cabin without even a knock on the door. "He's gut-shot, Doc. Happened down to Oliver's saloon. Card game. T'other man—some card sharp—hightailed it outta there 'fore a body could grab him. Kin ye help him?"

Todd had just finished his supper of a thick bean soup and had given a big bowl of it to Champ. He directed the men to place the victim on the cot in the "office" half of his cabin and turned up the coal oil lamp to full brightness. The injured man's eyes were closed but he was gritting his teeth and obviously still conscious.

"I'm Dr. Todd, sir. I'm going to examine you and see how badly you are injured. I'll try to help you," Todd said.

The man merely nodded his head in acknowledgement.

Todd unbuttoned the man's bloody shirt and underwear, stripping the garments back away from his hairy belly. A neat hole that oozed only a small amount of blood was present far to the left of his umbilicus, as though he had been turning when he got shot. Todd rolled him to his right and loosened the clothing to see if there was an exit wound; one indeed was present in his left flank, two and a half inches from his spine. A spent and bloody slug was entangled in the clothing at his back and Todd picked it up.

Holding it out to the man's companions, he said, "Here is the offending bullet. It might be well to keep it if it could help in convicting the man who did this shooting." Then to the patient, he said, "We don't have to worry about removing the bullet; it came out of your back. Hopefully, we may be very lucky and that it passed through without hitting your bowel, but it came out near the area of your left kidney so that is almost certainly injured. I'll bandage your wounds, sir, and we'll just have to watch you for some time in order to determine the extent of your damage. Do you need something for pain?"

The man hissed through still gritted teeth, "It surely smarts some, Doc. I'd not turn anythin' down that'd help that."

Todd had been pouring a small glass of laudanum and gave it to him before he bandaged his entry and exit wounds. "I'm going to keep you here where I can keep an eye on you for a few days," Todd remarked casually as he gently herded the man's friends out of the cabin. "I'm not going to offer you supper, though. We want to let all your insides rest for a while." The man seemed content simply to lie there on the cot.

Todd read for several hours, as was his usual evening activity, and his patient slept fitfully, undoubtedly from the drug effect of the opiate. Whenever he roused, Todd gave him a small sip of water and, at bedtime, gave him another dose of laudanum. The man still had not shown any desire to pass his water, and Todd found that a bit worrisome. Before he retired, he said, "I should know your name, sir."

The man said in a dialect of sing-song Scandanavian-flavored English, "Erickson. Olaf Erickson, Doc."

"Well, Olaf, here is a little hand bell. If you need me for anything during the night, I'll be over there in my bed. Just ring it—for anything at all. Do you understand?"

He nodded. "Thank you, Doc."

Early in the morning hours, Todd awakened to the tinkling of the bell. The fire had burned out and the cabin was cold and dark. When he lit a lamp and went over to his patient, Erickson said, "I mus' pee, Doc. I just hafta' pee. The pain's somethin' awful."

Todd turned him on to his side and gave him a basin in which to void. The man tried and tried but to no avail. Finally, he said, "'Tis no use! But, I still hafta' pee somethin' fierce."

The man was in obvious distress and Todd got a metal catheter from his bag. "I'll try putting this inside of you to let out some of your urine. It will hurt you a little, I'm afraid."

He greased the catheter with lard, bared the man's penis and, with some difficulty, worked the metal tube into the urethra. There was nothing at first, but with manipulation of the catheter, a string of blood clot followed by a small spurt of bloody urine issued from the metal tube. Working the catheter back and forth a bit produced another long string of clotted blood and then a mighty burst of bloody urine. Daniel continued this treatment intermittently until the basin was full of reddish-black urine and blood clots. When the urine flow finally stopped and Daniel removed the catheter, Erickson sighed in obvious relief and collapsed back onto the cot.

"I'm afraid, Olaf, that this means the bullet hit your left kidney and that is where the blood is coming from. These blood clots blocked your bladder; they may be plugging up your kidney, too, in what we call urinary colic. That's why you couldn't pass your water—almost like a stone was blocking it, no matter how much pressure built up behind it. We'll just have to wait and see how your body handles the injury now. It may be days. Do you need something more for pain?" Todd asked.

"Ah, no. I feel mightily relieved, I do. Thank ya, Doc. I'll be yoost fine."

Todd blew the lamp out and returned to his bed, worrying now whether the bullet had just hit the pelvis of the kidney or had injured the renal artery as well, and that was pumping blood out into his retroperitoneal space. This bleeding might even be indicating some damage to the cortex of the kidney, he thought. He finally drifted off to sleep accepting the reality that he would know nothing until morning and probably not even then. The emergency and the necessary treatment did succeed in blotting thoughts of Cordelia from his mind.

- - -

Dawn was a cold, anemic grayness that seeped into the tiny cabin before either the patient or his doctor was awake. Champ put his chin on the bed near Todd's head and gave a gruff whine that indicated his need to be let outside. Todd obliged and then lit a fire in his rude fireplace before jumping back into the relative warmth of his bed. He had barely made it there when the scratching on his door meant that Champ wanted to regain the refuge of the cabin, safe from the brutal cold outside. Daniel got up and let him in.

All of this activity made Erickson stir and Todd called over from the comfort of his bed, "How do you feel, Mr. Erickson?"

"Not yoost fine, but not terrible, neither," was the reply.

"Well, lie there and rest and when the cabin warms up a bit, I'll get up and check you to see if you might be up to some breakfast."

Todd pulled the covers higher against the cold and guiltily thought that Cordelia was probably already up and busily preparing breakfast for her charges. He thought he must ask her if she needed any of his food supplies in order to continue her boarding operation. People were complaining bitterly now about the food shortages everywhere.

So that it would be cooking in the fireplace, Todd optimistically prepared a pan of oat mush out of the rolled oats he had originally bought in case he got another horse. He then went over to his patient and pressed gently on Erickson's belly through the blankets. There was no flinching of discomfort so he laid the belly bare for a better exam. There was dried blood on the bandage on the front of the man's belly but, when he rolled him onto his right side so he could examine his back, Todd was perplexed to see a mounding of the tissue under the exit wound of the bullet. It was slightly firm but fluctuant and tender when he pressed on it. He rolled Erickson onto his back again and settled back to think.

"Not good, Doc?" Erickson asked.

"No, it's not, Olaf. Let me give you some laudanum because we have to do something about this," Todd answered. He poured a jigger of the drug and gave it to Erickson to drink. "We'll wait for that to take effect," he said.

He then put his tube stethoscope to Olaf's belly and heard faint bowel sounds. "When we're done, we may give you a little something to eat. All right?"

"Ya." Erickson drank another jigger of laudanum when Todd gave it to him and settled back to rest on his cot.

Todd poured himself another cup of coffee and, going over to the fireplace, leaned against the mantle and stared into the fire. That swelling has to be either a hematoma from bleeding into the tissues, he thought, or it's extravasated urine that has also gone into the surrounding flesh. Either I have to operate to explore and repair that damaged kidney or just try to drain whatever is in there by probing through the bullet hole in his back. He went over and felt of Erickson's belly again and was quite confident no peritonitis had set in. Why not just drain him through the bullet hole and watch to see what the liquid is and how he gets along, he thought.

When the man's breathing became slow and regular, Todd decided that the laudanum had reached its maximum effect, so he rolled Erickson on to his right side and laid bare his back. He wiped his gunshot probe with a rag soaked in whiskey and said, "This is going to hurt, Olaf." He insinuated the probe several inches into the bullet wound and, except for an initial wincing movement, Erickson did not move. Suddenly, bloody urine issued from the tract and, as it continued, the swelling of the area gradually diminished. There was no fresh arterial bleeding

"There, Olaf, that is what we wanted to do," Todd exclaimed jubilantly. "You'll be better now, although we may have to do that again later." Erickson did not answer but simply ducked his head resolutely and breathed heavily.

Todd placed a fresh bandage over the wound and rolled the man onto his back once more. "Do you feel like a little something to eat now? I'll give you a good swig of whiskey afterward and let you sleep? Want some food?"

Erickson nodded his head and Todd dished up a small ladle of mush. He sprinkled it liberally with sugar and spooned it into his patient's mouth. After a bite or two, Olaf seemed to enjoy the taste and eagerly waited the next spoonful. When the bowl was empty, Todd fulfilled his promise and gave the man a generous glass of whiskey. Erickson licked his lips and settled back to rest.

Daniel went back over to the fireplace and added wood to the fire. He couldn't help but wonder what they might have done differently in Boston. He did decide, though, that he should wait until the long-term effects of his treatment were made manifest before he even mentioned any part of this to Cordelia. Then he realized that he shouldn't say anything about this to her anyway because of the ethics involved. Surprisingly, the concept of not sharing any of his thoughts about his patients with her bothered him. Of course, she might not care a whit about his thoughts, and he became very melancholy at such a notion.

CHAPTER TWENTY-SIX

The days of the week that followed wore on both the patient and the doctor. The entry wound into Olaf's belly was healing well. A fistula had developed in the exit wound after Todd had probed it twice more; now, it drained clear urine in small amounts more or less constantly. A bandage was kept in place at all times to soak up the urine and to keep anything foreign from entering the fistula. Although Erickson was comfortable, he never became talkative and his presence deprived Todd of his usual solitude. Also, the doctor had no private place to treat other patients who dropped by. With no real mining being done because of the wintry weather, medical complaints were mostly limited to coughs, the ague, and belly aches. The one exception was Mrs. Talbot, one of the few women in camp other than Cordelia, and she was having trouble with her pregnancy as she neared term. Todd had to go to her shack to examine and treat her because of Erickson's presence in his cabin.

Today, Mrs. Talbot was sweating in spite of the clammy, smoky interior of her cabin. Oscar, her husband, had tried to keep the tiny shelter warm for her but its porous exterior allowed the heat to leak faster than the crude fireplace was able to supply it.

The woman seemed to be sleeping so Todd asked her husband, "How has she been during the night? Any labor pains?"

"Naw. No labor pains but jus' this bad pain in her head. She bin like this all night," was his response.

The patient's face looked unnaturally full to Todd, so he uncovered one of her legs and was disturbed to see marked swelling of the tissue of her lower limbs due to edema. Her pulse was bounding when he felt of her wrist. Headache and swelling due to edema in very late-term pregnancy—he had seen this, accompanied by severe hypertension, in his training and it could lead to disaster. He had seen patients go on into convulsions, and one woman even died of apoplexy with this array of symptoms. Perhaps if Mrs.

Talbot went into labor very soon, she could be spared such a complication. Todd felt of her abdomen and could almost convince himself that the baby had moved downward since yesterday. He hoped so, although there was no sign of uterine contractions yet.

She groaned pitifully, and he couldn't help but wonder if he were to find Cordelia in this state, how detached and professional could he remain. This thought sparked a hunger in him, and he could imagine nothing more desirable than for Cordelia to be this near to delivering *his* baby, an infant that would blend her body and his into a new human being that was *theirs*.

A twitching in Mrs. Talbot's face jolted him from his reverie and he recognized perhaps the first signs of puerperal convulsions in this patient. He felt her pulse and it was even more bounding; the muscles in her arm twitched even more forcefully than those in her face. While he fumbled in his bag for a lancet, he explained as simply as he could about her condition to Oscar.

"I must bleed her to reduce the pressure in her system. If you think it might bother you, I suggest that you go carry in more firewood from outside or something."

"I'll stay, Doc," was the response.

Todd got a wash basin from a back shelf of the cabin and opened a vein in the patient's hand. She started bleeding profusely into the pan and then arched her back. He thought it was the beginning of her convulsions, but when he placed his hand on her abdomen, the bulging uterus was rock hard.

"Thank God she has started into labor," he announced to her husband. "That's the treatment we really need for this."

Todd bled her more than he would have ordinarily done and it seemed to be effective because she never did really convulse; she just complained intermittently about her headache or her labor pains. Then her water broke and, about noon, she delivered a fine, healthy little girl. He placed the infant in her arms. The placenta seemed intact when it delivered soon afterward. After helping Oscar get his wife into a clean, dry nightgown and remake the wet and bloody bed, he sat back to enjoy the scene. The parents were beaming, the wrinkly baby tried unsuccessfully to nurse, and Todd was relieved that all had come about without Mrs. Talbot going into convulsions. The danger from that was likely past now. It was a good day's work.

He donned his coat and headed out into the cold. It had started to spit snow again and he was tempted to go down to Del's Kitchen, but he could think of no logical reason he might offer for his visit and so he returned home.

- - -

Erickson's condition stabilized and he left to return to his own tent. Todd carefully instructed him before his departure in the proper care of his draining fistula and assured the man that it would close up with time; it was easier to convince the patient of this than it was for Todd to persuade himself that such a thing was likely to happen. He hoped it would.

After a whole day of working himself up to it, he walked down to Del's Kitchen to offer her some of his stockpile of food supplies. He found her baking bread. He offered to share some of his food reserve with her, using the explanation of concern for her boarders, since food had become as scarce as it was. Actually, he was concerned only with her financial welfare and her ability to continue her business.

"Oh, Dr. Todd, I couldn't possibly accept any of your food. We'll get by until some pack trains make it through to us," was her response.

"If you would accept some of my supplies, it would relieve much of the guilt I feel in having so much while others in town are going hungry. Please take it, Mrs. Evans."

"I thought we had it settled that you were going to call me Del," she replied with a coquettish smile. After a moment, she added, "Well . . . I'm certain that my boarders would welcome better fare. Perhaps we could work out some sort of an arrangement for me to buy a few of your things, but you would have to agree to take your meals down here also, Doctor."

"And you were going to call me Daniel, as I recall."

Excitement surged in him, but he said hesitantly, "I have this dog, Champ, that I sort of inherited. I have to care and cook for him, you see."

"That's no problem," Del replied. "We always have some leftovers here; or, we did until recently. There will be food for him, I'm sure. Please agree. I would enjoy that."

Todd was jubilant, but still he responded with reserve. "You are too kind, Del. I have beans, bacon, salt, tea, coffee, sugar, flour and a gunny sack and a half of rolled oats. It's all yours as a gift if I am to take my meals at the famous Del's Kitchen."

He thought briefly about what others in Jacksonville would think—all of those who wanted more than anything to gain such an honor, and he just suddenly becomes one of Del's boarders. He decided that he didn't really care what others might think. He smiled graciously at her.

"Oh, Doctor . . . Daniel . . . my little group of boarders will be so happy about this turn of events. If you would be so kind as to bring your supplies down and put them in my sleeping tent, I shall set about seeing what culinary delights I might prepare for the evening meal." She reached over and squeezed his forearm in gratitude and he tingled at the sensation.

"I'll . . . I'll be right back," he stammered and beat a hasty retreat through the flap of Del's cook tent. Daniel Locke Todd, M.D., was supremely happy as he waded through the drifts up the hillside to his cabin. "Isn't she simply beautiful?" he murmured to himself and managed to slip clumsily on the trail in his rapture.

- - -

Dinner consisted of dumplings in a rich bean soup that was heavily spiced with onions and several red peppers. The quantity was greater than that to which the boarders had been accustomed recently, and there were loaves of freshly-baked bread and endless pots of rich tea to accompany it. Dessert was rice custard that was garnished on top with some of Del's meager supply of dried apples which she had cooked up into a deliciously sweetened sauce. Todd was heartily welcomed into the group when Del announced that his supply of food had helped make this meal possible. She also announced that there would be sweetened oatmeal for breakfast, along with strong, black coffee for a change. The men gave Todd three cheers.

Daniel stayed to help Del with the dishes, although she made a half-hearted objection. As they completed the chore and even enjoyed several cups of tea afterwards, they talked endlessly about their old homes and times gone by. Daniel was reluctant to tell her very much yet of his year on the whaler because somehow he felt it diminished him from the way he pictured himself now as the town's only physician.

He learned about her early childhood and the fact that she had two sisters and only one brother. The latter would take over the family farm soon if he had not already done so, and Del's sisters were married to other farmers in the vicinity of her home. Todd asked her if she would enjoy teaching here in the west if the opportunity presented itself.

"I'm quite homesick," she replied, "and I think I shall return to New York state when I have sufficient funds."

Todd found this disappointing and asked her if homesickness was her only reason. He really wanted to ask if there might be somebody else back there to whom she wished to return but restrained himself.

"Oh," she said, "I enjoy this country well enough. It's beautiful. But I find the coarseness of the men, the violence, the very frontier nature of life here to be so depressing. I would like to be closer to my roots, I suppose. Why do you wish to practice here, Daniel?"

"I feel that I have been given a fine medical education and I would prefer applying it wherever it might do the greatest good." He was tempted to tell her about Lottie Jo but thought that might sound too melodramatic, and now he felt he might even have sounded boastful in his earlier statement about his training.

He simply added, "And I find that I am thoroughly enjoying life here in the West." He didn't wish to overstay his welcome and clumsily explained that he should be getting back to his cabin.

"Thank you for all of these food supplies. You saw how welcome they and you were with my little brood here. Breakfast will be at seven o'clock sharp. Have a good night, Daniel," she said with a smile.

"You also, Del. I look forward to breakfast. Good night." He went out into the night and Champ followed at his heels. The fire was out in his cabin and it was very cold inside. He quickly lodged himself comfortably in his bed and relived every minute of the evening, playing the scene over and over in his mind. With a deep sigh, he decided Cordelia Evans was absolutely the perfect woman.

CHAPTER TWENTY-SEVEN

Christmas of 1853 came and went, marked by little change in the town's routine except for scattered acknowledgement of the Yuletide season with a few discordant carols. No new pack trains made it through the drifts, and food supplies became even more scarce; holiday fare at Del's Kitchen was an elk stew and a bread pudding, but everybody found even that simple menu festive and greatly satisfying. How Todd would have delighted in introducing the boarders there to thick whale steaks and some spicy *muctuc*. The weather moderated for a few days but that was followed by more snow. Following the last paralyzing blizzard, the sky cleared, and a wave of bitter cold settled on Jacksonville.

Supper that night was a thick bean soup with fresh bread so there were few dishes to wash. When those were finished, Todd grew adventurous and hazarded making an invitation for Del to accompany him for a walk in the cold, clear night. He could barely believe it when she said, "Yes, I think I will enjoy getting outside in the air for a little while. Wait until I get bundled up. We can fill the wood box for morning on our way back in."

Chase James and Laurence Whitsell, the only two boarders who had not joined the others for the nightly migration to one of the saloons, looked up from their cribbage game with as much surprise at Del's response as Todd felt. Del donned a heavy coat and a pair of felt boots and said, "Shall we go?"

Snow on Jacksonville's single street was packed down only by foot traffic and they picked their way carefully along its uneven surface until they were at the far edge of town. When they were beyond any feeble lights, Todd stopped and looked up at the overarching dome of the Milky Way. "Isn't that spectacular?" he marveled.

"Oh, I could just stare at it by the hour," she replied. "Don't you wonder how far away those faintest stars are? Surely there must be an end to space out there *somewhere*."

Todd and Reverend Edwards had enjoyed peering up at the stars following their suppers together back in Sacramento City and Simon had imparted much of his knowledge of the constellations to his friend in the process. Tonight, Daniel enjoyed pointing out the Northern Cross where it stood erect in the west. A little way to the north, Vega was just setting. To the south, the comparatively vacant area between Eridanus and the bright, solitary Fomalhaut crowned the brilliant Orion region in the southeast. The triangle formed by Betelgeuse in Orion, Procyon in Canis Minor, and Sirius in Canis Major stood on its base in the east, while Capella in Auriga was high in the sky, approaching its zenith. In the north, the Big Dipper was almost on the end of its handle, beginning another round; the Little Dipper, with handle bent backward, was hanging down from the North Star.

As Daniel pointed out these delights, Del said, "My goodness, where did you learn all of that?"

"Oh, I was at sea for some time—of course, that was almost entirely in the southern hemisphere and we had a markedly different view of the sky. I learned most of what I know about our stars from a very close friend in Sacramento, though. A very good and very intelligent friend," Daniel added.

"It sounds to me as though you have had an extremely interesting life," Del said. "I wish you would share more of your experiences with me."

"Perhaps we can on another night when it's not this cold. Are you getting uncomfortable?"

"Yes, but this is so beautiful that I can't bring myself to go back inside just yet." Staring up at the limitless heavens for a long moment, Del finally suddenly asked, "Do you believe in God, Daniel?"

"Yes, I believe in something of the sort. I don't see how all of that," he swept his hand skyward, "or the miraculous complexity of the human body, or just any part of Nature for that matter, could happen entirely by chance. I believe that some central intelligence had to set it all in motion. Do I believe in the God of our Christian Bible or the Old Testament? No, I don't. I can't help but think that God is an entity of Man's own creation."

Daniel looked up again toward the stars and said, "I truly don't know what I believe about our relationship to that central intelligence; why we're here, what is expected of us, whether there is anything in our future after death, or whether death is simply the complete end of it all for that person or animal or plant. I just don't know. I wish I did. Do you believe in God?"

"Oh, yes I do. And you're right. I am getting cold," Del replied.

Her seemingly abrupt change surprised him, and he felt he had said too much too soon. Why don't you learn to keep your silly mouth shut, he scolded himself silently. "Well, let's get back and fill that wood box, then," he said in what he hoped was a pleasant tone of voice.

They slipped and slid their way back toward Del's tents, both hunched deeply into the collars of their coats, their breath clouding the frigid air. Todd gathered a huge armful of firewood from her stack as she entered the cook tent ahead of him to light the coal oil lamp. There was still fire in the cook stove, and they crowded close to it for warmth.

Daniel was a little surprised when Del smiled up at him and said, "I don't know when I have enjoyed an evening as much as tonight. The stars are simply beautiful and I'm impressed by your knowledge of them. And you have given me things to think about. That's a good thing, and I thank you. Remember, breakfast is at seven o'clock sharp. Good night, Daniel."

"Good night, Del. I enjoyed it very much also. I'll see you in the morning." Champ reluctantly abandoned his spot behind the cook stove and followed Daniel out into the night.

- - -

Daniel's appearance began to improve in the days that followed. He concerned himself more with how carefully he combed his hair, how neatly he trimmed his mustache, and he even considered growing a full beard; although not pressed, he now kept his garments as carefully brushed as was possible while living in a frontier mining town; he even found himself longing to own a cheval glass so that he could observe his full appearance. He thought about Cordelia much of the time and always from the perspective of how he might make life better for her. Was she warm enough down there in those tents? Was she fatigued from her long hours of cooking? Was she lonely? And, he was embarrassed by the lust he felt for her; the puritanical rearing he had received in his childhood and youth had left its mark on him. He wanted more than anything to make her his wife, but he tried to crowd such thoughts from his mind because he felt it highly unlikely that she would ever accept such a proposal from him.

In the meantime, life went on. The winter seemed interminable. Todd's practice grew steadily although most of his patients would not be able to pay him until they could start mining again.

One day in late January, great excitement stirred the town when a fourteen mule pack train came plodding through the drifts from the south. Whoops and shouts spread from tent to tent and men spilled from every saloon in a mindless melee when word reached them. The packer slogged his way toward his goal, the mercantile store, where he hoped to discharge his load and then finally to enjoy some warmth, comfort and endless drinks at the nearest saloon.

After seeing the many bags of food supplies, the question that almost every miner shouted at the packer was, "Did ya bring tabacca?" After mumbling his response to the first half dozen questioners, the packer climbed up on a stump and shot in the air with his pistol.

"Goddamnit," he shouted. "Listen up! I'll jus' chew my cabbage *one more time* . . . jus' onc't more. Some rich sonuvabitch met me on the trail back there a piece an' axt me if'n I had tabacca. 'Yessir,' I said, 'but 'tis all mantied-up on one o' them mules back there.' 'I'll buy the whole shiteree' says he. An' b'God, that's jus' what the Jasper did; pulled out a whole goddamn pouch o' gol' dust an' bought ever' damn leaf o' the stuff. Any dealin' in tabacca ye men have in mind'll hafta be wi' him, I reckon. I ain't seed him since, but unless he has one powerful hunger fer tabacca hisself, I'll wager dollars to green apples he won't head nowheres else but this direction 'cause ain't nothin' but drifted snow ass-deep to a tall Injun back t'other way. 'Sides that, they's all kinds o' tabacca back Willamette River-way."

There was stunned silence among the crowd and then a chorus of groans and invective followed. Ignoring them, the packer proceeded to unload his mules and get his freight checked by the storekeeper. It wasn't until late afternoon that Orville Jackson rode into town with bulging saddle bags. He got no farther than the board sidewalk in front of the Nugget Saloon when word spread amongst the men that their fellow miner had tobacco for sale. Consternation spread equally as fast when everybody learned that Orville was charging $50 for a single twist of the popular product. Neither persuasion nor threats caused him to yield ground on the monopoly that he held. His only comment was, "Did any you Jaspers share anythin' wi' me when I was gut-empty hungry? Hell no, ye didn't. A man's gotta eat somehow. If'n ye want to chew now, ye'll have to pay the piper, b'God."

And chew and chew everybody did. By popular demand, though, Orville Jackson moved on to another camp by sundown, tobacco-less but with a fat poke of gold dust. Some said that in the days that followed, a man would work a single chaw around and around in his mouth until the tobacco leaves became as white as cabbage before he would allow himself to spit.

- - -

A southeast Chinook wind set in the following week and led to a massive thaw. The single street of Jacksonville, now called California Street, became a giant loblolly of mud. Miners who had gone broke during the long winter returned to their claims with great enthusiasm; those who still had a bit of gold dust left from their previous autumn's work grudgingly emerged from their slothful winter hibernation in the saloons. Mining once more turned the creek into a thick slurry that was almost as much mud as it was water. All hoped they had truly seen the last of winter but if not, most wanted to take advantage of any respite, regardless of how brief.

- - -

Only a faint grayness of early dawn had begun to touch the interior of his cabin when Daniel stirred from his sleep and heard the moan of a raw wind outside. Or perhaps it was a knock that had roused him, because when a pounding noise jarred him to full wakefulness, it almost had the familiarity of repetition. He bounded from his bed and rushed to throw the latch.

Three Orientals stood outside his door in the dim light; two in the rear supported a slumped figure and the one nearest on the low step spoke haltingly and with pantomime, "Cut bad. Maybe die."

Todd beckoned them to enter. He hastened to close the door after them because of the wind and helped the patient to a chair before he lit a coal oil lamp. Seeing that the blood was dried on the man's clothing and his crude bandages, Todd took time to build a fire before he proceeded with the examination and treatment. Champ stirred and peered about him but did not get up.

When Todd turned and moved the lamp close in order to examine the patient, he realized for the first time that the man was Gung Pi, the Chinese doctor. Eyes that had always glowered so malevolently at him whenever the two had met on the street were closed now and he seemed unconscious, but apparently was not because he had walked with help to the cabin.

The three companions stepped back silently and Todd cautiously removed the swath of cloth that had been wrapped around Gung Pi's neck. A gaping wound in his skin no longer bled; a large clot of dried blood tended to outline, rather than obscure, the slash that cut almost completely across the left sternocleidomastoid muscle. If the patient had his head tipped back instead of forward, Todd was sure it would fall to the side like the half-transected head of a chicken. He had trouble imagining how the jugular vein or carotid artery had escaped injury; the slash, just above the left clavicle and barely below the jugular arch, must be superficial and hit the anterior branch of the jugular; a deeper wound would have cut the internal jugular and probably the carotid artery as well. If it had, Todd would not have a live patient here now. The fact that the bleeding had been controlled by the pressure of the bandage almost proved his analysis.

When he got another cloth unwound from the patient's right hand, he found a deep defensive wound in the flesh, and the shattered fifth metacarpal bone was exposed. That large cut began to bleed again with the removal of the bandage so Todd re-wrapped it tightly. Not until then did he notice the large, blood-soaked rent in the upper left sleeve of the padded jacket. He was tempted to cut the garment away in order to examine further but, realizing it might be the only warm wrap in Gung Pi's possession, he enlisted the help of the spokesman and inched the coat off over the arm. The involved movement brought a grimace to the face of the stoic patient, but he still did not open his eyes. Another bandage, heavily clotted, had to be unwound and he found another yawning wound beneath. Here, a large tongue of deltoid muscle was exposed and had retracted the overlying skin upward. It looked as though the cut had either been made in an upward direction or that the arm had been lifted to ward off a downward blow.

Todd asked the spokesman what had happened. The Oriental looked to his companions for assistance in expressing himself and gesticulated with a chopping motion; then, turning to represent the victim, he raised his left arm for protection and made a grabbing movement with his right hand. He indicated a glancing blow on the left upper arm and then a ricocheting strike on the left side of his neck.

Todd went to his kitchen table and picked up a knife. Holding it up, he looked questioningly at the spokesman. That man shook his head and looked around. He picked up a hatchet from the wood box next to the hearth and made a chopping motion with it. Todd took the hatchet and with another questioning glance, pointed first at one Oriental and then the next and finally at the spokesman. That man shook his head each time, but took the hatchet and made wrestling movements; he then made a slicing motion across the throat. Todd understood that the culprit had been dealt with.

Gung Pi still sat in the chair and Todd decided that with his extensive wounds, it would be best for him to be reclining for the repair and so moved him to the cot. He poured a jigger of laudanum and placed it in the Oriental's hand. Gung Pi sniffed it and, still not opening his eyes, shook his head and refused to drink it. Todd decided that was the man's own choice, however misguided, and he proceeded to lay out suture material, needle and needle holder, tissue forceps and scissors. He then cleaned the skin around the wound in the neck with whiskey. He was certain that it caused great pain when some of the liquid spilled over into the wound but again, Gung Pi showed no response but merely kept his eyes closed. Todd placed the sutures deeply so that, in bridging the wound, they incorporated layers of both skin and muscle together; he planned to leave these in place, barring infection, many more days than if they were only through skin alone. He now concentrated on repairing the severe cut on the shoulder, leaving the hand until last.

Gung Pi's stoicism did not waver as Todd inserted stitch after stitch along the full extent of the cut that nearly laid the shoulder joint bare. The doctor finally straightened his tired back and would have welcomed a rest period but couldn't permit himself that luxury until the hand was repaired.

The Abductor Digiti V muscle was completely transected and the Opponens Digiti V almost so. He closed these both together as one layer of muscle and again brought the sutures out through the skin. He bandaged the hand and then created a splint that bridged from the bend of the wrist to the tip of the little finger to immobilize the fifth metacarpal. He had taken more than an hour and yards of suture material in his treatment, but Gung Pi had remained calm throughout it all, as had his companions who stood in a small circle as observers the entire time.

"There, I'm finished," Todd exclaimed as he sat back on his stool and straightened his back. To his great surprise, his patient now opened his eyes and looked at him.

In a high-pitched but very cultured voice, Gung Pi said, "Thank you very much, Dr. Todd. I appreciate what you have done. I did not wish to take your laudanum because I had ingested a small pill of opium before we left my quarters, and I did not wish to overdose myself."

Todd was almost speechless in his surprise. He finally stammered, "I . . . I am sincerely sorry that you received these injuries, but I am honored to have you as a patient, sir."

Gung Pi bowed graciously but avoided any movement of his wounded neck. "We shall be going now."

"I am very concerned about infection of these wounds. You should stay here for a few days." The Chinese physician swayed his entire upper body from side to side to indicate the negative without shaking his head. Todd added, "Well, at least allow me to come to your home daily to inspect them, then."

Once again the Oriental bowed and said, "You will be most welcome," as he moved toward the door. He swayed in his weakness and his companions crowded close to assist him. "Thank you again, Dr. Todd," he said softly in his high-pitched voice and stepped out into the raw wind.

Todd mused over the entire incident and realized that he now had an entirely different opinion of Jacksonville's "other physician."

- - -

Breakfast had been completed by the time Daniel arrived at Del's Kitchen. Knowing that he probably had had a patient visit him at the last moment or had been summoned to the aid of someone needing his attention, Del had saved some oatmeal for him. While he ate it and drank a cup of her strong coffee, he ached to share the story of the morning with her but resisted the temptation. That she talked endlessly about the first freighter who had reached town yesterday made it easier for him to remain silent, but that was not much of a comfort. He still longed to share everything with her.

Daniel felt a bit rejected when Del said, "Now that you have finished your breakfast, Daniel, you must run along because with all of those new supplies brought in by the freighter, I want to prepare something very special for all of you gentlemen tonight. No," she said, holding up an index finger to shush him, "I won't tell you what it is to be. You can just be surprised with everybody else tonight."

With what he felt to be a definite demotion to a rank equal to all of the other boarders, Daniel dejectedly left Del's Kitchen with Champ trailing along faithfully behind.

The wind brought rain later in the day and, although some miners labored throughout the cold, drizzly storm, Daniel was content to stay indoors and read. Two patients drifted in during the afternoon, but their problems were minor and could just as well have gone untreated. Todd gave one some liniment for his sore back and the other an unguent of opium and pulverized nut-galls for his piles.

In the evening, he went down to Del's to sample whatever culinary delight she had prepared. He could smell the aroma of dinner at least twenty feet from her tent and it was beguiling; the rich, smoky essence of roasted meat was accented by the tantalizing spiciness of sauerkraut that hung heavily in the air. He detected the redolence of fresh-baked rolls also, and he suspected that Del's baking might even have included a pie. When he entered the tent, the other boarders were already sitting around the table.

Although politely patient, their eagerness was obvious as they peered in the direction of Del's stove. Daniel sat at his usual spot and waited with the others. He suspected that Del dawdled in her serving of the meal just to tantalize her brood.

Finally, she announced, "Gentlemen, I am delighted to provide you with the cornucopia of food transported to us yesterday by Mr. Jarvis, the freighter. She placed a large baked ham on the table; next came mashed potatoes and gravy followed by a bowl of sauerkraut. She had sliced fresh potatoes and onions into vinegar as a salad and there were fresh rolls and real butter. When this was all in place, Laurence Whitsell held his cup of tea in the air and said, "Gentlemen, let me propose a toast to Cordelia Evans, the Queen Cook of the West!" Everybody cheered, but only briefly, before plunging into the food with gusto. Cordelia observed their enthusiasm with obvious satisfaction and, as usual, took her meal at a little side table.

Dessert was pie that she had made from dried peaches. When all appetites were sated and the last of the tea poured, Cordelia unobtrusively faded from the tent, probably to rest from her labors before cleaning up. Several of the men lit pipes or just sprawled back in their seats, uncomfortably gorged but content. Chase James commented to nobody in particular, "When I saw Doc, here, a'talkin' our Del into a stroll under the stars—in spite of it's bein' brutal cold—thinks I, b'God, she jus' might welcome some o' ol' Chase's company as well on some other night. She smiled politely, sure 'nuff, but showed me the road. No deal, whatsomever. What's yer secret, Doc?"

All eyes peered in Todd's direction. He chuckled and said, "Well, it must be at night in order to see the stars—can't be daytime, Chase—and not raining or cloudy. Timing is important." Everybody laughed, James included, and took his response as a joke, but Daniel found great satisfaction from Chase's story and thought that perhaps he might indeed enjoy some special place in Cordelia's estimation.

He was so jubilant that he added, "After such a meal as that, why don't we clean up these dishes and pots and pans so that our Queen Cook of the West doesn't have to?"

Nobody objected.

- - -

Todd made his way down the creek to where the Chinese had gathered in their crowded and rude shelters. He was surprised by the many clusters of the Orientals he saw there. Some were still gathered in groups outside, eating their morning meal, but many were already moving down toward the creek where they were probably panning abandoned tailings for whatever gold might remain. Several times, Daniel announced the name Gung Pi and tried to indicate by pantomime that he wished to find this man. He was met by mute and uncomprehending expressions. He was surprised by how sparingly all of these men were dressed, because the clouds hung very low and were threatening rain. He was certain the temperature hovered not far above the freezing mark. Finally, he encountered a man who bowed deeply and motioned for him to follow. They moved along a maze of pathways and the man pointed to a structure that was larger and more substantial than all of those around it. Todd bowed in gratitude and knocked on the flimsy door.

A few words of Chinese sounded from deep inside and, in spite of his uncertainty whether that indicated an invitation to enter or a warning to go away, he opened the door and went in. The subdued light made it difficult to observe his surroundings, but a figure on a sturdy bunk at the back stirred and he made his way toward it.

"Gung Pi? It's Dr. Todd. I have come to see how your wounds are doing. How are you feeling this morning, sir?"

"Ah, Dr. Todd," the familiar high-pitched voice replied. "My limbs are as stiff as bamboo, but I am not in great pain. Thank you for coming. I doubted that you really would venture into my world."

"And why would I not come to see my patient, sir? I had no idea that the Chinese community was as large as it is, however," Todd said.

"Yes. They were brought here from China as cheap labor to work as miners, but I fear that most of them have bolted and now prospect for themselves to recover what gold others have chosen to leave behind."

Seeing no lamp, Todd asked, "Do you feel well enough to come over near the door so that I might have enough light to examine your wounds, doctor?"

Without replying, Gung Pi lit a lamp and placed it near his bed. He lay back so that the doctor could remove his bandages. First, Todd loosened the swathing around the man's neck and was very pleased by how neat and clean the suture line appeared, although some new bleeding had occurred and clotted around it. He bound that wound again and next checked the right hand. It, also, was doing well and showed no sign of abnormal inflammation. After bandaging that and replacing the splint, he inspected the left arm. Here, he was disappointed, because there was considerable swelling and marked redness surrounding his line of sutures. As Todd paused and took in a deep breath, Gung Pi surmised that all was not well and tried to get a better view of the wound himself.

Before Gung Pi could comment on his observation, Todd said, "I'm afraid that we have a somewhat worrisome condition here, doctor. This wound has become badly inflamed. I don't know why it should be any different than the others, but it is. Let me re-bandage it loosely while I go back to my cabin and get some medication for you."

Gung Pi held up a restraining hand and said, "Allow me to use some of my own treatments on it, Dr. Todd." With difficulty, he rose from his bed and went to one of the crowded shelves which lined every wall. He took down a jar of dried leaves and came back to his bed. "This is *Tze-lan*, a plant belonging to the same order that I think you call the Chrysanthemum flower. Make a poultice out of these leaves and crushed stems and place over the wound, if you will, Dr. Todd. I think we shall both be gratified by the results."

Well, I suppose it *is* his arm, Todd thought. How can I do anything but humor him? "I shall be happy to do that, doctor. I will re-bandage it and then come by this evening to see how you are doing." He fully expected he would find then a further deterioration in the man's condition. "Do you need any medicine now for pain?"

"I am very comfortable. May I offer you a cup of tea?" Gung Pi replied.

"I would be honored to take tea with you, sir, but I have other patients to see," Todd lied. "I would be delighted to have some with you some other time, however." Feeling his medical expertise was somehow in question by the Oriental's desire to use his own treatments, all he wished to do now was to leave as soon as he could. He bandaged Gung Pi, bowed to show his respect, and left. He hurried down to Del's Kitchen so he would not be late for breakfast again.

- - -

It was a busy day at his "office." Tug Foley came by complaining of being "costive as hell, Doc," and was sent on his way with some of Dr. Rush's "thunderclapper pills" as well as a packet of "renovating pills" made from an imported root that, when shaken with water, produced a suds similar to Castille soap and had a remarkable purifying effect on the bowels. Charlie Mason had a painful and badly decayed tooth. It was so far gone that Todd was sure it would fragment if he tried to pull it so he compounded a paste of gum opium, gum camphor and spirits of turpentine and plastered it into the hollow of the tooth and instructed Charlie in follow-up treatment.

Several patients complained of "acid stomach" and Todd treated them with his stomachic bitters. This was such a common complaint that he kept a preparation of this on hand and "working" all of the time. It was a mixture of gentian root, dried orange peel, cardamom seed and whiskey and, if allowed to steep for at least a week before being prescribed, it almost always proved very effective. If that treatment didn't produce relief, the old and time-proven remedy of filtered wood ashes and soot in water *never* failed.

Ace Garrison came in because of his chilblains and received a mixture of sulfuric acid, turpentine and olive oil. Todd opened two boils and bled several patients for a variety of more serious symptoms. He would have wagered that it was still way too early for snakes to be out, but when Cletus Richards' friends brought him in, they also brought the dead rattlesnake they had killed after it bit had him. The companions had already cut through the fang marks and said they had sucked quantities of blood from the site, so Todd merely removed from the shelf a bottle of the antidote he had prepared months earlier and hoped it would still be effective. It was a preparation consisting of iodide of potash, corrosive sublimate, and bromine. He gave Cletus ten drops of this in a small amount of brandy. The snake appeared rather small and, although the leg was swelling badly, Todd was quite sure Richards would survive.

"Take him to his tent," Todd directed his friends, "and give him ten drops of this in brandy or whiskey every two hours. I'll drop by later to check on him."

Todd worked right through his noon hour without a break, so he was ravenous when suppertime came. A drizzly rain had settled in on Jacksonville and star-gazing was out of the question. When he and Cordelia had finished their usual after-dinner cup of tea together, he excused himself from helping with the dishes saying that he had to visit Cletus Richards and Gung Pi before returning to his cabin. He wished her a good night and said he looked forward to breakfast, hoping tomorrow would not be as hectic as today had been. Although her schedule had been no picnic, either, and she still had much to do, Del nodded tolerantly with understanding and wished Daniel a good night.

He went to Richards' tent first and found his patient was feverish. He wished that some of the snow banks still remained so he could pack the leg in something extremely cold; of course, if snow were still around, there wouldn't have been a rattlesnake about in the first place.

"See if any of the saloons still have ice in their ice-houses. If they do, get some and pack that leg in it after you have crushed it into fragments. Keep doing that all night, but don't stop that medicine you have been giving him by mouth." Todd silently castigated himself for not ordering this earlier but, in truth, he had underestimated the severity of the problem. "I'll come back in a few hours to see how he is doing."

With that, he headed up to Gung Pi's place. Although Todd was generally pleased with the way he had treated most of his cases that day and how they had gone, his visit to Richards' tent had put him in a pessimistic frame of mind. He fully expected Gung Pi to be worse and he contemplated going back down to his cabin to get some of his own poultice material to treat the inflammation in the manner he should have done in the first place. He knocked at the door and entered when bid. He was startled when he saw the Oriental sitting on his bunk sipping tea. The man was very carefully using just his right hand to do this.

"Good evening, doctor," Todd said and bowed slightly.

Gung Pi very courteously rose and bowed as well. "Welcome to my humble lodgings, Dr. Todd. Would you join me in a cup of tea?"

"No, thank you, doctor. I have just finished my supper. How is your arm, sir?"

"It is quite comfortable." He put his cup of tea down and sat on his bed so that Todd could examine him.

Todd brought the lamp closer and helped Gung Pi extract his left arm from his garment. Removing the bandage, he was amazed at how much the inflammation had diminished over the course of the day. "Oh, Gung Pi, this is amazing! Your arm is tremendously improved since this morning. I can hardly believe my eyes."

" Ah, so. *Tze-lan* is usually very effective in matters such as this. Perhaps you would like to use it in some of your other patients, Dr. Todd." The oriental face was essentially inscrutable, but Todd felt he could read a hint of triumph in the good doctor's features, He stammered, "Yes . . . yes, indeed I would." As an afterthought, he added, "Certainly not to encroach on your practice, doctor . . . not in the least, but purely in the interest of science and my own professional edification."

"Our science, as you call it, dates back hundreds of years. My basic text of medicine consisted of eighteen volumes. I would be honored to share my limited knowledge with you, Dr. Todd, in return for yours. I appreciate the care you have given me."

Todd said, "I will look forward to any instruction you feel you can bestow upon me, doctor," and proceeded to re-bandage the man's left arm. He felt uncomfortably chastened and beat as hasty a retreat from Gung

Pi's presence as he could do with politeness. "I shall return in the morning and check your other wounds, sir. I bid you good night." Gung Pi rose and bowed until Todd exited the door.

As he descended the hill to his cabin, the thought that echoed back and forth through his brain was, "That had to be an aberration, a fluke. I'm certain that the rest of his treatments can't be that successful. Mine certainly are not!"

Champ was waiting for him at the door and rushed inside ahead of him. In a frustrated and unsettled frame of mind, he quickly prepared for bed without even adding wood to the dying embers in the fireplace. He got into the bed, but sleep didn't come that easily. "How good a doctor am I? Am I really doing any good at all for mankind?" Those questions and doubts niggled at his brain until, long last, sleep finally overtook him.

CHAPTER TWENTY-EIGHT

When the daily rains of early spring became more intermittent, an occasional clear evening sky allowed Todd once again to take Cordelia on a star-gazing walk. Tonight, they enjoyed the view while gathering darkness gradually allowed one constellation after another to gradually blink into view. Discordant notes from the Nugget Saloon's new piano sounded in the distance. As always, the vastness of the seemingly endless space above overwhelmed them.

This evening, Del seemed more fatigued than usual and Todd hesitated to initiate the conversation he had silently practiced all day. He finally embarked on it anyway. "Surely you are having second thoughts about going back to New York, Del. I mean, so many people here depend on you."

Still staring up at the heavens, she took a deep breath and then exhaled slowly. After a pause, she said in a rather depressed manner, "My role here seems to be nothing more than that of a servant—cooking meals and cleaning up day after day for a group of hungry men. Don't misunderstand my meaning. They are pleasant, they are polite, and I am extremely fond of every one of them. I know they appreciate me and would miss my presence. But the individuals come and go as they proceed onward with their lives. I simply remain. I am like a mouse in one of those treadmill cages, running day after day but going no place. There must be more to life than this, Daniel."

Her response was not the one for which he had rehearsed and Daniel became slightly flustered. "Certainly, the long winter and now, this endless rain has . . . I mean, those things have worn terribly on all of us. Now that it is possible to get out and around more, perhaps we could . . . you know, see more of one another. I mean . . . walks and so forth. Would that be all right, Del?"

There was another pause and, for the first time this evening, a mischievous smile crept across her face and she said softly, "I thought that was what we were doing already—and I have enjoyed every minute of it." Her smile broadened to match the expression in her eyes.

Excitement clutched at his chest with this hint of encouragement and, as though his tongue were an alien thing over which he exercised absolutely no control, Daniel blurted, "Oh, Cordelia! Cordelia, I love you! Thoughts of you overwhelm me and crowd everything else from my mind. You obsess me. Become my wife and let me free you from the drudgery of Del's Kitchen. We could have each other, a family, and a wonderful, beautiful life together." He had spoken all of this in a single breath and stopped, panting to renew himself.

Although more or less expecting this outburst because of Daniel's behavior over the past weeks, Cordelia thought it best to appear undecided. "Oh, my goodness, Daniel, you surprise me. Such a tremendous change in my plans would require some time to consider and a great deal of very careful thought. Since Lukas' death, I have simply assumed that I would never re-marry. I think we should not discuss it any further this evening but merely enjoy the stars. But," she looked up at him with tenderness, "being honored by such a proposal, I think, is deserving of a kiss." She reached up and kissed him lightly on the cheek.

Elation and disappointment simultaneously swept over Daniel. He was disgusted with his own clumsy eruption but delighted by Cordelia's kiss. And he was encouraged that she had not simply answered with an immediate "no". They continued to stare up at the brightening stars in silence, both with thoughts on matters other than astronomical. Daniel reached over and hesitantly took her hand.

Del did not draw away.

- - -

At breakfast the following morning, Daniel was disappointed that Cordelia seemed completely unchanged and acted as though the events of the previous night had never happened. As she had been last evening, she seemed quite tired this morning, but she greeted each of her boarders with her usual smiling "good morning."

Daniel lingered for a few minutes after breakfast but, when Del still said nothing and acted as though he was just a boarder like all of the rest, he hesitantly went about his usual duties.

He still visited Gung Pi daily and over the past few weeks had learned about many of the medications in the Chinese doctor's formulary. These included *Shis-jue-ming*, which was ground abalone shell and was used in eye infections, for fever due to consumption, and as a diuretic or to treat gonorrhea; *Ren-chung-pai*, a dried substance derived from urine and then boiled with ginseng, was effective as a disinfectant on abscesses, gumboils and eczema; *Wu-ling-chih*, derived from Nightingale guano, was helpful in treating uterine bleeding, dysmenorrhea and snake bites; *Sheng-pa-tou*, from croton oil, a poison, but used in the treatment of diarrhea, apoplexy and toothache. There was *Hu-huiang-lien, Ch'ing-hsiang, Ta-chi, Chuan-pei-mu*, the *Tze-lan* that had been so effective in treating the inflammation in Gung Pi's wounds. Many, many others. In return, Todd described his own treatment for these various disorders and even taught the Chinese doctor the rudiments of setting fractured bones and the making of strengthening plaster casts. It turned out that Gung Pi was very knowledgeable about anatomy.

Cletus Richards had recovered from his rattlesnake bite but a sizeable area of tissue surrounding the original wound had sloughed and now proud flesh was beginning to fill in the defect. Todd had learned that he must be more aggressive in his treatment of snakebite in the future and, also, should not be misled by the size of the reptile.

There had been an outbreak of pip in camp and he had bled all of them, not being in possession of any leaches. As he had learned on the *Ellie Mae*, saline gargles and painting the tonsils with iodine was also quite effective. Acacian balsam proved quite potent in its therapeutic qualities.

The day dragged on endlessly and he had trouble concentrating. Instead, his anguished thoughts were, "Has Del made her decision? Will she give me her answer this evening? Lord, what will I do if she says no? Would I move back to New York and try to convince her there? This obsession is destroying me!"

Finally, suppertime came and he slowly drifted to Del's Kitchen. He lingered outside and hesitated entering. He thought, if I don't give her the opportunity to say no, perhaps in time she will actually agree to marriage. Realizing that he could not tolerate another day like today, he straightened his back, took a deep breath and resolutely entered the tent.

Most of the men were already seated. Del stood on the other side of the table with a large dish of potatoes in her hands. She looked across at him and as a greeting merely said, "Yes, Daniel, I will."

Todd was transfixed for an instant but then raced around the table to where she stood, nearly knocking Claude Charters off of his seat in the process, and gathered Cordelia in his arms, tipping the bowl of potatoes between them. He embraced her with pent-up emotion and then stared into her smiling eyes for a moment while curiosity and stunned silence gripped those at the table. Daniel turned to the other boarders and said with great pride, "Gentlemen, allow me to announce the pending marriage between Cordelia Evans and me."

While the others recovered from their shock, Daniel turned and embraced Cordelia again.

CHAPTER TWENTY-NINE

While Todd and Cordelia dawdled their way through washing the supper dishes, they started making their wedding plans and talking about what should be done regarding Del's Kitchen. She thought it would be an abandonment of her boarders if she closed it immediately. Todd was opposed to her continuing to work and, although he argued against the idea, they finally compromised by agreeing temporarily to move the cooking/eating tent up beside Todd's cabin and keeping it going . . . "just for a while." Since there was no minister in Jacksonville, they also agreed to ask Simon Edwards to come from Sacramento City to perform the ceremony. They would have the wedding as soon as he could be contacted and able to make his way north.

No more than an hour had passed after supper until word of the pending marriage had flashed from saloon to saloon and throughout the whole community. Of course, Cordelia's current boarders were filled with dread and worry about what lay in their gastronomic future; those non-boarders who were low on her extremely long waiting list had mixed feelings about the probable closing of the Kitchen. On the one hand, their jealousy was allayed somewhat in knowing that the current boarders would lose their coveted role. but on the other hand, closure would preclude any possibility that they themselves might someday become one of those select few to enjoy Cordelia's cooking. Speculation on the matter remained the primary topic of conversation for several days.

- - -

Life returned to normal over the next three weeks; mining went on apace and a new arrasta went on line as more and more rock required crushing to extract its gold. Along with his other cases, Todd had two patients who had become so mentally unhinged that both required restraint. He diagnosed each case to be the result of mercury poisoning from fumes inhaled by the men as they "cooked-off" quicksilver in the gold extraction process. He warned others at every opportunity so they could avoid the same fate. Del's Kitchen continued operation without interruption, and when she announced her decision to simply move its location following the wedding, the worries and emotions of everyone in town were considerably alleviated.

One day in early June, a large bearded man rode into town and inquired at the first saloon for directions to Dr. Todd's office. When he reached Todd's cabin, he tied his horse to a low-hanging branch and went inside the cramped structure. A voice from the back room said, "Have a seat. I'll be with you in a minute."

Simon Edwards looked around and was disappointed to see a combination waiting/examining/treatment/living room that was smaller and more crude in its appointments than the one used simply as the doctor's waiting room back in Sacramento. A simple screen apparently had to suffice here to afford privacy to a patient during the actual treatment. Of course, Jacksonville was very obviously not Sacramento in any respect.

Just then, Todd entered, still rolling down one of his shirt sleeves. "Simon! You're here!" He rushed forward and grabbed his friend's hand in both of his. "I had no idea word would reach you and you could get up here this quickly. Welcome! I'm delighted."

Simon's voice boomed, "It's not every day that such news reaches these old ears. When do I get to meet the future Mrs. Todd?"

"We'll go there immediately. Bring your things into the cabin while I move the medication I'm brewing off the fire. Oh, I'm so anxious to show off my Cordelia to you, Simon. I'm sure you will fall in love with her also." Edwards deposited his single valise inside Todd's door. Daniel donned his jacket and the two men strolled down the hill toward Del's Kitchen.

Cordelia was kneading bread dough as they entered the cooking tent. When she saw Todd, she said, "Oh, hello, Daniel," as she attempted to smooth an errant lock of hair into place with her upper arm, both her hands being white with flour. Then she saw the stranger entering behind him and said, "Oh! Why don't both of you have a seat while I finish this dough. I'll just be a minute."

Daniel said, "Del, this is my very good friend, Reverend Simon Edwards. Simon, this is she. This is Mrs. Cordelia Evans." He beamed his pleasure.

Cordelia was obviously annoyed at Todd for surprising her with this particular introduction before she had an opportunity to freshen her appearance. But, displaying extreme refinement and showing no hint of pique, she said, "Oh, Reverend Edwards, it is such a pleasure to meet you. Daniel has talked endlessly about the good times you two had together in the past. It almost makes me jealous."

With equal grace, Edwards bowed and kissed her hand. "The pleasure is all mine, madam. It is immediately obvious that you are much too good for my friend Daniel, here."

Del smiled coquettishly and playfully said, "And are you married, Reverend? Perhaps I am chasing the wrong man." She giggled and teased Daniel with her eyes.

He thought that was the first time he had heard her girlish laugh and was delighted by it. Placing an arm around each, he said, "My two favorite people in the whole world! How can we celebrate?"

"Well," she replied, "we can start by getting married. Let's set the date."

"Is today Wednesday?" Simon asked. "I've lost track of the days while I've been on the trail."

"Yes," Daniel replied. With a questioning glance at Del, he asked, "Can we get organized to have the wedding by Saturday?"

"Of course," she said. "Can you secure a large enough location by then? I may sound boastful to you, Simon, but social events are rare in Jacksonville. I suspect we will have a large attendance if there is no horse race or other earth-shaking event taking place on Saturday."

"Madam, stranger though I am to your fair community, afford me the pleasure of arranging for a location," Simon said. "Some say that I have some skill in the art of persuasion."

"There are no churches in Jacksonville, you know, Simon," Daniel countered.

"That was all too obvious to me when I rode into town," Simon replied. "But let an old miner see to organizing the ceremony, even though that is not the minister's traditional role."

"Done!" Daniel exclaimed with enthusiasm. "Do you suppose you can find something to feed a wandering mendicant man of the cloth tonight, Del?"

"Of course," she chuckled. "I'll give him your supper."

- - -

Eli Trump, the owner of the Nugget Saloon, warily eyed the large man across the bar from him. It was only when the man had turned his head and looked around that his flowing dark beard, of which even Joshua would take pride, was pulled aside and revealed the parson's white collar beneath. It was a sharp contrast to the blackness of his other clothes. Even these garments, though, did not convince Eli that this man really was a bible thumper; somehow, he had a more worldly look about him. An' what'd a preacher be doin' here anyway, he wondered silently. We ain't e'en got a church. Mebbe he's some kinda' gunfighter; more'n likely he's nothin' but a damn thimblerigger what's after somebody's claim. Then the sobering thought dawned on him that perhaps this jasper even had an eye on his Nugget.

Then the man spoke. "I seek an audience with the owner of this pleasure emporium. This *is* the El Dorado, isn't it?" The sheer volume of his voice was a challenge in itself.

"Hell, mister, if'n you could read, you'd a'seen the Nugget sign plain as day on your way in. What'ya want with him?" Eli asked.

"Actually, I seek to contract for the use of a hall for several hours, but I shall take that offer up with the owner of the El Dorado. Would you be so kind as to direct my path in that direction?" the man said in his booming voice.

Greed overcame Trump's caution. Sensing possible profit, he ventured, "I'm Eli Trump an' I own the Nugget, here. Mebbe we can fill your bill an' save you a long walk to t'other end o' town." Also, curiosity seethed inside him and he wondered why in hell would this jasper want to rent a hall. Does he plan to hold a prayer meetin' here in Jacksonville? Good God! Mebbe I don't want any part of it. Could put a hex on my place, it could.

"Ah, my distinct pleasure to meet you, Mr. Trump. Allow me to introduce myself. I am Reverend Simon Edwards of the Grace Evangelical Tabernacle of Sacramento City."

He seemed harmless and Eli reached out to shake the proffered hand; his was soon crushed in the giant paw. Trump winced and, even in his discomfort, continued to puzzle over what "the reverend" could possibly want with a saloon for several hours.

"What does this preacher man want with any saloon, you might be asking yourself," Simon continued. "Well, I shall tell you, sir. Dr. Daniel Todd is a very good friend of mine and has afforded me the honor of coming north in order to unite him and Cordelia Evans in the holy bonds of matrimony. You know them both, I trust?"

Trump nodded, feeling some relief.

"I wish to arrange the use of some spacious facility here in Jacksonville in which to perform the ceremony Saturday next—in the morning, of course," Simon boomed with exuberance. "And what would the charge be if we were to select your fine facility, Mr. Trump?"

With hardly a moment's hesitation, Eli replied, "I couldn't possibly shut down my saloon during such a busy time as that for less than $300." After a pause during which he noted not a flicker of emotion on Simon's face, he continued, "And then 'nother $100 for the use of the place, 'course."

Simon merely looked him in the eye with his penetrating gaze. "Ah, brother, the evil beast of greed slathers inside you—and thereby disgraces you, sir. I, as a man of God, am ashamed of you for trying to take advantage of your fellow residents in this shameful and covetous manner."

Eli didn't even flinch at this rebuke so Edwards felt he had to alter his tack. He leaned forward casually with his elbows on the bar and said in an almost conspiratorial manner, "But I can understand, Eli. You know, I ain't always been a parson. I've seen my share of tough times, too. You gotta make hay while the sun shines, right? Catch every buck and work every angle, right? Bet your bottom dollar, you do. I understand that better than most. But look at it this way—say, how 'bout you and me sniffin' a cork here? Let me buy you a drink, Eli."

Trump poured two glasses of rye whiskey, sipped at his slowly and marveled at the practiced manner with which "the reverend" downed his drink in a single gulp and then wiped the beard around his mouth with an experienced finger. "Where was I? Oh yeah, the wedding. Now, if a saloon worked it right, it could make a fortune out of this opportunity. You know what I mean? If a person could convince the Doc to throw his affair on an afternoon instead of the morning, why that crowd would stick around and drink all night. The licker would flow like milk and honey. Maybe a feller could get the Doc to chum the waters, so to speak, and buy a cask of *your* whiskey to get the celebration rolling—you know, toasts an' such."

Edwards could see the clockwork of greed ticking away in Trump's mind and ordered another round of drinks. This glass he savored more slowly and, pursing his lips appreciatively, held the glass to the light in order to enjoy the passage of light through the amber liquid. "Ah, let me complement you on the quality of your rye, Eli." Then he continued, "And, from what I gather, Mrs. Evans enjoys great favor among your citizens. Memory of the raucous merriment of her wedding will undoubtedly linger long—these miners just might even get in the habit of drinking wherever that glorious event takes place. Let me buy you a final drink before I seek out the El Dorado." When it was poured, Edwards sipped it slowly and finally toasted the Nugget owner, saying, "To your very good health, sir, and thank you for this most enjoyable respite and these moments of camaraderie"

As Edwards turned to leave, Trump stopped him with a wave of the hand and said, with slightly thickened tongue, "Wait up, Parson. Whyn't you jus' go an' tell the Doc if'n he agrees to buy a whole damn cask of my whiskey an' changes the time to Sat'day afternoon fer his weddin', b'God he can have the Nugget free fer nothin'. Let me stand you to a drink now, friend."

After this final glass of whiskey, Simon gave the barkeep a casual two-fingered salute and departed. "See you, Eli," he called back over his shoulder.

Later, as a somewhat inebriated Eli Trump reviewed the whole conversation in his mind, he mumbled to himself, "That jasper prob'ly is some kind of thimblerigger, but aye God, I got the best o' him." He nodded his head for emphasis.

When Daniel saw Simon that afternoon, he asked, "Did you get the Nugget for Saturday afternoon?"

Simon replied, "No problem there, Daniel. I'm afraid it's going to cost you a cask of whiskey for the toasts and so forth, though."

"No problem. Thanks, my friend," Daniel replied.

Cordelia finished stoking the stove with enough wood to finish cooking the roast of pork she was preparing for supper. The potatoes were peeled, the kraut in the pan was ready to cook and fresh bread had been baked that morning. She had nearly an hour with nothing to do so she went to her sleeping tent to lie down for a while. She didn't know why she felt so tired of late, and it seemed as though these backaches had become a daily thing. They never seemed to totally disappear.

She lay down on her pallet and stretched, luxuriating in the relief it produced. Her leisure gave time for her thoughts to wander once again over the many concerns she had had lately. *I wonder if I am doing the right thing in marrying Daniel? I know Lukas would understand and urge me to do it. I would like to return home but, at my present rate of earning, it would take several years before I could afford it. Papa would send me the money, I know, he and Mama both argued against my marrying Lukas in the first place. No, I won't ask them for the means to return home. And Daniel is a good man. I'm sure he loves me, and he is certainly better in every respect* than anybody I have met here. Do I love him? I think so, but probably not as much as he seems to love me. Whatever I do, though, I can't keep running the Kitchen much longer. It makes me so terribly tired. There are times I hardly seem to possess the strength to move one foot ahead of the other. I wonder why? It didn't used to be this way.

Cordelia stretched again and pulled a light coverlet over herself. Just think, she reflected, this time tomorrow afternoon, I'll be Mrs. Daniel Todd. She liked the sound of it. Certainly, any of her women friends back home would jump at the chance to marry a doctor. Yes, she thought, in all respects, I'm very happy that he asked me and that I accepted. Under the circumstances, though, wearing my original wedding dress would not be proper and besides, it would be disrespectful of Lukas. She decided to wear her pale blue organdy gown. It complemented her eyes, she thought. Then panic gripped her. Does it still fit? I haven't worn it since that promenade Lukas took me to in Binghamton before he came west. So much has happened since then.

She struggled to her feet and rummaged in her trunk to uncover the dress. She quickly found it; there were not all that many clothes competing with it for space. She stripped off her gingham work dress to try it on and was relieved that it fit easily over her body. As a matter of fact, it seemed looser than she remembered its being in the past. She took it off and started to fold it but found a hanger and suspended it from a nail on the tent pole instead so that the wrinkles would shake out by tomorrow. Even though only a few minutes remained before she would have to set the table and do the final steps in preparing dinner, she lay back down to get what relief she could for her back.

CHAPTER THIRTY

Daniel studied himself in his tiny mirror yet again to make sure his hair was as presentable as possible and then nervously brushed his trousers for the final time. Simon, casually sprawled in Todd's swivel chair near the desk said, "If you fiddle with yourself any more, I swear I will head back to Sacramento and leave you here on your own. Are you about ready to head down to the saloon?"

"Yes, I suppose," Daniel replied. He had seen several patients that Saturday morning but had been unable to devote his full attention to any of them. He couldn't concentrate and was surprised at being this nervous. After all, people get married every day, he thought repeatedly. Why do I feel as though my life is changing for anything but the better? How could *anything* but endless happiness result from today's ceremony? I wonder if Del is nervous? She's been through this before, of course. Is she as nervous as she was the first time?

Finally, when he almost gave Tor Svenson a strong laxative instead of some laudanum for his bad cough, Daniel recognized his incapacity and made a sign for his door that simply read, "Office closed for the day."

"Is it time to head down to the Nugget," he asked

"Yes," Simon replied, shaking his head in disbelief. "The clock hasn't moved backward. It still is ten minutes 'til two. Let's go."

"You have never told me whether or not you have ever been married, Simon," Daniel said as they closed the door of his cabin behind them.

"No, I've not talked about it. Yes, I have been and it's not fatal," Edwards replied but did not elaborate.

The sun was shining for a change, but no more than a handful of Jacksonville's miners were working at their claims. It appeared likely that the attendance at the wedding would be tremendous. Todd wanted to believe this was an indication of Cordelia's or his popularity, but he thought it much more likely that the hope of a free drink or two was the main attraction. Already, they could hear the faint tinkling of the Nugget Saloon's piano as Clarence, the ageing piano player, banged away at its keyboard. The tune was not completely identifiable but sounded more like "Oh Susannah" than anything matrimonial. Todd and Edwards picked their way down the trail toward California Street.

The crowd in front of the Nugget was huge and undoubtedly indicated even more jamming inside. As he and Simon edged into the fringe of the throng, Daniel was treated as the hero of the day with much back-slapping and hurrahing. He knew many of these men only by sight yet he was being accorded celebrity status. He knew it had to be because he had won the hand of the popular Cordelia and not because of himself.

Suddenly, a hush settled over the crowd. Daniel looked in the direction where all eyes had turned and were staring. A vision of loveliness in a blue gown was approaching along the street from the east. Del, appearing more beautiful than he had ever seen her, was being escorted by the entire group of her boarders, every one of them decked out in his best bib and tucker. At her insistence, Daniel had not eaten at Del's Kitchen that day. She had said it was not proper for the groom to see his bride before the ceremony on the day of the wedding, so he and Simon had prepared their own bachelor fare. Daniel felt guilty and almost like a voyeur to be seeing her now when he shouldn't and pushed Simon ahead of him into the Nugget where they could assume their positions for the ceremony.

The minister's giant frame served as an effective wedge as they moved through the melee inside and headed toward the rear of the room. In his booming voice, Simon shouted, "Silence men! Cordelia Evans is approaching on the street. Stand by with that music, Clarence!"

There was a sudden stillness, a stark contrast to the clamor of only seconds before. Daniel's breath quickened and then seemed to be completely stolen from him when Cordelia dramatically entered through the swinging doors. Shafts of afternoon sunlight, in which danced the tiny dust particles stirred by the crowd, framed her from behind and highlighted her in such a way as to create a halo around the tiny bonnet on her head. The throng dissolved ahead of her, forming a human aisle that led toward Daniel and Simon. Her honor guard of boarders gathered closer around to protect and cushion her passage as she moved forward. Clarence slapped his keyboard in a typical bar-room manner, and a tune that only vaguely resembled the hymn "The Overarching Love of God" filled the room. The music was more or less familiar to Todd from his youth but did not seem particularly appropriate to the occasion. The crowd had gone completely silent.

Cordelia smiled up at Daniel, her eyes shining with happiness, as she was deposited beside him and he returned her smile. Reverend Edwards held up both hands as though to quiet the gathering, but it was totally unnecessary because not even a foot shuffled. The only sound was a stifled cough by somebody near the door.

"Friends, we are gathered here to witness the vows of Cordelia Evans and Daniel Todd as they pledge their troth in holy matrimony. You know and love them both, and I am certain you join with me in boundless good wishes for their future happiness. So, without further ado, we shall proceed with the ceremony."

Simon turned to the bride and asked, "Cordelia Simpson Evans, do you take this man to be your lawful husband, forsaking all others and keeping yourself only unto him, to have and to hold, in sickness and in health from this day forward until death do you part?"

"I do," Cordelia answered in a firm voice.

"And Daniel Locke Todd, do you take this woman to be your lawful wife, forsaking all others and keeping yourself only unto her, to have and to hold, in sickness and in health from this day forward until death do you part?"

"I do," Todd said.

"Hearing no objection from anyone present, I, as a minister of our Lord and the Christian faith, now pronounce you man and wife. You, sir, may kiss your bride,"

Simon announced this last in his booming voice. Daniel complied in the most tender fashion. A tumultuous cheer rocked the Nugget Saloon and was immediately echoed by those still standing in the street.

Daniel and Cordelia turned to make their formal exit, but the press of the crowd kept them where they were. Clarence made an heroic attempt to play the tune from Mendelssohn's "Midsummer Night's Dream" that Edwards had hummed and tried to instruct him in playing—"It's all the rage at weddings in the East," he had said—but it still sounded more like a raucous barroom ballad than the Wedding March. Nobody was paying any attention to him at this point anyway. Those not close enough to pound Todd on the back or deposit a kiss on Cordelia's cheek were already rushing toward the bar where Eli Trump was frantically pouring shots of whiskey from the "marriage barrel". The quicker it was gone, the sooner he could start peddling from his own stock.

- - -

When the "reception" had progressed beyond the toasts, the clumsy speeches of congratulations and all of the hearty well-wishing, it gradually unraveled into a simple frontier drinking spree. Raucous laughter, profane shouting and the thunderous rumble of voices swelled to the point that the purpose for the whole celebration was defiled. Daniel became angry at the liberties being taken by some around Del; she appeared increasingly fatigued and her remarkable tolerance of the mounting crudeness began to disappear. Even Reverend Edwards' ability to assume worldly roles when the occasion demanded was fading. The three of them managed to slip out of the crowded saloon just as the afternoon sun was touching the top of the tallest pine to the west. They fetched Del's trunk from her tent and took it up to Daniel's cabin.

Simon said, if it were all right with Del, he would move into her tent until he returned to Sacramento. They deposited his valise there on their way back down the hill and then went to Lawrence's Café to have supper. They had the place almost to themselves.

All three had responded repeatedly to the toasts at the Nugget and strong, black coffee was even more welcome than the roast beef dinner they were served. Soon, their mood improved and the conversation drifted to their plans for the immediate future, accompanied by much laughter and good humor. Daniel and Del both tried to include Simon in their dialog, although he couldn't help feeling his presence was an encroachment on their wedding supper. It was almost a relief to him when, just at dark, the cacophonous crowd gathered outside the café and Clay Peters and Charlie Stevens came in to announce that the newlywed's carriage awaited them outside in order to take them to Daniel's place.

The "carriage" was a handcart with separate stools in it for the bride and the groom. When they were settled on to these, the legion of miners pressed close to push and pull the barrow not only along Jacksonville's single street but also up and down its many trails. Their bumpy passage throughout the town site was accompanied by the sound of hammers or spoons or sticks clanging on gold pans, bawdy shouts and songs of encouragement to the newlyweds, much drunken nonsense and even the discordant peal of somebody's cow bell. When darkness, fatigue and the desire to return to the Nugget's refreshments overwhelmed the crowd, they deposited Dr. and Mrs. Todd in front of their home.

The Todds graciously thanked all for the spirited "chivaree", waved goodnight to the throng and disappeared into their cabin. They were supremely happy to be married, honored by the genuine, albeit crude and noisy enthusiasm of Jacksonville's residents, and relieved that the festivities were finally all over. After Simon left to go down the hill, Daniel kissed Cordelia with a very gentle passion and then clumsily suggested an early retirement because of the exhausting strain and rigors of the day. His bride agreed.

- - -

Under the protective cloak of darkness, Todd found it infinitely easier to pour out his thoughts to his lovely bride. A gentle rain had swept over Jacksonville with the onset of night, and its soft tattoo drummed on the roof as an accompaniment.

Daniel whispered, "Ah, Cordelia. I can't begin to tell you how much I love you and how thankful I am that you consented to marry me." He hugged her closer than even the narrow bed required and softly murmured, "The thought of being able to share my most intimate thoughts, my desires, my innermost fears with another human being—our very bodies uniting as though the two of us were only one individual—it is all so new, so inconceivable to me that I can barely grasp the fact that it is finally real," Daniel admitted. "To look forward to a life together, to having children who spring from just the two of us, to grow old, side by side, in trusting love—oh, darling, I suddenly feel complete for the first time in my life. I have someone to care for and who cares as much for me . . . it . . . it simply is the fulfillment of my life."

Daniel held his wife close and continued to pour out his love. He said, "Now I know there was another in the past for whom you undoubtedly had the same thoughts that I describe, and I realize that you may well not feel exactly the same communion of spirit with me that I feel for you right now. But, please, just give it time. Del, my dear, I promise to be the best possible husband for you and to love you always as I do tonight. In time, I hope you will feel the same way toward me."

Del nestled her head under his chin and teased his beard with her fingers. "I love you too, Daniel, and I promise to be a loving wife of which you can be proud. Thank you for taking me." She reached up and kissed him tenderly on the lips.

Gathering her even closer in his arms, Daniel stroked her face with his fingers and then hesitantly reached on down to unfasten the buttons of her nightgown bodice that crowded high against her chin. His heart pounded and the thought flitted through his mind that he had touched and examined dozens—perhaps hundreds—of women's bodies in his medical career, but that this was the first time he was about to touch one in this manner because of passion. He slipped his hand down across her left breast; its satin skin and dough-soft texture caused the breath to catch in his throat. He kissed her passionately on the lips and gently kneaded the yielding tissue around her erect nipple.

Unbuttoning her gown on down to her waist, he exposed both of her breasts, although both darkness and the coverlet over them hid their beauty. He kissed the left nipple and then kissed her on the mouth again. Grasping a breast in each hand, he suddenly became transfixed! A FIRM MASS LAY UNDER THE AXIAL TAIL OF THE RIGHT BREAST!

In disbelief and attempting to be unobtrusive, Daniel gently massaged its surface with the heel of his left palm and then his fingers. There was no mistake! A relatively hard mass lay there, deeply and tightly fixed to the chest wall. It did not move under his disguised, but clinical, touch.

My God, he thought—how could Del *not* be aware of this? Suddenly, Daniel felt as though he was unable to breathe. He could not move. It was as though a death sentence had just been proclaimed for the two of them. How could this be? One minute, we were planning a long life of family and ecstasy together; the next—cancer of the breast! Maybe I'm wrong, Daniel thought. Maybe it is merely fibrocystic disease of the mammary. It doesn't move, though; it's fixed to the chest wall! He felt paralyzed.

Recovering, Daniel hugged Del close to him, trying somehow to instill his health into her body. What am I to tell her, he wondered? Do I ruin her wedding night? She has already had the passion of *one* wedding night; am I thinking more of the happiness of *my* wedding night? I must tell her. This is more important than anything else in the whole world, and the happiness of our wedding night is already destroyed. I should tell her; but what if I'm wrong and alarm her in this way for no reason at all? That would be terrible! What do I do?

"Is something the matter, dear?" Del asked, drawing back as though she could see him and judge him visually even in the darkness.

He didn't realize he had reacted so noticeably. What had he been thinking earlier? Sharing our bodies and innermost fears with another human being? Communion of spirits? After a painful pause, he decided that he must settle this now. "How long have you been feeling this fatigue that you've mentioned recently, Cordelia?" he asked.

"What a strange question," she replied. "I don't know—a few months—worse for the past three or four weeks, I suppose."

"And the backache that has become so bothersome?"

"About the same. Why?"

Without answering, Daniel ran his hand up into her right armpit and, feeling the localized areas of enlargement there, swept his hand down over her breast again to palpate the enlarged liver that could just be felt under the lowest rib of her chest cage. He felt drained of strength and movement and almost of even life itself.

"What is it, Daniel? What's wrong?" she asked in a voice now touched by alarm.

He couldn't answer for a long moment. Finally, his great love for this woman compelled him to choke out the words, "Cancer. I am . . . God, I . . . I'm so terribly afraid that you have cancer of the breast, Cordelia." He slumped against her now rigid body.

"What?" she exclaimed. "What did you say?"

"Haven't you noticed that firm area in your right breast? Surely you touch yourself there sometimes . . . perhaps during your bath or in getting dressed? How long have you had it?"

She moved her hand over the area, at first very gingerly and then with worried vigor. "No. No, I've not felt that before. It has been slightly tender, but I thought I had lifted too much wood. That's the arm I carry the wood in for the cook stove, you know. Did that have anything to do with it?" she asked.

"Let's be calm, Cordelia," Daniel replied with deliberate restraint. "I am probably all wrong and have stirred up both of us for no reason at all. Just be calm, my dear." He was sick with the certainty that he was *not* wrong and that this tumor had already spread to the area around the breast, to the bones of her spine, and to her liver. "Let's just settle back in bed and try to forget my outburst." He hugged her close and ran his hand through her hair. "It has been a very long and arduous day, my dearest Del. Just close your eyes and relax."

Both were rigidly silent as they lay in each other's arms, trying to dispel their fears through love, attempting to blunt this terrifying possibility by concentrating once again on their plans for a long and happy life together. Cordelia, typically optimistic, found it easier to be hopeful for the future; Todd's medical experience accorded him little hope.

He kissed her again, tenderly, but with all of his pent-up passion.

CHAPTER THIRTY-ONE

The soggy dawn was a melancholy gray, its gloomy atmosphere matching Daniel's troubled mind. Sleep had been fitful, elusive until only an hour ago. Awakening and looking about him, he wanted to believe with all of his soul that the tumor he had discovered last night was nothing but a horrible nightmare, although the fact that Del lay there asleep in his arms lent it reality. Her face was barely visible in the dim light, but she looked so peaceful, so seraphic that love surged in him, and the thought that this lovely creature could ever wither and die was more than he could bear. He closed his eyes to blot the thought from his mind. Then the image of her quiet repose was so vivid that he panicked; she might already be dead! He hugged her closer to him and with great relief, realized that she breathed!

Cordelia stirred but did not awaken. His heart pounding wildly, Daniel was suddenly aware of the cold that had gripped him and he slid from between the covers to build a fire in the fireplace. Rain drummed steadily on the roof and even the sound made the air feel more clammy and cold.

Their marriage had not been consummated, although Del's hopeful spirit, even in the face of the disastrous news conveyed to her by her new husband, might still have allowed such a possibility. Perhaps she even needed the emotional charge it would have given them, but Daniel had been so drained by his discovery, he was incapable of making love. He relived the long night in his mind as he nursed the hesitant fire. By the time it finally blazed into life, he realized he had ruminated a long time and was thoroughly chilled. He edged back into bed, careful not to awaken Del.

He was so completely convinced that his diagnosis was correct that he had trouble even allowing himself to hope that he was wrong. What can I possibly do to reverse the course of the disease, he wondered. If the tumor has indeed spread, there is no point in removing the breast. He knew of absolutely nothing that might have any effect on metastatic tumor. He pondered the possibility that Gung Pi might know of something that might be helpful. I could take her back to Boston, he thought; they would know, if anyone does, of any recent advances that have been made in treatment. How would we get her there, though? A trip overland would be terribly long and grueling. We could go down the Willamette and take a ship from Portland. Would we get there in time? Questions, questions, nothing but uncertainty.

There seemed to be very little that could be done at this point and thinking back to the almost casual way Del was handling the news by the time they finally drifted off to sleep, Daniel decided he should just be supportive and take his cues from her. Can I be that good an actor, he asked himself. I can be as cheerful as necessary for Del's sake if nothing else can be done, he thought, but I shall keep searching, and I will bend every effort to find some sort of cure!

The fire was crackling merrily now so he once again slipped from between the covers and dressed. He settled the coffee pot near the flames. His movements caused Cordelia to stir and then sleepily sit up.

"Good morning, Mrs. Todd," he said with a forced smile and came over to the narrow bed. "How did you sleep?"

She smiled and stretched. "Marvelous. I have been sleeping on a pallet on the ground for so long that I had forgotten how good a bed could feel. What time is it? I should be getting down to the Kitchen and get breakfast ready."

He sat down beside her and embraced her, saying, "Your only duty today lies within the confines of this cabin, Del, my dear. Simon is a very good cook, and he is taking care of your boarders today, although I'm sure not as well as you would do. Later today, he, a few of the boarders and I will attend to moving the cook tent up here as we had agreed. Now, I'll prepare *your* breakfast for a change. What would you like?"

"Not likely," she challenged. Swinging out of bed, she began donning her clothing. He marveled at the way she demurely wiggled garments up under her nightgown without uncovering herself at all and finally, in a sort of reverse chrysalis-shedding maneuver, pulled the gown up over her head and emerged completely dressed.

"It's not that I am unduly modest," she said with a giggle, "it's just that I have had to dress in my cold sleeping tent for so long that I have learned not to expose any skin unnecessarily."

To match her mood, Daniel laughed and held her close again.

- - -

Walking down the hill toward Del's Kitchen, Todd found it hard to believe that Cordelia had been such a classic example of the happy bride throughout breakfast, as though they had never even discussed his findings of last night. One could think that she was completely denying the possibility of anything being physically wrong with her. Perhaps that is best, he thought. If it turns out that my diagnosis is in error, she is better off not to have spent any time worrying; if it is cancer and nothing can be done about it, why not enjoy each hour of every day that she has left as though the problem did not exist. After all, he philosophized, none of us can be assured of even living to see the sun set on this very day.

When he was still a hundred feet or so from Del's cooking tent, he could hear Simon's familiar thundering voice as he carried on his usual monologue. As he entered the "Kitchen", Edwards announced loudly to all, "Behold, the bridegroom enters. All hail, Daniel. We shall not inquire into your present state of wellbeing."

"I thought my services might be required down here to treat any food poisoning you might have created, Simon," Todd countered. He waved at those present; it was obvious that they were captivated by Edwards' performance and were dallying over coffee rather than going about their day's work.

"I shall not claim even to be a somewhat adequate substitute for Mrs. Todd's artistic cooking," Simon replied, "but I think these gentlemen will be able to survive until supper."

Chase James said, "Whitsell here an' me will help move Del's tent up to your place this mornin' so's we can have *her* cookin' fer supper. Nothin' 'gainst the Reverend's cookin', but nothin' can touch Del's—that is, Mrs. Todd's."

"Thanks, Chase," Daniel replied. "I think we should take this tent down and then move the cook stove up there first, and get it located. That's going to be our biggest challenge."

"These fellers'll get it loaded on to a cart an' help pull it up there," James responded, indicating his fellow boarders. "Won't be no trick 'tall after that."

"Fine. You men go ahead and finish your coffee while I do a little planning with Reverend Edwards, here," Todd said, and motioned Simon outside with a nod of his head.

"Anything wrong?" Edwards asked as soon as they stepped outside.

After they had moved well away from the "Kitchen", Daniel said, "I don't know how to tell you this, Simon. Last night, I discovered a mass in Cordelia's breast . . . and . . . I'm almost certain that it is cancer. Quite far advanced."

"Oh, my God," his friend exclaimed. After a moment of silence, he asked, "Did you tell her about it?"

"Yes, I did. At first she acted quite alarmed and then just seemed to dismiss it from her thoughts. As though . . . as though she doesn't want even to consider its possibility."

"Can you treat it?"

"No, I think that it has spread too widely throughout her body to be treatable." Daniel's voice caught in his chest. When he recovered sufficiently, he continued, "I have decided to try and match her mood, attempting to make each minute that we will have together as happy as possible. I shall search for any treatment, of course."

Simon looked at the ground and shook his head in frustration. "I will be praying for you both, Daniel. I'm not certain that I can dissemble enough in front of her to hide the fact that I know about the problem, however. As much as I would like to be supportive of you both, I think I will leave very soon for Sacramento—unless, of course, you wish for me to remain."

"No, this is something that Del and I have to confront on our own. Thank you, anyway, old friend. I doubt that she will be able to continue much longer to cook for her boarders. She tires easily and has back pain from this, but I suppose it is well to let her go on as long as possible just the way she is. She feels a strong bond and an obligation to the welfare of these men. They obviously feel that way about her also."

"She is a jewel," Edwards said. "Such a shame. Such a shame. I'll pray that your diagnosis is totally wrong, Daniel."

"Thank you," Todd replied in an emotional whisper. After a moment, he said in a more vigorous voice, "Come on. Let's get this tent moved before we lose all of those strong backs in there."

- - -

Supper was the usual fine fare, another example of Cordelia's culinary skills. With spring, herds of cattle had arrived, meat was available and her table was loaded with a platter of steak. Along with it, she prepared potatoes, pan gravy, fresh rolls, sauerkraut and baked beans. Pie from some of her lemon extract provided the final touch. Every one of her boarders, as well as Simon and Daniel himself, had worked diligently much of the day to relocate her "Kitchen". When it was done, she had surveyed the way it nestled beside Todd's small cabin and announced that, except for the distance her boarders had to walk up the hill to get to it, she was much happier with the location.

Tonight, at everyone's insistence, Mrs. Todd had sat with all the men and enjoyed the meal along with them. It had been something of a wedding feast and when it was over, everyone lingered longer than usual before drifting off to a variety of evening activities. Daniel and Simon helped Cordelia with the dishes and then all sat around the plank table to visit.

After an appropriate time, Simon reached into a bag and produced a bottle of French wine, saying, "I had meant just to leave this with you two lovebirds, but it seems fitting, since this is my last night in Jacksonville, that together we toast your future happiness and our enduring friendship."

"Oh Simon, must you leave so soon?" Del asked.

"Yes, I'm afraid so. You might say that this trip was an unexpected one and, in rushing to arrive here as quickly as possible, I left things in quite some disarray back in Sacramento. Besides, you two don't need a third wheel on your cart around here; you have big plans to make and things to do. I'm only a few days ride down country and will come back. Better yet, the two of you should come to the big city and take a little vacation from your labors here."

By this time, the wine had been opened and was poured. Silently, but with an emotional nod of his head, Simon held up his glass to toast them in friendship. With only the three words, "To your happiness," drained it and placed it upside down on the table in front of him. Daniel and Cordelia, arms around each other, acknowledged the toast with a salute of their glasses and did the same.

Edwards rose and said, "I am going down the hill now. I want to get a good night's sleep and prepare for an early departure in the morning."

"You must come up here for a good breakfast before you leave, Simon. Promise?" Cordelia asked.

"It would be a genuine pleasure, madam," he replied and bowed. Daniel shook his hand and then embraced him.

"Thank you for coming all of this way, Simon. I can't tell you how much your presence has pleased both Del and me. I really hate to see you leave, though," Daniel said.

After a warm exchange of "goodnights", Simon left. Daniel and Cordelia followed him out into the night and watched him pick his way down the trail. The sky was clear and the nearly full moon was bright in the east.

"You told him about me, didn't you," Del said, more as a statement than a question. "He has acted differently all day."

"Yes, I thought it best," Daniel admitted. "He is extremely optimistic and said that he will pray for both of us but felt he had to get back to Sacramento. He is a true friend and has the greatest love and respect for you, my dear."

The fact that Cordelia had asked the question in this manner made it evident to Daniel that, although she had acted carefree throughout the entire day and evening, the problem of the tumor was very much on her mind.

"Why don't we put out the lamp in the 'Kitchen' and get to bed. It has been a very tiring day for both of us," Daniel suggested.

With no more than an appreciative look at the brilliant heavens, they went inside.

- - -

In spite of their drained emotions and physical fatigue, the night was one of great and loving tenderness. With the whispered exchange of their innnermost thoughts, they caressed, explored, and embraced in a beautiful bonding of bodies and souls. The marriage of Daniel and Cordelia Todd was finally consummated.

CHAPTER THIRTY-TWO

The rest of May and all of June passed all too rapidly. Daniel's and Cordelia's love for each other deepened and filled them both with an almost religious fervor. Neither could bear to think of anything but a shared life because they felt fused in their thoughts and hopes and desires. Nor did they mention the problem that both knew with increasing certainty would cut short this idyllic existence.

Daniel secretly searched high and low but could find surprisingly little written about cancer of the breast. He read an account of Baron Larrey, Napoleon's private surgeon, surgically removing, without anesthesia, the breast of Madame d'Arblay because of cancer in 1811. The barbarity of the procedure was chilling. He found reference to the use of powder of arsenious acid and muriate of morphia being spread over skin ulcerations when the tumor caused dermal breakdown, the medication said to cause eschar formation and drying of the wound, but Del did not have this complaint. Gung Pi recommended and provided *Shu-ti-huang*, the steamed roots of a plant with hairy leaves, red flowers and large, juicy roots, that he claimed was effective in wasting diseases. Nothing helped, and Daniel finally treated Del's increasing pain only with gradually larger and larger doses of laudanum.

Her discomfort, continuing weight loss and increasing weakness finally necessitated the closing of Del's Kitchen. Cordelia seemed to feel this event as a more cruel blow than her actual physical deterioration. The former boarders began bringing daily bouquets of wild flowers and their loyal solicitude was very touching to both of the Todds.

On any clear night, Daniel and Del stood outside their cabin and used the spreading heavens above as the venue for a communion of their souls. Speculation filled their conversations—about the limits of space, about the force that had created it, about whether or not their immortal future might lead them to its farthest reaches, about the manner in which either of them

246

might have earned such a future if it existed—endless questions that they had pondered so many times in the past. They found no answers, of course, but partly as a result of their mutual questioning, the bonds of their love grew and matured as though the two of them had spent a lifetime together.

Cordelia continued to maintain her optimism. Although he struggled to conceal it, Daniel grew ever more despondent. The thought of losing this lovely creature for whom he had searched all of his life was agonizing. Whether he thought as a doctor or as a husband, he felt utterly impotent. Why, oh why, his soul screamed its anguish, doesn't Medicine have the treatments for diseases such as this?

- - -

"I don't think the laudanum is working anymore, Daniel," Cordelia announced one day in late July. "My back pain seems to travel all the way around my chest now. There is no position I can assume either in bed or a chair that relieves it. Is this a new batch of medicine that you have prepared?"

"No, it is the same that you were taking a week ago." In his mind's eye he could visualize invasion by the tumor into the space between the ribs of her chest wall and increasing involvement of the intercostal nerves. "I have resisted increasing your dose of drug because I didn't suppose you wanted to sleep all of the time. We'll give you as much as you need, though. Do you want some now?" he asked.

"Yes. I think I really do need it," she replied.

Daniel measured out nearly twice as much as he usually gave her and she drank it down. They sat, silently holding hands, and within ten minutes, her head slumped over on her shoulder. Daniel lifted her onto the bed. Every time he did this, her frail body seemed lighter. It was as though the cancer was simply devouring her day by day. Her abdomen was becoming distended with accumulated fluid; both she and Daniel were conscious of the rapidly progressive alteration of her body that once had been so beautifully proportioned, so goddess-like, and was now so wasted.

In the past, Todd had encouraged patients to drop in at their leisure; he wished to be available at any hour of the day or night. More and more now, except for emergencies, he had been restricting his office hours to a brief period in the afternoon so that he could devote most of his time to the care of Cordelia. Gung Pi had become a daily visitor and, when sleep overtook her, the two men quietly discussed Del's case and any new symptoms. They each diligently searched their minds for *any* drug or procedure that might be of help. Todd had long since stopped any bloodletting because his wife was becoming so weak.

One day, Gung Pi handed Todd a small box containing a black pill the size of a large bean. It was soft and doughy and when Todd smelled of it, he quickly identified it as opium.

"My countrymen," the oriental doctor said, "take the 'black pill' themselves when life loses its appeal or solicitously give it to a friend when hope no longer exists and nothing but suffering remains." He bowed and took his leave without another word.

Daniel stared at the box in his hand and had to admit that this thought had crossed his mind more than once. He always convinced himself, though, that Del's suffering was not so great but that every breath of what life remained should be treasured. Was this selfishness on his part? He didn't think so; Del seemed to draw strength and hope from him. Daniel cast the small wooden box into the smoldering fire on the hearth. He went over to the bed and stroked the hair of his slumbering wife's head and, with tears streaming, he kissed her.

- - -

It was August 3rd and Del was sleeping most of the time now because of the ever-increasing amounts of laudanum she needed for control of her pain. The breast tissue had ulcerated over the enlarging tumor and Todd employed the arsenious acid and muriate of morphia mixture that he had read about. He was by her side day and night.

A great clamor arose down in Jacksonville's main street and Daniel went to the door to see if he could detect the cause. A milling crowd was rushing up the hill to the north, and a stranger was running up the trail to Todd's cabin. "Cave-in!" he shouted. "Cave-in!"

He arrived so out of breath that he gasped several times very deeply before he could talk again. "Cave-in up at Warp Taylor's mineshaft an' Warp's trapped. Ya gotta come, Doc." The stranger bent over and braced his hands on his knees while he caught his breath.

Todd didn't want to leave Del, but he couldn't refuse to go and help. He grabbed his bag and followed the stranger on a trail to the north. When they arrived at the mouth of a mine tunnel, the stranger shouted, "Doc's here. Let us through! Make way there! Get the hell outta the way."

Some of the crowd retreated out of the tunnel, and Todd muscled his way on through. Someone shoved a lighted coal oil lantern in his hand and led him along the shaft into the depths of the mountain. The ceiling of the tunnel dripped water and puddles of liquid mud covered the floor on either side of the metal tracks. Todd was no miner, but it seemed to him that the supporting timbers lining either side, and the ones that held up the ceiling were uncomfortably scarce and insubstantial. An apprehensive shudder passed through him. He hated caves and tunnels.

They approached a small cluster of men who were crouched on their knees; the tunnel ended in the cave-in just beyond them. At a word from his guide, they crowded to one side and Todd could see the trunk of a man projecting from beneath the jumble of rock and timber. The man was conscious and groaning in his pain.

"His right leg is caught an' crushed under them rocks, Doc," Cletus Richards announced. Todd recognized Richards as last year's snakebite injury. "We're 'fraid the whole shiteree'll give way if we move 'nuff rock to free him."

Todd bent over the patient and tried to illuminate the scene as well as he could with the feeble light of his lantern. The dirt around the left leg had been scratched aside and that limb was free. The right was horribly crushed between a ceiling timber and rock; obviously, it was not salvageable below the knee. The course of treatment seemed obvious.

"Can you hear me, Warp?" Todd asked of the patient. "Hang on there, man. We're going to get you out of here, but your lower leg is too crushed to save. I'm going to have to take the lower part of it off in order to free you. Don't worry, we'll be relieving that pain in just a little while."

Todd patted the man's shoulder and then announced to the crowd, "I'll have to go back to my cabin and get some instruments. I'll be right back. In the meantime, why don't all but two or three of you go on outside before more of this tunnel caves in. See if you can find several more lanterns." He rose and forced his way through the cluster of men. "I'll be right back," he repeated.

At the mine entrance, Todd quickly reported the situation to the crowd and then hurried over to his cabin. Del was asleep, but she felt feverish to his touch so he removed all of her covers except for the sheet.

He got some cloth for bandaging and inspected the wooden case of amputation instruments; it contained everything he needed. He placed those things in a box along with a bottle of alcohol. He reached for the nearly full bottle of laudanum that was at Del's bedside but decided that drug would be too slow in taking effect so obtained, instead, a treasured can of ether from his cabinet.

Todd was so preoccupied by his concern for Del that he was well on his way back toward the mine before the realization settled into his cluttered mind that he couldn't use explosive ether there in that confined space with only lanterns for light. He dropped the medical supplies and rushed back to his cabin. He got the last bottle of laudanum from his medical cupboard so he could leave Del's by her bedside and sprinted back along the path. Recovering the other supplies, he rushed to the mine.

More miners had gathered at the tunnel entrance, but they parted to let him through. He hurried along the tunnel and, at its abrupt end, found the things as he had requested. The dank blackness of the mine seemed simply to absorb the light of the three lanterns and left little to illuminate the scene. The shadows of the men who had remained with their injured comrade were swallowed and lost in the surrounding darkness. An ominous groan of timbers lent urgency to quick action.

Todd knelt beside the patient and explained, "Warp, I can't put you to sleep to do this operation. What would do that would also cause these lanterns to explode. Drink a big charge of this liquid," he said, uncorking the laudanum, "and it will take the edge off." The patient nodded and struggled to swallow the liquid in his awkward position. He choked a bit as he drank and coughed before he settled back. Todd would have waited at least a quarter of an hour for the drug to have more effect, but a groaning timber back toward the tunnel mouth reminded them all of the impending danger of their situation.

Todd asked, "Are you ready?" Warp Taylor's eyes were closed, but he was conscious and nodded. Cletus Richards knelt at Taylor's head and held Warp's arms firmly, as instructed. Todd cut and removed the pantleg and flannel underwear all the way from Taylor's crotch down to where the leg disappeared into the debris and then poured alcohol over the limb. He felt the man go rigid in anticipation and would rather have done anything other than what he was about to do. He couldn't suppress the image of the thrashing of Captain Corbet on the *Ellie Mae* so long ago when he performed that amputation.

"Are you all right?" he asked of Richards, who nodded as he tightened his grip.

Todd applied the tourniquet tightly on the thigh and made quick work of amputating the leg right at the knee. Warp bucked and twisted. His screams were pitiful until he mercifully lost consciousness. Todd felt like a carpenter in doing an amputation, especially when it came to sawing through bone, and he was thankful that was unnecessary here since he had operated right at the knee joint. Fortunately, he had developed greater skill in the operation since his *Ellie Mae* days, and he was finished in just several minutes.

The timbers groaned again so ominously that he hurriedly wrapped cloth around the stump and, without removing the tourniquet, sharply ordered "Get him out of here! Quickly!"

The three men who had remained had all turned their heads away from the sight of the gory operation. They sprang into action now and hurriedly carried the patient toward the mine entrance. Todd gathered up his instruments and had to help Richards, by now all but overcome by the sight he had witnessed. They all fled in a rush for safety and were almost out of the tunnel when they heard more of the shaft collapse behind them.

Spurred onward by this danger, they rushed out into the sunlight. A shaken Richards sat down and sucked in great gulps of the fresh air. Todd knelt by his patient, felt his pulse and then tied off vessels so he could remove the tourniquet and properly bandage the stump. Warp Taylor's friends offered to take the patient, who by now was thoroughly obtunded from the laudanum, to his tent. Todd said he would meet them there after he went back to his cabin and checked on his wife.

- - -

The cabin was hot and, as soon as he entered, he saw that Cordelia lay sprawled on top of her sheets but was fast asleep. He put his instruments on the desk and decided he would wash and dry them after he had again visited Taylor. Then, the bottle of laudanum caught his eye because he noted that it was no longer where he had left it. Del must have been awakened by the heat and took more for her pain, he thought. Then his breath caught in his throat! The bottle of laudanum, which had been almost full, was now nearly empty!

"Oh, my God," he screamed and rushed to his wife's side. She still breathed but in a very shallow and infrequent manner. She had *poisoned* herself with this immense dose of the drug and her respirations would just gradually diminish until they stopped entirely. He quickly draped her on her stomach over the side of the bed and introduced a tongue blade into her mouth in order to make her vomit, but she was too obtunded even to respond. To compensate for this shutting down of her respiratory system, he pumped and pushed on her back to simulate breathing, but finally he could feel no pulse at all. Daniel simply sat on the edge of the bed, holding her in his arms, and rocked back and forth in his misery.

"We didn't even have a final goodbye," he sobbed softly.

Stroking her beautiful hair, Daniel thought back and tried to remember if he had ever intimated to Del that laudanum, in excess, could have this fatal effect. He was certain that he had not, but Cordelia had been a very intelligent woman and undoubtedly had divined that fact on her own. He held her away from him and looked into her face; how animated and full of life it had been just such short, short weeks ago. The eyes were closed and the mouth slightly agape. He kissed her and held her close again. His beloved Cordelia was dead; as dead as he himself now felt.

For a long moment he was tempted to consume a bottle of laudanum also and join her in death, but then he thought that, in case there was no hereafter, she would live now only in his memory and then only as long as he was alive to remember her.

"Oh, Cordelia, my dearest—I shall never, never, *never* forget you." He again broke out into sobs.

He laid her out on the bed as though she was just sleeping and straightened the covers over her. He crossed her arms over her chest and taking several of the wild flowers that he picked daily to put at her bedside, placed those in her hands over her breasts. Smoothing her hair into place, he wanted only to remain there with her but knew that he must go down to check on Taylor. A crushed and utterly despondent man then picked his way down to the tent of Warp Taylor.

His patient had regained consciousness but was reliving the emotional trauma of the cave-in and thrashing about almost beyond control. Todd gave him another stiff dose of laudanum but had to remain with him for well over an hour. The man settled into a subdued, drugged state and Todd explained in detail to Warp's friends what Taylor could expect in the future.

"I'll keep checking on him later on," he promised and left.

The afternoon sun was dipping into the western treetops, but Daniel felt he had to detour down into town to request that Charlie Stevens, the local carpenter/undertaker, make a suitable coffin tomorrow for Cordelia. Finally, almost dreading to climb up to his cabin and once again witness the sight that awaited him there, he resolutely turned his steps homeward.

Cordelia looked so peaceful and serene as she lay there on the bed that he felt a twinge of guilt that he had denied her this tranquility and freedom from pain when she apparently wanted it so badly. He kissed her lightly on the cheek and then set a shaded lamp to burning at the head of her bed. He sat for hours and simply absorbed their togetherness because he knew that all too soon she would physically be taken from him forever. Reliving every minute that he could remember of their time together, he tried to reinforce and burn them into his brain so indelibly that they would never fade.

When he realized that night had settled on the community, he got up and walked outside. The stars were blinking into view in a cloudless sky, and he thought back to the way he and Del had enjoyed this great vastness of space on so many occasions. It seemed to him that the universe about him, so limitless in its extent, was the epitome of the powerful bonding force between Cordelia and him. It seemed strange to him that such a space, so imponderable in its limits and complexities, should be the dominant symbol in his mind of the love that existed between them, but it was. They had speculated about it on so many occasions that he vowed this was where he would always come to commune with her in his loneliness.

While she was still here, though, he would remain as close to her as possible. He went back inside and lay down at Cordelia's side.

CHAPTER THIRTY-THREE

Every weary hour of the remaining days and nights of summer and even those of early fall seemed endless, and the passage of time did nothing to diminish Daniel's grief. The soul-wrenching image of his beloved Cordelia's burial on that hillside slope of Jacksonville's new cemetery persisted and became an obsession. Even the hollow sound of each shovelful of earth drumming onto her coffin as the grave was closed continued to echo in his brain. This pain was like nothing he had ever experienced in his life, not even with the death of his mother so many years ago.

He did see patients, hoping that activity would divert his thoughts, but he went about his work mechanically and felt guilty that he could muster no empathy for the pain or suffering of his patients. Todd even left for several weeks and traveled to Sacramento, trying to find some solace in Simon's company and counsel. Nothing helped. It seemed to him that grief was a huge, empty hole that had suddenly developed in his life and the only two things that would ever diminish it were the limits of his memory and those of his love. His memory was extremely keen and his love for Cordelia had been and still was boundless. The hole remained unchanged, a gaping and miserable chasm.

Simon had urged him to accept Cordelia's death as another milestone in his life; certainly not to forget her but to put that experience behind him and find some peace of mind through establishing, if not a religious belief in God, at least a philosophy of life and death—one that was complete and meaningful to him, a type of personal theology that answered his intellectual and emotional needs. To that end, the good reverend had almost emptied his library, sending along with the departing Todd books on the teachings of Socrates and several volumes about world religions. Daniel had not been moved to open even one of those since returning to Jacksonville.

For him, life simply flowed onward. He was like a ship without anchor or bearing, drifting on the tide, day after tiresome, purposeless, endless, lonely day.

- - -

"Doc, ya gotta come. I think Asa's got the pox," the stranger said as he burst through the cabin door.

Todd, roused from napping in his chair, scratched at his tousled hair and unkempt beard. It took an instant to clear his head. "Asa? Asa who?" he asked.

"Sorry. Asa Clark. I'm Stu Reynolds an' Asa's my pardner. We only come to town a week ago, or so. Come up from on down Sonoma way. Asa's been feelin' poorly an' pukin' fer some time but just last night started gettin' spots on him. They was lots o' smallpox down in Sonoma an' I'm hopin' this ain't that, but I'm rightly feared," Reynolds blurted out.

"Let me get my bag," Todd replied and followed the man back out of the door with an overweight Champ tagging along close behind. A cold fall wind whipped his clothes, and he wished he had donned a coat before venturing out. The Reynolds' tent was way up the creek at the far end of town and when they got there, the stench of sickness hung in the stale air inside. Stu lit a lantern and stood aside for Todd to work.

The patient was sweating in spite of the cold. Todd drew back the blanket and noted the red petechiae on the man's face and wrists. On closer inspection, he saw that several of these blotches even had a tiny serous-filled blister in the center. He asked if there had been any back pain, nausea or vomiting. The patient didn't answer, but Reynolds volunteered, "Yeah. He had all them things an' runnin' off of his guts, too."

Daniel unbuttoned the man's underwear but could find no other spots. So far, nothing but the face and wrists were involved. He held the lamp so he could inspect inside of the patient's mouth and could see no lesions on the tongue or pharynx. No doubt about it; this was the early eruptive phase of smallpox. He motioned Reynolds out of the tent with a nod of his head.

"I'm certain that you are right, Mr. Reynolds, your friend has smallpox. Do you know if he ever had a vaccination in the past?" he asked.

"Not as I know 'bout," Reynolds replied. "We been together these past two year. He ne'er mentioned it."

"It's very early in his course. We'll know over the next several days how dangerous this is for him, but he could even die. You know that, don't you?"

"Yeah. Lots of 'em 'crossed over the bar' down Sonoma way. Can ya help him, Doc?" the partner pleaded.

"I'm going to leave a purgative powder for you to give him—calomel and emetic tartar—I want you to give him this with all of the water he will drink," Todd replied. "I'm concerned about you, also. You've been with him through all of this early period so there's no point in trying to separate you now. The best thing is for you to take care of him but to keep your contact with everybody else in town to the absolute minimum." Todd looked closely at the sick man's partner and asked, "Can you do that? Perhaps I should quarantine this tent. but I don't want to alarm the town. Let's just keep it quiet for now, but you will need to stay away from everybody else."

"Yep. I'd do 'most anythin' for Asa. We partnered up two year ago an' he's a good 'un," Reynolds replied. "We got beans an' bacon. I'll jus' stay close by him here."

All the while that Todd was preparing the powders for the patient, he was thinking about the possibility of inoculating other Jacksonville residents. Ever since Jenner had introduced cow pox as the medium to be used in vaccinations a half-century ago, it had become almost universal. He himself had been vaccinated in that manner in Boston, but Todd knew that the actual serous fluid from small pox lesions themselves had been used for many decades in Turkey and in England before Jenner. Of course, so many patients died as the result of that procedure that it had been discontinued. Since he had no cow pox serum and he was very possibly facing a serious outbreak here, Todd wondered if he would have to resort to the older method if it turned out that he had no other choice. He couldn't imagine that he would become that desperate.

On the way back to his cabin, he detoured to Gung Pi's place to discuss the problem with him. The Oriental informed him that in the past, earlier Chinese doctors had inserted fabric moistened with the variolous matter from pox into a nostril in an attempt to produce a milder form of the disease in those they were trying to protect but had discontinued the practice there also because of disastrous results. Gung Pi had nothing more to offer that Todd felt was worthwhile, or that he didn't already know about. Followed by his faithful Champ, he went home to pick at his worries throughout the night.

- - -

Concern about a possible impending epidemic diverted Daniel's thoughts from Cordelia for at least a part of the many hours of darkness. He did find some solace in this new reminder of how many, many ills can afflict the human body, and what a miracle it is that *anybody* survives as long as most do. Cordelia's death became not the isolated and unique occurrence as it had seemed in his mind for so long. Such thoughts did not ease the emptiness that was always with him, though.

When he awoke in the morning, he hastily prepared a breakfast of mush for himself and Champ and was anxious to make the house call on his new patient to check his progress. He thought it strange for a case of smallpox to be coming on this late in the fall; most physicians considered its cause, like most of the other fevers, to be related to some state of the atmosphere, although Todd was certain that a few victims undoubtedly contracted it due to a vitiated condition of the humors of the body. Of course, this pair of miners had come up from Sonoma—different area, different atmosphere—so perhaps the disease would affect only the two of them and not spread. Todd fully expected Stu Reynolds to come down with it because of his prolonged contact with his partner, but perhaps nobody else in Jacksonville would contract smallpox. Again, he considered the possibility of vaccinating Reynolds with some of the serum from one of Clark's lesions but, more than likely, that would only double the number of smallpox patients to two instead of one and make it just that much more likely to spread.

Daniel ruminated on these thoughts all the way through town on his way to the Clark tent. The night had been cold and frost crunched under his feet as he walked through patches of grass. Fog shrouded the creek below, but some hardy miners were already at work on their claims. Jacksonville's robust boomtown days seemed to have ended as the placer claims gradually pinched out and many miners either just moved on to work new digs in the northeastern part of Oregon Territory or had gone to work as day laborers in one of the scattered shaft mines that now penetrated the earth around the town.

Smoke issued from the stubby chimney of the sheepherder stove in Clark's tent so he knew that Reynolds was awake. Todd hoped against hope that Clark's lesions would still be limited just to his face and wrists; with only a few papules developing, the disease could be classified as being of the *distinct* variety rather than the *confluent* and, therefore, more likely to be mild.

He called to Reynolds, "Stu. Stu, it's Dr. Todd. May I come in?"

Reynolds stuck his head out through the tent flap and said, "Oh God, I'm glad you're here, Doc. Ol' Asa's a lot worse, certain sure. That medicine you give him las' night made him shit himself silly an' he's e'en been passin' some blood. I think he's a lot worse, Doc."

Disappointed, Todd entered the little tent. The stove had heated it warmer than necessary and, as a consequence, Clark had thrown off most of his covers. He just lay there, moaning in a pitiful fashion. His lesions had greatly increased in number and as Todd unbuttoned the man's underwear so he could look at his trunk, he saw that the early papules on Clark's chest and belly were almost confluent. The skin there had taken on a nearly uniform red and blotchy appearance and was flaming hot.

"When did you men leave Sonoma?" Todd asked.

"It'll be two weeks come next Sunday," Reynolds replied. "We catched us a ride with a freighter an' made it all the way up at a right smart pace."

So, he could even be into the maturation phase of the disease, Todd thought to himself, while reviewing in his mind the incubation period of smallpox as established by Sydenham.

"Why don't you make him some tea?" he said to Reynolds as he stepped outside of the tent to think.

This confluence of lesions was a bad sign. So was the restlessness and moaning, as was the mounting fever. Todd knew that most of the patients who died in the first week of the disease did so because of "malignant fever." Although he was no great proponent of bleeding, it was certainly the recommended treatment, so he went back inside and opened his bag.

"I'm going to remove some blood," he announced to Reynolds and to the patient, "to reduce some of the phlogistic properties of your disease."

He opened a vein in Asa's left arm and removed a full twelve ounces of blood. Then he said, "I'm going to leave some senna with you, a different aperient from what I gave you last night, and we'll see how you are by this evening."

To Reynolds, he said, "With this fever, you should give him all of the water or tea that he will drink. All right?"

Todd retreated from the tent, grateful that there had been no lesions in the patient's mouth to complicate the course.

Still wishing to keep the case of smallpox a secret, he returned to his cabin, followed by the faithful Champ. Throughout the day, Todd treated minor cases of ague, a lacerated shin from an axe wound, and a case of gonorrhea, although he had no idea where the miner might have contracted the disease; no new "lady of the evening" had arrived in town for several months. After supper, he returned to the Clark tent.

To his dismay, he found lesions forming in the patient's mouth and throat. In his mind's eye, Todd could already picture a purulent, gray mass of secretions coagulating into a thick, obstructing membrane, very similar to that found in Diphtheria, and that could close off the man's larynx, thereby choking him to death. He knew that was the most common cause of smallpox death in the second week of the disease, but it seemed too early for it to be developing in this case. His hopes for Clark's survival plummeted. Should he take some serum from one of these lesions and inoculate Reynolds? He decided against it.

"I'm going to have to quarantine both of you," he finally said to Clark's partner. "You understand, it is to keep this disease away from the rest of the town."

"Yeah, we saw a lot of that down Sonoma way," Reynolds said, making Todd's stern position easier for him to maintain. "Kind'a like havin' leprosy, ain't it, Doc?" the man observed.

"In that respect, yes, and I'm sorry but it's very necessary. I'll look in on Asa in the morning. I'm going to leave some laudanum with you to give him tonight in order to help him sleep better," Todd added. Again, he retreated into the night, feeling guilty that he was not making more progress in this case. He walked on down to the Nugget Saloon and downed a shot of rye whiskey before he made his announcement.

"Men, listen to me!" he shouted over the discordant sounds of the out-of-tune piano. He had to repeat his shout again but when the noise diminished, he announced, "Men, we have a case of smallpox in town." A loud murmur erupted among the crowd. "Quiet men," Todd continued. "It apparently has come up from Sonoma, and we hope that it will not spread to the rest of Jacksonville. After all, it's not the season for this sort of disease to strike. I have quarantined the patient and his partner."

In an effort to calm the men's fears, Todd said, "From the best information we have in Medicine, the disease is probably caused by the season or by a specific poison or contagion that spreads from the blood. As I said, this patient's tent is quarantined and it's now autumn, so we probably have nothing to worry about from its spreading to the rest of the town, but I thought that I should tell you about its presence."

A voice piped up, "You been with him, ain't ya, Doc? Why ain't you spreadin' it to all of us right now?"

Todd replied, "As I said, it's fall but you are absolutely right and so keep away from me, also. And I have to emphasize this, if you should start having ague, or belly cramps, or fevers, or red blotches on your skin, contact me right away so we can start treatment on you at the earliest possible moment. I'll be in my cabin."

He downed the second shot of rye that stood on the bar in front of him and departed the saloon.

- - -

Reynolds contracted the disease within the week and Clark died on the twelfth day. Reynolds' malignant fever killed him one day later. Todd and Gung Pi, whose pock-marked face testified to his having been infected with smallpox earlier in life and having survived it, worked nearly around the clock every day caring for some 270 patients over the next five weeks. It seemed as though it was the onset of another severe winter that put an end to the epidemic. The two doctors nearly collapsed from their chronic fatigue but could take only limited satisfaction in the waning of the epidemic because eighty-four men, six children and three women had died during the deadly outbreak. They had quarantined, burned clothing and bedding, bled and purged patients and even resorted to Gung Pi's assorted Oriental remedies which included *Tung-kuei-tze*, an extract of seeds resembling those of the elm, *Reng-chung-pei*, a dried substance obtained from urine and mixed with ginseng, and *Peng-sha*, the white salt of borax. Nothing had been completely successful and so nothing helped those ninety-three who now lay in the Jacksonville cemetery.

In his exhaustion, Todd was humbled, and the seemingly endless but deadly experience of the epidemic only added to his resolve to settle in his own mind his questions about the meaning of life and death. Why would a Creator give Cordelia to him and then take her away so cruelly and so quickly; why give these men and women and children life and then snatch it all away from them in their prime? He could see no logic to or any explanation for a Creator who would be such an intelligent and gracious giver of life but then seem to take it away so capriciously. In the end, he merely retreated to the sanctuary of his cabin and collapsed on his bed, attended by the recently much-ignored and hungry Champ who nestled in his arms. Daniel would think about his personal theology on another day.

CHAPTER THIRTY-FOUR

1856

Over the course of the snowbound winter months and interspersed between a few birthings, a dozen cases of pneumonia, countless cases of piles, ague, strained backs, pip, gleet, and the occasional shooting or knifing, Daniel finally managed to read some of Simon's books on religion. He studied Judaism more than the others, probably because he was familiar with much of its history through his knowledge of the Old Testament upon which he had been drilled endlessly during his childhood.

He knew that Abraham claimed God gave the land of Judah, or Israel, to "His People" as described in the Jewish Bible. He remembered learning that this writing, considered so sacred by the Jews, was contained in the *Torah*, the first five books of Moses that begin with creation and end with the death of Moses himself; the *Nevi'im*, that describes the period from Israel's settlement in Canaan after Moses' death to the destruction of the first Temple by the Babylonians, thought to be in 586 B.C.; and the *Ketuvim*, which consisted of books of wisdom, literature, poetry and history. Todd also read the books of the Maccabees about the clashes of Hellenistic rulers of Judea and the Jews; the *Midriash*, a commentary on the *Torah*; the *Mishnah*, the central legal text of rabbinic Judaism on religious and social behavior; and the *Talmud*, an embodiment of 300 years of rabbinic learning. He even read Maimonides' formulation of Judaism's principles which he outlined as:

1. The existence of God.
2. God's unity.
3. God having no corporeal aspect.
4. God being eternal.
5. That God alone should be worshipped.

6. One's requirement to believe in prophecy.
7. That Moses was the greatest prophet.
8. Belief in all of the Torah (the Pentateuch).
9. That the Torah will not be changed or superseded.
10. That God knows the actions of man.
11. That God rewards those who keep to the Torah and punishes those who transgress.
12. The belief that the Messiah will come.
13. A belief in the resurrection of the dead.

He found that much of this, and even Mohammedanism as described in the Quran which he finally managed to read, were both similar to Christianity in many important aspects. He was not finding enlightenment and answers that satisfied him.

They all conceive of God as a person who can do anything, knows everything, is good and created the world around us. In Todd's and Cordelia's eyes, this God created even the endless heavens they enjoyed so much contemplating. All of these religions believed Him to be interested in humans, intricately involved in our affairs, rewarding us for good behavior and responsive to our prayers, our sacrifices, our rituals. Todd pondered, what if He really is totally indifferent to humans and cares more about the welfare and eternal life of mosquitoes or earthworms. Supposing there are things this Creator is unable to perform or that He is sometimes wrong, sometimes embarks on efforts that just don't work out. Supposing all of those stars in the heavens were creations of that sort and were mistakes. Supposing there are other worlds out there that are perfect and more satisfactory to Him—that our world is one of those mistaken creations and will be left to molder and wink out on its own. Perhaps this Creator doesn't care one whit about what happens here.

Surely, Todd thought, wiser men than I have had these same thoughts and doubts. Why aren't there as many volumes written about those doubts and possibilities as I have been reading these past months? Why do we have to accept these beliefs on faith and not have tangible proofs about their concepts?

Questions, questions, questions. He was not any closer to finding an answer to the meaning of life than he had ever been.

- - -

One afternoon, a man who was rolling from side to side and writhing in agony was brought to him in a wheelbarrow, as so many seemed to be transported. The bumpy ride through the patches of late snow did little to relieve his discomfort.

"He couldn't poke his rupture back in," his companions said. "Kin ye he'p him?"

Sure enough, once Todd got the patient into his cabin, laid him down on the cot and removed enough of his clothing so he could examine him, he could see that an angry, inflamed and swollen mass filled the right side of his scrotum. Before Todd could proceed further, the man began to retch and then vomited into a basin that Todd held for him.

"How long has this been going on?" Todd asked the two men accompanying the patient.

"We was lifting some timbers this mornin' an' it popped out, I guess," was the reply. "He laid down an' tried to poke it back in, but couldn't. He rested fer an hour or so, but it din't change an' purty soon he started pukin'."

Several hours, Todd thought. The bowel might still be viable. I'll try to reduce this strangulation. He could picture the small intestine, held tightly by the small ring of aponeurosis of the inguinal canal through which it had slipped out of the peritoneal cavity and down into the scrotum; no doubt the blood vessels were being throttled to cause this swelling and the strangulation that was causing the vomiting. All of which would eventually cause the bowel to become necrotic. If he could not reduce the hernia one way or another, the bowel would simply die and, eventually, so would the patient. Todd shuddered at the thought of having to operate to relieve this strangulation. It would mean entering the peritoneal cavity.

He dragged his bed, with its sturdy headboard and footboard, into the main room from the adjoining lean-to and said, "You men help me get him onto this."

The move was painful for the patient, but when the discomfort subsided, Todd got a thin rope and tied the man's feet to the footboard. Then he and the companions of the patient moved the desk over and placed it under the foot of the bed so that it and the body were tipped, head down, at an angle of about forty degrees. The semi-suspended man voiced his bewilderment, but it was no less than that of his companions when Todd fetched a pan full of snow from outside and packed it around the swollen scrotum.

"What in hell ye doin', Doc?" the man screamed at this new addition to his discomfort and tried to wriggle away from the frigid poultice.

"Stop it," Todd ordered sternly. "If we don't get that swelling down, you may die. Do you understand?"

The man began to shiver and retched again but did not vomit. He panted because it was difficult to breathe in this position, but his scaphoid abdomen was testimony to the reduced pressure in his belly. "God! This is pure misery, Doc," he wailed.

Todd had to replenish the snow several times because of its melting and the shaking of the patient's body, but within a quarter hour, the swelling began to diminish. With gentle pressure and great care, Todd slowly began to work the distended intestine up and out of the scrotal sac. Finally, the last of it disappeared up into the abdominal cavity, and Todd breathed a sigh of relief. He could only hope that the blood supply to that section of bowel had not been compromised for too long or that, in addition, his manipulation had not damaged it too greatly. Only time will tell, he thought.

"I'm going to keep you here for the rest of the day and tonight to keep an eye on you and then tomorrow, we'll try to fashion a truss for you so this doesn't happen again. What's your name, by the way?" Todd asked.

"Charlie Phipps, Doc. Thank ye. But, by God, ye know how to torture a man, certain sure," was the reply. "Cain't ye flatten me out some now, Doc?" Todd obliged, embarrassed that he had not already done that. He was positive that Charlie's friends would spread tales of this bizarre treatment far and wide. Oh well, he thought, it turned out all right. I hope!

– – –

For months after Cordelia's death, Todd went to her graveside daily to converse with her. He knew this seemed immature and carried on his conversation silently and in thought only if any other person were within earshot. He was fully aware of the fact that no part of her could hear him, and he was quite certain that not even her soul could be aware of his words. Still, under that patch of dirt lay the only earthly part of the beautiful person who had been the most precious and treasured experience of his entire life.

Because, throughout their time together, they had such great satisfaction in looking at and speculating about the significance of the universe that stretched endlessly above them, Daniel gradually began to commune with his soul mate only under those high arching heavens, although he still visited her grave frequently. Somehow, he grew to feel that he was closest to her there under the countless stars. Tonight, with brilliant moonlight playing on the clouds of his breath, he quietly discussed his judgment with her of the religions he had studied thus far.

"I'm no scholar, Del. You know that. And I'm probably entirely wrong about these faiths—heaven knows, a lot of men more brilliant than I have pondered endlessly on religions and found great comfort in the various teachings. I can't envision a creator, God or a central intelligence or whatever you want to call it, who would have a "chosen people", as each group seems to think they are, and reward them exclusively. Of course, each group seems to feel compelled to convert everybody else to its belief. What about the rest of humanity who never get the word, if that is true? And, what about all of the other life forms? They have all been created, too. Are they just forgotten by this creator? It's taught in Judaism that God rewards those who keep to the teachings of the Torah and punish all of those who transgress.

"What about the countless people who have never even heard of the Torah? Are they to be simply forgotten when and if the resurrection of the dead occurs—if there is such a thing? I'm certain, Del, that if anybody ever gets resurrected and finds a reward in some later life, it will be you. There was never a more beautiful spirit than yours; I'm sure you have never read many of the things I have been studying. I'm afraid I have to find other answers to my puzzlement of the how, who, and why of all of this.

"Sometimes I can't help but believe that Man has conjured up his many beliefs and religions simply because he can't accept the possibility that this life—this here and now—is all there is going to be, and that there really isn't any grand purpose to it all. I'd hate to think that and so I'm going to keep on searching and studying to find a philosophy that is meaningful and credible to me.

"Wherever you are, Del my dear, it's my prayer that you can hear me and somehow guide my thoughts. Lord knows, my thoughts are almost entirely with you many hours of each day, anyway. Goodnight, my love."

When Todd grew silent, Champ, who had been quietly sitting on his haunches, stood up and rubbed against his master's leg. A rumble sounded deep in his throat; perhaps an affirmation of Todd's thoughts, but perhaps nothing more than a complaint about the penetrating cold. The two of them moved across the creek and up the hill to the warmth of the cabin.

CHAPTER THIRTY-FIVE

Spring had come but the rains continued unabated, as though they were determined to wash every vestige of Oregon Territory down the mountain and out into the sea. Heavy clouds hung low over the canyon and continued to vent tons of water that surged down the creek bed in a plunging torrent. The deluge didn't affect the major placer claims now worked by giant monitors; the small claims had long-since failed to yield more than a rare flake of the gold and mostly had been abandoned. The shafts of the deep mines were being sunk deeper and deeper into the mountain in the optimistic belief they might one day encounter the "Mother Lode" that everyone hoped and even a few dogmatically, but prayerfully, predicted now lay only a few feet beyond tunnel's end. For some, this often-voiced prediction was all too barren and they and many placer miners had drifted away from Jacksonville, broken and destitute. Some stayed but many businesses that once had flourished failed, claims were abandoned, and cabins were left to molder in the decay of a failing boom. Even Todd wondered if he should move on to some area with greater potential, but there were still people here, and they still needed medical care.

He stood, staring out of the front window of his cabin, observing the destructive flood of Jackson Creek down below. Perhaps this scourge of the canyon might uncover new deposits of gold, he thought, and might even be the resurrecting force of the town.

Champ lay in front of the fire, chewing the bone left from tonight's elk roast with obvious satisfaction. Todd almost felt guilty because his evening meal had been such a feast; he was certain that many of the other inhabitants of the town had made do with much less. On his way over to his chair in front of the fireplace, he bent and patted the head of his faithful companion. He lit the coal oil lamp and picked up Simon's book of Hawthorne he had chosen for his evening's enjoyment. He also felt guilty that his most recent *Lancet* lay unopened on the bureau against the wall. This copy of the only journal to which he subscribed was already seven months out of date but was his closest tie to modern Medicine. He should be sharpening his medical skills studying its contents but tonight he just wanted to relax and had chosen "The May Pole of Merry Mount" as Hawthorne's story to enjoy. He had read no further than "Bright were the days at Merry Mount, when the May Pole . . ." and there was a knock at his door.

When he opened it, a sodden figure almost seemed to dissolve back into the liquid darkness outside but said, "Doc Todd, my name's Stewart. My missus has reached her time an' she's havin' trouble. Terrible night, I know an' I hate to drag ye out, but can ye come?"

"Of course," Todd replied. "Come in out of the rain."

Daniel donned his oilskin and bent down to pat Champ. He left the lamp burning but said, "Stay here, boy. Lead on, Mr. Stewart." The two men headed back out into the downpour.

They slid and stumbled through the sopping darkness and Todd, familiar though he was with the terrain they were traversing, became lost. Finally, they arrived at a sagging tent, drenched but weakly illuminated inside by a single coal oil lantern. A painful scream greeted them as they entered and was followed by grunts of exhaustion. A wide-eyed and frightened child stood as a sentinel and peered at them from a crib. "Lay back down, Caleb. Mother's all right. The doctor's here," Stewart said.

Todd peeled off his oilskin and went over to the woman. "Mrs. Stewart, I'm Doctor Todd and I'm here to help you." He offered the words in what he hoped was a soothing voice.

"Thank you for coming, Doctor. This one is taking so much longer than Caleb did. I think I'm in trouble," the woman managed to say in a weak and weary voice.

Todd dropped his oilskin on the floor, looked around and seeing a basin and ewer, washed his hands with soap and water. He did not empty the basin. Laying back the covers of the rude bed, he examined the patient. Her belly was hugely distended but she was not having a contraction at the moment. Her water had broken some time ago and the bed was sodden. "Are your pains coming frequently, Mrs. Stewart?"

"Yes. Just every few minutes for the last—oh, I don't know—it seems like hours and hours."

He introduced his hand and examined her. She was dilated about one and a half inches; not fully. Exploring a little farther, he felt the soft tissue of the infant—not the firm resistance of a skull nor even the reassuring outlines of a cranial fontanel, but rather what he was certain was the gluteal cleft between the buttocks. This was a breech presentation! That was why it was taking such a long time and that was the reason the patient's cervix was not more dilated. The head was not there to act as a dilating wedge. Palpating the abdomen externally, he could not feel the baby's spine so it was a sacro-posterior presentation. Todd considered trying external version, the shifting of the infant end for end by gently massaging the outside of the abdomen while pushing the infant up from the inside, but decided against it because the membranes had already ruptured.

He washed his hands again and said, "We will simply have to wait a while longer, Mrs. Stewart. You are just not ready to deliver yet." He made no mention of her breech situation. "Why don't you make a cup of tea for her, Mr. Stewart. I think she might enjoy the comfort of that."

While the husband set about that task, Todd wrung cold water from a cloth and placed it on the patient's forehead. "Just try to relax for a while, my dear," he said. He felt a real solicitude for the patient's comfort and peace of mind, an outlook that was much more comforting and satisfying to the sufferer as well as to himself. Daniel had found that this empathy was much easier for him to render since he had now experienced the personal devastation of Cordelia's death. He was sure he had become a more caring doctor since tragedy had touched him so personally.

They all settled back and waited. With time, the patient's pains gradually became more intense and frequent. When Todd checked her again, he found that the cervix was finally fully dilated. He helped her move so that her hips were at the edge of the bed and asked her husband to hold her legs up in a flexed position. She grunted her misery and writhed with each contraction, one that occurred even while she was trying to move herself. Caleb cried at the commotion.

Neither foot of the infant had appeared at the vaginal opening, so it was a total breech. Todd gingerly introduced a hand and, between contractions, drew down first the right leg and then the left. The feet were slippery so he wrapped them in a remnant of the towel he had used and applied gentle traction.

"Take deep breaths between contractions, Mrs. Stewart, but push when the pain comes again," he told her.

The calves and then finally the thighs of the baby appeared through the vulva.

He reapplied his grasp to the sacrum and eventually the scapulae appeared. Finally, the right axilla emerged, but no arm could be seen. Todd rotated the body until the right shoulder was up and then teased a finger up and over the right shoulder, gradually extracting it and the arm. Next, he did a similar maneuver on the posterior shoulder and the left arm. Now only the head remained inside. He rotated the baby so it lay, belly down on his left hand, gingerly passed his hand forward and performed a Mauriceau's maneuver by inserting his left index finger into the infant's mouth, and then placed the fingers of his right hand over its shoulders and gently pulling, extracted the curving body up over the mother's abdomen until the head was fully delivered. He laid the baby on her belly, milked the blood in the umbilical cord toward the baby, tied off the cord and then cut it. Only then did he pick up the child, a fine little girl, and swat its buttocks. The newborn cried and Todd wrapped her in the towel that her father handed him.

Placing the baby in the panting mother's arms, he jubilantly announced, "You have a beautiful daughter, Mrs. Stewart!" He finally delivered the placenta and began cleaning up the patient and himself with several basins of water.

Stewart was now holding his other child in his arms so the boy could better see his mother and new sister. Todd felt tremendous relief and great satisfaction at the happy sight. Some breech deliveries simply don't go this smoothly. He donned his coat and said to the mother, "Let her nurse, even if your milk hasn't come in yet, Mrs. Stewart. I'll look in on both of you in the morning. You did very well even though this was a harder delivery than most. I'm proud of you."

"Thanks, Doc, until you're better paid. We really appreciate it.," Stewart said as he wrung Todd's hand. "Thank you, so much."

With a nod of the head, Todd inched into his oilskin and went back out into the rain. He was eager, after the worry of performing a breech delivery, to return to the sanctuary of his home. "Thank God it turned out so well," he muttered, hardly realizing that he was reciting an almost silent prayer.

\- - -

The fire was only embers in his fireplace. Still hoping to enjoy Hawthorne's story, Daniel rebuilt the fire and retrieved Champ's elk bone from under the bureau where it had gotten pushed. Before taking up the book, he sat before the fire and gloried in the ecstatic dance of the newly-revived flames.

His thoughts drifted to Cordelia, as they always did in his moments of leisure, and he pondered on what actually constituted love and attachment between two human beings. He was certain that either a man or a woman was more comfortable when accompanied in life by another living being—consider even the human penchant for pets, he thought. He reached down and stroked Champ's head as the dog chewed again on his bone at Todd's side. To have another living being attached to your life in some manner produces a very pleasurable feeling, he decided.

Then, he thought about one's tolerance for one's own self. One puts up with one's own body odors, even those very gross ones associated with bowel activity. No matter how bizarre they might seem, we find excuses for almost all of our own shortcomings, our failures, our appetites. We find reasons to justify, or at least accept, almost all of our own actions. True, a pole star in all of this, is our conscience—perhaps more blunted in some than in others, but nevertheless it is some sort of a beacon in guiding our way of judging our actions. If a man can find another person, so attuned to him that that person will tolerate his imperfections in the same manner that he himself does, will excuse his shortcomings as freely as he forgives his own, will take the same pride in his actions as he does himself, will share his concerns, will care for his needs—physical, mental, pleasurable—all in a manner most gratifying to him, then that is a person who is most desirable. And if he can fulfill a similar role for that other person, then the two of them can truly cherish and love each other. If one person should be a beacon in the eyes of the mate, a vision of perfection whose guiding light one considers superior to one's own conscience and who practices a code that inspires duplication, then that shining individual becomes a soul mate who deserves to be worshipped. Certainly physical beauty helps in the equation, but a man's idea of beauty most likely mirrors himself in some manner.

Had his love for Cordelia been of this basic nature? They had not had many days together in order to test his theory. Perhaps they would not have had that enduring tolerance for each other forever and ever. Discovering a disappointing lack in a mate undoubtedly would explain why some people fall "out of love" with each other once the initial attraction has been dissipated. Daniel couldn't imagine he would ever have fallen out of love with Del. In the past, he had always thought the mention of "the two becoming as one" in marriage ceremonies actually had referred to the physical union of husband and wife, but now he devoutly believed it referred to a couple becoming of *one mind*. He believed, above all else, that he and Cordelia had achieved that. And now, his memories of her were gradually becoming a type of worship.

That realization led him to think about the parallel between love and the need for another person as a life companion and the whole realm of religion.

After all, Daniel thought, we pray that "God" will forgive our transgressions; we hope "He" will accept us for what we are; we look to Him for support, for guidance as a beacon; for forgiveness or reward. We use "His" omniscience to explain the unexplainable. Man seemed to have a basic need for such an all-powerful "companion" and had always created gods to worship.

In his quest for a personal theology, especially after Cordelia's passing, Daniel wondered if he were merely shopping for another acceptable soul mate, a personal "Todd-God" who was in tune with Todd himself.

Such introspection seemed to spark a thirst and Daniel rose to pour himself a half-tumbler of rye whiskey. He rationalized this action by deciding it *had* been an extremely difficult delivery and he needed the whiskey's comforting effect to soothe his troubled mind so he could get a good night's sleep. After a moment's reflection, he went back to the cupboard and filled his tumbler all the way to the brim.

CHAPTER THIRTY-SIX

Throughout the weeks of early summer, Daniel read and reread the one book on Hinduism that Simon had given him and learned about the *sanatana dharma* or the Eternal Religion of the early cultures of the Indus Valley of India. While it taught tolerance for those who practice and worship differently, it was filled with so many Vedic gods and goddesses that he had trouble keeping track of them all. It seemed, above all else, that the followers worshiped *Siva*, the god with tremendous reproductive energies. He read about *sanskrit* and wished that he had some material written in it and that he could read it because that medium seemed to be the official language of Hinduism so perhaps it would allow him to understand these concepts better. Apparently, it was the medium for Buddhism and even was the base for many European languages.

To the best of his understanding, the Aryans had moved from central Asia down into the Indus Valley of the Indian subcontinent around 1500 BC but were quite unorganized pastoral nomads and horsemen rather than agriculturists. They had an oral tradition that they called *Veda* which was memorized by the Aryan priests. It was so secret that it was only now being revealed to Westerners and consisted of hundreds of hymns addressed to scores of Aryan deities. It seemed to be the basis of Hindu belief.

In times past, Daniel would have made every effort to learn more details of this religion that inspired so many millions of people, but somehow he just didn't have the energy or intellectual hunger to search out answers as he once might have done. Spring slowly drifted into summer and finally, autumn approached.

Daniel slept fitfully at night and took no great pleasure in food or in his surroundings. Even the fall colors failed to inspire him. He gradually became unconcerned about his appearance and felt no urge to study his books or to critically analyze the articles in *Lancet*. Instead of meeting each day with enthusiasm, he now faced it with worried anticipation. He became obsessed with agonizing over what problem he might encounter next that he had neither the skill nor knowledge to treat. He went about seeing his patients mechanically, and he was tired and short-tempered. He did continue to treat the great variety of routine medical problems that confronted him, and he dispensed the appropriate nostrums as he always had in the past, but he took no pleasure in even talking to his patients. He couldn't escape the suspicion that they all would have gotten better, even without his care. He simply could find no satisfaction in anything he did. If he were observing this condition in a patient, he would certainly make the diagnosis of Morbid Melancholia and would at least prescribe a change of scene, but his self-analysis was clouded and faulty. Instead, he simply sought what solace he could find in communing with Cordelia while staring into the star-filled sky, or in the company of the faithful Champ, or by consuming increasing quantities of rye whiskey which he justified by convincing himself that it was to help him sleep at night.

- - -

The patient who came to Todd's cabin under his own power, walked gingerly and bent forward at a painfully hesitant pace. He knocked at the door, but it was already halfway open so he looked inside and, since he could see nobody there, shouted "Doc. Doc Todd. I got me a heap o' trouble. Are ye here?"

Todd stirred from his drunken slumber and rose unsteadily, stretched the cramp out of his back and shuffled through the clutter of his cabin toward the door. "I'm here. Come on in." He squinted against the glare caused by the backlighting sun but could not recognize the patient. "Sit down over here," he said as he undraped his shirt from a chair.

The man struggled painfully forward and slumped gingerly into the seat. "I'm Seth Chambers, Doc. I cain't piss a'tall at times an' when I can, it's half blood an' hurts like hell. Ya gotta do somethin', Doc. I cain't stand this much longer."

Todd shuffled toward the back of the room and removed the wooden box of canned goods from his examining table. He blinked his eyes several times to sharpen their sleep-clouded focus and said, "Come over here, Mr . . . Mr. Chamblis. I'll examine you."

"It's Chambers, Doc." The man struggled to his feet and slumped his way painfully to the table. He lay down, hesitating in mid-motion as a stitch of pain caused him to stop. He grimaced and finally settled back in a supine position. "Oh, God! This is pure misery, Doc."

Todd licked his parched lips and stared down at the patient. "Tell me how this came about, Mr. Chambers."

"I've had short bouts o' this in times past—ya know, pain an' blood in my piss—but never nothin' like this. I mean, when I cramp down to go an' cain't, this feels like my guts is tryin' to come out an' then there'll be a few drops o' blood. Oh God—'tis hellacious."

"Do you feel as if you have to go right now?" Todd asked.

"I'd give anythin' if'n I could, Doc."

"I think you probably have a bladder stone, Mr. Chambers," Todd said, trying to suppress a yawn because he knew how unprofessional that would look. "I'm going to pass a catheter into your bladder. That will be uncomfortable, but it will allow you to void, and I can use it as a probe to see if I can feel a stone."

"Do what ya gotta do, Doc, but do it quick."

Todd went to his bag and selected a metal catheter. "Take down your britches, Mr. Chambers," he said as he smeared some lard on the slender tube. Next, he emptied assorted clutter from a basin to have some vessel to receive the urine and turned to the patient. Grasping the man's penis, he introduced the catheter into the meatus and gingerly worked it up the urethra. Maneuvering the nearly right angle through the prostate gland, he finally introduced the brutal instrument into the bladder after overcoming a hard but yielding resistance. The man's agonizing grunts suddenly stopped and then faded into a huge sigh of relief as urine gushed into the basin. "Oh . . . oh God. That's . . . that's wonderful. Thanks, Doc."

Todd's diagnosis had been confirmed. A large stone was present in the bladder and had blocked the upper opening of the urethra, preventing the patient from voiding. Todd knew it had to be quite large because of the severe obstruction it had created and from the feel of it against the upper end of the metal catheter.

"You do have a bladder stone, Mr. Chambers," Todd said, suddenly more alert and regaining a somewhat professional attitude. "If we don't break that up or take it out, you'll simply have this same problem again and again and again. I think it is very large. If we can't crush it, we will have to remove it surgically."

The patient was silent and only moved his head from side to side in his relief as he savored his new-found comfort. Todd had crushed some small bladder stones in the past but never one as large as he suspected this to be. He knew it would be a great risk for the patient if he had to remove it surgically; incising above the pubis led to a very high mortality. Unless Todd was lucky enough to find the bladder quite anterior so he could enter it just above the pubic bone and not intrude into the peritoneal cavity, his patient might not survive. He had never approached the bladder by surgery through the perineum below, but he knew this was reputed to be the safer approach even though it was said to be much bloodier. No procedure that he might undertake would be a pleasant experience either for himself or the patient. The immediacy of the challenge was removed, however, when Chambers thanked him and said he would now be on his way.

"You don't understand, Mr. Chambers," Todd said. "Your bladder stone is only going to get larger and you will have more episodes just like this one or worse. We need to treat this problem now."

"Mebbe ye're right, Doc, but I've got along good so far with this. I'll jest see what some time'll do here. Might not happen again. I had me a helluva lot of beer last night. I'll not do that again," Chambers promised.

When Chambers left, Todd was stimulated to dig through his jumbled and dog-eared copies of *Lancet*. He thought he could remember an article about bladder stones in one of them. He was suddenly repulsed at the slovenly appearance of his quarters and, not immediately finding the journal he sought, set about cleaning and organizing the place. Champ, not moving from his spot under the table where he lay with chin on crossed paws, observed it all through sad and droopy eyes.

- - -

Todd's prediction of recurrence of the bladder stone problem was not long in coming. Chambers came back in the middle of the night, in greater distress even than before and begging for relief. Todd directed the man to lie down on his examining table and, once again, went through the procedure of catheterizing him. As before, the metal catheter encountered a hard obstruction and, after displacing it and releasing a large quantity of bloody urine, Chambers seemed to sink comfortably into the examining table, so relieved was he from his earlier distress. Todd told him to rest before they did anything else and, in this brief respite, he recovered the copy of *Lancet* that he had sought earlier and which he had located in the tidying of his quarters.

He quickly refreshed his memory on the mechanics of *Litholapaxy*, the procedure of crushing stones in the bladder. His lithotrite, the only instrument in the fine collection that Dr. Channing had sent him so long ago that he seldom used, nestled in its felt-lined wooden case, and he took it out. It was an ominous-appearing tool, only slightly larger in diameter than the catheter he had just employed. Like the catheter, its tip curved upward in about a thirty degree arc of a circle. The serrated jaw, when closed followed the curve of the arc and created a smooth curved tube that could be introduced into the urethra. When the part of the instrument that was the inner curve of the jaw was retracted by unscrewing the knob at the operator's end of the handle, its ferociously jagged teeth disengaged from the matching pair on the outer curve of the arc. Screwing the knob back again created tremendous crushing force between the two segments of the jaw. Todd mixed a solution of boric acid with tepid water from the teakettle and roused Chambers.

"Mr. Chambers, as I explained earlier, we will have to crush that stone in your bladder or you are just going to continue having these attacks. If the stone proves to be too large for me to grasp in my instrument and break it into fragments, I will have to operate and take it out whole. I strongly recommend that we try to crush the stone right now," Todd explained.

"Will it hurt?"

"No more than it did when I drained your urine," Todd replied.

"Have at it, Doc," Chambers finally said after some hesitation.

Todd greased the neck of the lithotrite with lard and tried to introduce it into the urethra, but it was enough larger than the catheter that Chambers couldn't tolerate it. After several painful attempts, Todd said, "I'll have to put you to sleep in order to do this."

"Ya really think ya gotta do this?" Chambers asked.

"No doubt at all about it. Now, just settle back for now, and we will have to wait for daylight so it will be safe to put you to sleep with this medicine," he said indicating the can of ether. "Move on over to this cot—you'll be more comfortable."

Todd gave Chambers a small glass of whiskey and took a long drag on the bottle himself. "There now, we'll both get some sleep and then do it in the morning."

- - -

Todd had dragged the examining table around until the foot of it was toward the front window of his cabin and had positioned Chambers on it. He started dripping ether from its can onto the rag over the patient's nose. Chambers resisted breathing the irritating vapor but Todd said, "Just blow it away, Chambers."

The thrashing patient calmed enough to comply and with each inhalation before blowing again, sucked in great quantities of the gaseous air. After some more physical resistance by Chambers that required Todd's draping himself over the patient's upper body to control him, the man finally slumped into a drugged sleep.

Todd quickly introduced dilators of increasing size that accompanied the lithotrite and urine followed the removal of each. He partially inflated the bladder with boric acid and then introduced the instrument itself. He pushed it in until he was certain that the curved arc at its leading edge encountered the far bladder wall and then unscrewed the knob as far as it would go in order to open the jaws to their maximum. He gingerly screwed them shut again but encountered resistance after only two turns of the knob. The jaws had gripped the stone; apparently, it was small enough that he could get a bite of it with the lithotrite jaws. He moved the instrument back toward him a fraction of an inch. It rotated freely, so he had not also gripped the bladder wall in the jaws. He turned the knob further, now with great difficulty, until suddenly it moved freely again. He had either crushed the stone or it had slipped out from the jaws. Repeating the procedure many times revealed to him that he was encountering smaller and smaller fragments of the stone, so he was making progress.

The patient began to stir. Todd removed the lithotrite and dripped more ether on the rag. When he again had satisfactory anesthesia, he inserted the catheter and irrigated boric acid into the bladder to start washing stone fragments out. There was minimal blood in the liquid as the gravel from the disintegrated stone was flushed. When nothing but clear liquid returned, he reintroduced the lithotrite but encountered no more pieces of stone. He was through and had been successful!

Todd realized that he was sweating profusely and feeling a little light-headed himself from the ether-filled room. Putting instruments and basins aside, he opened the door to ventilate the stale air from the cabin and, waiting for the patient to recover from the anesthetic, poured himself a tumbler full of rye whiskey. He slumped on his bed as he drank thirstily, feeling triumphant that he had succeeded but shuddering at the possibility that he might have had to remove the stone, had it been larger, through a perineal operation. He wondered if he, indeed, would have had the courage or if he even remembered enough anatomy to successfully perform that procedure had it become necessary.

His tortured thoughts wandered and he asked himself, what would I have done if I had bitten through his bladder wall with that vicious lithotrite?

Perhaps I did and didn't realize it! No, no, I'm certain I didn't; he had no bleeding at the end. If I had, would I have had the courage to enter his belly and repair it? I have gone into the peritoneal space of the belly before, he recalled, but I've killed patients doing it.

Daniel shook his head, emptied the glass and sat, slumped forward in his exhaustion. Chambers began to stir.

CHAPTER THIRTY-SEVEN

1861

Seasons came and seasons passed. Todd remained in Jacksonville and treated every manner of affliction that presented itself to him although frequently he was not altogether pleased with the outcome. He was all too aware of the shortcomings of Medicine and the limits of his own abilities. The boom-town days of Jacksonville had long since ended, but it had begun maturing in its own right. There was now a lumber yard that furnished the materials for construction of more substantial buildings; a bank with a large, reliable safe was established; hardware stores, dry goods stores and even two churches appeared on the scene. The town center, still quite unattractive, had migrated to the mouth of the canyon. Todd welcomed two new doctors in town, but their response to him had been guarded; he felt that since they had both only apprenticed in Medicine, they undoubtedly felt uncomfortable because of his M.D. diploma that he had proudly framed and hung in his office once the Medical College of Harvard University had finally seen fit to replace the one lost in the shipwreck.

Many of the Chinese miners had drifted away and Gung Pi along with them. There had been no goodbyes, no exchange of sentiment between the Chinese doctor and Todd in spite of the fact that they had consulted one another in the past and even coordinated their professional efforts at times on some cases. One day, the seemingly ageless little man was just gone.

Champ became more and more crippled with rheumatism until he could hardly walk and he finally died. The loss of his companionship and loyal presence was devastating to his master.

Todd visited Simon in Sacramento several times, but the distance and the years seemed to have eroded their friendship until it had changed as drastically as had the appearance of the now cosmopolitan city itself. It seemed to Todd that Edwards had become unbearably rigid in his thoughts; it never occurred to him that disapproval of Todd's appearance, of his drinking, of his increasing sloth and Simon's frustration at trying to counsel and change him were the seeds of the good reverend's altered attitude.

Daniel's rhythm of life seemed to contract. He found little pleasure in any of his usual activities. His practice was increasingly routine and unrewarding. He lacked the interest or energy to search his few medical texts when diagnostic or therapeutic conundrums presented. He quit reading for pleasure or even looking at poetry that once had inspired him so powerfully. No longer did he puzzle over a personal theology or search for some meaning in his life. During his hours and hours of insomnia, his thoughts were scattered, disorganized and simply troubled. The two anodynes to which Daniel always resorted to soothe his lonely and troubled mind were his increasingly frequent discussions with Cordelia whom he somehow imagined to be out there in the farthest reach of the starry universe and the rye whiskey to which he had become addicted. The first made him feel better at the time he was pouring his thoughts out to Del, but these dialogues with her memory gave him no lasting relief. The whiskey's effect persisted much longer; indeed, he sometimes had to be roused from a drunken stupor in order for a patient to get treatment.

Most of the residents of the town understood that Daniel had never really recovered from his wife's death. They tolerated his drunkenness simply as an understandable human weakness because, over the years, he had become such a local institution. Many newcomers to Jacksonville sought their medical care from the other practitioners, Dr. Andrus and Dr. Childers. The older residents seemed to feel a loyalty toward Todd and, even if he drank, he still was more or less available whenever they needed him, and he never withheld his service if the afflicted couldn't pay. But all would agree that his addiction seemed to be progressing and most were amazed at his capacity; it went even beyond what most thought possible. In a mining town such as Jacksonville, such limits regarding alcohol consumption were almost infinite.

- - -

Matilda Thorpe came to Jacksonville in 1860. Since she was willing to accept the challenge of becoming the town's first actual school teacher in return for the mere pittance that was offered, she was given the job. Previously, one or another of the town's handful of mothers had undertaken the task of educating their small group of youngsters but each had given up sooner or later. Each claimed that the spread in ages of the charges placed too great and varied a demand on their untrained capabilities. The more likely reason was that none wished to continue being harassed by the often cruel pranks sprung on them by some of the students; to retaliate effectively risked the anger and disapproval of fellow parents.

The class consisted of seventeen children ranging in age from five to fourteen. The school was the old abandoned cabin of Finian McGarrity, the loft of which Miss Thorpe, soon to be known as "Old Maid Mattie", was allowed to use as living quarters.

Mattie Thorpe was tall, ungraced by beauty, somewhat awkward and of an extremely spare frame—her detractors even called her "stringy"—but she was capable of giving a very good accounting of herself when challenged physically, as the fourteen-year-old Tad Wilkins found out when she subdued him handily and led him, crimson with shame, around the schoolroom by his ear. She was patient, well-read, and religious, but a strict authoritarian who insisted on politeness, attentiveness and a commitment to learning in her classroom. Mattie was a twenty-six-year-old spinster and because of that magisterial nature of hers, those who felt they knew her predicted that such would *always* be her marital status. She was, however, so solicitous of the needs of others that she fed stray cats or dogs and always seemed to find the time to care for a sick miner when there was nobody else to help. Out of the classroom, she was gratefully recognized as the local angel of mercy.

People were curious about her background and it pleased her to keep it to herself. She felt it was nobody else's business that she had once taught school in Salem after coming west with her parents. Her competence as a teacher, she thought, would soon become obvious to them, and that was all that was important. In truth, she had had an affair with a man in Salem who led her to believe he was anxious to join her in marriage, but when she became pregnant, he had simply faded away to some distant place in the dark of night and left her to face the world alone. When she began to show signs of her condition, Salem residents were indignant at her indiscretion and felt she had acted too shamefully to be teaching their young. They had fired her from her position and would not consider rehiring her even after she tragically miscarried. Once fallen, she was never to be forgiven! Consequently, Mattie packed up and moved south to Jacksonville where, even though she allowed her past to remain shrouded in mystery, she was gladly accepted because she was the answer to the town's great need.

In the following months, her role of ministering to the sick led her to cross paths with Dr. Todd on a number of occasions. They came to depend on each other in some measure, but no close friendship developed. To Daniel, Mattie just seemed conveniently there; to her, Todd always appeared preoccupied and distant when he was not inebriated but, nonetheless, she respected his learning and the results of his efforts. She admired the way he had saved Mrs. Taylor's life when she hemorrhaged so terribly with her bloody miscarriage, his handling of the trauma with which he was frequently confronted, and so many of his other medical accomplishments. His drunkenness offended her terribly, and she felt that she could see a gradual decline in his appearance, in his attitude and, judging by the results, even in his professional competence. Such senseless waste of talent angered her.

If the town, in its blind tolerance, chose to excuse Dr. Todd's conduct, Mattie Thorpe did not.

She felt that the man had responsibilities to the world, in general, and to Jacksonville in particular. He had taken an oath to provide mankind with the best medical care he could furnish, and he was failing to honor that pledge through his weakness, through his excessive appetites, through his sloth. His professional competence was withering away, she felt, due solely to alcohol rotting away his brain. Matttie's anger over this disgraceful situation mounted ever higher the longer she was confronted by it.

The matter came to a climax one night when Mattie was summoned to the Sylvester's cabin because Bess Sylvester's labor pains were increasing in frequency. She sent Tom, Bess' oldest boy and one of her third grade students, for Dr. Todd. Tom came back and said, "I can't rouse him, Miss Thorpe. He's drunk!"

Mattie fumed and snorted her disgust but, the urgency of the situation did not allow for her to send for one of the other doctors, and she delivered the little baby girl on her own. Fortunately, the delivery was routine and uncomplicated so, after the cord had been tied and cut, the placenta delivered, the mother and baby cleaned and made comfortable, Mattie marched militantly up to Todd's cabin. Her wrath was beyond containment.

She threw the door wide and was nearly overcome by the stench of stale body odor, of whiskey and of vomit. She marched over and threw wood onto the dying fire that smoldered on the hearth, and then she lit a lamp. Todd lay sprawled face down on his bed, his slow rhythmical breathing raspy but not a true snore. He was in shirt sleeves but when Mattie glowered down at him and vehemently threw back the covers, she discovered that was all he wore. He apparently had collapsed while undressing and had been just too drunk to completely disrobe.

Sickened by her overwhelming disgust, she slapped him viciously across the bottom and growled indelicately, "Oh, you awful, awful man! Get your . . . get *yourself* out of that bed, you drunken *sot*!"

Todd awoke with a start from the pain and looked around him in confusion. "Who . . . what . . ." He blinked leaden eyelids and tried to focus. "Who, in the name of Heaven, are you, madam?" he finally croaked drunkenly. Discovering his nakedness, he fumbled with the covers to hide himself and slowly focused his eyes enough to recognize the schoolteacher/nurse. "What are you doing in my house?" His voice was thick and hoarse.

"I, sir," she said, drawing herself up to her full height and towering authority, "am Mattie Thorpe. We have met in the past—when you were not so drunk and more capable of carrying out your bounden duties as the physician for Jacksonville. I have just delivered Mrs. Sylvester's baby—in your *absence* due to your drunkenness, I might add. And I have come to put an end to this orgy of self-destruction."

Todd wiped his hand down over his face, as though to make this vengeful specter disappear but ended the futile effort by just hanging his throbbing head. He licked his lips and thirstily looked about for some sort of alcoholic reinforcement. "Please vacate my home, madam, so that I may decently clothe myself," he said, his words tumbling out, one crowding upon another in their jumble.

"Not likely, Dr. Todd. You would just avail yourself again of demon rum or whatever it is that you drink. You *stink*, sir, and I am going to prepare a bath for you. Your degenerate race toward death from whiskey is at an end. You, sir, have had your last drink! Stay where you are while I heat water for your bath."

"Listen, you stringy old *witch*! You can't intrude into my life like this," Todd screamed, furious at the behavior of this vengeful spitfire.

Mattie was already pouring a bucket of water into the iron pot. As she swung it and its supporting arm over the newly-rekindled fire, she replied with self-assurance, "Stringy women, Dr. Todd, live longer than whiskey-sodden derelicts such as you are becoming. Remember that, sir."

He heard a splash of liquid and looked around just in time to see her emptying the last of his rye whiskey into the chamber pot. "Ohhhhh! Now you're going too *damn* far, madam," he shouted and started to rise. Halted by the paralyzing burst of pain in his head and the sudden recollection of his nakedness, he sagged back down onto the bed and under its covers. He lay there, confused and wondering if all of this was illusory. He closed his eyes and shook his head, but when he looked again, the scene was the same.

Waiting for the water to heat, Mattie approached Daniel and stood over him, her arms folded in the most authoritative stance. "You have the reputation of being a good man, Dr. Todd. You certainly have the training and the opportunity to do a great deal of good in this community—a community of good people who respect and need you. And here you are, *squandering* your talents and *pickling* your brain in this disgusting display of self-indulgence. I, for one, have had enough of it. I simply will not allow you to destroy yourself and deprive Jacksonville of medical care. If you knew . . . if you were only *able* to stand back and look at yourself, you would be filled with loathing and too ashamed of yourself to continue as you are. You live in filth and clutter and you stink as badly as you have come to look. In your present condition, I am certain you spread more disease than you treat."

Shocked into relative sobriety, Todd blurted, "Just shut up and get out! You don't know me or what goes on in my mind. You meddle in things you know nothing about, Miss Thorpe. Just get out and leave me alone." Todd now spoke in carefully measured words. "I can't put it more plainly than that."

She turned on her heel and went to the door but, instead of departing, merely fetched the washtub that leaned against the cabin wall outside. Carrying it into the cabin, she placed it behind the screen Todd had made to preserve the modesty of his female patients as they prepared for an exam. She felt the temperature of the water in the kettle and dumped it into the tub. "While I get another bucket of water from outside, you get behind that screen and get ready to bathe yourself," she ordered and went out into the night.

Daniel couldn't believe this woman actually would have the audacity to come back, but she did. He now feared that if he didn't bathe, she would do it for him so he struggled to his feet and went behind the screen. All he had to do was take off his shirt, which he accomplished with fumbling fingers. Mattie scooted the screen aside far enough to allow her to add her bucket of cold water to the tub, and then her hand holding a bar of soap appeared over the top of it. In her stern voice, she commanded, "SCRUB!"

In contrast to the almost antiseptic aroma of the lye soap, Daniel had to admit that he detected a foul stench hanging about him like a cloud and wondered if that was really the way he smelled to his patients. He settled down into the tub, his legs bent at the knees and hanging out over its rim.

As if she did not trust him, Mattie soon peeked around the screen to make sure he was doing as ordered. "Miss Thorpe! PLEASE!" he screamed. Satisfied, she ducked back and waited.

Now more sober, Todd asked in more restrained tones, "And just how do you propose to keep me from getting more whiskey? Do you plan to invade the privacy of my home and watch me day and night so that I can't take another drink? Is that what you plan to do?"

"I suspect that there are many in this town who are just as pained as I am at your drunkenness. I shall enlist their aid. Are you ready to defend your right to kill yourself by alcohol each and every time you go about buying a drink for yourself? How about when one of your patients says to you, 'I hope *I'm* not the patient you kill because of your being crazy from your booze sometime.' Have you thought about that? Have you wondered if you always do the right thing by your patient, no matter how inebriated you might be when you have to act. You couldn't even come down to the Sylvester's tent tonight because you had passed out. What if she had gotten into trouble? What if I had not been able to deliver her baby? My God man—you're intelligent. Think what you're doing to yourself and to all of those around you. And then there is Dr. Andrus and Dr. Childers. Think of how satisfying it must be to them to witness you and your debasement."

By now, Mattie Thorpe had edged around the screen and was staring him straight in the eye as he sat in such an ungainly manner in the tub. "I'll leave you now, sir, but think of the shame of all of this if it should be spread about the town what I've done here tonight. They might even fire me from this job, too."

Todd didn't understand this last comment, but it did make him curious. Somehow, he was neither as drunk nor as indignant when he heard her noisy exit from his cabin as he had been earlier. He was just mortally ashamed of what he had become.

- - -

Memories, slowly emerging into his consciousness as he gradually awakened, were spotty and perverse. It all seemed like a nightmare. Todd slept late and, in great confusion, reviewed in his mind the vague images of the night before. It all seemed too surreal even for a dream. He dragged himself to his feet and staggered over to peer behind the screen and there was the tub he apparently had used sometime during the night. It couldn't all have been a nightmare, but how much of it was real? He sniffed under his arm and detected the strong aroma of lye soap. Shuffling to his kitchen and inspecting his whiskey supply, he found nothing but empty bottles. It *wasn't* a dream! She had actually appeared, had dumped his whiskey, and had even forced him to bathe. He was too humiliated to think straight.

"Yes, I know I've been drinking quite a bit," he mumbled to himself. "It's the only way I can get the sleep I need. Nobody has ever complained about it before. What was it she said? It was something about the Sylvester baby. Oh, yes. Mrs. Sylvester was getting close to term, wasn't she? You don't suppose that witch went ahead and delivered the Sylvester child without me? Oh! All they had to do was give me a call. Why didn't they come and get me?" He decided to have a drink before getting breakfast to settle his stomach. "Oh," he groaned loudly as the pain in his head was accentuated by another roiling wave of nausea.

He moaned and rubbed his forehead, "I feel like I have cholera morbus! Oh, my God ! No whiskey here! That witch emptied it all! Did she throw it out? No . . . she dumped it in the pot. I remember." He stared at the brown liquid in the chamber pot and even considered trying some of it but his revulsion overcame his need. "I'm not an addict," he affirmed with an exaggerated nod of his head. "I don't need whiskey bad enough to drink out of *that*."

He wished that Champ were here. He still missed that ugly mutt's face staring up at him and waiting to be fed his breakfast. Todd searched his cupboard. There was no bacon to cook and when he smelled the milk, he found it was sour so, if he had oatmeal, it would have to be plain. He decided to go down to the café to get some breakfast, although he was not sure that the knotting in his stomach would even tolerate food. What he needed was a drink and he doubted that any of the saloons would be open yet. He slumped back down on his bed and considered just sleeping some more, but he was too uncomfortable.

He sat for a long while and tried to call to mind what had been said last night. That witch said I was a drunken sot, he remembered. She said she'd try to shame me into not asking for any more whiskey. She said something about how satisfying it would be to Andrus and Childers to see me drinking myself into oblivion. Well, they won't see that and neither will she! I don't need whiskey! I'll show them. Now, I'll just go down to ol' Maudie Rogers' café and get some bacon and eggs. The thought set his stomach to griping all the more. He grabbed a basin and heaved into it, but nothing came up. More dry heaves ripped at his guts. Exhausted by the wrenching, unsuccessful effort, Daniel slumped onto his bed and wept once again, sobbing pitifully. "My God, Cordelia, I'm so miserable!" he whimpered. "Oh!"

CHAPTER THIRTY-EIGHT

1862

Years earlier, Daniel had engaged in a life-and-death struggle against the sea and had barely survived, thanks to the chance passing of the whaling ship, *Ellie Mae*. Had it not been for her captain's lusting for a tiny bit of floating booty in the form of some fuel and perhaps a few nails, Todd surely would have perished. Now, his salvation had come in the person of Mattie Thorpe, more altruistic than Captain Corbet, but every bit as motivated. It seemed that she had so taken his restoration to health and medical competence as a personal and community challenge, that she would allow nothing to discourage her. She promoted her cause with everybody who would listen. In spite of repeated suggestions that she would do better to mind her own business, she recruited a cadre of supporters who were genuinely interested in seeing Dr. Todd become an effective physician once again. They made it so embarrassing and uncomfortable for him to buy liquor that he finally could rely only on the supplies of medicinal alcohol he received from Portland along with his other pharmaceuticals. Even then, he could never know when Mattie Thorpe might invade his cabin and confiscate anything that smelled alcoholic, even when it was mixed with other ingredients. Daniel had taken to doctoring his supplies with simple cherry extract to disguise its odor.

On several occasions, when he was totally deprived of his supply, he demonstrated what he, had he been mentally competent to do so, would have diagnosed as Wernicke's Acute Alcoholic Hallucinosis as described in *Lancet*. At those times, his screams of panic caused neighbors to come to his aid. Once he claimed to be seeing rats as large as horses and he was convinced that they were bent on devouring him. He cowered under the covers of his bed and wouldn't come out until convinced that the monsters had been slain. He was given a drink to settle his nerves.

One other time, his hallucination was auditory, and his conversation was conducted in a screaming exchange with God—his father seemed to be a willing spokesman. This time, Miss Thorpe was one of those coming to his rescue, and she refused to allow any alcoholic remedy to be given. Instead, she supervised his being tied down to his bed and continued to apply cold compresses to his brow until he finally settled into a deep sleep.

Mattie undoubtedly would have eventually despaired and given up had it not been for the gunfight at Saddler's Saloon. A gambler by the name of Castleman was shot in the chest by the dealer over a game of Faro. He was carried up to Todd's cabin in a blanket on the urging of the saloon's owner. What the men found there was an inebriated Todd who was in no shape to operate. Andrus was reported to be off hunting and Childers had gone on a trip east to Salt Lake City, so Todd was absolutely the only doctor available. By the time the men got enough black coffee into him for him to be halfway responsive, the gambler had died. Most believed that probably nothing could have been done to save him given the severity of his wound; others were of the opinion that Jacksonville was far better off the way things turned out anyway. Only Dr. Daniel Todd felt a heavy responsibility for the man's death.

Slowly, one by one, the men who had brought the injured gambler to Todd's cabin filed out and disappeared, leaving behind nothing but Todd and the body in the blanket—and one other. Framed in the open door was the familiar scarecrow specter who had been Daniel's nemesis; she stood looking at him as she shook her head in merciless disapproval.

"Do you see what it has come to?" she asked, her words cutting into him like a lash.

Todd was in no mood to be lectured. Nothing could make him feel any worse than he did at this very moment. He felt as though his life had become worthless and was at its lowest ebb; he simply sat on his bed, silent and with his head bowed in wretched shame. He was surprised when she came and sat down beside him. Haltingly, she placed an arm around his shoulders and pulled him toward her. He surrendered and even was surprised at the faint lilac water scent about her. He expected to hear more of her diatribes of the past, her caustic criticism, her threats; but, there was only silent compassion.

She stroked his head and finally, after a long and quiet moment, said, "We can lick this, Daniel. You are a good person—a good doctor. Let's build on tonight's tragedy—this failure—and together we can restore you to what you once were. Now, lie down and sleep. I'll fix you some breakfast in the morning."

With that, she was gone.

- - -

Todd had long been aware of the strong arguments for reshaping his life, compelling events of the past that should shame him into change. They were factors that nobody else would even know about; what Dr. McClure, his original benefactor, would think of seeing him in the depths of his depravity; what Dr. Channing, who had started him in his practice with all of those instruments that he still used, would feel about his investment in Todd's future if he could see him over these past months; the shame Cordelia would suffer over the depths of his debauchery.

Those powerful reasons and the pride he had once felt in himself for actually becoming a doctor should have been sufficient stimulus to overcome his addiction. Countering those factors, though, was the hatred he had developed for that damnable Mattie Thorpe and her harassment of him. It became a challenge to him not to let her win. Gradually, however, he began to feel less and less of anything. It was as though his brain and his emotions were just dying. It was now, in this state of suspended mentation, that his drunkenness had rendered him totally incapable of treating a dying man. But even that had not been enough until Mattie demonstrated her stubborn, unyielding faith in him. He felt it demeaning to her to compare that allegiance to the loyalty always shown by old Champ, but it had the same unquestioning quality—the same blind devotion. It was finally the inspiration he needed.

When his guts cramped and the almost unbearable hunger for alcohol tore at his brain, he would simply grit his teeth and walk down by the creek, placing one foot very deliberately ahead of the other, struggling to convince himself that he had to deal with his addiction one step at a time—one *minute* or one *hour* or one *day* at a time. When he felt that he was on the verge of slipping, he would seek out Mattie and just go talk to her. She knew that her support was important and very necessary; she no longer lectured him but would probe with bits of conversation until she found just the proper topic that seemed to inspire or distract him at that moment. She discovered that poetry was very helpful and sometimes read long passages from her two well-worn books of her favorite art.

Daniel suffered indescribable hell, but he persevered and did not take another drink. He experienced only one more episode of hallucination, and this was followed by the gradual quieting of the turbulent seas of his mind. Todd slowly regained an interest in life and once again even became concerned about his appearance. Jacksonville found it difficult to believe the change that took place in Dr. Todd over the next several months.

Even when Todd no longer required Mattie Thorpe's emotional support, he found excuses to see her with increasing frequency. Over the weeks, he came to recognize an entirely different person than he had ever thought her to be in the past. Instead of simply seeing a plain, stern and mostly disapproving face, he became aware of a remarkable inner beauty in her. He no longer thought of her as the marshal of his conscience nor even a critical judge of his behavior; she had become a true friend. He was comfortable with her and felt no hesitation in sharing even his innermost thoughts or fears with her. Where he once had found her intrusive and meddling, he now recognized her involvement and concern with other people as true empathy for anybody she felt was suffering or in need. She was the embodiment of what his father had preached over the years but had failed so miserably to practice; she was a truly good and beautiful person.

Daniel finally realized that he was falling in love with Mattie Thorpe.

- - -

Chester Abrams dropped a wrecking bar down into a drill hole so he could pry away some layers of rock by using the steel shaft for leverage but, unfortunately, there was an unexploded stick of that new dynamite at the bottom of the hole. The explosion blew the wrecking bar many feet into the air and along with it went Chester's left hand and half of his right. Fragments of rock were embedded in his face and he was a bloody mess when they brought him to Todd. After giving him laudanum to control his pain, Todd set about cleaning the various wounds.

He excised the torn tissue and ragged remnants from the left wrist where that hand had been and made a clean amputation above the carpals. Abrams' shock was still so profound that no additional anesthesia was necessary for that. Todd cleaned the head wounds, controlled the bleeding and found that no further treatment was necessary there. The right hand, or what remained of it, was another matter. If he didn't save what was left there, the man would be a helpless cripple with nothing but stumps at the ends of his forearms. He studied the problem very carefully and then put the miner to sleep with ether.

Todd debrided the badly damaged bone and soft tissue and was left with the thumb, the index and middle finger, and half of the palm to which was attached some soft tissue that still looked as though it might survive. He removed what was left of the hamate, pisiform and triquetrum carpal bones and hoped that the exposed remnant of median nerve and the apparently intact radial artery would be viable. He was able to wrap fragments of skin and soft tissue around the remaining exposed metacarpal bones and the partial stump, praying all the while to some ill-defined god that somehow the remainder of the hand would survive.

With Mattie's help, he nursed the patient through the following weeks and was jubilant that the claw he had fashioned seemed to be doing well in spite of the swelling; Abrams was even able to move his fingers and thumb in a weak, abortive gripping motion, although the wrist had lost all flexibility. At least half a dozen fracture patients sought his care during that time period and, in treating all of them successfully, Todd's pride and confidence were greatly fortified. He was indeed considering himself a doctor again. He tried to express his gratitude to Mattie for her aid and everything she had done to restore to him this measure of professional competence, but he was overcome by emotion. He knew all too well that he could never have overcome his terrible addiction without her help. He just could never put the words together to tell her that.

CHAPTER THIRTY-NINE

1863

It was early June and school had closed just a day earlier. Mattie Thorpe had been painting her quarters in the loft of the old McGarrity cabin but had come to Daniel's cabin to dine on his clumsy attempt to cook a pot roast of venison. He had long ago used up the last of his winter's stock of onions that might have made the meat more palatable and unfortunately, it had come from a very randy old buck that tasted just as gamey as it was tough. The two laughed off his failure, crediting it to Daniel's inexperience as a gourmet cook. Now they relaxed and enjoyed the lazy spring evening.

Mattie took up a position near the single window at the front of the cabin so she could use the light to read from Shakespeare's "The Merchant of Venice". Daniel settled back on the patient's cot to once again enjoy the sound of her voice reading poetry. Her animated rendition of the play made it come alive for him and before he realized how much time had passed, she was all of the way into Act II and was reading from Scene I.

> "Portia: In terms of choice I am not solely led by nice direction of a maiden's eyes;
>
> Besides, the lottery of my destiny bars me the right of voluntary choosing:
>
> But if my father had not scanted me and hedg'd me by his wit to yield myself

His wife who wins me by that means I told you, yourself,
renowned Prince, then stood as fair as any comer I have looked
on yet for my affection."

Todd was aware that the light was fading and almost gone. He wondered
how Mattie could see to continue reading. He looked over at her and was
amazed to see that she was not reading at all but was staring out of the
window and was simply reciting Shakespeare completely from memory!

Sitting up in his surprise, Daniel exclaimed, "Oh Matilda, you really are
something! How long have you been reciting instead of reading?"

Mattie ducked her head in her embarrassment. "Not long," she lied.
"Actually, some of his other plays please me considerably more than this one."

A wave of tender thoughts swept through Daniel's mind. This woman
was like the huge icebergs he had encountered around the Horn; the depth
and magnitude of her unsuspected dimensions were absolutely astounding.
Matilda Thorpe, such a plain and almost unattractive creature, but one
so brilliant in her works, her intellect, her depth of understanding and so
charitable in all of her actions, was a jewel of untold value. The impulse
overwhelmed him and, in a wave of passion and without even a moment
of hesitation, he said, "Matilda, will you marry me?"

Almost like a cat toying with a mouse, Mattie looked at Daniel for a
moment, drew her head back and asked in a challenging manner, "Why?
Because I can recite Shakespeare?"

"Don't be silly," he bristled. "I'm serious. Without you, I would at this
very minute be either dead or just the same as. I have grown to love you
because you are as essential to my life as the very air I breathe. You know,
there are cultures in which a life that you save becomes your ward forever.
I'm that ward for you, so marry me. I swear that I will do everything in
my power to make you happy and will never again give you cause to be
ashamed of me."

As she looked at him in that magisterial manner of hers, appraising him
as she might peer at one of her students, Daniel shrank small inside and
thought, this is absolutely crazy! What would Cordelia think? This is not
like me. I've not even courted her. Why would she even want to take on a
drunk like me?

"I'm truly honored that you asked me, Daniel. Truly," Mattie said softly.
"I wonder, though, if this might not just be part of your recovery. Perhaps

you are merely grateful to have been restored to health. Don't some of your patients express their gratitude with much greater friendship for you than they had ever shown in the past?"

He was certain there was an element of this attitude in his behavior, but it was so much more than that. "Mattie, I have had one great love in my life. I've probably told you so much about Cordelia that you are tired of hearing about her. Our very limited number of days together will always be a rich treasure chest of memories, and she will be there in my thoughts as long as I live. I wouldn't try to convince you otherwise."

Mattie remained silent and Daniel went on, "It's true that I do have boundless gratitude to you for what you have done for me. But this love I have for you is very real—very intense. You are such a superior being, Mattie; a true paragon of womanhood. You are saintly in your goodness, a Solomon in your wisdom; you are tender and warm and I desire nothing more than to make you the other part of my life for the rest of my days—for us to hoard our own treasure chest of yesterdays together. I am now well beyond breathless passion and will never have that for anybody again, I'm afraid; but I have a very mature, very rational and extremely well-reasoned love for you. Be my wife," he implored again.

"I am quite beyond breathless passion also, Daniel." She gave him that appraising look again and, after a long but tender moment, finally said, "Yes, I accept. I will marry you."

- - -

The wedding had none of the raucous festivity of Daniel's marriage to Cordelia. Mattie's minister, the Reverend Peters of the Methodist-Episcopal Church, officiated and his wife was both the organist and the witness for the event. Mattie's gown was a slightly faded blue dress that came almost to the floor and, instead of a veil, she had some early pansies pinned in her hair. After the ceremony, they went down to Maudie's Café and had their wedding supper. Even with such a simple celebration, the bride seemed radiant.

"Daniel, I must confess to you that I had given up expectation of ever becoming a bride. I know that I'm not fair to behold; I know I am abrasive and that I rub most people the wrong way. I will do my best, though, to be the best possible wife for you," she promised just after their plates of food were placed in front of them.

"Most people can see flaws only in others—*you* imagine blemishes in yourself that simply aren't there. You are beautiful in my eyes; you are observant and analytical although, I will admit, sometimes painfully truthful. I wouldn't have you any other way, Matilda. Thank you for becoming my wife. I love you very much. Now, eat up and let's see what else the evening holds in store." Daniel toasted Mattie, his new wife, with his glass of water.

- - -

Both Daniel and Mattie found that their passion grew much more intense over the following weeks than they had ever imagined possible before their marriage. He discovered fervor in their love that even spawned guilt feelings, as though he was forsaking his love for Cordelia; he struggled to overcome these and not reveal them to Mattie. Matilda felt only rapture beyond anything she had ever imagined possible. She settled into her domestic chores, and Daniel finally rediscovered true satisfaction in his practice of medicine. No longer did he feel the need or desire for the rye whiskey that had become such a constant necessity for him in the past. He did occasionally wander alone into the starry night and try to explain all of these happenings to Del in whatever distant realm she might now reside.

Before school started again in the fall, Daniel convinced Mattie that they should make the trip to Sacramento and share their new happiness with Simon Edwards. With the insight that seemed to come with his new grasp on life, Daniel realized that his drunkenness had been the cause of the gulf that had developed between Edwards and him. He was now intent on setting things right. But even more than that, he wanted Simon to meet Mattie.

The trip south was a wilderness holiday that both Dr. and Mrs. Todd enjoyed tremendously. Daniel thought back to the fear he had felt of the now long-subdued Karok and Okwanuchu Indians that he had experienced on his initial trip north through this country. In spite of enjoying their present safe passage, he couldn't help but feel a sadness for the change brought about by displacement of a people who had resided here in the past, perhaps for centuries.

The two were confounded by the metropolitan bustle of Sacramento City. There were now many buildings of stone and brick and wood; not a tent was to be seen anywhere. They saw several churches and there was even a park near the center of the city. The Grace Evangelical Church was still at its original location, but it was now an imposing structure surrounded by permanent buildings and even had several young trees growing out in front. There was nobody inside the building itself, but the front door was unlocked and offered a welcoming portal to any who wished to enter. The sign out front provided the address where the Reverend Simon Edwards could be reached in case of emergency.

Daniel and Mattie got a room at the Colonnade Hotel before seeking out his friend. Whether bashful or because of feelings of insecurity, Mattie decided to stay in their room while Daniel located Simon and said, "We can have a pleasant dinner, just the two of us together, and I will be fresh and rested to meet him tomorrow. You need some time alone with him in the beginning."

What Todd found at Edwards' suite of rooms was very disturbing. Instead of the robust giant of the past, Simon was weak and wasted, his face extremely drawn and pale. In spite of his debilitated appearance, he rose and greeted Todd warmly.

"What a wonderful surprise," he said, his voice also a mere distant echo of the bellow it had been in the past.

As Daniel shook his hand, he couldn't help but notice the massive tumor that swelled the lower half of Simon's throat, imperfectly hidden by his full but graying beard.

"Hello, Simon. I'm sober! I'm completely recovered, and now I have once again become a truly temperate physician," Todd announced proudly in his greeting. "I couldn't bear to think of the way we parted and left our friendship in such terribly fragile circumstances when I left here before. I realize it was entirely my fault because of my condition, and I simply had to come back to make amends. I am now truly ashamed of the way I was at that time. Also, I wanted to bring my new wife and introduce her to you. She thought it best if that meeting were postponed until tomorrow; the trip has certainly been strenuous and exhausting for her."

"A new wife! I'm amazed," Edwards croaked. "I never thought you would ever remarry."

"Nor did I," Todd replied. "Mattie was amazingly successful in engineering my salvation from a certain death from alcohol, and I will be eternally grateful to her. You'll find her to be a remarkable woman, Simon."

"I will look forward to tomorrow," he said and edged back to recline once again on the *chaise longue*. "Pardon me, Daniel, I must lie down again. I have become remarkably weak of late."

"You look terrible, Simon," Todd said, his brutal frankness warranted by their past friendship. "When did all of this start?"

"Perhaps six months ago," the minister said in a hoarse, throaty voice that faded to little more than a whisper. "The doctor here told me I had a goiter and put me on raw oysters several times a day and iodine water." He paused and took several deep breaths to restore himself. "But I have only gotten worse as it has just continued to grow and get bigger." Apparently from habit, Simon rubbed his hand appraisingly over the surface of the tumorous enlargement.

Todd asked, "May I examine it, Simon?"

"Of course."

Expecting either the fluctuant firmness of a goiter or the heat of an inflamed thyroid, Todd was saddened to encounter an extremely hard and almost cadaverously cold mass. This could be nothing other than a tumor of the thyroid. The hoarseness of Simon's voice gave evidence that the problem had spread to the larynx or, at least, involved the nerves in that area. Todd ran his hands up toward the angles of the jaw and felt nodular masses on either side—further evidence that the disease had spread. What should he tell his friend—that this would kill him?

Finally, he said, "I'm afraid this is not good, Simon; not good at all."

"I had reached the same conclusion, Daniel. I don't suppose you can do anything for it," his voice rustled coarsely.

"I would give absolutely anything if I could, Simon, but I don't think so."

"How long do you think I have?" Simon asked in that painfully raspy voice.

"You said that this started about six months ago. I would guess that you have only months to live, but I shouldn't predict until I can examine you more completely," Daniel replied.

"I suppose if I truly believe what I preach, I should welcome that end as merely a passage to Heaven and a better life, shouldn't I. This is a test of my faith." Edwards settled back into a completely supine position.

"I suspect that even a drowning saint would struggle to stay afloat," Todd countered. "Can I get anything for you now, my friend?"

"My mouth is always horribly dry. I would enjoy a glass of water."

It has even invaded his salivary glands, Todd thought as he went to the pitcher and poured glass of water. "Listen, if there's nothing else I can do, I should get back to Mattie. I shall bring her around tomorrow morning, you can meet her, and we can all have a good visit."

Daniel was having trouble staying focused on his role as a physician, and he was most uncomfortable as simply a sympathetic but very helpless friend.

"No, there's nothing you can do for me. My housekeeper will bring soup in for me this evening. I have trouble swallowing anything else. I shall look forward to meeting your Mattie and learning about everything that has transpired in your life." Totally exhausted, Edwards closed his eyes and seemed to sink deeper into the lounge.

Todd took Simon's hand and gave it a supportive squeeze. "I'll see you tomorrow, my friend. Rest well until then." He retreated out of the front door and leaned against the outside wall, weakened in the knees by this turn of events. He felt as impotent and unable to help as he had when he discovered Cordelia so close to death. Overcome by grief, he stumbled out onto the street and cursed his own inadequacy as a healer.

When once again in the comfortable presence of Mattie, he took her in his arms and hugged her protectively and surprised her with a kiss of remarkable passion.

"My goodness," she exclaimed, "To what do I owe this flood of emotion?"

"Oh, Mattie," he replied and hung his head in his sad feeling of impotence. "Simon is dying. I'm sure it's cancer of his thyroid gland and there's nothing that anybody can do at this point. How fragile our grip is on this life and on those we hold dear." Then he told her the details of the meeting with his friend and, though totally without appetite, took her down to the dining room for their dinner.

- - -

The Todds waited until ten o'clock the next morning to call again on Reverend Edwards. They were both surprised when he answered the door neatly dressed, his beard freshly trimmed, erect and altogether very different from the picture Todd had painted of him in his description to Mattie. He bowed and said, "Mrs. Matilda Todd, I presume."

Mattie curtsied slightly and replied, "Reverend Edwards?"

"Simon, please," he said very graciously. Even his voice seemed stronger than yesterday, Todd noticed. "Please come and sit down. Would you care for some coffee? This pot is freshly brewed."

"That would be delicious," Mattie replied. She wanted to help him serve it but felt that would countervail the impression Simon was striving to make, so she merely seated herself alongside Daniel.

"Sugar or cream?" Simon asked.

"No. Just black for both of us," she replied.

"Well, Mattie, tell me about yourself. I can never trust the bragging ways of your husband." Edwards' voice was beginning to lose some of its vigor, fading almost to a whisper at the end.

"I was a simple farm girl back in Ohio. My father also taught school and so insisted on a rigorous schedule of reading and arithmetic for me. When my parents decided to make the adventurous move westward, I came along, of course. That led to my becoming a teacher in Salem, and then I eventually moved on to Jacksonville where I met Daniel."

"And rescued him from his Bacchanalian self-destruction, he tells me."

"Well, yes. Daniel was certainly not at his best in those days," she replied. She smiled and squeezed Todd's hand.

"I salute you, madam," Simon said. "His perverse attitude was more than I could deal with. What part of Ohio?"

"Near Chillicothe," Mattie responded.

"Oh, the historic old Indian village on the Miami, I suppose. Then you are familiar with Simon Kenton who spent much time around there and eastward decades ago. He had extensive dealings with Tecumseh, you know."

"Oh yes, everybody there knows about him. Are you from Ohio, Reverend?"

"No. I have just been a dedicated student of the Shawnees. They had a remarkable confederation of tribes there in the time of Tecumseh—almost like the Iroquois League of New England. It is sad to think of it all collapsing. It makes you almost embarrassed to be one of the invaders of their lands and the cause of that demise." Edwards sipped his coffee and swallowed with difficulty.

"Of course, we have been just as disruptive of the western tribes of Indians out here," Mattie replied.

Todd interrupted. "Let's talk about more pleasant things. It looks as though your church is thriving, Simon."

"Yes, it is considerably different from the tent that you and I turned into a make-shift hospital years ago, isn't it, Daniel." His head sagged as his raspy voice reminded him of his present condition and he continued, "I don't know what might happen to it in the future if I . . ." He paused and was silent for a short moment. "I meant to say that I have spent my fortune in making it into what it is today, and I don't know if it can be self-sustaining in the future."

Todd put a hand on his friend's arm and said, "Simon, there was a world already here when we came into it, and there will still be one when we leave it. It's painful to think that it might just be able to go on without us, but I'm sure it can. I accept that and hope that Medicine will be even better in the years ahead than it is now regardless of what I may or may not have done for it. There will still be sin and salvation when you are gone, too. It's the same for Mattie; the same for you; the same for me, in spite of what we might wish to think."

Simon smiled and nodded his head. "You're right, I'm sure. I'd offer you both some wine to celebrate this reunion, but I don't think that would be appropriate under the circumstances of your recovery, Daniel. Let me refill your coffee cups and then let's plan a celebratory dinner here this evening to honor the occasion. Mrs. Lacey, my housekeeper, will prepare it." By now Edwards' voice had become almost inaudible.

"Yes, we'll leave for now and complete some of our many errands in the city. We will be delighted to join you tonight, Simon," Daniel said. "Thank you for the coffee."

No more had the Todds rose, shook hands and left than Edwards shuffled to his bed and collapsed in exhaustion. His show of strength in playing the gracious host and receiving the new bride so hospitably had completely drained him.

The act had not deceived Todd. As they reached the street, he said, "Simon would rise from his death bed to try and appear his old, indestructible self. I'm afraid he's not long for this world, Mattie."

"Oh, surely not. He's such a pleasant man," she replied as they strolled into the downtown district.

- - -

Todd was proven right when they returned that evening. Mrs. Lacey greeted them at the door and said, "Oh, you must be Dr. and Mrs. Todd. When I came this afternoon, I found the Reverend collapsed on his bed and almost in coma. He told me about the invitation for tonight, but he is totally unable to even get out of bed. I'm so worried about him, Doctor. Can you do anything for him?"

Todd went to Simon's bedside and pulled up a chair. His friend's breathing was labored and had a constricted wheeze about it. He looked as different from this morning as the contrast had been between the morning and last night. Simon half-opened one eye and recognized his friend. "I'm afraid I've preached my last sermon—staked my last claim, old friend," he wheezed in a whisper. "Wanted to welcome Mattie properly—sorry . . ." His words trailed off in a feeble cough.

"Don't talk now, Simon. I'm so thankful we arrived when we did. You are my friend, and I will always love you like the brother I never had." Daniel stammered and couldn't express all the feelings that welled up inside of him. He grimaced and wanted to scream, "WHY MUST ALL THOSE I LOVE BE TAKEN FROM ME?" but he simply bowed his head in silence.

"We'll remain here with you, Simon. Just rest for now."

- - -

Todd and Mattie remained in Edwards' suite for three days and nights as death slowly overtook their friend and finally snuffed out his life. He was in coma for the last forty-eight hours, fighting to get his breath from around the constricting tumor, and there was no necessity for sedatives; any other medications obviously would be futile, and so Daniel administered nothing. He and Mattie were constantly at Simon's bedside, though, contributing what little comfort their presence might afford. When Simon died, Todd made the funeral arrangements and left the disbursement of Edwards' assets to the diaconate of the Grace Evangelical Church after bestowing the household items on Mrs. Lacey in recognition of her devoted care. Todd wasn't sure what the legal basis might be for these arrangements, but he was confident these certainly would be his friend's wishes.

Following the funeral and the interment in Sacramento City's burgeoning cemetery, the Todds left to return to Jacksonville. The journey back was a bleak contrast to the honeymoon atmosphere that had marked the trip down to Sacramento. Mattie's strength and staunch support created an even stronger bond between the two newlyweds. Daniel's need and love for Mattie knew no bounds.

CHAPTER FORTY

When school started, Mattie's time was completely occupied by her duties there and Daniel was much busier than either of the other two physicians in town. He continued to wander almost nightly to Cordelia's gravesite, bemoaning to her memory his anguish at losing both her and Simon. He strived to maintain a sunny disposition the rest of the time around Mattie, but his emotional struggle did not go unnoticed by her.

When she feared he might once again resort to whiskey for some relief of this mental strain, she said one night as they lay side by side in bed, "Daniel, I know what you are going through. Jacksonville has become home for you; it is where you and Cordelia once found happiness; it is where she is buried. It is also very closely related to all of the memories you have of your friend, Simon. I fear I am witnessing your gradual destruction by all of those reminders of the past that are slowly consuming you. I know it will be very difficult for you to do, but let's think about moving to some place new. Ours is a whole new life together; let's find a new setting for it—one that is no longer burdened with the sadness of yesterdays that we can neither relive nor change. Think about it, Daniel," she said as she snuggled close to him under the thick comforter.

Daniel feigned sleep and did not respond, but he had to admit to himself that there was wisdom in Mattie's thoughts. How painful such a move would be, he thought; leaving Cordelia there all alone in that cemetery, though she did lie in her grave beside that of her first husband. Daniel had always just assumed that when he died he would lie on the other side of her. And, of course, he would be abandoning the final resting place of his friend Simon, although, to his shame, he hadn't returned to Sacramento to visit it since the funeral. And it would mean starting a new practice all over again. Could they even afford to abandon what they had here and start all over again somewhere else? He lay completely still with his back to Mattie and tried to go to sleep; he would think about all of this some other time.

- - -

When it became obvious that Mattie was pregnant, and as she continued pleading daily for them to leave Jacksonville, Daniel started giving serious consideration to such a move. Of course, winter once again was approaching and the trip would be impossible once it held the little mining community in its grip. One minute, that threat lent urgency to start making the move immediately, but the next, Daniel was convinced that nothing should be done until spring came and school was out. But, Mattie would be near term then, and it would be very dangerous to travel without risk to her and the baby. The problems weighed heavily on Daniel but he resisted, thanks to much spousal support, from finding solace in rye whiskey.

For some reason, good health seemed to settle like a cloud over Jacksonville.

Todd scarcely had more than one or two patients a day. At first, he wondered if his patients were shunning him for some reason but, on his strolls around town, he consistently saw either Andrus or Childers wandering around also, seemingly as much at loose ends and as free of patients as he. They were certainly not capturing h*is* patients. It was just that nobody was currently sick or injured. Inactivity spurred him to make his decision. That night, he asked Mattie if she could find anybody to take over the school if they should decide to leave Jacksonville before winter.

"Where would we go?" she asked in her surprise.

"They say that there is a new gold strike over in the Boise Basin in Idaho, or Washington Territory, or whatever it is called now," he replied. "I think we should go there."

"My only memories of that miserable country is when we were crossing it on the Oregon Trail. It consisted of endless miles between water with nothing but sagebrush and Jackass rabbits in between," she objected in that stiff authoritarian way of hers.

Daniel recited the list of reasons she had presented nightly that favored such a move but added to it the declining medical practice he was experiencing. He could neither admit to himself nor to her that deep down inside he somehow missed the excitement he had first found in Sacramento and then again in Jacksonville when he came to those towns during their infancy. They had been raw, boisterous boomtowns spawned by the madness of gold discovery and not yet having been suffocated by civilization. There had been a wildness and turbulence of life, not unlike that of his whaling days, that had now disappeared from either place. Perhaps his desire to move was an effort to regain his youth; he hadn't factored in this reason but certainly part of his desire to go was that he simply needed to follow another gold rush.

"Where is this Boise Basin?" Mattie asked.

"In the mountains of southern Idaho Territory," he replied. "I think it has recently been split off from Washington or Montana Territories. They say it's some thirty miles or so northeast of Fort Boise."

"Will we go all of that way by wagon?"

"We can go by boat down the Willamette to Portland and then, I'm told, we can continue on as far up the Columbia as Umatilla. From there, yes, it will be by wagon or horseback," he answered.

"You seem to have explored this thoroughly," she said in an accusatory tone. "We'll have to cross the Blues. Do you think the trip will harm the baby?"

"Not if we get started right away," he replied. "How soon can you leave your job?"

"My students would be delighted if I didn't show up tomorrow morning," she joked. "I think a week and a half is adequate notice. Can you be ready to leave by then?"

"I can have things packed in a day," he said, sweeping his hand around the cabin.

Daniel found it disturbing that he seemed to be dismissing his life here so easily but once his decision was made, he could hardly wait to execute it. He wondered how long it might be before he looked back in sorrow on this choice. "I'll make the arrangements," he said. They blew out the lamp and went to bed, both a little fearful because of the momentous decision they had just made.

- - -

Then it happened. Just before dark the very next evening, a frantic Mrs. Terrel, with mounting panic, went from cabin to cabin searching for her son Andy.

"He just went out after school to play and has disappeared. Have you seen him?" she wailed plaintively, time after time.

Nobody had laid eyes on the boy but several friends tried to reassure her, saying he would undoubtedly come home when supper was ready, boys being boys.

He didn't return and that resulted in a new round of inquiry. Many townspeople now became alarmed also. A bear? A mountain lion? Some demented stranger? A search was mounted.

When no trace of young Andy was discovered, Silas Devereaux volunteered the use of his Blue Tick hound, Toby. Mrs. Terrel produced an unwashed pair of Andy's drawers and, after sniffing them thoroughly, Toby bounded off across the countryside to the east of the Terrel cabin. The hound occasionally bayed his mournful howl, as though to urge the searchers to follow him; then, suddenly, he began to bark stridently, summoning one and all to his discovery. When the crowd reached Toby, he was staring down into the vertical shaft of the old abandoned Harris "Golden Princess" mine.

"Oh, my God," exclaimed Arch Lacey. "Not down there."

Todd was one of the next to arrive on the scene. After looking down the gaping and unprotected hole, he hollered, "Hello down there. Can you hear me?"

A weak cry that was little more than a moan was his answer. He then asked, "Does anybody know anything about this mine?"

A voice from farther back in the gathering crowd said, "I worked the Princess more'n two year ago. The two horizontal drifts take off from the shaft about thirty feet down."

Todd immediately assumed command and ordered, "Get me a length of stout rope and somebody go back to my cabin for my medical bag." As several people rushed off in the direction from which they had come, he asked the miner, "What else can you tell me about what it's like down there?"

"Not much," was the answer. "Used to be a windlass up here to hoist ore out, but it was took when the vein petered out. One drift goes out more or less northerly an' one sort of northeast. The shaft don't go no deeper. Didn't seem no point."

A lantern was seen bobbing along the hillside as the person with the rope returned, and Todd immediately tied a double bowline in the end of it to create a crude Boatswain's Chair. When his bag arrived, he grabbed it, put his legs through the loops in the rope and ordered those around to lower him into the hole. The shaft entrance was heavily overgrown with dead vegetation remaining from summer and, as Todd went over the edge, two thoughts crowded his mind; first, how panicked the boy must have been when he started to fall, not knowing how far into the darkness he might plummet; second, the memory of the fear that Todd himself had felt when first confronted with the foretop of the *Ellie Mae,* and how he had shamefully found it necessary to resort to using the "Lubber's Hole."

Down, down, down he went in jerky and hesitant spurts, one hand holding the coal oil lantern and the other grasping his bag and the rope as those above tried to lower him slowly but securely. Suddenly, his foot encountered a soft mass that didn't move but emitted a weak sound, more groan than cry.

"Andy! Andy, it's Dr. Todd and I've come to rescue you. Can you hear me?" The only answer was another feeble groan.

Todd set his lantern and bag down on the muddy floor of the shaft and set about examining the boy. His face was almost obscured by clotted blood from a nasty cut on his forehead. That could explain the boy's almost unconscious state. His neck and upper extremities seemed to be intact; the right lower leg was fractured—both bones—but Todd could feel no bone protruding so it was not a compound fracture. Further examination would have to wait until they were out of this hole.

"Andy, if you can hear me, I'm going to fasten you to a rope and your papa is going to pull you up out of this hole," Todd said and then hollered to the surface, "I've found him, and he is alive. He's unconscious and has a broken leg. Get a short length of rope so I can tie him to your rescue rope and I'll send him up."

Almost as though someone had anticipated the need for such an item, a rope fell down onto him, along with the belated warning, "Look out below."

Todd worked Andy's legs through the loops of the double bowline and then tied the boy's body to the main rope with the short length that had just been dropped.

"All right, haul him up slowly. Be careful because he's unconscious."

The rescuers immediately complied. In only minutes, the rope was lowered again for Todd to come up. He mounted the "chair", picked up his lantern and bag and called, "Haul away. I'm ready."

He had to bounce himself away from the walls of the shaft with his feet as he was pulled up, and he immediately began to worry about any damage that might have been done to the unconscious boy's head if it had snagged when he was being hoisted. When he reached the surface, the crowd was knotted around the inert body of little Andy.

"Take him to my cabin so that I can examine him further, set his leg and sew up that cut on his head," Todd ordered. Only then did he take a great breath of relief and tally up in his mind the many disastrous consequences this event might have had.

- - -

Andy Terrel recovered from his concussion within twenty-four hours, and Todd felt comfortable turning his care over to Dr. Andrus after he had splinted the broken leg and placed the patient at complete bed rest. He was sure that injury would leave the boy lame in later life but, after all, Andy was very lucky to have even survived the terrible fall.

Along with packing their belongings, Todd exerted gentle pressure on those who had outstanding accounts with him, but he was too kind-hearted to apply very much pressure; most of his debtors would have paid already if they had the money. As a result, the collections, his savings at the bank and the sale of the old cabin yielded only $772. Mattie had $88 saved and with $860 of gold in his pocket, Daniel and his wife headed out of town. His medications, instruments, their books, household items and clothing made only a modest load for the freighter who took them to the Willamette River.

As they left the comfort of the now respectable little town of Jacksonville, Todd looked back at the settlement as it slowly was lost from sight among the hills and thought of the many joys and sorrows he had experienced there. He had matured as a doctor; he had found the love of his life and then lost her; he had sunk into the depths of drunken depravity and then, near death, had been rescued by the love of another woman whom he had grown to love passionately. He couldn't help but compare this experience of separation to the one when he had watched his shipmates and close friends from the *Ellie Mae* sail away in their whale boat, leaving him on board the *Calliope*. It seemed as though his life was divided into definite chapters and now he was ready to open the pages on the next one.

Daniel had taken leave of Cordelia at her gravesite last night under the glory of a clear sky with its exuberant display of brilliant stars. It was as though Fate had ordained such an elegant setting for their goodbyes. Mattie, in her wisdom, had understood his need for this final ritual and had silently watched him go out into the night. He had stood by the grave that he felt to be hallowed ground and that he had tended so neatly, and placed his hand on Cordelia's grave marker. Silent, he stared for the longest time into the familiar heavens.

Finally, blinking through his tears, Daniel softly had choked out his parting words. "Del, I will always love you, my dear. I'm leaving you and your grave but I will always have you in my heart, and I will talk to you often in the heavens that we enjoyed so much." He had tearfully but tenderly patted the head board for a final time and stumbled home through the starlit night.

- - -

Daniel reached over and squeezed Mattie's hand as she sat on a bundle of bedding, surrounded by their other possessions, all neatly stowed on the freight wagon, and asked, "Are you warm enough, my dear?"

"Yes, I'm fine. We're embarking on a whole new adventure, aren't we?" she asked, as though she had been able to fathom the thoughts that were going through his mind. "We'll soon have a little companion to accompany us in our new life, though." She patted her slightly bulging but definitely pregnant belly and smiled lovingly at her husband. He smiled in return.

PART FOUR

1864

THE BOISE BASIN

CHAPTER FORTY-ONE

Daniel and Mattie looked out at the broad Columbia as it stretched eastward as far as they could see and even farther up the broad stream, on into their future. They had just come from the tiny railroad café overlooking Celilo Falls where they had had a Spartan meal of roast beef and potatoes and were waiting to board yet another paddle wheeler to continue their journey on upriver to Umatilla. Both, by now, had begun to doubt the wisdom of having uprooted themselves from their home and what they had had in Jacksonville in order to embark on this venture.

Daniel reached over and eased her shawl up over her shoulders to protect Mattie from the now raw, late-October wind and the mist from the nearby falls, saying, "We should be able to get a good night's sleep on the boat during this next phase of the trip."

In the beginning, the freighter had taken them up the well-traveled track from Jacksonville to the main fork of the Applegate and then along its course to the Willamette River, where they encountered their first financial shock. The captain of the small sternwheeler, *Sandpiper*, had weighed their gear on the crude scales at dockside and informed them that transporting their freight to Portland would cost $95 and that passage for the two of them was an additional $100. Daniel paid him and then, with mounting concern, realized that he now had only $600 after paying the freighter to bring them only this far from their home. Supposing we don't have enough even to reach the Boise Basin, he worried.

All the way down the Willamette, he and Mattie had been regaled with stories about the steam sternwheeler *Elk* whose boilers blew up back in '55, the fearsome explosion blasting its Captain Jerome into the top of a tree on the bank. Even more gory were tales of the *Gazelle* that had blown the following year and killed 28 of those on board. Though unnerved, Mattie had merely squeezed Daniel's hand, giving him a brave and reassuring smile. She was a real trooper, thought Daniel.

Their next shock had come in Portland when they went into the offices of the Oregon Steam Navigation Co. to secure passage up the Columbia. After talking to various knowledgeable people, they had determined that they should go upriver as far as Umatilla and then travel overland from there to Idaho City. They were told that the charge was $100 per ton for freight to their destination on the river and passage for each of them was $75. Even if they could leave right away, Daniel knew that reducing their funds to $350 would even further jeopardize their ability to reach their final destination. He and Mattie had conferred and decided that the only alternative to turning back was either to try going overland up the Columbia's shore or to take passage on this boat. Resigned to their situation, the couple sorted through their belongings and sold, for a mere pittance, whatever they thought they could spare. Paying the OSNC $227 for their tickets and freight charges, they went on board the *Tenino*.

They were pleased with the accommodations that included a tiny stateroom and tolerable food. As the puffing sternwheeler, a trim craft with a freshly-painted white wheelhouse and piles of cargo cluttering the deck, moved away from the dock, they were surprised at how swiftly the shoreline now swept backward past them and at how much more rapid this passage was than the trip would have been had they traveled utilizing a wagon freight outfit.

They soon discovered why the freight costs were so expensive. When they reached The Cascades, passengers and all of the cargo had to be off-loaded onto a train that conveyed them on a six-mile portage along the Washington Territory side of the river where they were loaded once again onto another sternwheeler. Daniel never did get a look at its name, but they were on board her only as far as The Dalles where they again boarded a train, this time on the Oregon side of the river. It took them fourteen miles up the river bank to a point above Celilo Falls.

When Daniel commented on all of this effort to get upriver, a deck hand had said, "Oh yeah, but 'tis a bodacious thing that there's been so much rain upriver. Last year 'twas a dry 'un. When water's skinny like that, we had ta handle cargo more'n a dozen times twixt Portland an' Lewiston, up in Idaho country."

But now, it looked like clear sailing to Umatilla, although Daniel couldn't help but be apprehensive over what new barriers they might encounter there. He had been advised to seek out John Hailey, the freighter, when they reached that milepost in their travels.

- - -

Umatilla was little more than a tiny settlement with a dock protruding out into the river a few yards from the shore. It was surrounded by dry, barren hills, their monotony broken only by a sparse growth of willow along the stream that emptied there into the Columbia. The town itself consisted of a huge livery barn, a hotel/café, a mercantile store and two saloons. Todd quickly discovered that John Hailey had departed less than a week before, and that a man called Trace Stevens was now the only other packer who was available to move freight over to the Boise Basin.

After getting Mattie settled in the Orleans Hotel, Todd sought out Mr. Stevens, finding him in the Columbia Queen, the slightly more elegant of the two saloons. Trace Stevens was a big, raw-boned man who sat at one of the tables at the back of the establishment.

"Mr. Stevens, my name is Todd. I'm a doctor and I'm headed to the Boise Basin. My wife and I have some freight and I would like for you to transport it and the two of us to that area. Can you help me?"

To Daniel's surprise, Stevens rose from the table to shake his hand. "Yes, I'm Stevens and packing is my business, Dr. Todd." His voice, in contrast to his appearance, was soft and restrained. His manner was most gentlemanly. "How much gear do you have?"

"The steamship line claimed that we had 1240 pounds but I think that is an excessive measurement," Todd replied. "Of course, you will have to weigh all of that yourself."

Quickly calculating in his head, Stevens said, "That would be about $310, Dr. Todd. I charge twenty-five cents a pound, and I move freight on pack mules. Do you and your wife have mounts yourself or are you going to travel by stage?"

"We're afoot, sir, and I did not know that stage travel was possible. My wife is five months pregnant, but I think she could ride all right," was Todd's hesitant reply. "Tell me about the stages."

"Well, Ish and Hailey have been running coaches the 300 miles or so from here to The Basin for five or six months. Thomas has a line going from Wallula up over the Blues on the Thomas and Ruckles Road northeast of here. They each charge $150, I think, per person but carry no freight to speak of. On the other hand, if each of you ride with me, that will require two more animals, each of which could move two hundred pounds of freight if I were packing them. Along with your found for the trip, it will cost you $100 each, in addition to your freight." The brutal news was delivered in the most kindly manner, but it was devastating to Daniel, knowing that either amount would completely deplete their funds.

"And if I walked?" Todd asked.

"Then it would be a total of $125, travel and found, for both you and your wife. I would warn you, though, sir . . ." Stevens took a deep breath before he proceeded. "And I don't want you to think I'm bleeding you for money, but it's a hell of a long trail—mighty steep up over the Blues—and we move pretty damn fast. I'd hate to have to abandon you, footsore and worn out, halfway twixt here and there."

"We want to go, Mr. Stevens. I'll talk to my wife and decide if we can whittle down our freight a bit. When do you leave?" Todd asked.

"Five days, if I get my load all lined out."

Quickly balancing a $125 charge by Stevens against $300 for the stage, Todd said, "Count us in. We'll have our freight ready by tomorrow."

When he got back to the hotel, he found Mattie lying down on their bed. She wasn't asleep and the bedsprings skirled their loud protest as she turned to face him when he entered. "Did you find the man?" she asked.

"Yes, and we can leave in five days but it will take just about all of the money we have left," he answered. "Mattie, I hate to do it, but we just have to abandon some more of our things to cut down the cost of the move. Can you help with that?"

"My family had to do that when we came out on the Oregon Trail; we grudgingly made a number of *gifts* to the Indians along the way. I suppose I can do it again. Let me rest a while, and then we'll go down and make our decisions before supper." She turned back and faced the wall. Knowing that the move had been mostly on her insistence didn't make the moment any easier for her.

- - -

The small bureau that Mattie's sister had laid out her dead baby in years ago back in Ohio was one of the casualties. There was some consolation in knowing that it would be very difficult to transport it on a pack mule anyway and that made the parting with it easier. Leaving cherished books and all but the most basic cooking utensils was more difficult. They cut their food supplies in half, hesitating all the while because they knew that these items would cost much more in the Boise Basin than they would get for them here in Umatilla. They estimated that they still had about 500 pounds of freight when they got all through. That would make their bill $325 if

Daniel rode—$250 if he walked. When he counted the gold in his money belt again, it had not grown from the $352 Daniel knew was there. That confirmed his decision to walk and would leave them with only about $75 after they paid their hotel and board bill for the next five days. He hugged Mattie and gave her a deceptively brave smile.

"We'll be just fine," he said. "Now, let's go and have our supper. Are you feeling more rested?"

- - -

The days that followed were filled with what seemed needless delay to Daniel, but Stevens was carefully weighing and making up his packs, sorting food supplies so he knew exactly where everything was located and putting his tack and animals in the best possible condition for the long journey ahead. Mattie took daily walks along the dusty streets of the little town. On the third day, she rushed back to the hotel in panic when a band of Indians rode into the village and looked about them with an imperious air as though the place was theirs and every white person was an interloper.

Daniel gathered Mattie protectively in his arms and asked the hotel man who these savages were.

The answer was, "Oh, that's young chief Homily of the Umatilla tribe. He'd sure 'nuf like to bust loose and drive all us'ns off into the river, but the Army done tolt 'im they'd confiscate all his people's horses was he to give any misery to the whites. Them Umatillas damn sure prize their horses—they's mostly appaloosi what they took from the Nez Perce. So, they's fair tolerant of us, fer the time bein', 'cause of that threat."

Daniel had noted the big prize stallion that the Indian leader was riding and could understand why he would want to protect it. He only wished he owned that sturdy mount for the long trip ahead.

The Indians made several passes at a gallop through town with much shouting and waving of their bows in the air but did nothing more threatening than that. It had been enough, however, to restrict Mattie's exercise to brief walks very close to the hotel from then on.

On the evening before their departure, Todd sought out Stevens, gave him the $232 fee for the freight charge and his and Mattie's transport fee. He informed the packer that he was going to walk.

Stevens simply nodded his head, grimly accepting the decision, and said, "I guess you know what you're doin', Mister. Just don't whine and ask for a ride somewheres on down the trail, 'cause we won't have a mount for ye."

Very early the next morning, Stevens and his two helpers lined out the cantankerous string of pack mules, all very heavily laden, and headed them out in a southeasterly direction across the dry, sagebrush hills that stretched all the way to the horizon. Mattie rode sidesaddle on a horse with spotted withers that resembled the Indians' ponies and stayed far enough behind the string of pack animals that she escaped their dust. Daniel walked along behind her mount and wondered how he was going to feel at the end of this day. The sun rose in a cloudless sky some forty minutes after they had hit the trail.

- - -

They learned in the days that followed that the routine rarely varied. It consisted of a large breakfast of bacon, fried potatoes and coffee prepared by one of Stevens' helpers while the packer and his other man packed the mules. Mattie couldn't resist lending a helping hand. Departure from the camp site was always before sun-up and brief stops were made about every two hours for the animals to "blow" and for people who felt it necessary to relieve themselves. Coffee was boiled at the nooning, but no other repast was offered. At least an hour before dark, the evening camp was pitched near a stream, whenever possible, but on open prairie if not. In those cases, water for camp use would be drawn from the casks carried by one of the mules, and the animals themselves would have to wait until the first water course was encountered the next day for their ration. Todd was pleased to note that Stevens' water casks had none of the "bilgey" taste that he remembered from those on the *Ellie Mae*.

The same "cook" who prepared breakfast always put beans to boil and began peeling potatoes just as soon as they stopped for the night, while Stevens and the other packer stripped the mules, hobbled them and put them to graze on the dry bunch grass of the prairie.

Mattie was tolerating the journey very well and always cheerfully responded to any of Daniel's inquiries about her welfare. After nursing very sore feet the first two nights, he was keeping up with the pace of the string. He was thankful, though, that he did not have to carry his blankets or a pack of supplies on his back; he doubted he would have been able to keep up as well if he had had to bear much of a burden.

After four days, the trail began steadily to ascend and the dark shadows of wooded hillsides became visible in the near distance. "The Blues," Stevens cryptically announced that night in camp. "Thank God we don't see any snow on 'em yet. This probably will be the last trip we get in 'fore winter, though, I fear."

That night, the cook made Dutch Oven biscuits and added some onion and molasses to the beans to celebrate the completion of the first phase of the journey.

They plodded upward through dense forest, crested the summit without being beset by blizzards and then descended the eastern slope until they crossed the Grande Ronde river. This late in the season, it was little more than a creek. For the next three days, they traveled south-southeast through a broad valley between what Stevens said were the Blues on the west and the Wallowas on the east until they finally crossed the Burnt River. This stream also was shrunken to little more than a creek.

The low water of the season was truly a blessing when they encountered the broad Snake where the autumn flow allowed Todd simply to wade across; the water scarcely even wet the rider's stirrups. Stevens said that the silt deposited by the Boise River dumping in just upstream created this ford, but that during the spring flood, even this spot needed to be crossed by a ferry. Proceeding up the course of the Boise for only a few miles brought them to the crumbling ruins of old Fort Boise, a commercial trading post established by the Hudson's Bay Fur Company some thirty years earlier, but which had been abandoned for the past six or seven years. The walls and square bastions now guarded nothing and were attacked by nothing more violent than Nature's elements.

A cold drizzle enveloped them as they approached the old fort, and Stevens indicated that they would find shelter for the night in some of its abandoned buildings. As they entered through a squeaking and unhinged front gate, Daniel couldn't help but think about all of the effort that had gone into the construction of the fort and wonder if the protection it afforded had ever been required for the safety of the establishment and its people.

After the evening meal, which included two fine, large trout that the wranglers had caught in the river, Mattie called Daniel aside and said, "I'm afraid that I have been having some spotting of blood today, Daniel. No great amount, you understand, but enough for a bloody show."

"Have you had any cramping?" Todd asked.

"No. Absolutely nothing of that sort," she replied.

Daniel forbade her helping with the meal preparation and, when she prepared for bed, he brought a lantern and inspected her undergarments. There was no odor of corruption so he doubted the death of the baby *in utero,* but he went to Stevens and told him that Mattie was having difficulty with her unborn infant and that his wife needed some bed rest.

"We've got to press on to Idaho City to beat the winter weather, Dr. Todd. I'd like to lay over for her, but this rain we're getting is surely putting snow down in the mountains," was his answer.

"How far from Boise City are we?" Todd asked

"Day an' a half," Stevens replied.

"Travel slower and make that two days," Todd pleaded, "and my wife and I will stop there; we won't continue on to Idaho City. Can you do that?"

"Yes," Stevens said after careful consideration. "It won't make that much difference in the time it takes for us to get to Idaho City."

Daniel spent the evening and night solicitously caring for Mattie and hoping against hope that there would be some accommodations in Boise City where he could put his wife at bed rest to protect her and their unborn infant. He didn't give the crumbling surroundings of the fort another thought except for being thankful for the protection the place provided against the rain which by now had become torrential.

As he lay down beside her in the warmth of their comforters, Daniel said, "Don't worry about this bleeding, Mattie. We'll stop over in Boise City for a while and give you complete bed rest. I'm certain that you won't lose this baby like you lost the last one. Are you feeling all right?"

"I'm fine, Daniel. Thank you for your care. How will we afford staying in Boise City?"

"We'll manage just fine," Daniel replied, hiding his worry with brave words.

CHAPTER FORTY-TWO

Boise City consisted of a single broad and muddy street. Although just a little over a year old, the community already had buildings constructed from sawed boards. The two-story Columbia Hotel was one of these. It could boast of an attached restaurant and, bowing to the demands of the times, a small bar near its entrance. So luxurious was this hostelry that its upper story was even served by a two-story privy at the rear. Lining the street on to the east was a mercantile, a gunsmith, two blacksmith shops, a livery stable and a barber/bath shop. Across the street was a row of four saloons, a café, a second livery stable with a large hay barn, a meat shop, a Chinese laundry, and the assay office. A rather elaborate repair station had evolved to work on wagons of the Oregon Trail trains that passed through town constantly during the summer. None of these were evident; no trains had passed through Boise City for the past month.

Daniel and Mattie rented a room at the Columbia for an indefinite period of time. Their accommodation was located at the rear of the second floor, and from its window, they could look out to the north at the military Fort Boise and the foothills stretching upward behind it to the ring of mountains beyond. Substantial barracks and horse barns had been built, but the barrier walls surrounding the fort appeared to be more for show than protection. A snowstorm blanketed the town with a soft, clean tranquility, and Boise City was far from the boisterous mining town that Daniel envisioned Idaho City, their destination, to be. It was with mixed emotions that he imagined Stevens and the pack string heading out early the next morning toward that town without the Todds or their belongings. But, Mattie and the baby were the most important thing for Daniel to consider at the moment. He went over and stroked her forehead where she lay comfortably in the room's squeaky bed. "Can I get you anything?" he asked.

"No. This bed feels wonderful. I don't want to move for a week," she replied and languorously stretched.

"I'll go down to the restaurant in an hour or so and bring up some supper for both of us," Daniel said. He set about emptying their bag and placing their clothing in the marble-topped bureau. That chest, a wash stand and a chair were the only pieces of furniture in the room, besides the bed.

Daniel didn't have to inspect their dwindling gold supply to know how inadequate it was. He would have to earn some money soon if they were going to spend the entire winter in this hotel. He had nearly panicked when the desk clerk had told him that this room would cost $11 for the week. Suddenly very aware of the chill of their lodging, he went over and lay down beside Mattie and pulled another comforter up over them. Just then, their snug cabin in Jacksonville, with its roaring fireplace, presented a most appealing memory.

- - -

After breakfast the next day, Daniel waded through ankle-deep snow to explore Boise City. A faint dusting of flakes still sifted down over his shoulders. For Mattie's sake, he was thankful that the weather had held until they reached this town. The thought of her, in her condition, sleeping out in a snow bank was abhorrent to him. There was no sign of Stevens' mule string; he had no idea how far out of town the packer had gone to camp yesterday after leaving the Todds.

As he had done in Jacksonville years ago, Daniel went from business to business and introduced himself. Most of these were already open and their inhabitants hard at work. If he had any thought of practicing Medicine here during the winter, Daniel had to make himself known. Even more important, he had to find space to rent so that he could set up an office. Mr. Jacobson at the mercantile was giving the store its morning sweep out. He didn't miss a stroke of the broom, but he seemed willing to visit with Dr. Todd.

"No, I don't know of any place you could rent to set up an office," Jacobson commented. "Buildin' was goin' on here like there warn't no tomorrow until a few weeks ago, but ever'body was just buildin' fer their own needs. Ain't no rentals in town that I know of."

Daniel was very discouraged and wondered if he would have to rent another room at the hotel to use as his office, but the outrageous price there was almost prohibitive. And with Mattie at bed rest, there was no way he could use their present room for both an office and their lodging.

He dawdled, inspecting Jacobson's wares in a desultory fashion as he turned these problems over in his mind.

Two soldiers, presumably from the Fort, entered the store, their navy blue capes lightly matted with the snow. They went directly to Mr. Jacobson and asked if he had any liniment. Todd overheard one of them say that since the Army doctor was laid low, they had no sick call anymore. Daniel approached them to explore this situation further.

"I'm Dr. Daniel Todd and I just arrived in town. Did I understand you to say that you have no doctor at the Fort?" he asked.

The troopers were slow to answer, both suspiciously appraising Daniel from head to foot. Finally, one said, "That's right, mister." He looked at his partner as if to question whether or not he should share any more of their information with this stranger.

Finally, the other man said, "Yep, more'n a week ago, our troop went out on a punishin' raid against the Paiute. They'd massacred some homesteaders a dozen miles to the southwest. Our Doc Watkins went along in case anybody had survived out there. All dead, but them Injuns warn't gone. They stormed o'er the hill an' hit us like a shovelful o' shit. Wouldn't ye know it—they done hit the Doc an' jus' 'bout done fer him."

The other trooper joined in at this point and added, "We got 'im back to the Fort, but he may cross o'er the bar any time now. Don't look good."

Todd volunteered, "I will be happy to come out and see to him. Who's your commanding officer there?"

"Major Lugenbeil is in charge of the Fort. We ain't s'posed to be out o' the compound so's ye didn't hear any o' this from us'ns, but I'm sure ye'd be welcome out there was ye to show up."

The trooper pushed the liniment back across the counter to Jacobson and said, "Guess I'll take a few seegars 'stead o' that, mister. Might not need it." He paid up and nodded to Todd before they left.

Jacobson grunted, "How's that fer coincidence, Doc? Yer office may be out at the Fort from now on."

Daniel couldn't wait to share the news with Mattie and go out to the military post to introduce himself. He thanked Jacobson and left.

- - -

Major Lugenbeil was a tall, graying man, and he moved around his office with a limp, perhaps the result of some wound received on Civil War battlefields back east, Todd speculated. He had had some difficulty in getting past the sentry at the gate of the Fort but when Todd identified himself as a doctor and said that he might be of assistance to Dr. Watkins, he was ushered immediately into Lugenbeil's office.

After the introductions, Todd got directly to the point. "I heard in town about your doctor being wounded, and I came to see if I could be of any assistance. My wife and I just arrived on a mule saddle train from Oregon Territory yesterday, and we are staying in Boise City."

After shaking hands, the Major replied, "Yes, Dr. Todd, we are in a bind. Because of the conflict back east, I don't know when we might get a replacement for Dr. Watkins and, at the moment, his very life hangs in the balance. I would be most grateful if you would see what you can do for him."

Todd eagerly agreed and was quickly shown to Watkins' quarters. The man was feverish and in delirium. He had a gunshot wound in the right lower abdomen, but it seemed to Todd that it was far enough to the side and the man was obese enough that it might not have penetrated the peritoneal cavity. But when he put his ear to the abdomen and heard no bowel sounds he decided that, with no peristalsis present, peritonitis had probably developed. It was a through-and-through hole so there was no retained bullet, but the area was definitely very inflamed. The man was dehydrated with dry and caked lips, a bounding pulse and a parchment tongue. The bedclothes were a mat of dried blood and secretions from the wound. Todd stripped the patient, cleansed the area around the wound with water, teased a plug of tunic cloth from where it had been blown into the anterior portion of the wound and then, after re-bandaging, clumsily remade the bed underneath him with clean linen that he found in the cupboard.

He returned to Lugenbeil's office. "My medications are packed away in town," he told the Major. "May I inspect Dr. Watkins' pharmacy for his medical supplies? If I can control his inflammation, I hope I can save his life, but I think he has peritonitis from the abdominal wound and, so, I'm not too hopeful."

"Of course," Lugenbeil replied. "Orderly, show Dr. Todd to the Infirmary so he can obtain whatever medicines he needs."

Todd was not surprised by the scantiness of medicine that he found. He took some laudanum, chlorate of potash, spirits of nitre, a lancet, a small basin and returned to the doctor's quarters. He asked the Orderly to prepare a large pot of tea and also to see if he could obtain a quantity of beef broth. The room was chilly, so he built a sagebrush fire in the stove first and then set about compounding some of the medicine he would need.

In light of the patient's bounding pulse, Todd's first action was to bleed about eight ounces from Watkins' antecubital vein although he continued to have serious doubts of the wisdom and effectiveness of this procedure. He was somewhat surprised when he found the doctor to be so comatose that he made absolutely no response to the pain of the venesection. Todd was also unable to rouse him enough to take any medicine by mouth, so he merely wet the patient's lips and tongue with a cloth moistened in water. He then instructed the Orderly, who was watching all this with great curiosity, to give Watkins tea and broth if he should awaken enough to accept it. He went back to the Major's office and informed him that he would have to return to town and get the medical supplies necessary for properly treating the Army surgeon.

After first checking on Mattie and telling her he might be at the Fort until dinnertime, Daniel went to the livery barn where they had temporarily left their freight and fetched flaxseed, some extracts of butternut and of jalap, as well as some of Gung Pi's *tung-kuei-tze* and rapeseed oil. He hurried back to the military post, not surprised to find the patient's condition unchanged. The room was now comfortably warm so he stripped the blanket off Watkins, tore up a bedsheet and used it to bind a flaxseed poultice in place over the skin wounds and then set about dripping broth and some of his medications into the man's mouth. Several times the patient coughed when Todd, in his eagerness, supplied the liquid too rapidly but, all in all, he was satisfied with what he was able to administer.

Watkins' brow was still flushed and hot, but he now moaned occasionally and soon, Todd thought, would be able to sip some liquids. He instructed the Orderly on what to give and then once again returned to town so he could obtain his own and Mattie's meal and take the food to their room. The sun had set when he and Mattie finished their supper and he trudged through the snow back toward the Fort. The sky had cleared, the stars were out, and the black rim of mountains behind the military post framed the night sky. Todd looked at the heavens for his usual communion with Cordelia. Although not making a sound as he plodded along, his thoughts conveyed to the old love of his life what the current situation was that faced Mattie and him. He even stopped in his tracks when a shooting star streaked across the sky and peered long at the path it had traced through the heavens, wondering if its passage had been any sort of a message from his departed Del.

He identified himself at the Guard's challenge and was admitted through the gate of the Fort. Only scattered lights showed through windows here and there. What he assumed was the horse barn and feed storage area on the west and north was darkened. Flanking the front gate were barracks for the troops and only pale light showed through the windows. All but one of the cottages crowning the slight rise on the north edge of the parade ground had lights showing; these were Headquarters and residences for the officers. The Infirmary where he had gone to pick up medications earlier, the mess hall and kitchen, and some storerooms made up the eastern wall of the Fort. They had been constructed of logs and the back wall of all of these structures composed the outer walls of the Fort.

When he arrived at Watkins' quarters, Todd was dismayed to discover that the Army doctor was much worse, in spite of his treatments. He felt hotter to the touch, his pulse and breathing had increased and, occasionally, his abdominal cramping broke through the anesthesia-effect of his coma and he writhed in pain on the narrow bed. In spite of anything that Todd could do, the patient died shortly before dawn.

Todd had always felt very empathetic with his patients, but this man's death, although probably inevitable, was particularly devastating to him because of the circumstances. Not only was this event catastrophic for Watkins himself and whatever family he might have, but Todd had wanted so very much to impress the Army with his medical skills. This defeat reflected poorly on his abilities. He sought out Major Lugenbeil before the formalities of the morning formation to report Dr. Watkins' death and found him coming out onto the parade ground from his office.

The Major shook his head at the news and simply said, "I would like for you to remain until after the Colors Parade, Dr. Todd. I must talk to you." His orderly handed him the reins of his horse, and the commanding officer mounted to ride out in front of the long file of mounted troopers. All came to attention as the bugle sounded to accompany the hoisting of the flag, and then there were shouted reports from along the line of men. After the long night at his patient's bedside, Todd was anxious to get back to the hotel and Mattie who would be worried; it seemed to him that this pageantry was needlessly long.

When the whole ceremony was finally finished and orders issued for the day, Lugenbeil returned. Dismounting, he invited Dr. Todd into his office.

"I may seem callous to you if I speak of these things before Surgeon Watkins is even in his grave, Dr. Todd, but this is wartime and I have the welfare of two companies of cavalry to concern me. Those troopers are experiencing almost daily encounters with hostile Paiutes. I now have only the Surgeon's striker to administer medical care to my men. As I told you yesterday, with the war still raging in the East, there is practically no prospect of receiving any replacement for Dr. Watkins in the immediate future. Could I interest you in filling that role, sir?" the Commander asked.

"Do you mean to recruit me into the army?" Todd asked in his surprise.

"No, of course not," Lugenbeil replied. "I have authority to contract for certain services although, I admit, funds to pay for such things are somewhat erratic in arriving at such a remote post as this. You could use Dr. Watkins' quarters and I could guarantee compensation—eventually—although the funds might not arrive until spring."

"My wife is with me, Major," Todd said, not very enthusiastic about the offer. "We were on our way to Idaho City but she developed medical problems, and we had to lay over here in Boise City, perhaps even for the entire winter."

Lugenbeil was not to be deterred and argued, "Granted, we have not yet constructed quarters suitable for wives—even mine will not join me until next spring or summer—but I'm certain that we could arrange accommodations for the two of you if you would consent to help us out."

"Would I be able to conduct some private practice on the side?" Todd asked, "On civilian patients in the town itself? I would have to have some sort of continuing income with which to purchase medical supplies if the funds from the army are often as 'erratic' as you suggest."

"Of course. Do we have a deal, Doctor? Will you aid your country in this manner?"

Perhaps it was because, from time to time in the past, Todd had experienced an occasional twinge of guilt for not being personally involved in the great war between the states that he now thought he detected a hint of accusatory judgment in Lugenbeil's attitude. Perhaps not. In any case, the offer provided a temporary solution to his and Mattie's financial problems so he replied, "Yes, I will be most happy to assume these duties. Would I be able to move my wife out here by the end of the week?"

"Yes, even sooner if you like. I will order some of my men to prepare your quarters for you immediately. I assume you can start holding sick call even today, though, if necessary."

"Of course," Todd replied.

CHAPTER FORTY-THREE

November and early December brought about a dramatic change in the lives of the Todds. Two rooms in Officer's Quarters at Fort Boise were made available to them and Mattie, who was active and on her feet again, was able to transform the lodging into very comfortable living quarters. Todd's professional practice on the post consisted of simple medical problems, for the most part, because the troops were generally in very good health. He was able to find space in the back of Agnew and Riggs' adobe saloon in town where he could hold private office hours for a part of each day. He found the nearly-half-mile walk to and from the Fort pleasant even though the early winter had deposited considerable snow.

Mattie became the darling of the post. With her returning health, she resumed the "nursing" role she had filled in Jacksonville, although it was seldom necessary. The Todds took their meals in the Officers' Mess, and Daniel was extremely proud of the grace and charm Mattie exhibited there. Of the six officers, three had seen action on battlefields back east earlier in the war, two had been promoted from the ranks after extended duty on the frontier itself, and one was a recent graduate from "The Point". The latter, Second Lieutenant Davis, presumably coached the two "mustangs", the ones promoted from the ranks, in the social graces because all three were models of proper etiquette and charm in the presence of Mattie. She, in turn, always displayed wit, intelligent judgments and offered well-considered opinions when it was appropriate for her to voice them. Her grammar was precise and faultless, her tone always melodious and, although now a little over six months pregnant, she always sat with head high, her proud spine never touching the back of her chair. She was a *grande dame* of magnificent dignity and Daniel could not have been more proud of her. When taking her daily stroll about the post, though, Mattie was equally warm and friendly to the enlisted men but so dignified that she maintained a somewhat regal aura that provided her with an armor that not a single man would think of breaching by showing the slightest sign of disrespect.

Boise's growth was slow because almost everyone who arrived there was merely passing through on their way to Idaho City, Centerville, Placerville, other mining camps to the north and east or to the new gold strikes to the southwest. Boise City had become a transportation and supply center. Only months earlier Ben Holliday had established the stage line going through Boise City from Salt Lake City to "the Double Wallas" and Wallula in Washington Territory. Now, lumbering freight wagons had started following the stage road carrying grain, flour, hay and other provisions from the Mormon farm communities of Utah Territory and the eastern end of Idaho Territory to supply the mining camps.

Daniel was already aware that jackrabbits tremendously outnumbered people in and around Boise City. Whereas the town's population numbered only in the hundreds, Idaho City boasted of over 6,000 inhabitants with some 300 women and more than 200 children. That burgeoning mining town was said to have over three dozen saloons, many law offices, two bowling alleys, a mattress factory, a photographer's gallery, and even a hospital of sorts. Daniel had not been able to learn how many doctors were practicing there, but he suspected there was no shortage. All of this growth, as well as that of the other mining communities, had taken place in the brief two and a half years since gold was first discovered in the Boise Basin.

Their situation argued against Daniel's original plan to establish his practice in one of the mining camps of "the Basin". Now that the die was cast, he realized that he and Mattie were better off remaining in Boise City, at least until after Mattie had delivered, and then they could decide to stay or move on.

- - -

Fresh snow blanketed the parade ground when Dr. Todd stepped out of his quarters after hearing the bugler's mess call. He looked around him appreciatively, having grown accustomed to these surroundings. They were certainly more orderly than any mining camps he had been in, many of which were much longer established than this Fort. The harsh winter seemed to lend a relatively relaxed feeling of security to the post because nobody expected the Paiute to rampage during weather like this. They would undoubtedly wait until spring grass restored their horses before they embarked on any depredations such as they had in the past.

Today, Daniel had decided to eat with the troopers in their mess and evaluate how they fared. He had commented on their state of good nourishment to several troopers who had come to Sick Call. Each had given the same story. Army rations were tiresomely plain and consisted mostly of beans, bread and salt pork that was often so old that the fat had sloughed away from the lean. The government commissary department issued rations according to the complement of men that regulations called for in a company. Seldom was that roster ever full and so extra "issue" rations were sold by the mess sergeant to settlers, merchants or other townspeople and the money added to the "company fund," and then used to purchase more varied food items and fresh vegetables locally, products that everyone called "non-issue" items. And, Todd learned also that there was keen competition between the Companies as to which group could raise the best garden. The past summer had produced a cornucopia of potatoes, squash, carrots and cabbage so, for the time being, the rations were considered excellent.

But Daniel was disappointed when he sat down to share the troopers' breakfast. It was hash, bread with no butter, and black coffee; no milk or sugar graced the table. Even Fishcake's porridge breakfasts back on the *Ellie Mae* were preferable to this repast. When Daniel commented on that fact, he was assured that dinner was almost always better than breakfast.

The trooper across the table from him said, "You should eat field rations, Doc. When we're on patrol, ever' meal is fried salt pork, mashed-up hardtack fried in the grease, an' coffee. Ever' damn meal, I tell you."

Not reassured by that information, Todd chewed on his hash without enthusiasm and found that each bite seemed to get larger the longer he chewed it.

- - -

Mattie had asked Major Lugenbeil for permission to hold evening classes for any of the men who wished to learn to read or cipher. He had given his approval. and the mess hall was made available after supper three evenings each week. Daniel didn't want her to overdo, but her boredom had become so evident that he welcomed her suggestion. Although a few of the men were quite well educated, a great number were completely illiterate.

The first evening, only three men appeared. They seemed ill-at-ease and as though they were embarrassed to reveal their lack of education. Mattie had brought one of her books of poetry and after struggling to teach them the alphabet and the rudiments of phonics, she read several of the poems.

The meter, the beauty of the words spoken in her melodious voice, and the meaning of the works when she explained what she had read left them enraptured. The next session was attended by seventeen troopers, and Mattie had to start all over again. Eventually, field manuals, the occasional Bible, general orders, any printed material became a reading resource for the troopers. Everybody, Mattie included, enjoyed themselves tremendously.

Daniel was as concerned about the men's clothing as his wife was about their intellectual welfare. He had been so impressed that first day when he saw the troopers mounted and drawn up for inspection because they had been wearing their dress uniforms with the dark blue, roll-collar blouses, the light blue trousers with the yellow piping, their campaign hats and swords. They had been strikingly smart. But, out here on the frontier, supply was a difficult and serious problem. Shoddy, wartime-issue clothing soon wore out with the result that everyday clothing, except when the men were on parade, on guard duty or some similar work detail that was out of the ordinary, consisted of a highly variable patchwork of the "make-do" assortment instead of regulation uniforms. Boots and shoes were mostly those manufactured at the military prison at Fort Leavenworth, Kansas. The abominable things could be worn on either foot, and the leather uppers were held to the soles by brass screws. They were most uncomfortable and not very durable. Most troopers wore Indian moccasins and, saving their campaign hats for patrols, forage caps were worn around the post. Soldiers frequently bought clothing from those of their comrades who were being discharged or at the occasional post auction where condemned quartermaster stores or clothing of deserters was sold.

Some items, particularly winter clothing that was necessary here in this harsh climate, were quartermaster property and simply "loaned" to the troopers. Such articles included buffalo coats, leggings, muskrat caps and fur gauntlets. These goods were carefully logged and had to be returned to the quartermaster when spring arrived.

The men were given a uniform allowance against which clothing items could be charged but, since the supply was so erratic and the clothing quality was so poor, the soldiers usually just got along on non-regulation items when they could and let their credits accrue so that they could draw the money in a lump sum upon discharge.

- - -

Mattie's presence at table in the Officer's Mess resulted in much greater formality than might have ordinarily existed, particularly at the evening meal. The officers tried to outdo each other in displaying their chivalry and etiquette. In spite of their best efforts, all too often the conversation drifted to news of the war in the east or to the Indian situation, although the latter seldom involved any commentary about the local Paiutes. It would have been considered too unnerving to Mrs. Todd to discuss matters that might impact the immediate environs of Fort Boise.

Daniel had heard a number of times from people in town about how unruly the local Indians—the Paiute Shoshone, the Snakes, the Weisers, the Bruneaus, the Malheurs, and the Bannock—had been during the virtual absence of military might from the area during the war between the States. The impact on the miners had begun two years earlier, in 1862, when the Indians had killed George Grimes from ambush while he was panning his discovery of gold in Boise Basin near the present town of Pioneer City.

The depredations had gradually increased against miners, packers bringing supplies to the area, farmers, or just any white man. Killings were rampant, horses were stolen, and buildings burned. Finally, in the spring of 1863, the miners temporarily left their claims to form up two companies of men to go on punishing raids, mainly against the Paiute. One was under the command of Jeff Standifer and the other under one of his lieutenants, J. T. Sutton. They raided scattered bands of Indians, killing and scattering them and relieving them of huge bands of stolen horses. This had had a dampening effect on the natives, limiting their murderous raids for a while. The most significant result of all this activity was that the U. S. Army sent Major Lugenbeil and his troopers to the area to start Fort Boise. The presence of these men and establishment of Fort Boise had been a great reassurance to everyone in the Boise Basin, except for the Indians.

Major Lugenbeil and the two mustangs, Captain Townsend and First Lieutenant Chalmers, seemed to be the best informed about conditions of the Indian problem in the West and, from time to time, they discussed it in general terms after the evening meal. The Santee Sioux had erupted from Minnesota in 1862 and had flooded the Dakotas to join their western kinsmen. Since then, their war parties, along with the Cheyenne and Arapaho, had scourged much of the Nebraska, Kansas, Wyoming and Colorado country. On the southern plains, the Commanches and Kiowas fought the meager Union and Confederate forces alike.

Just a month earlier, the southern Cheyennes had negotiated for terms and had gone into winter camp near Sand Creek in southeastern Colorado. A force of Colorado volunteers under a man by the name of Chivington then tried to annihilate that camp of Black Kettle, and now it was feared that this massacre would fan the Plains Indians into a new outbreak of warfare. The northern Cheyenne and Sioux were already wreaking their vengeance. The Apaches and the Navajos had been at war with the whites in the Southwest since 1861. Kit Carson and his force had subdued the Mescalero Apaches almost a year earlier and had forced the Navajos to surrender at Canyon de Chelly. The Navajos had been quiet since, but some bands of Apaches were increasingly bothersome.

Violence had erupted everywhere and when such discussions about it started, Mattie usually excused herself, either retiring to her quarters to read or going to conduct one of her classes in the Troopers' Mess Hall. Daniel wanted to allay her worries and accompany her, but he was so fascinated by the tales told by the officers that he usually stayed behind. The settled country back around Jacksonville seemed very tame by comparison.

- - -

The outbreak of venereal disease started with what seemed to be an isolated case. Because of the preponderance of men living in the places where Daniel had practiced in the past, it had not been uncommon for him to see a moderate number of cases of gleet or gonorrhea or whatever the patients chose to call it. Most often, these were in the early stage of that disease, and a rather conservative therapy had been adequate to ease the symptoms. Daniel had occasionally seen the erythematous rash or early buboes of syphilis and there were times when some of the patients he had seen had papular skin eruptions, destructive lesions of bone or skin, or vascular or neurological findings that he strongly suspected of being due to secondary or tertiary forms of that disease which had such protean manifestations.

Venereal disease being common, Todd didn't consider it too unusual when Private Eli Kennedy came to Sick Call, feverish and in great distress. Examination revealed a painfully enlarged and inflamed penis with true phimosis; the foreskin was swollen and thickened into a ring so tight that the organ was bent sideways and only the urethral opening was visible—that pouting eye could be seen weeping thick pus. Kennedy reported the history of rapidly increasing symptoms that began just a few days after he had visited a "lady of the evening" in town. The trooper was fully aware that he had caught "the clap" but was amazed and frightened by its severity.

Todd set about initiating the usual treatment for this stage of the disease: ordering the patient to avoid rigorous exercise or horseback riding, which in Kennedy's case restricted him from duty; administration of a cathartic;

soaking the penis in hot boric acid solution for 15 minutes five or six times daily and oral administration of a mixture of bicarbonate of potassium, tincture of hyoscine and water every six hours. In the absence of improvement in the man's condition, Todd resorted to a variety of treatments; suppositories of sulphate of morphia, extract of belladonna and oleum theobromate; avoidance of an erection by using liquid Morphiae Magendie, cocaine muriate and water, irrigated into the urethra before retiring. He advised scrupulous avoidance of touching the eyes with fingers contaminated with the purulent discharge from the penis because the most recent issue of *Lancet* he had seen—over six months ago—had described blindness from such polluted transfer; and the total abstention from alcohol.

Kennedy was miserable because of the infection but also in great part from being restricted to the Dispensary, where his treatment could be supervised and the proscription of alcohol enforced. The Dispensary was inundated, though, over the next several days, beginning with three more cases. By the fourth day, a total of thirteen cases of severe gonorrhea had presented for treatment but, fortunately, none as severe as Kennedy's. This far exceeded the capacity of the Dispensary, so Todd set up a section of the barracks as his "hospital". At first, nobody would reveal the name of his contact in town but upon threats of restriction of pay during their disablement—which Todd was quite certain he could not implement—they, one by one, revealed the "soiled dove" who had favored them with such a gift. Todd was not entirely surprised when they all named the same prostitute—"Princess", who operated out of an upstairs room at Agnew and Riggs' Saloon.

Todd reported this to Major Lugenbeil. Except by invoking Martial Law, the Commandant was powerless to rid the community of this civilian woman, so Todd went to her with his own approach. Dissembling with apparent solicitude for her welfare, he warned her that some of those infected by her were in danger of "losing their manhood as a result"—a possibility he could not actually rule out because he had never seen cases of gleet with this severity—and that they were bent on violent revenge as soon as they were physically able.

There was soon a vacant room at Agnew and Riggs.

CHAPTER FORTY-FOUR

It was December and the frigid weather was brutal. Whether it was the boreal cold or, what was much more likely, the departure of the "soiled dove" from Agnew and Riggs, the gonorrhea plague had subsided. When it appeared that Kennedy might lose his organ from necrosis, Todd had incised the black, swollen and grossly phimotic foreskin. After a moment of agony, there had been almost instantaneous relief of the trooper's discomfort and the health of his "manhood" slowly began to improve.

The Indian problem remained quiet and except for the routine cavalry patrols, the troopers were quite at leisure in their quarters. Mattie, with her usual concern for the men's welfare, had petitioned Major Lugenbeil for permission to have some soldiers hunt the neighboring mountains for game for a Christmas feast. He had finally agreed and a detail brought four fine mule deer back to the Fort for whatever festivities might develop. Two other squads had hunted the Boise River downstream to the west and had brought back over a dozen Canada geese. As the game seasoned and the holiday drew near, the limitations of the cooking facilities to roast all this fresh meat became obvious to everyone.

Again, Mattie took the initiative and went into town to Pierre's Bakery. It was a small establishment producing bread and the occasional pastry for the small frontier town and eked out a bare existence for Dubois and his wife. He had built two large brick ovens, though, that he heated with wood-fired kilns. They seemed ideal to Mattie so she approached Dubois with a proposition. She said that if he would roast the geese that the troopers had shot, they would give one of them to him as well as some venison for his family's Yuletide. The offer sparked memories of his youth and the Christmas feasts of goose in his native land, and he readily agreed.

The post's cooking facilities still were not adequate to roast all of the venison. It was finally decided that the most monumental stew that had ever been undertaken at the Fort would be prepared. On Christmas Eve, every available pot and pan contained the makings of a rich goulash—venison, potatoes, carrots, onions, turnips, garlic, dried tomatoes and even some of the infamous beans that were such a staple for the cook.

All of the day before Christmas had been blessed by gently falling snow and the troopers extended an invitation to the officers and the Todds to join them in their mess for a Christmas Eve celebration. The hunters had brought a tall, well-proportioned evergreen back from their hunt and it stood regally, although undecorated, in the corner. The only musical instrument was Harris' harmonica, but the singing of carols was spirited. For Daniel, as well as many of the others, the music inspired memories of better times in the past sharing all the joys of the Christmas season with family. After "Joy to the World", "Oh, Little Town of Bethlehem" and finally, "Silent Night", followed by a number of toasts with punch that contained more than a hint of the sutler's alcohol supply, the festivities concluded. Daniel and Mattie were moved by the convivial and joyous Yuletide celebration.

As the officers and the Todds crossed the snow-blanketed Parade Ground, the mounting northwest wind was sweeping the clouds away, leaving a star-studded sky and sending the temperature plunging. Major Lugenbeil invited them all to the Officers' Mess for a final glass of wine before retiring. There were more toasts, as though all were reluctant to have the evening end.

Daniel and Mattie finally settled in each other's arms at bedtime, thankful for her health, their situation and the future that lay before them. He patted her protruding abdomen appreciatively. They even commented on how they looked forward to the feast they knew would take place tomorrow in the Mess Hall.

- - -

The usual "Sunrise Gun" sounded and the bugler blew Colors just as the lazy sun of the recent Winter Solstice rose over the mountains in the east. Even Sergeant Mulvaney slackened his discipline for the lazy holiday morning because Reveille had been more or less ignored. Few stirred as Christmas Day began.

A few days earlier, Daniel, in a sudden panic, realized he had no gift for Mattie so he had pleaded with Capt. Townsend to sell him his worn book of English Verse. When the good captain finally agreed, Daniel had that to give to his wife, which he did while they were still in the comfort of their bed Christmas morning. He was pleasantly surprised when she reciprocated by presenting him with a fine pair of mittens that she had knitted.

Breakfast was festive in the Officers' Mess and they were all treated to unspoiled bacon, fried eggs that were actually fresh, and griddle cakes with syrup. The delightful treat was interrupted, though, when a rider pounded past the sentries and galloped into the parade ground. Major Lugenbeil went out without even his hat to investigate the man's shouted alarms. When the Commandant came back into the Mess, he showed a troubled countenance and announced to all that the messenger was an employee of a stage company. Inskip Station, one of the relay points far to the west and some twenty miles south of the old commercial Fort Boise, was under attack and he had been sent to notify the army. The man did not know whether or not the Indians had struck any other relay stations on that line north from California. The officers took hurried last bites of their holiday breakfast and left to muster their men. Lugenbeil apologized to Mattie for the interruption and said that such Indian activity was totally unforeseen because of the winter season.

After the troopers were put on the alert, a hurried meeting was convened in the Major's Headquarters' office. Captain Townsend and Second Lieutenant Davis were to take their men of Troop A to investigate and the remainder of the soldiers on post would remain in reserve in case of having to deal with other depredations elsewhere.

The Major approached Todd and said, "Since we don't know the condition of survivors, if any exist, and since there will undoubtedly be action against the Hostiles, it would be best if you accompanied the Troop, Dr. Todd. Of course, I can't order you to do such a thing but, for the welfare of all concerned, I would certainly like for you to do it."

Although he was hesitant to leave Mattie alone, Todd replied, "I feel obligated to accommodate you and the men, Major. Of course I will go." He still felt some guilt about not being a Union soldier himself.

– – –

All too soon, Daniel found himself departing the front gate, riding the new McClellan saddle on a feisty sorrel cavalry horse and wearing a government-issue buffalo coat and muskrat cap like the rest of the men. With his hasty preparations for the trip, there was time only for a brief goodbye to Mattie. He had been issued a non-regulation "wallet" that was nothing more than a sack, sewn shut at both ends and entered through a hole in the middle. In this pack, he had placed his spare clothing, his rations and the medical supplies he thought necessary to take with him. It was tied by the whangs of the rigging behind his saddle, and his blankets and poncho were lashed across the top of it.

He waved reluctantly at Mattie as they departed the gate without ceremony and with little sound except for the rattle of cavalry sabers and the muffled drumming of horse's hooves as the animals pranced across the frozen, snow-covered ground. There was the occasional early morning cough from one or another of the troopers. The sun had climbed a cloudless sky above the mountains to the east, and the northwest wind was bitter cold. Already, Daniel wished that he had taken the advice of some of the men and wrapped his feet in the burlap sacks that so many of the troopers used for warmth. Mattie's mittens were most welcome.

Solid ice covered the Boise River where they crossed it below town, and as they climbed the bench beyond, Captain Townsend said, "Lieutenant, the men are to lead their mounts for thirty minutes every two hours. You may time that evolution at your discretion as terrain dictates."

A crisp "Very well, Sir," was the response. No other conversation took place for a long time as all hid behind mufflers and tried to protect their faces from the lacerating wind. Todd rode alongside Townsend at the head of the column.

When they finally stopped for a brief nooning, almost every man built his own tiny little fire of sagebrush twigs to boil coffee in his mess cup. Daniel followed suit, and as he waited for the water to heat, he took the opportunity to stamp his feet in an attempt to restore circulation. Stiffness and cold feet were the worst part of riding a horse in this brutal weather.

By late afternoon, the party had arrived at the site of John Fruit's primitive ferry across the Snake River only to find the smashed craft snagged on one end of its tattered rope and portions of it floating aimlessly in the ice-choked current of the broad river. They found no bodies or any survivors so, apparently, Mr. Fruit had made his escape before the Indians arrived.

"The Indians got here first," Townsend complained with a curse. "We can't swim the horses in all that float ice and in this cold. We'll ride down to the ford below the old trapper's fort."

Daniel clearly remembered the spot where he and Mattie had crossed with Steven's mule train. The best aspect of that event was that they had been able to use the ruins of the Hudson's Bay fort for shelter while they were there. Now, the prospect of getting in out of this frigid wind for the night filled him with eager anticipation.

Indeed, the Captain did order encampment there for the night. After picketing the horses on the lee side of the old fort's east wall and providing them with a ration of oats from the pack animals, Lieutenant Davis set up a rotation and posted vedettes for the night and then ordered the men to make camp inside the shelter. Daniel felt as much primal pleasure as the other men displayed as they all crowded close to their cooking fires, absorbing as much heat as possible as they fried their salt pork.

The crisp meat, fried hardtack and hot coffee of the field rations was far from elegant fare, but it was most welcome to all of the men. When he'd finished, Todd rolled up in his cocoon of buffalo coat and blankets and enjoyed the first relative comfort of the day. He wondered how the Indians could possibly survive in cold like this.

- - -

Morning dawned cold and clear. The wind had died down, but the subzero temperatures cut into flesh like a knife. Breakfast was a repeat of the previous night's Spartan menu; soon the troop was moving west toward the Snake River. The larger stream did not have a solid covering of ice like the Boise had, but it flowed only sluggishly because of the jam of ice flows. A bridge of these had formed upstream from the ford where the smaller stream had joined. The cavalry crossed with the frigid water scarcely ever wetting the animals much above their bellies. Nevertheless, when they lurched up and out of the river on the other side, Lieutenant Davis ordered the men to dismount, break off lengths of willows and wipe the lower parts of the animals to strip as much water from them as possible before it hardened into a crusting of ice.

As Daniel witnessed the rapid freezing of the thin crust on the hair of his mount, he was reminded of the rigid, icy sails that were so difficult to handle on the *Ellie Mae* as she rounded the Horn. This weather seemed every bit as cold and inhospitable as what he had experienced down there so long ago.

They circled back and proceeded south on the faint tracks that marked the stage road. It was nearly midday when they reached the first relay station, or what was left of it. The naked stone chimney stuck up like a skeletal finger out of a jumble of cold ashes. Two bodies, frozen in the shape in which death had overtaken them lay just beyond the rubble. Both had been scalped.

Observing no evidence of horse feed or any sign of where it might have burned led Captain Townsend to comment, "I think the Indians struck here to obtain fodder for their horses. We can expect more hostile activity out of them if their animals are well-fed in this weather. Damn!"

A detail of men quickly buried the frozen corpses under piles of stones, and the troop moved onward toward Inskip Station, the next relay point on the line. Darkness was approaching, accompanied by a mounting wind, when they reached the lonely outpost only to find the same devastation. Three mutilated bodies and the carcasses of several Indian ponies scattered about were mute evidence of tough but futile resistance here. Before making camp nearby, several troopers buried the men's remains across the road from the ruins. It was a somber and watchful encampment of cavalry around their cooking fires that evening.

Daniel missed the shelter that the relic of old Fort Boise had afforded the night before. After his hot coffee, fried salt pork and fried hardtack, he was delighted to strip off his boots, hug them to his chest to keep them from freezing and bundle up in his buffalo coat and blankets. He wished that he was cuddling Mattie close to him for companionship and for additional warmth. He worried that her bleeding might have resumed.

The second dawn brought not only a howling blizzard, but now the northwest wind also carried with it ominous yipping sounds that were readily identifiable as human and therefore Indian. Townsend and Davis quietly held a council of war; Daniel, although not included in the deliberation, was just able to hear the exchange.

Captain Townsend said, "The hostiles wouldn't be making all of this racket unless they want us to attack, and they wouldn't want that unless their position is a strong one. I can't understand why they didn't just quietly let us ride into an ambush or sneak in under the cover of this storm and stampede our horses. We'll simply sit tight until things clear and we can evaluate their position—I would hate to have them get away, but let's not make any rash moves. Double the vedettes, Lieutenant, and have the men dig in."

Davis circulated among the clusters of small fires the men had built to cook their breakfasts before the Indian disturbance started and quietly issued his orders. The troopers, although made nervously alert by the taunting sounds in the distance, reluctantly abandoned their cooking and went to their mounts. Todd teased his cup of coffee out of his small fire and jealously protected it from spilling while he sought out his horse as well. He could see no protected area where he could "dig in"; the flat prairie around the remains of Inskip Station offered no shelter from attack—it was a tiny island of visibility in a surrounding sea of blowing snow. He stood by his horse.

- - -

Out of the veil of swirling snow, a shower of arrows suddenly rained down on the encampment like a silent swarm of bees. Many missiles passed with only the soughing sound of a rustling evening breeze, but several delivered an ominous thud. These were immediately followed by surprised screams of human pain or the agonized neighing of stricken horses. "Indian attack!" was shouted as scattered pockets of troopers erupted into disorder amongst the milling horses. It was only the shouts of Lieutenant Davis that caused the men to grab mounts, twist the necks of the animals and force them to the ground so that they became a shelter of sorts from the arrows. Captain Townsend had been struck down where he stood and was silent.

"Squad one, fire into the teeth of the storm," Davis ordered. "The scouts have either been killed or will have taken shelter." Scattered shots, aimed at the unseen foe, were the response. A single scream ahead and off to the left was evidence of a hit, hopefully on an Indian. The shots brought another volley of arrows.

Todd could see Townsend and two troopers down and crawled to the officer first. An arrow jutted from his throat just above his sternal notch and a bloody froth flew from his mouth with each breath. Todd tried to pull the arrow out but got only the naked shaft—the head stayed in the wound which now pulsed a flow of blood that was impossible to stem. The Captain mouthed words, but only more blood bubbled out. There was nothing more Todd could do.

A silent arrow suddenly pierced the frozen earth next to him as he crawled on toward the next wounded trooper. A grunting and thrashing horse that had been hit was an obstacle he had to circle around but when he reached the next patient, he found him to be much less seriously wounded than Townsend. The man's buffalo coat had provided fairly effective armor, and only part of the head of an arrow, which apparently had been on a descending trajectory, penetrated the trooper's thigh. Todd pulled it out and, tearing a strip of cloth from the man's blouse as a bandage, tightly bound the wound. The last of the casualties was much more serious. An arrow had penetrated his coat and uniform and was deeply embedded in the left side of his chest. Not wanting to try to remove it under these conditions, Todd merely broke the shaft near the chest wall, threaded the remainder of the arrow out through the buffalo coat and laid the man out on his back.

The mounting volleys of rifle fire had apparently caused the Indians to retreat from their position because no more arrows assailed the cavalry. A trooper nearby shot his wounded horse and Todd, finding no more injured troopers, went back to the Captain. He was dead. The abruptness of the whole violent incident had much more impact on Todd than the grim spectacle of those frozen bodies at the two stage stations. It was the same as his experience on the *Ellie Mae*—sudden death rode on your shoulder constantly, simply waiting its chance to pounce and when it did, it could be precipitous and oft-times unexpected.

When he crawled to Lieutenant Davis to inform him of the Captain's death, he heard Sergeant Mulvaney ask about making a charge to the front.

"Into what? It does us no good to ride blindly after the Indians" Davis replied. "Send three more men forward as vedettes, and we'll wait until the storm lets up so we can see what we face."

The Lieutenant turned to Todd and asked, "What are the casualties, Doctor?"

"Captain Townsend is dead, and two men are wounded. One has only a minor wound, but the other has a chest wound that may very well be fatal," Todd replied.

Davis only acknowledged the report with a sad shake of his head.

Two of the original scouts returned to the troop, carrying a body between them. Clark said, "They got Stewart at the same time that we heard the ruckus back here amongst y'all. We never did see hide nor hair of any of 'em. Sorry, Sir."

Three other horses had been wounded severely enough to require them to be put down. Their tack was stripped and tied on to the pack horses. When they finally were ready to get underway, one cavalryman took the Captain's horse and placed the officer's body across the croup behind him. Several men rode double, and the man with the chest wound was held upright in front of another fellow trooper. When the column cautiously moved forward, they found evidence of an ambush that had awaited them if they had charged ahead, but the Indians had faded away. Todd could only guess how many of them had been killed or wounded; it undoubtedly had been enough to cause them to abort the attack, or perhaps their leader had been killed.

As the crippled column slowly picked its way homeward, Daniel thought back over the chaotic jumble of events that had just taken place. He realized that the action had been so intense that, at the time, he had experienced no actual fear. He did remember wondering, as the arrows had showered down from the snow-filled sky, if being struck by one was by design or the result of pure chance. Seizing on the hope that the former was true and that his fate would be unaffected by any action he might take, he had then proceeded to render what aid he could to those who were hit. He had not acted out of bravery; there was just no alternative at the time.

Now, as his horse plodded over the frozen ground, he had the opportunity to appreciate what the consequences might have been. What would Mattie do if he had been killed? How would she cope with raising an infant on her own? He compared the complexity of his life and responsibilities now to that of his days on the *Ellie Mae* and shuddered at the thought of what might have occurred during the recent battle.

Daniel also mused over what he would have done had he encountered a wounded Indian. Could he have rendered dispassionate care? Would he have bent every effort to save the man's life? A few of the troopers were almost strangers to him, yet he knew that he would not hesitate to care for any of them in whatever manner necessary. Why would he treat an enemy any differently? After all, he had done his best to save Corkscrew Trumbull after the bully had tried to murder him, hadn't he? Would an enemy of another race be any different? He hoped that the color of the man's skin would make no difference, but he wondered . . .

Todd was still puzzling over these questions when the column finally forded the Snake and once again reached the old commercial Fort Boise where they would make camp for the night.

When the make-shift camp had been organized, Dr. Todd decided he must try to extract the arrow from the trooper's chest, because he was now developing great difficulty in breathing. Todd puzzled over the fact that the respiratory distress had just been gradually increasing. He recalled gunshot patients who had had a sizeable hole blown into the chest wall—they had trouble breathing immediately and it continued until they died. He assumed that course was because of the large defect in the chest wall so that a hole the size of the arrow wound should present no problem. The arrow had penetrated between the eighth and ninth ribs on the left, just below the heart. He was reluctant to enlarge the wound to get the head of the arrow out, but the memory of the tip coming off in Townsend's throat made him hesitant simply to pull on the remnant of the shaft. His patient, however, was failing very fast, so he finally just gritted his teeth and pulled.

The trooper gasped and fainted, but the arrow head came out along with the shaft, and the patient's breathing gradually became more and more labored. Concluding that the arrow itself had indeed been plugging the hole, Todd tried sealing it with his thumb. The man's breathing was unchanged. Perhaps he was not sealing it effectively with his finger.

Looking around, Todd noticed that some of the troopers were already starting to cook their evening rations over scattered fires, so he ordered one of the fascinated onlookers to request all troopers to save the bacon grease they rendered from the salt pork and bring it to him. When they did, the frigid weather had already hardened it. He extracted some of Gung Pi's *Tung-kuei-tze* from his bag and mixed this powder with the hardened grease, choosing that powder because it was both a styptic and also combated inflammation. He smeared a thick layer of this ointment over the chest wound defect and bound a pack of lint over it all with strips of cloth that encircled the man's body. He hoped that this type of bandage would truly seal the defect.

Observing the patient's breathing for a few more minutes, he had to admit that the condition had even worsened with his efforts. Stripping off the lint bandage, he noticed bloody air bubbles oozing from the wound, through his poultice itself; the rate of the escaping froth seemed constant and bore no relationship to whether the man was breathing in or out. He decided that pressure had built up inside the chest and, since it worsened even when the chest wall was sealed, it had to be from leakage of air from the arrow wound in the lung itself. Scraping away the grease, Todd started sucking on the arrow-hole in the chest wall. He intermittently sucked and spat blood; it seemed to him that his patient's breathing improved slightly. He continued his efforts for another ten minutes and the trooper's breathing improved even more.

Todd thought that perhaps, with time, the hole in the lung would close. He continued with his efforts, nearly retching at the distasteful nature of the whole procedure. Some fifteen minutes later, it seemed to Todd that the patient's breathing was stable, although it still did not seem normal. Bundling the man under blankets and a buffalo coat, an exhausted Todd finally retreated to a cooking fire and prepared his own evening meal. The coffee tasted marvelous.

After Todd's hurried meal, he found that the trooper was again having trouble breathing so he repeated the sucking. When that man's condition stabilized again, he treated the other trooper's thigh wound with some of the poultice he had created and then settled down in his bedroll near his chest patient in an effort to stay warm. The relative comfort of his crude bed and his exhaustion made him very drowsy, although he struggled to remain vigilant. When he suddenly bolted upright in total darkness, Todd realized that considerable time had passed, and he could not hear his chest patient breathing. Indeed, when he moved to him and placed an ear directly over the man's face, there was no sign of any respiration whatsoever, nor did he find any carotid pulse. His patient had simply died quietly in his sleep while Todd himself slept. He felt miserable guilt in what he saw as his terrible neglect. His presence on this patrol had served very little purpose since three of the four wounded men had died and the other undoubtedly would have recovered without medical care.

He checked on the thigh patient and found him sleeping peacefully. He returned to the corpse, covered the man's face with a blanket, and once again crawled into his own bed. Sleep did not return readily to him that night.

CHAPTER FORTY-FIVE

Since no Indian raids occurred throughout January and most of February, 1865, officers at Fort Boise believed that the leader of the Inskip attack had indeed been badly wounded or killed during the snowy exchange. Since the Indians always made every effort to remove their dead or wounded from the field of battle, it was impossible to know for certain. In any case, the respite was welcome. All were saddened, however, that it had cost the life of Captain Townsend, such a seasoned and savvy Indian fighter, and that of Troopers Stephens and Stewart.

Stage transportation from the south was interrupted until Holliday's company could rebuild and restock the stations destroyed in the December raid. Todd's medical practice was fairly dormant, both at the Fort and in town, except for an outbreak of scarlet fever. As always, that led to several deaths, in spite of the best treatment he could give with either Occidental or Oriental medications.

Mattie moved closer and closer to term with no further sign of bleeding. Daniel cautioned her constantly to reduce her busy schedule of teaching, but she simply smiled and ignored his advice. He had decided that they must remain in Boise City until after her delivery. Then he would go on to Idaho City to locate quarters for them and an office space for his practice. He understood that recently there had been quite a fire there, destroying many tents and temporary structures. Todd hoped that some new construction would have taken place by the time of his visit and good accommodations would be available.

He notified Major Lugenbeil of his intentions.

- - -

Perhaps it was the Chinook wind that melted much of the snow, providing a false spring, that provoked the surprise attack—nobody could

344

explain the reason for the assault otherwise because there were few supplies to rifle at the site, only four old plow horses to steal, nothing that could be deemed of value for the Indians. The small group of farmers who had settled near one of the stage stations on the route to the east was too impoverished and near starvation to offer a very tempting target for a raid. In spite of this, they were attacked but able to send for help and to give a good accounting for themselves until the cavalry arrived.

There followed a punishing defeat for the Paiutes, although Todd ended up with over a dozen wounded troopers in his care. Five required surgery and two of these died, but the action was considered a major victory over the Hostiles. All of the excitement may have been the precipitating factor causing Mattie to go into labor three weeks before the date Todd had estimated as her time.

Obstetrically, the event was totally uncomplicated, but being both the father and the attending physician for the event was extremely unnerving for Daniel. When his son finally entered the world, emitted a healthy cry and wiggled in his hands, Todd drew a deep breath and said a silent prayer of thanksgiving. After tying and cutting the cord, toweling the infant nearly dry and making a hasty appraisal of his physical condition, Daniel placed little Edward (Mattie's father's name) into the eager arms of his mother. Breathless from her ordeal, Mattie smiled and held her son close.

- - -

Edward was a strong, healthy baby and, once his mother's milk began to flow, had started nursing voraciously. Todd, of course, kept Mattie at bed rest for a continuation of her confinement, but after one week, she rebelled and once again became ambulatory, resuming her duties as a housewife. The officers and many of her former trooper students paid their respects from time to time and showered the infant with a variety of handmade gifts, They brought whistles whittled from willow branches, a tiny carved horse, and a crude animal that somewhat resembled a cat because it had been made from furry rabbit skin. Even a wooden ball whittled intact inside a slotted wooden enclosure was included in the offerings. Both parents were mightily impressed by the outpouring of attention.

The baby only further strengthened the bond between Todd and Mattie. The inner beauty he had seen in her in the past now blossomed even more with motherhood. Added to her sensitivity and concern for others, her dignity and wisdom, and her happy and unselfish devotion, she exhibited a tender yet fierce concern for her baby.

Todd was extremely proud of his family, and he had become aware of changes in his own outlook also. The appearance of the infant in their lives sparked new questions in his mind about life itself. He would often sit for long periods of time and just stare at his child. Here was an actual human being that he had helped to create. This infant was of his own substance and would undoubtedly carry some of Daniel on into the future and be bestowed, in turn, on Edward's own offspring. Perhaps, in the "Grand Scheme" of things, this single contribution was the whole purpose of Todd's life. Perhaps this was his and Mattie's immortality, he thought, but what about Cordelia? All of her physical substance lay moldering in that grave in Jacksonville. Surely there was more purpose to her existence than that. Of course, Daniel told himself as he had so many times, Nature was profligate in wasting all manner of other life forms. Why not humans?

How many, many babies Todd had delivered over the years without fully appreciating the tremendous significance of each and every one of those lives. He had to admit that these events had become rather mechanical to him and that he was so concerned with facilitating the process—of avoiding physical pitfalls and complications—he had never considered the almost sacred aspect of the new lives he held in his hands as they drew their first breaths. Yes, Edward's birth put a whole new wheel on the wagon, as the troopers were fond of saying about any situation that was different.

Not only were the Todds becoming a family, Daniel himself was becoming a more caring and humane physician.

- - -

The drifts were still deep on the rude wagon road to Idaho City, a stark contrast to the thawed and muddy parade ground of the Fort at its lower elevation, but a concurrence of events had made this an appropriate time for Daniel to investigate the opportunities Idaho City might offer. Funds had arrived at Fort Boise for payroll and to allow Major Lugenbeil to purchase local supplies. These also enabled him to pay Todd. At the same time, word was received that Dr. Watkins' replacement, another Army surgeon, was now en route from Fort Walla Walla. His imminent arrival meant that the Todds would have to vacate their quarters. And also Mattie was becoming eager to get into permanent and more homelike surroundings because of the baby.

Todd was somewhat uneasy venturing by himself on this journey; it was early March and the anticipated spring raids by the Paiutes had already started. But, he felt reasonably secure on Bucephalus—he had jokingly bestowed the name of Alexander the Great's war horse on the sorrel cavalry horse that had become his mount. The animal was perverse, would lay its ears back in a threatening fashion even without provocation and was fond of biting, but it was very fast and seemed tireless. He patted the gelding's neck; the ears lay back in warning, as expected.

Daniel began to encounter scattered clusters of men who, even though the creek was still narrowed to only a trickle between icy slabs jutting out from either bank, were busily stockpiling dirt and gravel that they could wash for its gold when the thaw came. As he rode farther on, the snow became trampled and dirty, more tents dotted the low hillsides and, gradually, the hills opened into a large basin. The settlement in its center was blanketed by a gloomy pall of wood smoke. The entire area appeared inhospitable, crowded and dirty, and resembled every other mining town Daniel had ever seen.

As though to emphasize the malevolent atmosphere of the town, two almost simultaneous gunshots followed by a third echoed among the hills. Bucephalus' ears perked and Todd stopped to look around. The people he could see all turned and peered toward the center of town but then resumed their activities as though this event was not unusual enough to interrupt their activities. When he rode onward down the rutted street, he saw a small knot of people clustered around a body on the ground. One knelt beside the prostrate form. Even without dismounting, Todd saw immediately that it would be futile for him to offer assistance because the wound had carried away a good portion of the man's head above his left eyebrow.

He rode on since this was not his affair and as he did, he heard grumbled remarks from the crowd: "Chandler's gone an' done it again, ain't he"; "Who's gonna stop that sonuvabitch?"; "Mebbe we need a vigilance committee." He tied Bucephalus in front of a café and went in for warmth and food.

After his meal, Daniel rode throughout the town and found three doctor's offices, but since he was not interested in any sort of partnership, he didn't go in to introduce himself. Idaho City, spread over the surrounding hills, was mainly a sprawl of tents with an occasional rude cabin sprinkled among them. It seemed a typical mining boom town, but after the rumors he had heard about a recent destructive fire, Daniel was surprised to find many permanent buildings. They were mostly concentrated along two streets. As he inquired about available space, he found it quite scarce but that same name of Chandler he had heard earlier in the day kept being mentioned;

apparently the man owned a great deal of the local real estate. Indeed, when Daniel finally did locate three rooms that were available and that seemed suitable for lodging and an office, it was Chandler he was told to see about renting them.

Shadows were lengthening in the late afternoon when he entered Chandler's office on Main Street. From the snatches of conversation he had heard from the crowd this morning, he had mixed emotions about renting from this man. About Todd's age, Chandler had the physical build of a bull. The man didn't speak to the doctor standing before him but merely raised his eyebrows and tipped his head, giving Todd an inquiring, "what the hell do you want" look. Even seated quietly behind the large desk as he was, Chandler's imposing size created an authoritative presence.

"I'm Dr. Todd and I'm coming to Idaho City soon to set up a medical practice. I am told that you own the building between Harris Mercantile and the blacksmith shop. I would like to rent the three vacant rooms in it for my residence and office," he said, neither offering nor receiving a handshake.

After another moment of silent appraisal, Chandler said, "So, you're a sawbones, are you? We got several of them around here. Are you Reb or Yank?"

"I've never gotten into the politics of secession and all. I was born and raised in Massachusetts and have been a contract surgeon for the Union Army so I guess you would consider me a Yank," Todd replied. "I'm definitely opposed to slavery."

"Are you any good as a doctor?"

"I graduated from medical college at Harvard University in Boston. I've practiced medicine at sea on a whaler, then in San Francisco, in Sacramento City, in the mining town of Jacksonville in Oregon country and at Fort Boise as a contract surgeon, as I said before; fifteen years in all. I've had my successes and my failures," Todd replied.

"Ain't we all." As though testing him, Chandler asked, "Tell me about gout."

Todd was offended at being asked the question and being quizzed by this man, apparently having to justify himself in order to practice in Idaho City. But he answered, "Well, I could describe it as Cullen did: '*Morbus hereditarius, oriens, sine causa externa evidente, sed praeunte plerumque ventrucule affectione insolita, pyrexia, dolor ad artyiculum et plerumque pedis pollice*, etc. etc.' but, I suspect that doesn't tell you much.

"It has a constitutional component that we call the phlethoric state, which undoubtedly has a nutritional component but is manifested by inflammation of various parts of the body and fever, such as we also see in tempests of the thyroid. The usual case, however, is identified by pain in a joint. This is usually preceded by some sort of trauma or even exposure to cold. The meta-tarsal phalangeal joint of the great toe is the most common joint to be stricken. That is in the foot, Mr. Chandler."

"I know damn well where I ache when gout hits me," Chandler replied with what seemed barely restrained venom in his voice.

"Sometimes it involves the great toe on both feet, sometimes the instep, the ankle, the heel, knee or hand. The joint becomes very red and tender to the touch. The patient usually complains of the ague and fever. It is almost exclusively a disorder of males, although females are afflicted occasionally."

Todd was interrupted by Chandler who had been listening with apparent bored indifference. "You all talk or can you treat it? I got me a case of the gout an' if you can give me relief, I'll rent you them there rooms for $60 a month. Would cost you more'n a hundred, otherwise."

Todd looked him in the eye and replied, "For treatment, I advise bed rest, bleeding to reduce the plethoric state—although I have become less impressed with that treatment of late—avoiding rich foods, repressing hyperasthenic orgasm without inducing aesthenic debility, cleansing the bowels by calomel and colecynth and administering colchicum in moderate amounts. I have also found some benefit can be derived by drinking a tea brewed from the bark of *salix albus*, the white willow."

Daniel concluded, "That, sir, is just a bit of my knowledge of and the treatment for gout. I should be happy to include you as one of my patients, and I'm sure I can control your discomfort although, as I'm certain you are aware, gout is a disease from which you can never be permanently free of a recurrence of the symptoms. If you are afflicted at present, Mr. Chandler, allow me to examine you."

Following his examination of his new patient, Todd promised to start treatment as soon as he could return to Idaho City from Fort Boise with his supply of medications.

Dr. Todd now had accommodations to move into with his family and to start his practice.

CHAPTER FORTY-SIX

A late spring blizzard had struck Idaho City and shattered everyone's hopes for an early thaw. The furnishings of the Todd household were painfully sparse and the family crowded around the only one stove in which they kept fire to heat their three rooms, an economy measure because the price of firewood had nearly doubled over what it was said to have been last fall. And after paying the freighter to move their few belongings from Boise and giving Chandler the first month's rent, money was very scarce. Mattie, with Edward in her arms, had even traveled all the way to Idaho City on the freight wagon to save stage fare and Daniel had ridden along with a cavalry patrol to the Basin before he reluctantly turned Bucephalus over to them for their return to the Fort. In the week since their arrival, Todd had seen four patients, but none of them had paid. He went out every day to introduce himself to anybody who would stand still long enough for conversation.

Mattie still had a warm glow from the affectionate send-off at the two parties that had been given to wish them well on their departure. One had been organized by the troopers themselves with punch and even a huge cake the men had purchased from Dubois' Bakery. Much singing and laughter had made it a gala affair. After several glasses of the punch, Todd had hummed a couple of sea chanteys which Harris was soon able to pick up and play on his harmonica. The good doctor then surprised them all by singing a few of the many verses of the two tunes and telling some stories of how they fit into the work-a-day life of a sailor. Little Edward had taken it all in without crying until he finally got hungry and Mattie had to retire to nurse him.

The other affair had been a formal dinner put on by the officers in their mess. They had appeared in full dress uniform, complete with swords, and Mattie was feted as the matron of honor. She was embarrassed by the attention they heaped on her, but welcomed it because she had developed a deep, deep friendship for all of the men of the post, especially these officers with whom she and Todd had dined nightly. She hated to leave, although thoughts of moving into a home of her own made the separation easier.

But now, they weren't even as comfortable as they had been in Todd's old cabin back in Jacksonville. And to make matters worse, little Edward had become colicky. Neither of the Todds could understand the reason for this new development because his diet was simply Mattie's milk and that had not changed. The infant's distress was eased by his passing flatus and so the treatment was frequent warm enemas to which was added dissolved calomel and laudanum. Also, warm fomentations were applied to his abdomen. Daniel could only promise Mattie that everything would improve when his practice was established and they could move to an actual house. In the meantime, they made their coffee and mush on the same stove they used for heating and Daniel brought their evening meals up from the nearby café.

- - -

Todd remained relatively inactive and he began to wonder if having his office in a Chandler building was an obstacle to the development of his practice. He learned through his many conversations with the miners that Chandler had a very bad reputation with almost everybody. They claimed that the man tried to scam miners out of their claims whenever possible; exploited the bevy of "soiled doves" he employed in his saloon; gambled excessively with remarkable "good luck"; and was so extremely capable as a gunfighter that nobody had yet survived challenging his "good luck" at the poker table. Todd was hesitant to believe gossip of this sort, but that opinion of Chandler seemed to be so universal and the sparse trickle of patients who found their way to an office that seemed to link him to Chandler lent credence to the rumors. When he learned that Asa Glover, the president of the Miner's National Bank, was a very vocal enemy of Chandler, Todd sought him out.

He presented his medical credentials to the banker and described his years of experience. He confessed how his lack of funds had led to his unwittingly renting space in a Chandler building and recounted the problem that choice seemed to be spawning. He then learned that Glover was a fellow New Englander from Vermont, had been a sailor in his youth, and had even rounded the Horn a half dozen times. The banker knew of a miner's cabin that was for sale by the unfortunate man's widow and, on the basis of Todd's Harvard degree and the experiences they had in common, Glover loaned him enough money for the purchase. It was with great satisfaction that the Todd family made the move.

The new cabin was actually slightly larger than the one they had had in Jacksonville and even had a cook stove instead of a fireplace. The stove was smaller than the one Cordelia had had but Mattie was delighted with it and immediately started producing what Todd considered culinary delights. He had been able to wheedle enough of a loan out of Asa Glover not only to buy the cabin but also to add a small addition that he turned into another bedroom and an office so that family and professional life could be almost completely separated.

Only days after they had settled, a horrendous accident occurred that was so spectacular that it launched Todd into the midst of the medical scene in the whole Boise Basin. The premature ignition of some black powder resulted in an accidental detonation of a charge designed to fragment a huge boulder. This unfortunate event apparently launched into the air the small hand-bit that the miner had used to make the blast hole and then very foolishly had used to tamp home the powder. The blast killed him outright and his partner, who was already moving toward shelter, was struck from behind. The bit apparently had arched high into the air and then had come down, striking the partner on the top of his head. After penetrating the skull, it had exited through the left orbit. The partner was wheeled to Todd's office in a wheelbarrow, the bit was still lodged firmly in the skull. To everybody's amazement, he was still alive and breathing.

The fellow trotting along behind the wheelbarrow volunteered, "This is Tim McGeary, Doc. Didn't think there's much point in wheelin' him all the way down here but, b'God, he's still alive so's we thought we had to try. Can ye give 'im anythin' for his pain."

No analgesic was necessary since the patient was completely unconscious and Todd so informed the crowd. "Let's put him on the cot in here," he added.

When that was done, Todd examined the patient. The left eye was ruptured and hung, like an empty sack, from the orbit by a single muscle. There was considerable bleeding from both the scalp wound and from around the eye. The path the bit had taken carried it down through the left frontal lobe, Todd thought, and he had to agree with the assessment of the crowd: treatment was probably pointless, but he had to try. The broader head of the drill bit was sticking out through the orbit so he was sure there would be little resistance to complete extraction of it by pulling it on through.

Dr. Todd announced to those crowding around, "This injury is almost certainly fatal, but I'll do my best to save him. It's certain that he can't survive with this drill still in there, so I'm going to remove it while he's unconscious. I think all of you should wait outside."

As they filed out, Todd gathered what he thought he would need. The wound would undoubtedly bleed a great deal more when he removed the bit, so he gathered a good supply of lint. Since Gung Pi's *tung-kuei-tze* was not only good for infections but also as a styptic in wounds, he decided to utilize it. His dental forceps opened wide enough to grasp the flared end of the drill, so he gripped it with them and pulled. As predicted, the drill came out quite easily and was followed by a rush of blood. Todd debrided the wounds and then let them bleed freely for several minutes to flush out any debris. He finally bandaged both the entry and exit defects tightly. He was surprised that, throughout it all, the patient just continued to breathe with that same slow, regular rhythm and seemed to sleep peacefully. He removed the man's boots, arranged him comfortably on the cot and invited the people in from outside.

"I've removed the metal bar, and he's resting comfortably. I would appreciate it if you would notify any of his family about the accident. I shall keep him here so that I can care for him at present," Todd said with authority.

The man who had wheeled the patient in the barrow said, "My claim's next to Mac's and his dead partner's. I'm no close friend, but I ne'er ever heard neither of 'em speak of family, Doc."

"Well, he must stay here in any case so my wife and I will care for him," Todd replied.

The man's companions left and Todd reviewed in his mind the likely course he felt the patient faced. With all of the debris carried into the skull on that drill bit, he expected brain fever to develop from the inflammation and be attended by raving disorientation, convulsions and eventually death. The damaged vessels of the dura and the torn lobe would certainly continue to bleed; it and the cerebral fluid surrounding the brain would drain from the scalp wounds as long as the man survived. His expectations were very pessimistic. All he could do, though, was to continue the treatment he had started so far.

- - -

Todd sat with the patient throughout the afternoon and night. Mattie had brought his dinner to him and had offered to spell him off, but he was so fascinated by the man's peaceful and apparently comfortable state after such a mutilating wound that he insisted on remaining there to observe. On one occasion, the man did stir enough to mumble some unintelligible words but then simply settled back down once again and resumed the quiet, rhythmic respirations, his one remaining eye closed.

The next day, little Edward developed croup and Todd had to divide his time between him and Tim McGeary. Edward gradually responded to steam and the vapors of tincture of benzoin. McGeary remained unchanged, although the bandages were very wet and bloody when Todd changed them. Mattie offered what nursing care she could manage with the other demands on her time; she helped strip the patient's soiled clothes and removed the bedding, all of which she washed. Todd had expected deepening coma or convulsions or raging fever in the accident patient by this time. Instead, the man simply continued to sleep peacefully.

McGeary's acquaintances dropped by from time to time and continued to be amazed that he was still alive. Todd questioned them once again about any family or friends who might care for him in the future, should he survive, but there seemed to be nobody. Mattie continued nursing him and spoon-feeding him broth while he slept; Todd changed his bandages and applied Gung Pi's herb medication. It seemed as though McGeary was living in a suspended state.

As word spread about Todd's triumph in removing the drill bit and keeping his patient alive, the flow of patients to his office gradually increased. Todd was not sure whether it was simply people's curiosity, their growing confidence in his abilities, or the fact that he had severed any apparent relationship to Chandler that made the difference, but he was grateful. To make his office more available to patients, they moved McGeary into the room in the addition that had been planned as the nursery. Because of Edward's croup, Mattie kept the baby's tiny crib at her bedside in order to give him better care.

After a week, while Mattie was straightening the sick room, McGeary opened his Cyclopian eye and peered about him. He giggled in a foolish manner and said, "Don't know who you are, m'am, but I'm right glad to have you a'visitin'." He rubbed at his missing eye because he apparently thought something was obstructing it. Feeling the bandage there, he sat bolt upright in a puzzled manner as he fingered the dressing.

"There's been an accident, Mr. McGeary. You are in Dr. Todd's house and have had a severe injury to your head," she said in a soothing manner. "Would you like a cup of tea?"

"I best be a'getting' back to my claim," he said. "Charlie Chase—that's my partner—he'll be raggin' me somethin' fierce for lyin' a'bed like this."

"Is Charlie Chase your only partner?" Mattie asked.

"Yep. Has been for nigh onto five year now," McGeary replied.

"I'm afraid, then, that it was Mr. Chase who was killed in the explosion that injured you and sent you here. You just lie there and be comfortable for now and I will get you a nice cup of tea. Would you like to see Dr. Todd?" she asked.

McGeary laughed as though he didn't understand what had just been told to him. "Tea'd be good. I'm spittin' cotton," he mumbled

"I'll send the doctor in."

When Mattie interrupted Daniel and informed him that his patient had awakened, he said, "I'll be in as soon as I am finished here." She made the tea but when she returned with it, McGeary had drifted into sleep again.

When Daniel arrived, rolling down his sleeves, he observed the situation and asked, "He was actually awake?"

"Yes, and even talked quite coherently, although he seemed rather silly, I thought," Mattie replied.

Todd nodded thoughtfully and then returned to his examining room.

- - -

As the days passed, McGeary continued to recover. He had no convulsions, the drainage from his wounds did not become purulent, and he did not develop a significant fever. He conversed with Todd and Mattie but remained "silly", as she had described him earlier. There was no defect or impediment in his speech, he had normal use of his hands and arms and legs, and he had complete control of his bowels and bladder once he was no longer asleep so much of the time. But, he seemed not to be in contact with the reality of his situation. He giggled and stared off into space, quite unconcerned that he was seeing it only through one eye. He did continue to voice his concern that his partner, Charlie Chase, would be missing him; he couldn't seem to realize that Charlie was dead and several weeks buried.

McGeary was not able to care for himself and his wounds were still draining, but the sick room was needed for other patients. Some of McGeary's friends moved the miner's tent up alongside Todd's cabin and Mattie agreed to care for him out there.

This arrangement had worked well for a week when Taylor, one of McGeary's acquaintances, came and told Daniel, "Don't ask me how I know, but the word is that that sonuvabitch, Chandler, is fixin' to take over McGeary's claim as bein' 'abandoned'. Ol' Tim won't have a pot to piss in. Can ya do anythin' about it, Doc?"

"Is the claim worth anything?" Todd asked.

"It's as good as most. It kept Tim an' Charlie in vittles an' whiskey. I'd hate to see Chandler get his paws on it."

Todd thought for a moment. "Can Chandler legally do that?"

"That's minin' law—at least here. A claim abandoned for a month is up for grabs by any bastard what can take it and hold it," Taylor replied.

"If it's being worked by somebody working *for* the owner, then it's not abandoned. Right?"

"Sure. They's all sorts of absentee owners of claims. 'Course, some of them gets overrun by claim jumpers," was Taylor's opinion.

"Can we hire somebody to work McGeary's claim?" Todd asked.

"Ever'body thinks his pickins is still too rich to want to work for wages yet. Down the road a piece, when only the big outfits is makin' money, then all sorts o' jaspers'll gladly work for their beans an' bacon, but they'd be hard to find at present."

"Why don't we offer somebody half the earnings of the claim just for working it? That would essentially make them McGeary's partner," Todd said.

"Not if'n the man was to strike it rich. Then McGeary could just fire him an' have it all," Taylor said.

"Well, to be truthful, I don't think McGeary could be considered of sound enough mind to deed over half interest in his claim to somebody, but if he could, that would block Chandler and Tim would have just as much as he did when Chase was still alive. I'll give some thought to how that could be brought about, and you can scout around for a reliable miner as the candidate for the job," Todd said.

"Hell, Doc, I ain't that much in love with my own claim right now. I'd go for a deal like that myself," Taylor said with enthusiasm.

"Well," Todd replied reluctantly, "let's both of us give it some thought over the next twenty-four hours."

Taylor nodded his head and left, deep in thought and obviously envisioning great rewards that this opportunity might provide.

- - -

Just as soon as Taylor left, Todd went into the next room and explained the situation to McGeary. He seemed to listen attentively but then replied, "What you suppose Mattie is a'fixin' for supper? You got you one helluva woman there, you know it?"

"Yes, you're right but, Tim, listen to me! You can lose your claim if you appear to have abandoned it. What would you think if we found somebody else to work it if he gave you half of the gold that he finds?" Todd queried, realizing that it was like posing the question to a child or a fence post.

"He does the work an' gives me half the gold? Hell, sounds downright bodacious to me. Ol' Charlie makes me work like hell for half the gold," McGeary replied and giggled.

"Listen, Tim. Charlie's dead, as we've told you many times, and you are not physically able to work the mine. Chandler will take your mine, and you will have nothing. If we can find somebody to mine for you so you can still own your claim, will you let him keep half the gold and promise to make him a full partner if he should really strike it rich for you?"

"Charlie's dead?"

"Yes."

McGeary pondered his situation for a long moment and then hesitantly asked, "Who'd do the minin'?"

"Nobody knows about it yet. I wanted to see how you felt about it," Todd explained patiently.

"He does the work an' I get half the gold?"

"Yes."

"Hell, a man can't argue with that. What did you say Mattie was a'fixin' for supper?"

Todd said, "Pot roast." He then left McGeary's room.

As he walked down the hillside toward Front Street, Daniel wondered if any document with McGeary's signature would ever withstand a legal challenge and he was quite sure it would not. He decided that the first thing he should do was to make discreet inquiries to find out if Taylor's information was correct, and that Chandler actually did have designs on McGeary's claim. Next, he should find out more about Taylor himself. Would he be the proper person to take over the claim. Todd decided that his own son Edward, as a helpless infant, was less trouble than McGeary was turning out to be but, at least, the man was still alive.

Before he got downtown, however, Todd was intercepted by a small boy who said, "Doc Todd? Pa says my ma has reached her time an' needs you. Can you come?"

The next thirty-six hours were a marathon of medical emergencies. First, Todd delivered Mrs. Snyder of a little daughter, only then to be confronted with a gunshot wound, followed by a man who had sustained a fractured pelvis when his horse shied and fell over backwards on him. Then, a miner from over Placerville way was brought in with a broken arm and Carrie, a new girl at the Deuces Wild Saloon, had a seizure.

When Todd recovered from it all after a few hours of sleep, the realization slowly dawned on him that the next day would be the thirtieth day since McGeary's accident. With no time left for careful investigation, he decided that they must act if, indeed, there was any risk of his patient losing his mining claim. He sent for Taylor.

When the man arrived, Todd asked him, "Are you still interested in working McGeary's claim."

"Certain sure, I am."

"I suggest that you get a group together who know you and who also know McGeary," Todd ordered. "We'll have to get them to swear that they have nothing to gain from awarding you this position, and that they are willing to take responsibility for obligating a portion of what McGeary owns—that they're convinced he is not mentally capable of making this decision himself, and they are doing it on his behalf. Can you do that?"

"I'll be back in half an hour."

When Taylor returned, Todd explained the details of the situation to the five men who accompanied him. He then sent them in to talk to Tim so they could attest to his mental condition. While they were doing that, he wrote out a statement on a sheet of paper. It said:

"To whom it may concern: We, the undersigned, have conversed with Timothy McGeary and, having evaluated him to our satisfaction, determined that he is not mentally capable of reaching reasonable decisions for himself. None of us has anything to gain, financially or otherwise, from the action we are about to take, but we proceed with this action in the certainty that it will be economically advantageous to Mr. McGeary and that it is necessary in order for him to retain possession of his mining claim. Hence, we authorize John Taylor to mine the McGeary Claim, keeping half of the proceeds for himself and giving the remainder to Timothy McGeary as owner of the claim. One year from this date, to wit, July 17, 1866, if gold production from the claim over the preceding thirty-one days should warrant such an action by doubling the August, 1865, output, Timothy McGeary will award half interest in the claim to said John Taylor." Daniel then allowed space for each one of the group to sign the document if he chose to do so.

The men filed out of the sick room, each shaking his head in sympathy for the patient. "Couldn't find the barn door if'n he was locked right inside it," one of them said. Todd read the document to them and, one after the other, each signed it.

CHAPTER FORTY-SEVEN

Months passed and by early 1867, Todd's practice was so busy and lucrative that Daniel and Mattie sold their cabin and built a substantial house toward the north end of Front Street. Mattie was expecting their second child and their new home provided not only adequate living space for themselves and two rooms to serve as Todd's office, but a bedroom for Edward and a nursery. Another room served as a sort of hospital that Tim McGeary was using for the time being. Tim had become permanently dependant due to his disability. His cranial wounds had closed over many months ago and, although he was not physically weak, he was able to get around town quite well, his empty eye socket hidden behind a leather patch. Mentally, though, he failed to improve significantly from his state when he first recovered consciousness. He found it impossible to concentrate on any conversation, many of his actions were nonsensical and foolish, and some people took advantage of him. He mistook their attention for friendship and bought drinks as long as his money lasted or until a real comrade pitied him and escorted him back to his quarters.

Todd had opened a bank account for him with Asa Glover at the Miner's National Bank because his claim had become very productive, thanks to the hard work of John Taylor in locating a new and very rich deposit deeper in the earth, and who was now half owner. Todd allowed Tim only a limited amount of pocket cash since so many parasites were ready to exploit his condition for free drinks.

It was certain that Chandler knew exactly how his own plans for obtaining the McGeary claim had been frustrated, but he gave no indication of his displeasure although any contact he had with Todd was definitely not cordial. He even sought other medical care for his gout until he finally decided that he fared better under Todd's management and returned as a patient.

There were other doctors in town, several of whom had served in the War Between the States, but Todd's medical successes had spread his name and reputation even to neighboring mining towns. He eagerly took the time to learn from the war veterans about how to manage gunshot wounds better and there was ample opportunity to employ this knowledge in his practice because of the town's violence. Also, since Daniel's arrival in Idaho City, several large fires had destroyed significant portions of the vulnerable tent city. As a result, Dr. Todd had more burn-patient experience than he cared to have. Otherwise, his practice consisted mainly of obstetrics, mining accidents, care of the young, routine cases of ague, lacerations, consumption, gastric distress, urinary stones, venereal disease and enteric complaints such as ulcers, constipation, piles, "summer complaint" and diarrhea. He had failures, of course, but he was gratified that he had been able to help a great many.

Mattie was in the fourth month of her pregnancy and was feeling very well. Raising Edward seemed to satisfy much of her appetite for teaching and educating others, although tonight she was working with the small group of women who gathered weekly in the Todd home to receive instruction from her in reading. But, she still continued to be a caring and very effective nurse whenever that was required of her. Her devotion to Tim McGeary's condition seemed tireless and was essentially the same as caring for another child. McGeary was very dependent on her and idolized her as much as he did little Edward. Tim would sit for hours and play so tenderly and repetitiously with the boy that it was usually Edward who tired of the attention first and sought other things to do.

- - -

The sun had long since settled in the west as Daniel, breathing heavily, climbed the trail up the hill just east of town. He trod this path so frequently in his search for a few moments of solitude that it was familiar even now in the cloaked darkness, a hushed, moonless evening gradually being lit by the brilliant stars. The deep drifts of the winter snows had melted and the blossoming trillium scattered the hillside around him with faint white patches. Happy to be free of the shackles of the hibernal months, Daniel couldn't help but dread the summer season that would follow soon with its insects, the endless enteric cases of "summer complaint", the increased danger of typhoid and cholera, and cases of poison ivy and snakebite that always seemed to plague newcomers to town.

But tonight, he thought only of the glorious Heavens above as he used to do so often with Cordelia. He stopped and looked up, searching the sky for several long moments. He was suddenly saddened, though, as he realized that recently his thoughts related more and more simply to puzzling over the meaning of life and the immensity of the Universe and less to do with Cordelia than they once had done. He could still picture in his mind her beauty and her gentle ways; he would always love her and a passionate emptiness still welled up inside of him at the thought of her. But he also had a deep abiding love for Mattie and was very content now in his life with her.

Certainly he owed his present existence to Mattie for her rescue of him from alcoholism. He often wondered if that life-destroying drunkenness was a result of his anguish over losing Del or had he simply become suicidal and wanted only to join her? One possibility he tried to blot from his mind was the suspicion that his increasing awareness of the limits of his professional abilities had led to drink in an attempt to escape accountability for his inadequacies. In any case, Mattie had saved him, and he loved her deeply. She was a loving partner to him and a wonderful mother to Edward.

Tonight, the stars seemed to crowd the Heavens even more tightly than usual. Todd searched out his favorites. Are there people on any of those, he wondered? If so, do they wonder about their Creator as I do now? Do they love and hate and struggle as we do? Do they look upon death as liberation from the miseries and trials of life, as nothing more than a passage on to something better, or do they believe it is final and the end of everything for them. Daniel realized that he had repeatedly asked himself these same questions and had never come any closer to an answer. Perhaps, he thought, that knowledge will only come when I, too, die and cross over that bar. Probably not, though.

Todd lit his pipe and put aside his worries, vowing to do nothing but enjoy a few quiet moments of leisure and the beauty that was spread out before him.

- - -

June finally blossomed and with it came the sticky discomfort of a late spring heat wave. Tonight, the late evening breeze was pleasantly cool after the scorching heat of the past few days that had been more oppressive than anybody could remember its being before July or August in the past. Todd's sweat-soaked shirt clung to his back, and he carried his coat as he trudged homeward. Mrs. Trail's delivery had been difficult—long and emotionally draining for both Dr. Todd and his patient. The low-ceilinged cabin had been stifling and the breech presentation had taxed his skills to the utmost. But, the Trails' baby daughter was healthy, the mother had survived, and all was right in the world.

Instead of feeling elated by his successful management of the case, though, Daniel was aware only of the mind-numbing fatigue that seemed to consume his body. He was puzzled by this exhaustion because he had actually gotten more sleep than usual the previous night. He didn't feel ill in any other way, but over the last month or so he had become increasingly aware of this lack of energy. As he turned onto Front Street and saw the lights in his house on ahead, his pace quickened in anticipation of Mattie's cooking. The thought of a welcome pot of tea buoyed his spirits like a tonic.

Mattie was waiting at the gate in front of the house as he approached and addressed him in a very worried tone. "Tim hasn't come home this evening, dear, and I'm quite worried about him."

Anger welled up in Todd. His fatigue surged and he did not want to deal with a problem such as this now. "He's probably drinking with some of his hangers-on," he grumbled.

"I don't think so. At our nooning, he was complaining that you hadn't given him the money he usually gets on Wednesday. I don't think he had any money at all."

Daniel straightened the cramp out of his back and said, "Damn it! He can be a lot of bother at times. I'll go look for him, but I need a cup of tea before I do. Do you have any steeped?"

"Yes, but watch your profanity or I won't let you have any," she replied sternly.

After a brief rest, Todd started downtown to make the rounds of the saloons. Before he had even reached the first one, he saw a crowd congregated in the street, and he stopped to learn the cause. He found a raging cauldron of anger and speculation:

"I had a drink with ol' Tim not two hour ago."

"Sure as hell, that damn Jack Taylor had the most to gain from Tim's passin'."

"Yeah, an' he's got that goddamn big toad sticker, don't he?"

"That minin'claim o' his'n an' Tim's sure been churnin' out nuggets the size o' walnuts here of late."

"I say we bring Taylor in—anybody with me? We'll see what he has to say for hisself."

The crowd seemed to be growing frenzied.

Todd had to shout to make himself heard above the noise of the group. He asked, "Is this about Tim McGeary?"

"Yeah. Eli Stevens found 'im out back o' the Pink Lady with his throat cut; not an hour ago, 'twas."

"Where is he now?" Todd asked.

"The Marshal had him moved o'er to Agee's barber shop. He's there. I 'spect Agee's buildin' a box for him right now," somebody in the crowd volunteered.

Todd exclaimed loud enough for all to hear, "Don't do anything hasty! Tim's my responsibility. I'm going over to Agee's."

- - -

When Todd saw the body of Tim McGeary, he was surprised at his own reaction. He didn't realize how strong the bond was that he had formed with this man during the months that the miner had been in his care. Tim's body lay on a board, mouth widely agape and his head almost severed from his body, so vicious had been the slash across his throat. Just last night this had been a living person who had found great satisfaction in playing with little Edward. They had romped together and tumbled on the floor, Tim always taking great pains to be tender with the boy and not to harm him in any way. Both had laughed and enjoyed themselves immensely, but now poor Tim was cold and lifeless, never to move or laugh again. Todd mused, anyone would think that I would get used to death but I never do. Such a waste! So senseless!

He noted that there were no wounds on Tim's hands or arms. Apparently, he had either known his attacker or was taken by surprise with no chance to put up any resistance. There were no other visible injuries to the body; the throat trauma appeared to have been the only blow delivered in the attack. And so brutal! It was as though the attacker had so much pent-up anger that he had just suddenly exploded into action—deadly and with great resolve. And that crowd seems to suspect John Taylor! Daniel thought about how obsessive Taylor always had been about sharing the ever-increasing product of the mining claim, how meticulous had been his accounting of what had come out of the ground. Todd couldn't imagine Taylor doing something like this. It seemed to him that such an action was a complete impossibility!

His contemplation was interrupted when Marshal Stroud came in the front door and noisily made his way to the back room that served as morgue and funeral home. "They said you was over here, Doc. Nasty business, ain't it. I've already arrested Taylor."

In surprise, Todd asked, "Did somebody see John do this?"

"Yep an' everybody knows that Taylor packs a knife big as a saber an' knows he jus' couldn't wait to lay his hands on McGeary's share of the claim," Stroud said as he leaned against a door jamb and lit the cheroot he had been chewing on.

"Who was this who saw the attack?" Todd asked. "I would like to talk to him about it."

"Cain't. It was Cletus Ocker and he's left town on his way to 'Frisco," was the reply.

"So, you arrested Taylor purely on circumstances that you assume and the word of a witness who has suddenly disappeared. You don't have any specific and concrete evidence in hand?"

"Hell, everbody says he's guilty as hell." Stroud wagged his head and continued lamely in a more defensive tone, "An' besides, I've arrested him as much for his own safety as anythin' else."

"You know, Marshal, that I have known Taylor and McGeary as well or better than anyone else in Idaho Territory. I've been caring for McGeary ever since his injury; I helped negotiate his taking Taylor in as a partner; and I have received and banked all of the funds that John turned over as Tim's share. The accounting has been meticulous on everybody's part and Asa Glover will testify to that. John has been straight as an arrow. I say that he seemed very satisfied with owning half of the claim. He was grateful that it had been given to him in the way that it was. I think you're making a bad mistake in arresting John and putting credence in what you claim somebody said and everybody thinks. You should be out there looking for the real killer, I'd say." Todd was angry and made no attempt to hide it.

"You tend to your doctorin', Todd, an' I'll take care of the marshalin' in Idaho City. It jus' so happens that ol' Judge Johnson—he's a Territorial Supreme Court Justice, y'know—is in town, home from a circuit-ridin' tour an' will be here for the next three or four days 'fore he heads out again. We'll try Taylor day after tomorrow." Stroud relit his cheroot and shuffled back out through the barber shop.

"May I see Taylor?" Todd shouted after him.

"No. Only his lawyer," Stroud threw the words back over his shoulder as he went out the front door.

- - -

Todd went home just long enough to break the horrible news to Mattie and then he set out for Asa Glover's house. He found the banker in his shirt sleeves and sitting in a rocking chair on his front porch, enjoying a glass of lemonade.

"Hello, Mr. Glover. I'm sorry to disturb you at home, but have you heard the news about Tim McGeary?" Todd said, not waiting for his greeting to be acknowledged.

"Hello, Doctor. No, I've been home since late afternoon. Would you like some lemonade?"

Todd shook his head and, seating himself in the chair offered him, hastily briefed the banker on all of the facts of which he was aware and about the Marshal's actions.

Glover pursed his lips thoughtfully and then said, "It appears as though Stroud's in a hell of a hurry to get this all over and done with, doesn't it. I've always felt he was Chandler's lap dog, though he has been very careful to hide the fact. Ocker, too, for that matter. Makes a person wonder whether or not Stroud is being pushed, doesn't it? With McGeary and Taylor both out of the way, you can make a pretty sure bet as to who would end up with that claim?"

Glover gazed thoughtfully off into the night and took another sip of his lemonade. "Do you suppose any of Chandler's hangers-on were out there stirring up that crowd that you heard tonight?"

"I suppose, but I don't know," Todd replied. He had to admit that with the terrible shock of the whole situation, he had never given thought to the possibility that Chandler might be involved in this murder. Glover's hatred of Chandler was well-known. Todd couldn't help but consider that a factor in Glover's response, but what he said certainly fit Chandler's pattern and made more sense than the accusations against John Taylor.

Glover continued, "If Chandler is involved, perhaps the safest place for Taylor right now *is* in jail. That crowd might become a lynch mob. Did you say that it is Judge Johnson who will be hearing the case?"

"That's what Stroud said," Todd replied.

"I know Charlie Johnson well. I have a document down at the bank that he should see. I'm sure it could scuttle this suspicion of Taylor, but if the case goes to trial and the jury could be manipulated by Chandler, I wouldn't bet on an acquittal. I will give the information directly to Charlie. He will handle it properly. In the meantime, it's best to keep my information secret so, Doctor, just keep quiet about *all* of this. I have my reasons. Go home and rest easy."

Uncertain what the banker could be talking about but trusting him implicitly, a puzzled Todd shook the man's hand and bid him goodnight. The terrible fatigue that had been so overwhelming earlier in the evening, but temporarily erased by the surge of events, now returned. As he plodded homeward, he implored whatever force that might be guiding his destiny just to spare him any other emergencies this night. "Please, just let me sleep," he muttered half aloud.

- - -

The Eldorado Saloon was the temporary location for court proceedings in the Idaho City venue until the new Territorial court house could be completed and when the judge entered, he sat at a "bench" consisting merely of several planks laid across two poker tables. Judge Johnson surprised everybody when he struck his gavel firmly and announced, "Before empanelling any jury, I wish to hear the facts relating to the capital case being brought against John Taylor, which I see has been placed on the docket for tomorrow. Who is acting as Prosecutor in this matter?"

Rulon McBride, a lawyer with great ambitions, rose and said, "I am, Your Honor. Rulon McBride, Esq."

"Consider this a Preliminary Hearing, Mr. McBride. What is the evidence that substantiates the charges brought against the accused, Mr. Taylor?" the judge asked.

"The victim was nearly decapitated in the attack, and it is a well-known fact that Mr. Taylor is in possession of a knife of the Bowie variety which is of sufficient size to produce such a result as this, and that he uses it frequently. And then . . ."

Judge Johnson interrupted. "Uses it frequently? Has this man been charged or convicted of other assault crimes involving his knife?"

"Not to my knowledge, Your Honor."

"Ah, so he owns a knife and uses it frequently. How? Does he kill animals with it or destroy houses or chop down trees with this monstrous Bowie knife?" Johnson asked in a voice that dripped sugary innocence in its sarcasm.

"Ah . . . no, Your Honor. It is just that it is common knowledge that Mr. Taylor owns a knife capable of inflicting a wound such as the victim received. But more to the point, he had this weapon in his possession when he was arrested. He was the equal partner of the victim in a mining venture involving a valuable claim and stands to gain complete ownership of that mine with this death."

"Has there been any conflict or animosity between the deceased and the accused that you know about personally or about which you can present testimony? Did anybody witness the killing or any prior dispute?"

"Oh . . . yes, Your Honor . . ." McBride stammered as though recovering from a brief oversight. "Cletus Ocker says he saw a fight between Taylor and McGeary last night."

"Is Mr. Ocker in court?" the judge asked.

"No, Your Honor. He had to go to Boise City, on his way to San Francisco. But several other individuals think they may have seen the accused in the area that night."

"Do you have a deposition by this Cletus Ocker or do you plan to call him back to testify at trial, Mr. McBride?" Judge Johnson asked, staring in a dour and forbidding manner over the top of the spectacles perched on his nose. It seemed obvious that he knew the answer to his own question.

"Ah . . . no, I'm told that he left immediately on his way to California . . . but I need to elaborate on this matter of claim ownership, Your Honor," McBride stammered.

"It may interest you to know, Mr. McBride, that I have in my possession the last will and testament of the deceased, one Timothy McGeary," Judge Johnson said. "Because of the incapacity of Mr. McGeary, a fact familiar to all since the time of his accident, Mr. Taylor and several friends of Mr. McGeary went to the banker, Asa Glover, and drew up a will, fully cognizant of Mr. McGeary's incapability in such a matter and knowing full well the mounting value of his assets. Because Mr. McGeary had no known relatives and because of his great affection for and in recognition of the kindness rendered to him by the person named as beneficiary of his estate in case of his death, Mr. Taylor and the others advised that Mrs. Mattie Todd be designated as that assignee. This fact and the pertinent document were brought to my attention by McGeary's banker and the long-time shepherd of his affairs, Mr. Asa Glover. So, you see, Mr. McBride, the accused had absolutely nothing to gain from the death of the deceased. Therefore, unless you can present a witness or a single concrete fact, I find insufficient cause from what you relate to me today to bring Mr. Taylor to trial. You must search more vigorously for the culprit. Case is dismissed!"

A surprised buzz of conversation filled the saloon until Judge Johnson rapped his gavel and shouted, "Order in the Court. We will now select a jury for the first trial."

Daniel was speechless in his surprise.

CHAPTER FORTY-EIGHT

As the months stretched into early and then late summer, Mattie was entering her eighth month of pregnancy. She felt well although Todd was concerned because she had started having mild episodes of increased pulse, slight headache and perhaps a hint of peripheral edema. This condition was disquieting because these were the symptoms of toxemia that he had seen in some pregnant women in the past and some of these had died from apoplexy during their devastating convulsions. He attributed this course to hyperaemia of blood vessels in the brain and had tried such things as *aconitum napellus* for its sedative effect, but the initial excitation was more than the patients could stand. He had tried *phosphoric acid* and even *carbo vegetabilis,* which had always been helpful in depressing the aggravated state seen in typhoid, but they had been of no benefit. In those who survived, the symptoms almost always disappeared as though by magic soon after the delivery of the baby. He could only pray for Mattie's child to come early.

In turn, Mattie grew increasingly concerned about her husband's health. He was obviously very pale and anemic. He seemed to be losing weight although, if anything, his girth increased slightly and she chided him about developing a "beer belly". Of more concern to Daniel was his almost disabling fatigue, so severe at times that he could scarcely find the energy to move one foot ahead of the other. He decided that his spleen had enlarged because, at times, he could palpate its edge himself where it peeked below the rib margin on the left side of his abdomen. He attributed the enlargement of his belly to this splenomegaly and now even began thinking it was associated with the lumps in his axillae and under his chin, the enlarged lymph nodes that he had started noticing several months before. His own diagnosis puzzled him because, other than his fatigue, he felt quite well.

All of these concerns of domestic health were eclipsed, though, when Todd was called to see little Elvira Thomas because of her difficulty in breathing. The Thomas cabin of unpeeled logs was much too small for the gaggle of children who seemed to spill out of every nook and cranny when Todd made his entrance. His first thought when he heard the whistling wheeze of labored breathing was that he would be confronted with a child's case of the croup. This misconception was dispelled as soon as he saw the child; a reddish membrane filled each nostril and caused her mouth to gape open as she struggled to breathe. Todd lit a coal oil lamp and held it so he could see into the child's open mouth. A gray/red gelatinous membrane spread from each tonsillar area to become confluent in the center and he was certain this was the origin of the nasal membrane blocking the nostrils. He took a wooden tongue blade from his bag and tried to loosen the obstruction in the youngster's throat. Blood burst forth from the mucosa that was laid bare at the base of the membrane; some spilled from her mouth and much went down her throat. She coughed and gasped, choking and crying at the same time. Todd flipped her onto her abdomen and allowed the blood to puddle over the edge of the cot. When she had recovered sufficiently, Todd asked Mrs. Thomas about the onset of the child's disorder.

"She complained some of sore throat over the last two or three days but, ''taint bad,' she'd say. Last night, it started gettin' worse an' by morning, she was havin' this trouble breathin'. What is it, Doc?"

Todd stroked his chin in deep thought. He had seen such membranes in the past and, in many cases, the disease was fatal. A decade ago or so, this disease had been labeled *Diphtheria* in an article in *Lancet* and it had described this array of symptoms precisely—low grade fever, malaise, sore throat for several days and then a sudden turn for the worse with membrane formation and respiratory distress. Todd couldn't remember the name of the article's author. As he recalled, congestive heart failure and cranial and peripheral neuritis had been described as late complications there, but none of Todd's severe cases had survived long enough to develop those symptoms, having died too soon of respiratory distress.

"I'm afraid your little daughter has diphtheria, madam." Todd finally replied. "This is a very serious illness. We need to separate her from your other children. Then we need to move her cot close to the stove so she can breathe warm, moist air from your teakettle."

Mrs. Thomas looked about her at the severely crowded cabin. In despair, she said, "There ain't no way we can separate her from the other children. We have them stacked three deep in here as it is."

"Do you have some friends who could care for your other children in their homes until this child gets better?" he asked.

"Cain't think of nobody. Silas, that's my huband, sort of rubs ever'body the wrong way. We ain't got no real friends," she replied.

After a moment's pause, Todd said, "I'll take her to my place and care for her there." He was very concerned about keeping her isolated from little Edward and from Mattie, but he didn't feel that he could leave the child with this badly over-crowded family. He could keep her in the room that McGeary had used and practically isolate the child and himself from the rest of his family.

"Oh, Doc, that'd be a blessing if you would do that. Her name's Elvira an' she's a good girl. I'll get her ready to go," Mrs. Thomas replied, gratefully grasping his hand in hers.

"I'll go and get a room prepared for her at my place, Mrs. Thomas. I shall be back shortly."

On his short walk home, Daniel was not fretting over explaining the situation to Mattie but, rather, how he was going to impress on her how terribly important it was that she and Edward stay away from the patient's room and yet convincing her in a manner that did not cause panic. Mattie's first inclination would be to render nursing care and that had to be ruled out most definitely, but with her recent symptoms, he had to be careful not to create undue worry for her that might cause additional stress.

Daniel's foreboding was for naught because Mattie understood the problem thoroughly and agreed with him completely. When all had been prepared and he carried little Elvira to his house and placed her in the sick bed, though, Mattie was overcome with pity. The child's wheezing and labored breathing were almost more than she could bear.

"Oh Daniel," she wailed, as she surveyed the scene from the open door, "the poor, poor little thing. Imagine how frightened she must be. As though not being able to breathe freely were not enough, she is spirited away from her family and loved ones and into these strange surroundings. Can't her mother come and be with her?"

"She has her hands full down there with all the rest of her children," Todd replied. "I swear, the place is so crowded that you would almost think that she's taking in boarders."

With a sympathetic wag of her head, Mattie disappeared but returned a moment later with a small rag doll that belonged to Edward. "Give this to her, Daniel. It might be some small comfort to her."

The day had been unseasonably warm for early autumn but still Todd built a fire in the potbellied stove that heated this separate room so that he could get a teakettle boiling. When steam began hissing from the curved spout, he created a tent of sheet material and positioned the teakettle so that the hot, moist air was channeled into the space over the bed where it mingled with the vapors from a lamp fueled with tincture of benzoin. In spite of all this, little Elvira continued to struggle with each breath. Her body was soaked with sweat; she was burning up with fever. Over the next several hours, her breathing became worse. Finally, Todd called Mattie and asked her to go to the Thomas cabin and fetch the child's mother.

"I'm afraid we're losing her," he warned before his wife left.

By the time Mrs. Thomas arrived, Elvira was beginning to turn blue and, for want of some better course of treatment, Todd dislodged more of the obstructing membrane from the throat. Only moments later, Elvira expired, drowning in her own blood that flooded from the newly-denuded mucosa of her nasopharynx. Slumping from fatigue and his agony at this defeat, Todd was so overcome by the child's death that he was almost unaware of the hysterical wailing of the distraught mother. Finally, he pulled the sheet up over Elvira's face, now deathly still and no longer fighting for breath. Turning, he tried to comfort Mrs. Thomas and ushered her out of the room. Mattie took the whimpering woman in hand and seated her at the kitchen table, supplying her with a fresh cup of hot tea.

"Don't worry, Mrs. Thomas. We will take care of getting Elvira's body to Agee's and having a casket prepared for her burial," Todd said. "You just go home to your other children."

"We ain't got no money for a casket, Doc. A blanket'll have to do," Mrs. Thomas replied between stifled sobs.

"Don't worry about that, my dear," Mattie said. "I will get a proper casket for the little darling."

After her cup of tea and a final look at her dead child, Mrs. Thomas headed into the night to return to her cabin.

Mattie put a consoling hand on Daniel's arm and said, "I hate to tell you this, Daniel, but two more of those Thomas children looked flushed when I was there, and they were beginning to breathe in a noisy fashion. I believe they are getting diphtheria also."

Todd slumped even deeper in his chair, cradling his head in his hands. "What a disaster for this poor family," he finally said. "I must go back down there."

- - -

In the weeks that followed, not only four more of the Thomas children developed the disease, but it had now spread through much of the north end of town. More children than adults were afflicted and in almost all of the cases, it was the so-called *faucial* variety with the throat being the main target—only a few of the victims developed the nasal mass of membrane such as had obstructed Elvira almost completely. All the new cases started with sore throats and fever and for some patients, that was the extent of their symptoms and they recovered in ten or twelve days. Among those who went on to pharyngeal membrane formation, most of their deaths resulted from this cause of suffocation; two of the four afflicted Thomas children died in this manner. Several of the adults, after lingering long, succumbed to heart failure that Todd attributed to some sort of toxin that had developed in their bodies as a result of their inflammation.

In the days that followed, as death and misery of the epidemic raged, the effect of the pestilence on Todd was profound. He spent endless hours nursing the sick, sitting up with the dying while silently cursing his inability to alter their course, consoling the families of the stricken, and snatching only a precious hour or so of rest whenever he could. Mattie delivered a healthy daughter during this marathon, but Daniel had to hire one of the women in town to provide her care after the delivery because he was so completely occupied. He finally just collapsed from his exhaustion as the epidemic burned out. Daniel's efforts seemed to have broken his health that had been growing increasingly fragile even before the onset of the epidemic.

- - -

For many weeks, Daniel floated in a cloud of varying density—numbing darkness, the occasional awareness of hushed voices, blinding light from which he had to retreat into a cocoon of covers, the ebb and flow of chilling coldness, feverish heat. Through it all, Todd was overwhelmed by the crushing weight of a profound weariness that seemed to pin him to the bed like a bug skewered to a board. He could neither muster the strength nor marshal the will even to lift his hand.

Gradually, as he was able to sit up in bed with assistance, he began recognizing the things around him. Mattie fed him broth and even carried a baby in to show him. A little boy who looked very familiar clung to Mattie's long skirt and peeked around its folds as though he were frightened of what he saw. When Todd felt strong enough to sit on the edge of the bed, he caught a glimpse of himself in the cheval glass. The wasted figure that stared back at him was almost a stranger. Deeply sunken eyes peered hollowly from the slack and wasted face nearly hidden by a rat's nest of beard; slumped shoulders seemed to compress the sunken chest; cadaverous limbs looked as though they belonged on a stick figure. It was the picture of severe cachexia.

My God! How long have I been here? What's wrong with me? These unspoken questions were too much for Daniel to cope with and he collapsed back onto the bed. With that surrender, though, a black fog of deep depression began to envelop him and it became more and more profound as the days wore on.

The wasting of his flesh increased the prominence of the enlarged lymph nodes he had discovered on himself earlier; he was now able to palpate his spleen very readily. He searched his brain for a diagnosis but couldn't define his illness. He began to believe that some sort of cancer was devouring him from the inside. This diagnostic puzzle only reinforced his feeling of professional incompetence. How many hundreds of my patients have died over the years because I know so little and am such a poor excuse for a doctor, he asked himself. Not only have I not made any great discoveries or have I advanced medicine beyond hocus-pocus witchcraft, I have probably crippled or killed many, many people along the way. I *know* I have!

Tortured thoughts careened through his troubled mind, shredding Daniel's self-image mercilessly. Cordelia's death, Simon Edwards' death, failed operations, rampant epidemics—he was convinced that they all bore the imprint of his failure. He grieved over what he considered his inadequacy to be the "missionary of mercy" that Dr. Channing had expected him to be or even the fine physician Dr. McClure had hoped to produce with his bequest in the beginning. He thought of being cast out by his father and realized that neither of them now knew whether the other was still alive or not—and he discovered he really didn't care. Nothing but these morose thoughts crowded Daniel's brain and even these were always blacker during the long hours of winter darkness as the wind howled mournfully outside his window.

Mattie came to his room many times each day and stayed as long as she was able while still caring for their two children. She urged food on Daniel and constantly sought ways to spark his interest in life. She consoled, she cajoled, she challenged, she scolded, she brought the children in to try and interest him; sometimes she would just sit and hold him protectively, stroking his brow or reciting some of the poetry she knew so well. Finally, she insisted that he get out of bed and get dressed. She helped him walk to an easy chair by the stove in the parlor and, indeed, he was cheered somewhat by the fire. Not only was the warmth welcome after the cool bedroom, but even the dancing flames visible through the stove's isingglass window provided a primal comfort. Daniel sat and stared into them for a long time before returning to his bed with Mattie's help.

In the days that followed, he was able to spend longer and longer periods at fireside before becoming exhausted. He found that he could think more clearly in this upright position, but even this improvement did little to alleviate his depression. He did allow his mind to wander, and he pondered many things.

--- --- ---

Oh God, he whispered in angry frustration rather than out of reverence, why can't I have faith and believe in a Divine Being like almost everybody else? Mattie seems so totally content and secure in her belief. She has no doubt whatsoever but that she will see God and spend Eternity in his loving bosom when she leaves this life. Cordelia had that same faith. I am afraid that my own death is near, and I am as totally confused now as I have been for many years. What a peaceful blessing it would be just to feel as confident as they about the future, even if that belief were totally wrong. At least, he thought, I would have equanimity instead of the chaos that is always in my mind now.

I truly do believe there is a Central Intelligence that coordinates the infinite complexities of the Universe, this world, the endless numbers of creatures and plants around me—the miraculous machine that is my body, my mind, perhaps even my thoughts themselves. I suppose I shouldn't quibble over whether to call that Intelligence God, Brahma, Vishnu, Siva, Allah or any of the other names devised by man. It's just that I can't abide the thought that something as profound as that Central Intelligence would have to be could care one whit about the rituals we puny humans engage in, the sacrifices or supplications we offer in our formal religions. It is so egotistical to think that, somehow, we are that much more important than any other life forms.

But is there, Daniel wondered, such a thing as soul or spirit? Some tiny spark imparted by that force I'm calling Central Intelligence? Perhaps "being alive" is nothing more than the temporary possession of that spark. One instant an organism is alive and the next it is dead; probably in a chemical sense there has been no change at all—"death" is simply the absence of that life force, that spark, that "soul" and dying is just the state that exists when the body loses that energy. Perhaps it flows back into some huge "life force" reservoir to be distributed again to some other organism that is ready to spring to life—much as water is taken up as clouds from the ocean, falls as rain in individual drops, and then eventually finds its way back into the oceans again. Perhaps that same life force temporarily resides in all living things, animal *or* vegetable. Perhaps that makes me related to these pine trees outside of the house or the wheat in the field or flies or turtles—whatever lives, while it lives.

If that's the case, he mused, I wonder what my life force might come back as when it returns; perhaps it won't even be on this earth but somewhere else out there in that great Universe that Cordelia and I used to enjoy watching. And will what I do here and now as a human affect what sort of organism my spark might occupy? I can't believe that it is a matter of reward or punishment. A Central Intelligence brilliant enough to organize all of this could leave little to chance. What if we are all pieces in a magnificent chess game, each being moved around to accomplish a specific goal through our actions. If that is true, then there is no such thing as free choice and all of our actions are simply an extension of the will of that Central Intelligence. And if that is so, then there are no good or evil acts. We're simply tools, all part of some "divine" plan. There is no reward nor any damnation; no Heaven or Hell.

Todd dozed briefly, but roused in a moment with the sudden thought—if all of that were indeed true, what has been my purpose in being on Earth? Is it the contacts I have had with other people? Is it what I have done with my life as a doctor? Is it the beings that I have helped produce in little Edward and the baby Elizabeth and the effects that they, in turn, might eventually have? He couldn't believe the Medicine he had practiced all his adult years was of such an outstanding quality that it had been his reason for being.

He continued to puzzle over it all until his head drooped on his chest and he napped before being helped back to his bedroom.

- - -

Daniel's depression persisted but, physically, he did gradually become stronger. The snow was deep and much of December had been bitter cold. A few visitors dropped in from time to time but most of them were friends Mattie had made through her community activities; no patients were allowed to penetrate her protective barrier around Daniel. She decorated the living room with candles and garlands of greenery for Christmas; the carols she sang for Edward brought to Daniel's mind memories of the miserable efforts at Yuletide merriment the crew of the *Ellie Mae* had attempted. His depression spawned countless hours of ruminating and reliving so many of those past incidents. He wondered if Isaac Lawrence or old Captain Corbet were still alive. Cordelia was almost constantly in his thoughts. He still missed her terribly and had to actually force himself to recognize the blessings he enjoyed now in the present—Mattie, her love, Edward and little Elizabeth. He knew he was extremely fortunate to have them all. Of course, he felt that he didn't deserve their kind devotion, and it galled him that with his inactivity, they were forced to live off Mattie's gold claim earnings. His impotence as family head and source of support only added to his depression.

- - -

The year 1868 arrived in the mountain country around Idaho City accompanied by a howling January blizzard. Fortunately, Mattie had restocked the wood shed only days before and their pantry was equally well filled. Daniel watched the swirling maelstrom through the window of their warm front room for hours and, mesmerized by its violence, relived those frigid deck watches as the *Ellie Mae* had rounded the Horn, the struggles as all hands tried to reef those stubborn sails that were rendered board-rigid by their mantle of ice, the monotony of short rations, the tyranny of Captain Corbet.

The obvious contrast to his present comforts energized Daniel, and he began slowly to emerge from his black cloud of depression, in spite of his weakened physical condition. Slowly, his perspective began to change. Always aware of the precarious state his health seemed to have developed, in the days that followed he was able to accept for their true value the blessings of having loved ones, the comforts of his home and the success of his practice.

"I'm alive," he told himself. "As long as there is breath in me, I should be enjoying every minute of every day and not wallowing in a swamp of defeat."

Mattie exulted in Daniel's gradual improvement and credited the change to her constant prayers for him. Edward regained his earlier closeness to his father that had been temporarily displaced by fear of the man who had exhibited such a changed appearance weeks ago. Through it all, Todd's strength improved until he was able to take short walks through the snow-clogged streets. Mattie, the "gate-keeper", even allowed a few patients through her protective barricade and Todd was very happy to see and treat them.

CHAPTER FORTY-NINE

The lengthening days of February, 1868, had begun to melt the deep drifts and reveal the blackened scars of the most recent of the fires to sweep through Idaho City—severe ones had become an almost annual occurrence and the last one had devastated the south end of town. Todd's practice was back to only a portion of his usual load, but he paced himself and spent many hours abed each night to maintain the necessary level of energy. His general condition was so much improved that he began feeling guilty for suspecting that he had cancer. True, he still had enlarged lymph nodes here and there on his body, and his belly was still quite crowded by that enlarged spleen, but he was feeling remarkably stronger.

This optimism was dashed, however, when he blotted his mouth at dinner one evening and discovered blood-staining of the napkin. Soon, the bleeding was sufficient for him to taste the saltiness of his own blood. He excused himself and went to the bedroom where he lit a lamp. Holding it close and inspecting his mouth in the mirror, he found a number of petechial hemorrhages along the upper gum line and blood oozing from several of these. Immediately, memories flooded back of that young man so many years ago in Sacramento City who had presented with an abscessed tooth. What was his name? Travers, Taylor—something like that. He had developed severe bleeding, primarily of the mouth, accompanied by very significant lymphadenopathy making Todd suspect cancer of the bloodstream. In spite of Todd's treatment, he had died most suddenly with massive hemorrhage and apoplexy.

Panicked, Daniel pulled up his shirt and unbuttoned his underwear. Inspecting his bared skin, he was alarmed to see several hemorrhages, much larger than petechiae, under the skin of his chest and abdomen

He stared into the mirror again and muttered half-aloud, "Is this the beginning of the end for me also?" Surely not, he thought. I have felt so very much stronger over these past weeks. He placed a tiny lump of alum on the worst of the bleeding spots in his mouth and the flow of blood stopped. Rearranging his clothes, he returned to the dining table.

"Is something wrong, dear?" Mattie asked.

"No. I just thought of something and wanted to jot down a note to remind me of what I need to do about it tomorrow," Daniel lied. Her response was a nod and smile, but there was an admixture of worry and doubt as well in that look from his wife.

He concealed the bleeding inside of his mouth that recurred throughout the course of the evening and when he and Mattie retired, he donned his nightshirt in private in order to hide his blotchy skin. He turned with his back toward Mattie in bed and began breathing regularly as though drifting into sleep almost immediately.

Although he remained motionless and quiet, Daniel's mind raced in panic. Supposing this really is the end for me: what about Mattie and the children? I have so very little money saved. The house *is* paid for—at least they will have that. And she has her share of the mining claim, along with the money she has saved from that. Of course, most claims peter out eventually. She has taught school, though; that would always be a possible source of income for her.

Daniel picked and picked at these worries until, finally, he must have drifted into slumber because, suddenly, he awoke; he had dreamed that he was attending his own funeral and he remembered looking at himself in his coffin and asking, "Just what was the purpose of your being on this earth?"

It was a familiar theme that had recurred so often in his pondering over these last months that it now suffused his dreams, also. Now that he was awake, the question niggled Daniel's sleepless brain for hours.

- - -

The next day, an unlikely patient, bleeding and unconscious, was brought to Todd's office and eventually her plight set into motion a train of thought that could solve the dilemma about a purpose in his life. First, though, he called upon all of his skill to save the woman's life but the gunshot to her head had simply been too destructive and she died without regaining consciousness. Only then did Daniel have time to question the people who had brought the victim to him and who had stood by and watched during his frenzied efforts to save her.

The Lane's Café waitress who had wrapped several dishtowels around the woman's wounded head spoke up, "She was just walking past that man Chandler's saloon an' the window plum blowed out an' she fell. People screamed an' I ran out; Oh God, there she was, kickin' an' twitchin'. I fetched them towels an' wrapped her while we brung her here."

One of the men volunteered, "I was inside an' Chandler an' this other gambler jumped up from the poker table an' Chandler gunned 'im down. They was several shots so I s'pose one went through the winder an' nailed this poor lady."

Another man wagged his head and asked, "When we goin' to do something about Chandler? Don't expect that damn Marshal Stroud to rein him in. They's as thick as thieves."

Todd asked if anybody knew the woman's name and the waitress volunteered, "Castor. She's Nettie Castor."

"Do you know her family?" Todd asked.

"She's married to Ike Castor an' they have two kids. I'll get word to him, if'n you'd like," she replied.

"I would appreciate it if you would do that. In the meantime, I'll notify Stroud and then try to make the body a little more presentable before Mr. Castor has to see her," Todd said. "Thank you all for bringing her here."

As he ushered them from the office, he noticed a large area of extravasated blood that had raised a large bluish blister on the back of his hand; it had apparently developed just while he was treating Mrs. Castor although he couldn't recall bumping the area. If my bleeding has gotten so bad that I'm puddling blood like that right under my skin, I may not have much time left, he thought. When will the bleeding strike my brain and take me in a final fit of apoplexy like that young patient so many years ago?

The words "when we goin' to do something about Chandler" echoed through Daniel's mind and he began ticking off in his thoughts the many outrageous crimes Chandler was either known to have committed or suspected with considerable certainty of having perpetrated. They ranged from the countless stolen mining claims and murders labeled as "self-defense" to the slaying of Tim McGeary and now of this innocent bystander. Suddenly, he decided that an act he could perform that would be of infinite benefit to humanity would be for him to rid the world of this man once and for all.

"Oh, how I *detest* that man—no, not a man—how I have detested that creature since I first met him. But, I just wonder if I have enough time left to do anything about him," Todd muttered to himself as he donned his coat and went to find Marshal Stroud.

- - -

That night, as Todd prepared to join Mattie in bed, he blew out the lamp and, in the complete darkness, toppled over but, fortunately, it was in the direction of the bed itself.

"Daniel! Are you all right?" Mattie uttered excitedly.

"Yes, I'm fine. I just got my feet tangled," he replied. He pulled the covers over him, tucked them around Mattie, and stretched to kiss her. "Good night, dear."

He had not gotten his feet tangled. In reliving the moment of the fall in his mind, he realized that when that light went out, he had no awareness of his body in space—he was totally disoriented as to where he fit into the room around him. His sense of balance was now markedly impaired and totally dependant on visual images of the things around him. He realized that he had become increasingly clumsy lately but had not attributed it to anything like this; he had felt it was due to his severe weakness and the muscle-wasting from his recent illness. Then, his problem of forgetfulness came to mind. He had explained it away by admitting to always having had trouble with names, but even he had realized that the problem had been rapidly getting worse. He was having trouble applying appellations to diseases or medications that he had known very well. The horrible realization presented itself that these tiny vascular accidents which were producing hemorrhages all over his body were occurring in his brain as well. His mind was simply winking out, small pieces being destroyed one at a time. Would a massive hemorrhage be the way it would all end, he wondered.

He went rigid in his anxiety and was grateful that Mattie was not witness to his anguish. My God, he thought, a person's mind is everything! It is what makes me the person that I am. I suppose you could say that somebody really dies when his mind is gone. Could it be that the mind is the soul? That thought would ordinarily launch him into philosophical speculation, but tonight, he was suddenly just deathly tired. He sank deeper into the feather bed and muttered under his breath, "As always, what will come, will come."

He put his hand on Mattie's thigh and surrendered to exhausted sleep.

- - -

Several days passed. Nettie Castor's funeral was attended by many more people than she had ever known in life, so great was the indignation over the manner of her death. In spite of this wave of anger in the community, no official action was taken. As with previous killings perpetrated by Chandler and stemming from gambling disputes which Marshal Stroud declared to be acts of self-defense on Chandler's part, Nettie Castor's death was deemed by "the law" to be an unfortunate result of being in the wrong place at the wrong time.

Such a state of affairs confirmed in Todd's mind the need for him to act and removed any of his doubt that, even though the saving of life had been his life's work, killing Chandler was the mission Fate had proclaimed to be his destiny. Nor did it occur to him that even considering such a bizarre plan as this might in itself be an indication of how far the brain damage from his disease had advanced.

Fearing that Mattie's keen intuition might sense his thoughts and detect his plans, Daniel spent much time in the solitude of his office. It pained him to do this because if his days or hours indeed were numbered, he should be spending every second still left to him with his loved ones, but killing Chandler had quickly grown to become an absolute obsession with him.

"How do I do it?" he puzzled. "I'm not a gunfighter. There's no way that I can possibly kill him in face-to-face combat with a pistol. Perhaps I could ambush him and shoot him with a rifle from a distance but that would martyr him. In some people's eyes, such a death would be a persecution of him and would gain their sympathy instead of their having a sense of justice having been administered. It would be the same if somehow I were able to poison him, he thought. No, it has to be face-to-face and he has to be told at the time why he is dying. It must be in front of witnesses. But how can I possibly do it?

Eventually, memories of Corkscrew Trumbull crept into Daniel's mind. Images of the shadowy figure striking down Isaac Lawrence with the belaying pin and then advancing in such a menacing manner along that darkened deck were still very frightfully vivid. Todd literally felt himself groping and again finally encountering the handle of the razor-sharp mincing spade he had used to defend himself so many years ago. His muscles tensed and he could actually feel himself again striking Trumbull with all of his strength; in his mind's eye, he could see the man staring down at his intestines as they spilled from the gaping wound in his belly.

A mincing spade! What an unlikely weapon! Undoubtedly, it would spawn humor and derision among Chandler and onlookers alike when they saw it, and they would only ridicule him if he were to threaten the man with it. The more he toyed with that thought, though, the more it seemed to him that this temporary diversion might just give him the moment's advantage he needed to overcome such an accomplished gunfighter as Chandler—considering the many men he had gunned down in the past before they could even get a shot off at him!

He will probably kill me before he dies, Todd thought, even if I am successful in striking him in such a critical area as his throat. But that thought didn't frighten him.

He preferred a sudden end to a perhaps lingering death after an apoplectic stroke, which he increasingly feared would be his end. The important thing would be to wound Chandler *fatally*. Perhaps he should smear excrement or some other sort of corruption on the blade to render the wound more lethal even if Chandler didn't die immediately as a result of the attack.

Todd continued to fantasize details of the possible scenario until Mattie called for him to come to dinner. As he entered the lighted room, he noticed yet another large blister of accumulated blood, this time on the back of his other wrist, which he surreptitiously slid into his pocket to hide the lesion from his family.

Mattie had already fed Edward and the baby and was just finishing the carving of the chicken she had roasted. She was silent for a long moment after they seated themselves at the dinner table. Finally, she said, "You have been very quiet over the past several days, Daniel; almost secretive. Is there something that I have done to displease you?"

Todd was quick to reassure her. "Oh, no, Mattie. It is nothing like that. You have been such a rock through all of my illness. Just as always, you have been wonderful." He hesitated and looked down at his lap in embarrassment. He felt that he couldn't isolate her any longer. "I haven't wanted to mention anything about this before because I'm not sure—not even yet. But I realize now that I should have told you . . ."

Again he paused. The words came haltingly. "I think I may have cancer, my dear. I can't make a definite diagnosis, but I have seen this sort of thing before. With my very abnormal fatigue, the enlargement of some of my glands, and these . . ." He held out his hands to display the large hemorrhagic areas that defaced his skin. "As I said, I've seen this before and I'm afraid I have cancer of . . . I don't know . . . probably cancer of the blood. I suspect that I am going to die . . . and probably quite soon."

Mattie was mute in her thunderstruck astonishment and simply arose from her seat and walked around the table to embrace Daniel and hold him close to her bosom. After hugging him for a long moment, she said softly, "We will hope, just this once, Daniel, that your diagnosis is so fanciful and foolish that we will laugh about it heartily in the long years to come."

Holding him protectively close to her, Mattie bit her lip and could not bring herself to say anything more.

Daniel reached up, taking her hand where it still rested on his shoulder and kissed it. Trying gently to guide her back to her chair, he said, "Come, my dear. Let's finish this wonderful meal that you have prepared."

With uncharacteristic emotion, Mattie merely squeezed his hand, blotted a tear from her eye with her handkerchief, and fled from the room. Daniel's saddened gaze followed her, and then he hung his head. Death, he thought, involves not just a final, solitary spasm of pain; it is a composition—a gloomy symphony of many, many separate pains. Would my committing murder just add another discordant tone to it all?

Mattie remained apart from him until bedtime and even then, as they prepared to retire, she did not speak a word about Daniel's suspicions. Instead, she talked as though nothing was different, but when they embraced after getting into bed, she touched him very carefully as though she now considered him to be extremely delicate. They both thought their own worried thoughts, drifting silently into the mounting hours of the night which were as black as their spirits.

- - -

Todd's resolve to dispose of Chandler, although shaken somewhat by the exchange with Mattie, was still strong and the next morning, he went to the mercantile and bought a garden hoe.

"You planning on cultivatin' a snowbank, are you, Doc?" the proprietor asked.

"Can't get started too soon, you know," was Todd's rejoinder.

Next, he went to O'Donahue's smithy and instructed the burly Irish blacksmith as to how he wished to have the implement modified. "I'd like for you to straighten this so that the blade is in line with the handle, Mr. O'Donahue. Then, I'd like for you to round off the corners a bit to give the cutting edge a gentle curve and then temper the steel so you can put a keen edge on it. I would like to be able to shave with the thing."

O'Donahue, a man of so few words that one might easily consider him mute, merely conveyed his question about Todd's sanity in the long sidelong glance he gave the doctor as he took the hoe. "Two, mebbe three days," he finally said, and leaned the tool in the corner by the forge.

Next, Todd thought about going to a lawyer to have a will drawn up. He didn't have much of an estate to leave, but he wanted all of it to go to Mattie.

He was hesitant to share the news of his condition with anybody, although he knew that people draw up wills, just to get it done and over with, even when they are still in the best of health. There was no reason to explain anything specific to a lawyer. In the end, though, he decided to maintain his silence and merely write his will in his own handwriting and sign it. He was certain that he had heard such an instrument was legally binding—an holographic will, he thought it had been called. He would simply write it out, seal it in an envelope and place it where it would be found, when the time came, along with the note explaining to Mattie the purpose of his actions.

On the way back to his office, though, Daniel was intercepted by a small boy who said, "Doc Todd? Ma says to fetch ya quick. My sister's powerful sick."

CHAPTER FIFTY

Indisposed as he was, but like an old fire horse, Todd made the house call that eventually would prove so devastating. He found that little Elsie Cooper had high fever, a suppurative exudate on her enlarged tonsils associated with her sore throat, and the typical rash of scarlet fever. While he was painting her throat with iodine, she had coughed and gagged so violently that Daniel had been soaked by her sputum. During the next two days, Elsie's condition seemed to improve, but on the third day she took a dramatic turn for the worse. Todd remained with her for hours, sponging her with whiskey in an attempt to reduce her fever. Ever since the previous night, he himself had felt feverish and as the minutes dragged past while he treated his young patient, he began feeling extremely ill. He was certain that he was having a relapse of the illness that had devastated him so recently. During just the few hours that Todd remained with the child, he felt that he was plunging off a precipice—profound weakness, tightening of the throat, a worsened clouding of his mental state, and a fever that caused him to feel as though he was burning up.

Am I having that apoplectic stroke I have feared so much, he wondered? I have no headache, no paralysis. He had known for days that he was becoming more anemic; he had observed his pallor in the mirror and his usual test for anemia, the mere pinching of the earlobe and noting how quickly it recovered a pink and well perfused color, had shown conclusively that he simply did not have enough blood. And he had recently noted red blood in his stools. He seemed to be bleeding everywhere, but the precipitous nature of this collapse surprised him greatly. The worsening feverish weakness had progressed so rapidly over the course of just several hours that he entered a state of collapse so severe he was forced to ask Mrs. Cooper to get another doctor to care for Elsie. He had to be helped to get to his own home and even with that, barely made it.

Mattie immediately put him to bed and placed heated flat irons to his back to relieve his chills. She then summoned Dr. Stevens, one of the other Idaho City physicians, of whom Todd had always spoken favorably.

"Your husband is very ill, Mrs. Todd. I have trouble believing this malady came on as suddenly as you describe. I've never seen overwhelming ague of this terribly devastating severity. It's as though his body has absolutely no defense against it whatsoever; the inflammation is simply consuming him. I'll leave some powders with you that should be an aid in his recovery."

Daniel had a limited awareness of the activities going on around him. He had a warped impression of Mattie's comings and goings, of the children being brought into his room, of foul-tasting medications being spooned into his mouth, of the paralyzing inability and frustration that he couldn't go and pick up the flensing spade that O'Donahue had been so slow in preparing for him, of perhaps never being able to render justice to Chandler, of wanting to fetch some of Gung Pi's herbs to treat himself, but not being able even to move. It was as though he were immersed in a giant vat of molten tar that sucked at his every movement and from which he could not extract himself.

Todd remained unconscious for many more hours following that state of limited awareness, and he was totally oblivious to the conversations between Dr. Stevens and Mattie about his condition or his treatment. He would never hear the shocking news that rocked the town—Ike Castor had gunned down that man Chandler, killing the gambler with a single rifle bullet.

Finally, the misery of his painfully dry mouth and burning fever, the knowledge that he was actually dying seeped into Daniel's clouded thoughts. He realized that he had no sense of panic nor was he at all fearful. He did feel profound regret over leaving Mattie and Edward and little Elizabeth, of things left undone in his life, of having accomplished so little over the years. But perhaps . . . just perhaps . . . he would see Cordelia once again . . . and Simon Edwards . . . and possibly even the ends of that limitless Universe . . . and he finally would know if there actually was some sort of existence beyond death . . . or not . . .

Daniel summoned every ounce of his remaining strength and was able to inch his hand a short distance across the covers. Mattie's familiar grip, so strong and reassuring, closed around it as a profound darkness enveloped Dr. Daniel Locke Todd.

CHAPTER FIFTY-ONE

A chinook wind blew in for several days, melting the drifts and thawing the ground sufficiently enough for a grave to be dug. Now, the wind had shifted and was raw and cold again and whipped mercilessly at the small group of mourners gathered on the hillside of Idaho City's rapidly expanding cemetery. Todd's service had been a simple graveside affair; Mattie was certain her husband would not have wanted a lengthy sermonized funeral or some flowery eulogy. For her own comfort, she had asked her minister to speak and he had just finished saying very simply that Daniel Locke Todd had given tirelessly of himself in relieving the suffering of his fellow man, and he had asked God to receive this good man and reward him for those efforts.

Edward, bundled in a bulky coat, clung to Mattie's leg in his bewilderment at the events that were taking place. Mattie held Elizabeth and tried to shield the infant from the wintry blast as she nodded and acknowledged the condolences of well-wishers. She lingered on after the last of the mourners had quietly filed away down the hill toward town and watched as the workmen started to cover the wooden casket. The measured drumming sounds of shovelful after shovelful of dirt striking the coffin were muted by the wind and swept away from earth, on into eternity.

Mattie felt an overwhelming guilt for still being alive and, looking about her, felt a smoldering anger that those workmen still existed also. The town that sprawled beneath them was unchanged . . . the world was continuing on just the same as it always had. But . . . the world was *not* the same! Her beloved Daniel was *dead* and *gone* and *nothing* would ever be the same on this earth again! She knew it would be likewise when she left this life, but it was a reality she didn't want to face.

Edward hunched himself against the cold. His movement and the realization of her tremendous responsibility toward the children jarred Mattie from her reverie.

Now only a naked mound of earth marked the site of her husband's grave. Mattie edged close and held the headboard in place with her free hand as a workman tamped the dirt around it. When it was firmly in place, she and her children stepped back and observed the simple carved letters.

DANIEL LOCKE TODD, M.D.
1825-1868

EPILOGUE

Over the years of the late Nineteenth Century and early Twentieth Century, two generations of Idaho City children enjoyed the stern, but loving and devoted, teachings of Mattie Todd and revered her memory long after she died at the age of 73. She had witnessed the blossoming exuberance and eventual decline of the mining town of Idaho City, her adopted home. During that time, she experienced all of the joys and sorrows of a widowed mother. Elizabeth had a happy childhood but succumbed to pneumonia at the age of seven. Mattie found great fulfillment and joy, though, in Edward who grew to manhood and, although he always said he desired the simple life of a freighter, continued his education to become a University professor of Literature. In turn, he fathered four outstanding grandchildren for Mattie; grandchildren who had only fading childhood memories of their grandmother and knew nothing except for hearing a scattering of oft-told tales about the grandfather from whom they sprang and sometimes touching the strange and awesome contents of his black bag.

So it is with each of us. Almost none of those from whom we descend performed any outstanding accomplishments, led particularly noteworthy lives or left any breathtaking legacy to us other than life itself. Yet, how important it would be if we could know the details of the existence of our ancestors. The fact that they had fears, doubts, triumphs, defeats, loves, boredom—all of the emotions that fill our own thoughts—is a certainty but, all too often, is forgotten. If we could know more about their lives, their ordeals and the thoughts that they had, how great a richness it would add to their memory and how much more comprehension it might add to our lives. To know everything we can about them should be our goal. After all, perhaps we are their only immortality.

The author, a fourth generation Idahoan and a graduate of Harvard Medical School, is a retired physician who lives in Boise, Idaho with his wife, Nettie.